D0014489

NOV 05

DATE DUE

JAN 7 '00			
JAN 24 '06			
MAR 09			
MAR 25 '06			
APR 14			
APR 26 '06			
JUN 9			
JUL 28			
JAN 31			

GAYLORD PRINTED IN U.S.A.

the hounds of winter

the hounds of winter

A NOVEL BY JAMES MAGNUSON

UNIVERSITY OF TEXAS PRESS AUSTIN

JACKSON COUNTY LIBRARY SERVICES
MEDFORD OREGON 97501

Copyright © 2005 by James Magnuson
All rights reserved
Printed in the United States of America
First edition, 2005

Requests for permission to reproduce material from this work should be sent to:
Permissions
University of Texas Press
P.O. Box 7819
Austin, TX 78713-7819
www.utexas.edu/utpress/about/bpermission.html

∞ The paper used in this book meets the minimum requirements of ANSI/NISO Z39.48-1992 (R1997) (Permanence of Paper).

LIBRARY OF CONGRESS CATALOGING-IN-PUBLICATION DATA

Magnuson, James.
The hounds of winter : a novel / by James Magnuson. — 1st ed.
p. cm.
ISBN 0-292-70990-0 (alk. paper)
1. Murder victims' families—Fiction. 2. Fathers and daughters—Fiction. 3. Wisconsin—Fiction. 4. Secrecy—Fiction. I. Title.
PS3563.A352H68 2005
813′.54—dc22 2005009346

in memory of my parents

EVELYN AND ROY MAGNUSON

acknowledgments

I would like to thank all those people whose encouragement, deft observations, and gentle criticisms have done so much to shape this book: Marla Akin, Sally Arteseros, Sarah Bird, Andrew Cooper, Charles Crupi, Tom Esser, Steve Harrigan, Dick Holland, James Hynes, Mark Magnuson, Billy and Martha Magnuson, Laura Olah, Hugh O'Neill, Kathleen Orillion, Wendy Weil, Tom Whitbread, and Tom Zigal. I am indebted to the staff of the International Wolf Center in Ely, Minnesota, for taking me into the wild, but my greatest debt is to Hester Magnuson, for her unflinching honesty and unwavering support.

the hounds of winter

prologue

Maya tapped the brakes as she passed the ranger station, easing down the winding park road to the lake. Through the driving snow she scanned the silent woods. There was no sign of life; everything had taken shelter from the storm. But the stillness was deceptive. There would be wolves out tonight, wolves that she had spent the last four years helping restore to the wilderness; she imagined them loping across the pristine whiteness.

She needed a smoke badly. She leaned against the steering wheel, wiping the windshield with her hand. Bonnie Raitt crooned through the speakers, but the sad, bluesy voice did nothing to assuage the rawness of her nerves. Blanketed quartzite boulders loomed in the woods like gleaming cenotaphs. It was Christmas Eve.

It looked as if a plow had been through at some point, but a good couple of inches had fallen since then. Her father, flying in from New York, was supposed to have gotten in before her, but she couldn't imagine he was going to make his connecting flight at O'Hare in weather like this. If he was late, the good news was she would have time to get hold of the people she'd been trying so desperately to get in touch with all day.

All fall she and her father had barely spoken, and this was going to be a hell of a way to break the silence. She was going to have to tell him everything. The story she had to tell was not one that you could do in installments. The thought of it made her chest heavy. Maybe she would wait until after supper.

Coming around the last hairpin turn, she could finally see the high bluffs, the mile-long lake where the wind chased great shrouds of snow across the ice. The cabin that her father had purchased just four years before nestled in the grove of dark pines just below her. She was relieved to see that her father's car was not there yet.

Leaving the main road, the Bronco fishtailed up the drive, bucking through untouched drifts. Maya got out, gathering a bag of groceries from the front seat, and trudged to the cabin. A crow called from deep in the woods as she fumbled with her keys.

As soon as she opened the door she heard the phone. She set the groceries on a chair in the hallway and ran for the kitchen, grabbing the receiver on the fourth ring.

"Maya?"

"Hey, Dad," she said. She tried to disguise the disappointment in her voice. She had been hoping for someone else. "Where are you?" The room was bitter cold.

"I'm in the car. Maybe twenty minutes away."

"Are you really?" She undid the top button of her long Russian wool coat, shook out her tangle of black hair. "I never thought they'd let you get out of Chicago." As she moved across the room to adjust the thermostat she saw the small hard kernels scattered on the floor. "Oh God."

"What's wrong?"

"Nothing. It just looks as if the mice have gotten into the pantry again. Let me get off. I'll have a big fire in the fireplace by the time you get here."

"Maya, I'm really happy we're doing this."

"Me too," she said. She kicked the toe of one of her battered cowboy boots against a chair, knocking off the snow. "There's a lot to say."

"What do you mean?"

"I'll tell you when you get here. See you in a few minutes."

She hung up and opened the pantry door. A crumpled bag of Orville Redenbacher popcorn, a hole gnawed in one end, sat on the shelf. Shiny golden seeds were all over the floor, mixed with pellets of mouse droppings.

She got the worn broom from the closet and swept up the mess. As she was dumping it all in the trash she heard something bang upstairs, a door or a shutter. She froze for a moment, listening for something more.

"Hello?" she called out. "Is anyone there?"

The cabin was utterly still, and then there was a metallic rattle as the heater kicked in. She put the rubber dustpan on the kitchen table and walked into the hall, gazing up the dark stairway. The glass chimes tinkled softly on the front porch, and through the living room window she could see the pine boughs rising and falling in the storm. It was nothing, she told herself, absolutely nothing.

She went back outside and unstrapped her icy skis from the top of the Bronco, leaning them against the back door.

It was the first time she'd been back to the cabin in winter, and it felt strange. After her senior year in high school, Maya had come to Wisconsin for eight weeks to work as an intern with a group helping to restore wolves to the wilderness. It had been the best experience of her life. The following fall her father had bought the cabin, just ten miles in one direction from Black Hawk, the small town he'd grown up in, and ten miles in the other direction from the Wolf Center headquarters. At the time, Maya had found the decision alarming. It was so sudden, so extravagant, the sort of thing her father never did, but ever since the death of Maya's mother, she'd had to get used to him doing a lot of things he'd never done before. They'd come back to the cabin every summer. Now, as she limped her way through a desultory senior year at Macalester, the work at the Wolf Center had become the center of her life.

She swung two duffel bags from the Bronco and, head down against the snow, ran back to the house. She stomped her boots off on the worn mat and ascended the stairs. She dropped the duffel bags on the landing, stepped into her bedroom, and flipped on the light.

The first thing she noticed was one of her father's old photo albums, splayed open on the bed, but then she noticed more. In the far corner lay a soiled green sleeping bag and on the windowsill sat a nearly empty bottle of Jack Daniels. Outside a couple of chickadees flitted in a snow-covered apple tree.

When she nudged the sleeping bag with her foot, she uncovered a blue plastic soap container, a leather shaving kit, and a stack of old newspapers and *Field and Stream* magazines. Nearly every winter there had been break-ins. They had tried hiring a caretaker, a local man named George Kammen, to look in from time to time, but there was no way to keep people out, whether they were hunters or teenagers on a lark. But this looked as if someone had been living here. It scared her, and then it made her mad.

She went to her closet. Nothing had been touched. She opened her drawers. Shorts, T-shirts, scarves, socks, underwear—everything was just as she'd left it in August. She ran trembling fingers through her hair.

She tossed the newspapers, the shaving kit, and the bottle of whiskey into the center of the sleeping bag. Marching down the stairs, she held the stained bundle at arm's length, the way someone might hold a dead rat. She went out to the back porch and stuffed it all into the big plastic trash bin.

Her heart was racing. She stared at the undulating meadow, covered in snow, pristine. The cold stung her cheeks. God knew how long the intruder had been staying there. A week? A month? Hadn't George been checking? The man was utterly useless. She tried to calm herself. She and her father would discuss this. There was no point in letting it ruin everything.

She took a handful of the old newspapers and went back into the living room. She removed the fire screen and set two logs in the fireplace. Down on one knee, she balled up some of the old newspaper and wedged it under the logs. Her father would be here in minutes. She wanted the house to be warm. She retrieved the long matches from the mantel and lit the fire.

The paper ignited quickly, flames licking around the scabby oak bark, but after a few seconds the flames began to die. She reached back for the poker, but the poker wasn't there.

She turned. A figure in a ski mask of the palest blue stood in the middle of the room, holding the poker loosely to one side, the way a dog owner might hold a leash while his retriever went for a romp in the water.

"What the hell are you doing here?" Maya said.

There was no answer. The intruder was tall, in a bulky hunting coat, and behind the pale blue ski mask there was something in the eyes that was almost familiar. Wisps of smoke had begun to back up in the room, as if the flue was still closed.

Maya was still kneeling on the bricks of the fireplace. She rose to her feet. When she took a step to her left, the intruder moved to block her way. Maya's heart thudded in her chest.

She glanced out the window at the road, at the falling snow. Where was her father? He was supposed to have been here.

She grabbed the fire screen and tried to swing it, but the poker came up quickly, knocking it away. She tried to run, moving behind the couch, shoving the heavy furniture, trying to create an obstacle course, but as she did she stumbled on a piece of loose firewood. As she fell, the poker caught her across the back. The blow knocked her to the floor, took all the breath from her. Once when she was ten she had fallen from the loft of a barn. This was like that: the same metallic taste in her mouth, the same black dots swirling in front of her eyes.

She groped on all fours, reaching out for the wall. A second blow missed her hand by inches and smashed the window just above it. She felt the rush of cold air, of winter. She struggled to her knees. She stared out at the dazzling white meadow, searching the empty road and calling out through the jagged glass, "Dad, Dad. . . ." but there was no answer, just the sharp crack of metal on bone and engulfing darkness.

one

Following the wide diamond treads of his daughter's Bronco down the hill, all David Neisen could think of was that he should have warned her to put on chains. Not that she would have listened.

He passed the ranger station and the turnoff for the campgrounds. It looked as if no one else had been through all afternoon. The snow filled him with a mindless joy. Wasn't this what everyone was always hoping for, a white Christmas? It was so good that he and Maya had decided to do this. Their estrangement at the end of the summer had been allowed to go on too long, to grow into something more than either of them meant it to. This would give them a chance to back away from the ledge.

On the other hand, he needed to keep reminding himself that this was not Versailles; they were not deciding the fate of the Western world. All they were doing was getting together for a few days of cross-country skiing. They would open a few presents, sit by the fire and drink hot cider, have a little time to talk. He had the manuscripts of two clients in the trunk of his car, but if he didn't get to them until he was back in New York, he wasn't going to sweat it.

He slowed the rented Camry to ten miles an hour, creeping

along the guardrail. White flakes danced in front of the windshield, melted and slid along the glass, and, farther off, drifted and settled silently in the trees. If the storm kept up for another hour, the road would be impassable. A crow flapped low over a jagged outcropping of rock. The woods on either side of him were filling with shadows.

He still felt bad about the summer. He was aware of his faults as a father. He knew that he was too private, that he kept things in too much, that he had failed Maya after her mother's death in ways he was only beginning to understand.

But, good Christ, there was more to their relationship than that! When she was small and afraid of the dark, he would lie next to her in bed and tell her stories until she nodded off. Even then, in sleep, she would have her fist tight around his thumb so he couldn't escape.

Yet it wasn't as if he needed her to remain a child. Nothing made him happier than to look across the room at some neighborhood holiday gathering and see her surrounded by a group of college boys, see her regaling them with her adventures in the Wisconsin north woods.

She had a wonderful, wicked laugh, and she was a little too much for boys her own age to handle. Parents were always pulling David aside to tell him how gorgeous she was. It was true; she could be beautiful, with her great mane of tangled black hair and startling blue eyes. She had a rebel's charisma, there was no doubt, and seemed capable of a certain raucous exuberance, particularly when she was in the presence of people other than her father. She was just twenty-two. How much could he ask? In five years or ten, they would be laughing over the trouble they were having now.

He could feel a slight tug in his calf as he toed the brakes. For over a month he'd been doing an hour a day on the cross-trainer, plus weights and stretches, and he was in the best shape of his life. When you had Wilderness Woman for a daughter, you didn't assume that three days of skiing was going to be a stroll through the park.

Coming out of the hairpin turn, he glanced down at the cabin in the dark cluster of pines. He could see her car and the skis leaning against the back door. He eased off the pavement and then nearly got stuck coming up the drive, tires spinning in the snow. Rather than force it, he let the Camry roll back and tried again. On his second attempt he bumped through. He opened the car door, hitting the horn lightly with the heel of his hand.

"Hey, Maya!"

There was no answer. He stood, slamming the car door behind him, and stared up at the dark windows of the house. Great wet flakes caught in his lashes, blurring his vision for a second. He wiped at his eyes, then got his suitcase out of the trunk and walked to the cabin.

The first thing he noticed when he entered was the smell of smoke. A bag of groceries sat on the chair in the hallway. He turned and surveyed the living room, scanning the fire screen overturned on the rug, the couch askew, unlit logs, the smoldering papery ashes. His heart leapt with alarm, but it wasn't until he stepped forward to pick up the fire screen that he saw Maya on the other side of the couch. She lay face down, her arms outstretched, her head resting on a bloody towel, broken glass scattered around her. There was a second when he tried to tell himself that it was just an accident, that she had tripped and fallen and cut herself and that he could still save her, but as he knelt he saw behind her ear the tangled hair matted and, almost black with blood, the bludgeoned skull, and he understood that there would be no saving anyone.

He heard a terrible sound come out of him. He gently turned her over. Her nose was broken, blood still flowing from her left nostril, and one of her eyes was swollen shut from a blow. His beautiful daughter. He cradled her to his chest, her body still warm and limp. He could feel the cold streaming from the window as he rocked her, and then he saw the poker lying under one of the chairs.

He stared dully at it for a second before it occurred to him to wonder why it was there. He lay Maya down softly on the rug and rose to his feet. A thin band of smoke hung in the air. He swayed for a moment, nearly blacking out. He retrieved the poker and turned the cold metal over in his hands. A tuft of his daughter's dark hair trembled between the prong and the shaft.

His mind refused it; this could not be happening. He had just been talking to her, minutes before. He whirled around, as if looking for someone to help.

His thoughts were oddly mechanical, narrowed to a dim tunnel, but he still knew he needed to call someone. On his way to the kitchen he stumbled over a chair and almost fell. He glanced up the stairs and saw two blue duffel bags on the landing, an old *Field and Stream* magazine sitting on the top step. He set the poker on the breakfast table and reached for the phone. He dialed 911; it rang four or five times before anyone picked up.

"Black Hawk Police Department." It was a woman's voice.

"This is David Neisen. Something terrible has happened. Someone has just killed my daughter."

"And where are you now?"

"I'm at our cabin. On the north end of Sauk Lake. Just a half mile down from the main entrance." Wiping his hand across his chest, he realized that his coat was slick with his daughter's blood. "Please . . . Someone help me. . . ."

There was a sharp bang, like a screen door slamming shut, somewhere in the house. He whirled around and stood listening for another sound, but none came. He set the phone silently on the counter. The policewoman's voice still flickered through the phone, tinny and unreal. He picked up the poker and moved into the hallway.

The front porch door was open; it had not been open before. David stared dumbly at it for several seconds and then glanced over his shoulder. Through the living room window he could see a man in a bulky winter overcoat plunging through the heavy snow in the meadow. The air in the hallway was acrid with the smell of ashes.

David barged through the open porch door, down the steps, and out into the snow. The man was less than a hundred yards ahead of him, and at first David was able to gain ground by simply following his trail, leaping from one gaping foothole to the next. He narrowed the gap to fifty yards and then twenty-five. He was close enough to hear the man's wheezing and the crunch of his boots in the hard white crust—there was no other sound in the vast dazzling space—but then David fell.

He retrieved the poker from the snow and rose to his knees. "Murderer!" he shouted.

A crow called from deep in the woods like an answering cry. The man disappeared over a rise. David stumbled forward, falling again, then righted himself. There was the gutting sound of an engine starting up. He began to run, lunging through the snow like a lashed horse. The sound grew louder, clattering. He was almost at the rise.

A snowmobile flew at him. David threw the poker at the hurtling vehicle and the metal rod shattered the windshield. He dove to his left, getting his right arm up to protect his face, and the snowmobile drove right over him. It felt as if he'd been hit in the back by a wrecking ball.

He lay gasping in the snow, trying to get his breath back. He wondered if his right arm was broken. The buzzing of the snowmobile grew more distant and then vanished altogether.

He made a first tentative attempt to bend his arm and discovered that he could. He finally rolled onto his back and wiped the icy crystals from his face. Huge lacy flakes drifted down, and it felt as if the tops of the encircling trees were rotating slowly, first in one direction and then in the other. He closed his eyes again. Something cold trickled down his back. It was utterly still, and then, out of the stillness, he heard the faint whine of the snowmobile.

He sat up. Ten feet away, lying at the base of an ancient red oak, was the poker. He rose, clenching and unclenching his right hand; the pain was dull and constant, but at least he had motion. He scooped up the poker and stared back at the cabin. For a second it occurred to him that maybe he should go back and call the police, but then he heard the sound again, the droning of the snowmobile carried by some shift in the wind. The tracks leading into the woods were crisp and fresh; there was no way he was going to just walk off and leave them. He set out across the undulating meadow, the twin grooves in the snow drawing him onward. A squirrel bounded from branch to branch, chattering warning. David began to run.

He stood at the edge of a ravine, utterly lost, quivering like an exhausted pack animal. The ice-glazed poker swung at his side. He had no idea how far he'd come or even how long he'd been following the tracks of the snowmobile. Twenty minutes? Thirty?

The tracks had gradually grown fainter, and now had disappeared altogether, filled in by new snow.

He had made a terrible mistake. What person in his right mind could ever imagine a man on foot being able to overtake a man in a snowmobile? But he hadn't been in his right mind. He had been a fool to leave Maya, bloodied and cold on the cabin floor, but each time he'd been about to turn back, another low mechanical whine in the woods or over the next ridge had jerked him onward like the yank of a puppeteer's string. Now, finally, his rage had burned itself out. All that was left was grief and despair.

He swayed, steadied himself, and finally dropped to his knees. He tried to push himself up, using the poker as a crook, but hadn't the strength. He set the poker aside and lowered himself until he sat, propped up by his hands, his legs sticking out in front of him.

He watched the snow gather in the folds of his trousers. He knew that he wasn't thinking correctly. His attention bounced from thing to thing, like a wasp trapped between panes of glass. He remembered snowball fights he and his friends used to have on afternoons like this; he remembered promising Peggy on one of her last days in the hospital that he would see that Maya had a proper wedding; he remembered the Christmas presents still sitting in the trunk of his rental car.

It wasn't until he lifted his hand to wipe wet flakes from his cheek that he saw the discoloration on his jacket. Maya's blood, dried in the cold and wind, had made a stain as dark as coffee.

He rocked onto all fours and puked into the snow. When he was done, he sat on his haunches, panting, wiping at the corners of his mouth with the back of his hand. He could feel the tiny acid bits burning in his nose and throat. He rose to his feet and surveyed the silent woods. There was only one thing that mattered now, and that was being with his daughter.

Trudging down the road, he could see the cabin and the two squad cars pulled in behind his rented Camry. One of the cars still had its overheads on, blades of red and blue flickering across the snow and the side of the house.

He stopped and stared, momentarily befuddled. He had not counted on the police being here already. He should have, but he hadn't. The impulse to flee was deep and impervious to reason; he fought it back. If anyone could help him, these were the guys.

He left the road, stumbling down the slope behind the tool shed. The poker still swung in his left hand. He halted thirty feet from the house and stared across the meadow. The trail of gaping boot-holes left by Maya's killer had been reduced to a series of gentle indentations. He turned back to the cabin. Lamps flickered in two of the windows.

"Hello?" he called out. "Hello?" The last thing he wanted was to take anybody by surprise.

It was five or six seconds before the kitchen door opened. A young policeman poked his head out, stared for a moment, and then came down the steps. He stopped between the cars, rubbing the back of his neck.

"I'm David Neisen."

"I know."

There was something familiar about the boy, something about the way he moved, but it took David a minute to place him; it was Tommy Burmeister, the grandson of their old mailman. A second deputy, barely older than the first, had come to the open door. Shorter and grimmer than Young Burmeister, he exuded the glaring menace of a pit bull.

"Please," David said. "You've got to help me." Neither of the officers spoke. The poker in David's hands had Young Burmeister transfixed. "The man who murdered my daughter, he's out there. When I was on the phone, calling you guys, I saw him running from the house. I went after him, but he had a snowmobile stashed back in the meadow . . ."

"I think you better come inside," the Pit Bull said.

"But you don't understand. There's no time to lose. If we go now . . ."

"It would be best if you did like he said." Young Burmeister was backing up his partner.

David looked from one to the other of them. "Fine," he said. "Fine."

Young Burmeister retreated a step to let David pass. The Pit Bull held the door, stiffening as David ducked into the kitchen. The place was a mess: muddy footprints on the floor, a Sheriff's Department jacket tossed over a chair, a walkie-talkie and a couple of writing pads on the counter. David propped the poker against the wall.

"So what's this?"

David turned back. The two deputies stood shoulder to shoulder in the entryway, raw and wary. The Pit Bull nodded at the poker.

"That's what she was killed with," David said.

"You took it with you?"

"Yes."

The Pit Bull moved across the room, picked up the poker, and turned it over in his hands, frowning. David glanced over at Young Burmeister, who just looked sorrowful

"So where were you when you saw him?" the Pit Bull said.

"In the living room. I was on the phone and I heard a door bang, so I went in there and saw him through the window."

"Did you see his face?"

"No."

"Was he a large man, a small man . . . ?"

"I'm not sure. Large, I think," David said. Young Burmeister surreptitiously knocked the snow off his boots, using the mat.

"And where is he now?"

"I don't know. I followed the snowmobile tracks as far as I could . . ."

"Which was how far?"

"Maybe a mile."

"So you lost the tracks or you just gave up?"

"I lost them. It was hopeless." He could tell from their faces: they weren't sure he was lying, but they weren't convinced he was telling the truth either. "He's probably out of the park by now, but if we went now, I could show you where the tracks gave out. He was headed up toward the north entrance. At least we'd have a chance . . ."

Young Burmeister looked as if he was up for it. The Pit Bull didn't. He set the poker on the counter. "I'm sorry, we can't leave. We're expecting the sheriff any minute. He was supposed to have been here by now."

"You can't let him waltz away like this!"

The Pit Bull's neck began to redden. "Did you hear what I said? We can't leave. We're under orders. All right?"

Anger took like a struck match. David felt himself within an inch of doing something stupid. For several seconds the two men stared at each other like heavyweight fighters at a weigh-in, and, to David's astonishment, it was the Pit Bull who wavered.

"Let me get on the phone and see what we can do." He turned sourly to his partner. "Just get him out of here, OK?"

Young Burmeister ushered David into the hallway. Moving through the cabin had the quality of a dream where everything was simultaneously familiar and utterly foreign. David's suitcase was right where he'd dropped it, and the acrid smell of smoke was as strong as ever. The bag of groceries still sat on the chair. David fingered a quart of softening Ben and Jerry's ice cream perched precariously atop a loaf of bread.

"I'd like to see my daughter if I could," David said.

"I don't see how there would be any harm in that," Young Burmeister said.

When they came to the entrance to the living room, Young Burmeister took David by the elbow, making sure he wasn't going any further.

From where they stood, he didn't have a clear view of her. She lay on the far side of the couch, one arm reaching out, the towel that had been under her head now unfurled on the rug and dark with blood.

"Can I . . . ?"

"No, I'm sorry," Young Burmeister said.

David lowered himself gingerly into a sagging wicker chair. Something had changed. Maybe it was just that it was later in the day, the afternoon fading in the dark windows, the lamp glowing in the corner. The silence seemed so deep. Maybe it was just that death was settling in. When did the soul leave the body? All at once, in a twinkling, or could it still be there in the room with them, like fine ash, bitter and burning to the eyes? He stared at the worn-down heels of her cowboy boots.

David could hear the distant murmur of the Pit Bull on the phone. How much could there be to talk about? They needed to go now. How obtuse could these people be? David crossed his arms tightly, trying to keep himself in check.

He could not see Maya's wound. He could almost convince himself that she was merely asleep, that all he needed to do was go to her, pick her up, and carry her to her bed. Pine boughs rose and fell outside the window.

All his life, David realized, he had mishandled grief. It had always filled him with wonder, seeing footage of Middle Eastern women wailing over the bodies of their dead. When the worst happened, he had always gone into a fog. It was as if an aperture closed down to the narrowest slit.

He rubbed his knees with the palms of his hands. He could have been at a museum, staring in at an exhibition sealed off by velvet ropes. This place was not his anymore. He had to understand that. It was a crime scene, a site to be scoured for hair and fiber, bits of torn skin and fingerprints.

He noticed for the first time the huge dent in the fire screen, as if someone had fallen into it. Maya must have fought the man. For how long, he wondered.

A door slammed in another part of the house. Why couldn't he just have gotten here ten minutes earlier? She would still be alive. If the flight from O'Hare hadn't been pushed back a half hour, if the line at the car rental hadn't been so long, if it hadn't been snowing so hard, he could have stopped this from happening.

David looked up and caught Young Burmeister staring at him.

"You're Eddie Burmeister's boy, aren't you?" David said.

"Yeah."

"I knew your grandfather. He used to deliver our mail. Years ago."

"All right."

Voices rose and fell in the kitchen. It sounded as if somebody else had arrived and somebody was angry. This was not the way any of them had planned on spending Christmas Eve. This boy needed to be home, wrapping presents for his family.

"So how long have you been with the sheriff's department?"

"A little over a year."

"Your dad must be proud of you."

"I guess he is." In the corner the lamp flickered with the uncertain light of a votive candle.

"So how old are you?"

"Twenty-two."

"That's how old my daughter was. Twenty-two." David hunched forward. He could feel a fever coming on. "So have you ever seen anything like this before?"

"No, sir, I haven't."

"It's hard, isn't it?"

"Hard for everybody, I guess," the boy said.

"But let me tell you something," David said. "That's not her."

"I'm sorry?" Young Burmeister said.

"That's not her. What you see there. That's not her." Young Burmeister had no reply. There was the sound of footsteps in the hallway. The deputy turned to look, but David did not, focused only on his daughter's outstretched hand, the curled fingers, trying to fix it all in his mind.

"What the hell is going on here?"

Even after thirty-five years the voice had lost none of its bully-of-the-schoolyard belligerence. David pivoted in his chair. In his winter parka, Doug Danacek looked as big as a buffalo. When the Pit Bull had said that the sheriff was on his way, it hadn't fully registered with David just who that sheriff would be.

"He just wanted to see his daughter," Young Burmeister said.

"I understand that." The sheriff unzipped his jacket with one brutal motion. The Pit Bull had emerged from the kitchen looking thoroughly chastised. David leaned forward, looking from one to the other of them, on the verge of saying something. If they were going to have any chance of catching the man on the snowmobile, they had to leave now.

Ignoring the three of them, Danacek skirted the perimeter of the room with the gravity of a golfer sizing up a difficult putt. He had been big as a kid and three decades had only made him bigger. Ruddy-faced, coat open, heavy leather gloves flapping from his pockets, he seemed to blot out half the light in the cabin.

He moved finally into the space that David had been forbidden to enter, examining the overturned fire screen, the obstacle course of furniture knocked askew. David rose to his feet.

The sheriff toed the spilled ashes on the hearth, opened and shut the flue. He picked up the framed photo of David, Peggy, and Maya, taken on their trip to Tuscany, ten years before. In the picture, the three of them sat on a Roman aqueduct, tawny hayfield stretching out beneath them. Maya had been just twelve then, scrawny, with braces and big glasses.

Danacek set the photo back on the mantel. He surveyed the room, drinking it all in—the Navajo rug on the wall, the varnished log beams on the ceiling, the jammed bookshelves, the Shaker chairs. Danacek might not have known the price of Indian weaving, but he was no fool; this was not the kind of cabin a small-town sheriff could afford.

He knelt finally behind the couch to examine the body. After a minute or so he leaned forward to undo the buttons on Maya's long black Russian coat.

"Don't . . ." David said.

Danacek's eyes came up slowly. "I beg your pardon?"

If there was anyone in the world David didn't want touching his daughter, it was this man. "Nothing," David said. "Nothing."

Danacek lifted Maya's outstretched hand, examining the fingernails, and then let it drop. He pushed himself up; his knees were not good. "So where's the coroner?"

"He's on the way," the Pit Bull said.

Danacek hiked up his belt. Young Burmeister put a hand on David's arm, and David gave the deputy a quick glance. Young Burmeister knew the story; David could tell instantly from the flushed cheeks. Who in this town didn't know the story, the story that had linked David and Danacek for all these years?

The sheriff stepped around the fire screen. "I understand that you went after the man who did this?" he said.

"Yes."

"So where did you lose his tracks?" There was a full complement of gear on Danacek's belt, including a gun and what looked like a walkie-talkie.

"Somewhere in the boulder field. Below the ranger station."

"But you could still hear the snowmobile?"

"Off and on."

"And how long ago was this?"

"Thirty minutes, forty . . ."

Danacek glared at his two deputies as if he was ready to fire both of them. "Which way did it seem to be going?"

"At first I thought it was headed for the main road, but then I wasn't sure. It was more like he was trying to find a way up to the west bluff."

"I want you to show me."

"I don't understand."

"I've got a car outside."

"You mean, you and I . . ."

"That's right, you and I," Danacek said.

"But he's got to be long gone by now."

"Maybe so, maybe not, but one thing I can tell you, the way it's snowing, another half hour and there's not going to be a trace of anything out there." For the first time David noticed that Danacek's trousers were wet from the knees down.

"The coroner's going to be here any minute," Young Burmeister said to David. "It would be better if you went with the sheriff."

Bewildered, David glanced over at the deputy. Why, of the three of them, should Danacek be the one to believe his story? They were all staring at him.

He looked back at his daughter. Because of the way Danacek had repositioned her arm, all David could see of her now was her mass of dark curls. Her mother was the only one she'd let brush it. He remembered once going to the bedroom door and spying on them—Maya sitting at her desk in her flannel nightgown, her mother behind her, combing out the snarls. He could see Maya's reflection in the mirror, shining with contentment, see her mother whisk away an unruly lock. Maya had started to sing. She'd been in the chorus of *The Nutcracker* that winter, and she'd practiced her tiny part endlessly, night and day, the same twenty note refrain. He remembered thinking at that moment, standing outside the door, that the universe had never seemed so whole.

"OK," David said. "We should go then."

two

David followed Danacek to his car, a Jeep Cherokee with "Pelican County Sheriff's Department" in blue letters on the door. There was a packet of Red Man tobacco and a thermos on the front seat; David had to move them aside to get in. Danacek wedged himself behind the steering wheel.

"Let's go see what we can find," he said.

They made their way up the road. Without the presence of the young deputies, silence closed around them. David stared blankly through the windshield. There was nothing left for him to live for; it was a simple fact.

Danacek's quietness was so complete it could almost have been mistaken for consideration, but David knew there had to be a million things going through the man's head. How could there not be? How could either of them think about one death without thinking about the other? Maya sprawled behind the couch and Danacek's brother washed up in a stand of willows thirty-five years before, the floodwaters rushing over him for hours before anyone knew.

After a half mile or so, Danacek slowed the car to a crawl. He leaned forward, scrutinizing the slopes above them, looking for tracks. David stared at him. Danacek finally came to a complete stop and rolled down the window. He took a moment to listen, but the only sound was the hush of snow falling through ancient oaks.

David and his family had left Black Hawk when he was fourteen. What he knew of Danacek's history since then was sketchy, pieced together from a dozen different sources: that he had joined the army after high school, failed in three or four businesses before he was finally elected sheriff; that he had remained popular with voters, despite the rumors that he was on the take; that he spent July and August parked behind the billboards out on the highway, setting speed traps for out-of-state tourists; that twice a year, regular as clockwork, he would get his picture on the front page of the paper, once setting fire to a giant pile of confiscated marijuana, and once delivering a Thanksgiving turkey to the officially designated poorest family in Pelican County.

In the summers since David had been coming back, the two men had somehow managed to avoid running into each other, no mean trick in a place as small as Black Hawk. It was almost as if they had entered into an unspoken pact to give each other the widest possible berth. David had known that sooner or later they were bound to meet; what he never could have imagined was that it would happen like this.

They continued on up the road, stopping to listen every hundred yards or so. David pressed both fists to his mouth, staring blankly into the woods. Who could have done this? Who could possibly have had a reason? Danacek reached out to flick on the defrost.

"You cold?" he said. "There's coffee in the thermos. It'll make you feel better."

"I was just wondering," David said. "Maybe you could get some other people to help us."

"I already have," Danacek said. "I've got officers at both entrances to the park." Cold air poured in through the half-opened window. "Can I ask you something?"

"Sure."

"When you came into the cabin and saw your daughter, what did you do?"

"I don't know. I went to her. I got down on my knees. I held her."

"And that's when you got the blood on your jacket?"

David gave Danacek a quick glance. It was a policeman's job to notice things like that; David shouldn't have been surprised that he had.

"And what did you do then?"

"I went to the kitchen and called 911."

As they eased around a curve, David caught a glimpse of himself in the rearview mirror. Ashen, mouth agape, hair wild, he looked like a man drugged.

"There was a towel. In the living room. Tell me about that."

"It was there when I came in. It was folded under her head."

"You didn't put it there?"

"No."

"Huh." One of the windshield wipers was out of sync, the frayed rubber strip stuttering across the glass. "What about the poker? Where was the poker?"

"It was on the rug. About ten feet from her."

"When did you pick it up?"

"I'm not sure."

"Did you carry it with you into the kitchen?" There was a remoteness in Danacek, something impossible to read.

"I guess I must have."

"So when you went after the killer, you took it with you?"

"Yes."

David picked up the packet of Red Man tobacco and stared at the proud Indian profile. Danacek had chewed even as a teenager. To David, three years younger, it had seemed like a nasty but remarkable habit. The only people he'd ever heard of who chewed were baseball players and some of the old-time dairy farmers. It had all been part of Danacek's swagger, part of the act.

Danacek yanked the steering wheel hard to the right, and the car bumped off the road and up the ranger station's unplowed driveway.

"Where are you going?" David asked.

"I want to take a look at something."

Danacek put the Jeep Cherokee into park, reached under his seat to retrieve a pair of binoculars, and got out of the car. David hesitated, but Danacek motioned him to follow.

The ranger station, a low log building with green trim, was closed for the season, but it wasn't the ranger station the sheriff was interested in. David trailed Danacek across the parking lot to a scenic overlook. Most of the north end of the park was visible beneath them.

Danacek raised the binoculars to his eyes and surveyed the blanketed boulder fields. A chill gust of wind caught them full in the face. Turning, David scrutinized the woods behind them. As far up as they had come, the tops of the bluffs were higher still.

"Here, take a look." Danacek handed over the glasses. "If you need to focus, there's a little thing you can fiddle with in the middle." The nubbly black plastic was cold to the touch. "So you have any idea who could have done this?"

"No," David said.

"You and your daughter have been doing fine?"

David stared at him; how much did Danacek know? "We've been doing all right. Why?"

"I was just curious." Danacek swiped at his nose with a gloved hand. "Tell you what. I want to go back to the ranger station, call and see if they've spotted anybody leaving the park. Let me know if you spy anything."

David watched the burly sheriff lumber to the low log building. Danacek stood by the door, fiddling with his keys, and then disappeared inside.

David raised the binoculars, trying to focus on the bouldered incline beneath him, but the snow was coming too hard; everything was a white blur. He let the glasses drop, confused for a second. Danacek couldn't possibly have seen anything either. He turned.

Great plumes of exhaust curled up from the back of the idling Jeep Cherokee. On the far side of the road, five or six crows flapped up from the trees, making a commotion. David walked to the police car, boots squeaking in the new-fallen snow.

Through the window of the ranger station he could see Danacek hunched over the phone. David didn't understand any of it—why

Danacek had left him out in the storm, what he could possibly be talking about.

David opened the car door, tossed the binoculars on the seat, and retrieved the thermos. He unscrewed it and poured an inch of coffee into the red plastic lid. Sipping at the too-sweet liquid, he watched Danacek inside the shadowed building. The sheriff looked like a hulking sea creature lurking in the corner of an ill-lit aquarium.

There was a crash in the woods. David spun around, wild with hope. He scanned the slope across the road, but couldn't locate the source of the noise at first, because the woods were too dense. But after four or five seconds, there was more shattering of branches, a great racket moving down the incline toward him. Finally David spotted a five-point buck bounding through blackberry thickets.

When it got to the road, the exhausted animal paused and glanced over its shoulder, ears erect. Its rib cage heaved and steam rose off the wet, tawny coat; the buck had been running for a while. After a moment it leapt over the guardrail and disappeared.

David's heart raced. He stared at the slope. There had to be something up there, he figured. He remembered the explosion of crows. Something had to have frightened the deer, yet the hillside was utterly silent. He screwed the top back on the thermos and dropped his head, listening intently. At first the sound was so faint he thought he was imagining it, but then, after three or four seconds, he was sure that he wasn't—the distant, intermittent whine of an engine on top of the ridge.

David looked back at the ranger station. "Danacek!" he shouted. The sheriff had settled into a chair; all that was visible of him was the mound of his fur hat. "Danacek!" he shouted again.

The sheriff finally lurched to his feet and turned to the window, peering out, the receiver still at his ear; David gestured to the wooded slope. "He's up there! I heard him!"

Danacek gaped, uncomprehending, through the frosted glass, and then put a hand up as if telling David to wait. He pivoted slowly, still absorbed by his phone call, and disappeared into the shadows of the ranger station.

Why had David been so slow to understand? Was he a total idiot? Given what had gone on between the two of them, hell could freeze over before Danacek was going to lift a finger to help him find his daughter's killer. Danacek could make as big a show out of it as he wanted; there was going to be no help coming from here.

David tossed the thermos into the car and slid behind the wheel. He eased the door shut. Sitting for a moment, he stared at the gearshift. He was a person who detested rashness, but once, thirty-five years before, he had stood on the banks of a river and watched his best friend get swept away. That single event had changed his life. The promise he'd made to himself, so long ago, had been a child's promise, but a fervent one: no matter what it might cost him, the next time something happened, he would not just stand by numbly, watching. The transmission was in park. He punched the button and pulled the gearshift down a notch.

Looking over his shoulder, David eased the Jeep Cherokee down the driveway. He was halfway out in the road before he saw the door of the ranger station swing open and Danacek come running out, bellowing.

What struck David as most remarkable about the sight of the sheriff careening down the driveway was his own indifference to it. There was nothing anyone could do to him that was worse than what had already been done.

David shifted into drive and hit the gas. The tires spun and took. When he looked into the rearview mirror, he saw that Danacek had fallen in the snow, but in an instant the sheriff vanished, replaced by the reflection of dead tree limbs sliding across the rectangular glass.

He had come around a long turn and was out of harm's way. He was amazed at what he had done and amazed at how easy it had been, though he knew that what was coming would not be easy at all. In ten minutes every cop car in the county was going to be screaming down this road. He had to find Maya's killer and he had to do it fast.

The trick was how to get up on the ridge. For a hundred yards it looked impossible, the hillside marked by steep rock walls and dense timber. For the next hundred it was only marginally better, but finally, just beyond the trailhead markers, he spied a twenty-foot-wide corridor cutting through a stand of maples. An old fire road, most likely.

The Jeep Cherokee lurched off the pavement and slammed into deep snow, bucking and whining through the unplowed drifts. It was a good thing Danacek's vehicle had some weight to it, as well as chains. When David made it to the wind-scoured slope, traction was better.

At the top of the first rise, the fire lane angled left, unfurling through the dark forest. David took quick glances into the trees, but he knew that only a fool would try to maneuver a snowmobile through woods this thick. If he wasn't going to use the main road, the only place where he could make decent time was on top of the bluff, where there were trails and open ground. Maya's killer had outrun him once; he wasn't going to outrun him again.

David leaned forward and turned the knob on the police radio. At first there was just static and then, emerging out of the fuzz, the voice of Young Burmeister.

"He did what?"

"He stole my car!" Danacek's voice seemed further away, cutting in and out.

"But how did he do that?"

"What does it matter how he did it? I want you and McElroy up here, and I want you to call and make sure we've got road blocks on the entrances to the park."

"But I don't understand. What does he think he's doing?"

"What do you think he's doing? If you'd murdered your daughter, what do you think you'd be doing?"

Their voices disappeared in rolling breakers of fresh static. Disbelieving, David stared down at the glowing lights of the radio. This was crazy, utter madness. He was still stunned by his own foolhardiness, but even more stunned by Danacek's reaction. Much as the sheriff might have it in for David, he had to know that David couldn't possibly have killed his own daughter. What the hell was he thinking?

David grabbed for the receiver, but as he did, the Jeep Cherokee banged over a log hidden in the snow, and he had to grab the spinning steering wheel with both hands to keep the truck from plunging down into a thicket.

Engine straining, the Jeep Cherokee crawled up a second steep pitch onto the cliffs that overlooked the lake. He turned off the ignition and got out. The wind buffeted him for a second, the lake curling like a white snake, eight hundred feet below.

Still numbed by what he'd just heard, he tried to reason his way through it. His brain felt thick. Danacek had every right to be enraged. David had just stolen his car, shown him up. That still didn't make David a killer. What was he going to do? Get on the radio and apologize?

He trudged across the snow, looking for tracks, but when he reached the edge of the cliff he still had found nothing. He walked back across open ground, moving even more slowly than before, trying to focus only on the task before him, trying to ignore all the thoughts swarming in his head. He passed the Jeep Cherokee. The police radio crackled, but he paid it no mind. He went all the way to the edge of the woods. Nothing. He pivoted, mystified.

Could he have been outsmarted again? He'd seen the crows fly up, seen the buck come running out of the woods. Something had to have scared them. He had heard a snowmobile, hadn't he? Nothing felt certain anymore. Maybe the killer was on foot now, or maybe David simply hadn't come far enough. He remembered that there were three or four hiking paths that would take you down off the cliff tops and back along the lake.

He moved on down the bluff trail. Great outcroppings of rock jutted into the milky white sky. It was hard to estimate precisely how far he'd driven in one direction and then come back in the other, but he guessed he must be getting close to the spot where he'd first heard the buck thrashing in the timber.

He wondered how much time he had. It shouldn't take the deputies long to discover his tracks leading up the fire lane. The only thing working in his favor was that the Jeep Cherokee was outfitted to negotiate the snow and the smaller cop cars weren't.

The thought came to him, unbidden: Maya would need to be buried. He tried to imagine it: the meeting with some sad-eyed funeral director, the picking out of a coffin, the phone calls, the neighbors coming by with casseroles. He would have to decide about a plot. They would be there side by side, mother and daughter. He would have to go by the cemetery a day early to see that the ice was chopped from Peggy's grave, since the families would want to visit that too. All of Maya's college friends from Macalester would arrive, shuttling in from the airport. All the kids she knew from grade school in Westchester. There would be a motorcade after the service, maybe a small lunch for relatives at the church. Then, in the days after everyone left, David would have to go through her clothes and make some calls to see who might find them of use. It was more than he could bear.

The trail began to descend into what seemed like a narrow glen. Coming around a turn, he spied a chain draped across the path. A battered tin sign was nailed to one of the posts. He had to wipe away the snow to read it: BRIDGE OUT—DO NOT CROSS—WISCONSIN STATE FOREST SERVICE.

He walked a dozen paces down the trail. Whoever had posted the sign hadn't been lying. The narrow bridge was in a state of utter collapse, a jumble of splintered timbers angling from the rocks below. He cursed softly.

He stared into the glen, spying a stream running between huge rocks. It was only partially frozen, rushing water alternating with lacy patches of ice. A massive dark shape loomed at the water's edge; at first he almost thought it was an animal, a huge bear come down to drink, but there weren't bears here, there hadn't been for nearly a hundred years. As his eyes adjusted, he finally was able to make out the dull sheen of metal, the curve of a shattered windshield. It was a snowmobile, overturned.

Heart racing, David picked his way cautiously down the embankment. The smashed vehicle was a black Arctic Cat, with a billowing red flame emblazoned on the side.

Dusted with snow, it had to have been here for some time. When David ran his hand over the curved metal, he could feel that the motor was cold. He picked his way around the vehicle, looking for a registration number, some identifying mark. He opened one of the compartments and reached in. He pulled out a plastic sack of trail mix, an ice scraper, and an oil-stained pair of gloves. He tossed them aside and reached in again, retrieving a small plastic vial. It was filled with a pale yellow liquid. He popped the cap and gave a sniff; it smelled like urine. He snapped the top back on, put the vial in his jacket pocket, and reached down into the side compartment one last time.

There was one thing he'd missed. It looked like some sort of plastic baggie, rolled up tight, fastened with a rubber band. He undid the rubber band and held the parcel up in the failing light. He squinted at the profile of the Sioux chief in his feathered warbonnet; it was a packet of Red Man tobacco.

Cold radiated through the soles of his boots. There it was, the answer, staring him in the face. Danacek had murdered his daughter. Everything snapped together like a string of beads—the sheriff's belated arrival at the cabin, his trousers wet from the knees down, the way he moved through the room, putting his hands on everything, muddying any possible evidence. Even Danacek's taking him off in the Jeep Cherokee had served a purpose, given the sheriff a chance to find how much David knew, to bait him, get him riled. What a perfect set-up: walk off to the ranger station, leave the car running, and pray that David would be fool enough to steal it.

But what about the snowmobile that David thought he'd heard on the ridge? That couldn't have been Danacek. And that snowmobile couldn't have been this one. This one had to have been in the ravine for at least an hour, judging from the cold motor and the dusting of snow. There were a million possible explanations. Sound plays tricks in the cold; the snowmobile he thought he'd heard could have been miles off.

In the end, what did it matter? That spring afternoon, so long ago, came back to David, when Danacek and his friends had cornered him in the school playground. They had spat on him—in his hair, on his face and jacket. It was a month after the death of Andy, Danacek's brother. David had never once tried to hit back or defend himself, and that had only made Danacek more enraged. He had begun to push David in the chest, shoving him up against the chain-link fence. Through the whole thing, David had never uttered a word. Danacek had been the one to finally burst into tears. "One day you're going to pay for what you did," he kept repeating. "One day you're going to pay, I promise." So the day had finally come.

Everything felt so wonderfully simple; what was complicated

was deciding what to do next. He followed the half-frozen creek upstream, careful not to leave footprints in the snow, his boots splashing in the shallow water. Once he reached the top of the cliff he found refuge in a small cave.

Leaning against the rock wall with his legs out, he wrapped his arms tight around his chest, trying to fight off the cold. His back was stiff and sore, and breathing was difficult. He wondered if his ribs were cracked; being run over by a snowmobile certainly hadn't done them any good. He was unable to move, unable to think.

After an hour, or maybe a little longer, he went to the mouth of the cave and stood for a good while. At one point he saw a pale flickering down in the trees, but it quickly disappeared, and a few minutes after that there was a fierce beating in the air. David crouched as a helicopter zoomed low across the clifftops, a dazzling shaft of light scouring the rocks, but in seconds it too was gone. It did not come back.

David stripped some low branches from the nearby pines, hauled them into the cave, and arranged them into a makeshift bed. It would keep him high and dry and serve as at least temporary insulation against the plummeting temperatures.

He lowered himself carefully into the springy nest, needles and twigs stabbing and scratching at him, but it didn't matter. He fell almost immediately into a dead sleep.

He awoke several hours later, shaking uncontrollably. At first, he had no idea where he was or how he'd gotten there. The backs of his wet trousers were now stiff with frost; he couldn't feel his toes at all. He rolled over and got to his feet. He walked up and down the cave, stomping, beating himself with his arms, trying to get his blood going. The bite in the air was sharp and deep; it couldn't have been much above zero. He knew he couldn't stay here.

He walked to the cliff edge, snow crunching under his boots. The stars were luminous in the night sky. As far as he could see, there wasn't light anywhere in the park. All he could imagine was that they had given up the search for now and would be back with reinforcements in the morning.

He was not by nature a reckless man. If anything, he was a bit cautious, overly amenable, and almost pathologically sensitive about not hurting other people's feelings. But beneath all that, and closely guarded, there was iron, a line that could not be crossed, and if ever that line had been crossed, it was now. The gloves were off.

He began to pick his way down the rocks. Footing was treacherous, it was impossible to see where he was going, and he was not as limber as he'd been as a thirteen-year-old boy. Every few yards he would stop to regather his nerve. He slid on his rump and groped between boulders, lurching this way and that. He caught his ankle in holes three or four times and once, just below a pipestone ledge, nearly couldn't tug it free. He remembered that somewhere along the bluff there was an Indian rock shelter, twelve thousand years old; the range itself, a park geologist had told him once, had been around for more than a billion.

Halting to blow into his numb fingers, he stared at the north end of the lake. A single set of lights flickered through the trees. A police car leaving the cabin was his guess.

It took him three quarters of an hour to get to the bottom of the bluff. He walked out onto the frozen lake. Even with the new snowfall, there were still great open lanes of ice, scoured clean by the fierce wind, and David was able to work his way from one to the next, leaving no tracks, heading for the south shore.

The cold from the ice radiated through the soles of his boots. He was in the middle of the lake when the wind came up again momentarily, blowing snow.

There was a long, shuddering moan that echoed off the surrounding cliffs. After four or five seconds there was a second moan, somewhere off to his left. It was a sound that he had heard before, but not for years, the murmuring and shifting of the ice as it thickened.

He wasn't sure that he had a plan, except to physically survive the night. He knew that he needed to call someone, someone he could trust. He'd also had the beginnings of one other thought. It was infantile, but he had trouble getting it out of his mind. The thought was of making his way to Danacek's house.

It would be a difficult task, but not impossible. David knew Black Hawk inside and out. There was the city utility shed on the edge of town where they kept their snowplows and other vehicles. There were milk trucks that came into the creamery every morning. If a person could make it to the county trunk highway on the south side, it ran past the canning factory, and from there it would be possible to cross the bridge into the center of town.

He knew that Danacek lived somewhere near the old elementary school. David would have to wait until evening and hope that Danacek's wife was out. Their kids, he was pretty sure, were all grown. Danacek, without doubt, had weapons in the house.

Once he got within a couple hundred yards of the south shore, he could finally make out the dim shape of the old dance hall. It had been built a hundred years ago, along with a giant luxury hotel. The hotel had burned down decades before, but the dance hall remained, reduced now to a place where, in the summer, you could rent a canoe, buy postcards or hamburgers, use the bathrooms to change into your swimsuit.

As he approached the sprawling log building, an owl flapped up from the boat dock and glided into the woods. He moved into the cavernous space beneath the dance hall, where canoes and outboard motors were stacked. The outer door leading to the upstairs was locked, but the back wall of the storage area was crumbling rock, and it took David just a few seconds to work free a stone the size of his hand. The door had a window, caked with frost. With a safecracker's delicate touch, he tapped lightly on the lower pane with his stone. The glass broke suddenly, the sound of it shattering on concrete surprisingly loud in the still night air. David reached inside, fumbling with the cold metal knob and then flipping the lock. The door swung open on its own.

He felt his way up the dark wooden steps, holding to the railing. Once he got upstairs, it was better; moonlight shone through the huge windows, across the bare dance floor. It was timeless, this place: the racks of postcards, the bulletin boards announcing Friday night dances and nature tours and fish fries for the tourists from Chicago, the same cheap bow-and-arrow sets, decorated with brightly colored bits of fluff, that he had loved as a boy.

Near the front door was an old-fashioned cooler, unplugged, its black rubber cord coiled on the floor. It was too dark to tell exactly what was in it, but there was something. The problem was, it was locked. Using his stone, David smashed the curved glass top with one blow. He reached down and pulled out a plastic carton of cheese curds.

He ate greedily, finishing off nearly three-quarters of the container. He yanked four wool Indian blankets off the shelf above the cash register.

He spread one out on the cold dance floor, sat down on it, and then pulled the other three around him as best he was able. After ten minutes he finally stopped shaking. From somewhere far out on the lake he heard a long, eerie howl and, after an interval, an answering howl, much closer. This time it wasn't just the ice—it was wolves. Maya will be thrilled to know that I finally heard them, he thought, and then he remembered that she was dead.

three

After a week of steady rain, the skies had finally parted. The river had flooded its banks, the high school football field looked like a lake, and every March breeze shook fresh showers of icy water out of the trees, but David, delivering his Saturday morning papers, had a new baseball nestled in the bottom of his newsbag.

What did it matter if the diamond was going to be a little wet? The snow was finally gone, he'd called everybody, and unless they had another downpour, they were playing at two o'clock.

He tossed the last of his papers onto Mrs. Schroeder's porch, wheeled his bike around, and pedaled the two blocks up the hill. Andy Danacek was just coming around the corner of his house, lugging a trash can on his hip.

"Hey," David said.

"Hey."

Andy swung the trash can, gave it an extra boost with his knee, and deposited it at the curb. He was David's best friend, in part because Andy was even further down in the ninth-grade pecking order than he was. They were both outsiders: Andy's family had moved to Black Hawk just fourteen months before, and David's father liked to complain that after five years in town they were still being introduced at church as "the new people."

Andy looked a little like Ichabod Crane—all elbows and knees, with a large Adam's apple and huge eyes that seemed to swim like languid carp behind his thick, Buddy Holly glasses. Whatever measure of social acceptance he'd managed to achieve came from playing the class clown: he knew a million jokes, would break into odd bits of song whenever the teacher stepped out of the room, and could talk like Donald Duck so well you could actually make out the words. His brother, Doug, just a year older, a sullen bully who was building a reputation as a football player as well as the administrator of the nastiest Indian rope burns on the playground, gave him a wide berth.

"I just wanted to let you know I got hold of everybody," David said. "I think we've got at least twelve, maybe fourteen."

"Good." Andy wiped his palms on his jeans. As far as David knew, the Danaceks were the only people in town who didn't have a phone.

"Want to see what I got?"

"Sure."

David dug in the newsbag, pulled out the Spalding box, and tossed it to Andy. Andy caught it with both hands.

"Wow." He opened the flap and lifted out the shiny new baseball.

"I bought it this morning."

Andy set the white box in David's bike basket and faked a throw, twisting his wrist as if snapping off a Bob Buhl curve ball.

The truth was that the two of them weren't athletes. Neither had the kind of father who would bother to sign them up for Little League. David's father had no interest in sports and Andy's was a drinker and a drifter who worked some days at the lumberyard and other days didn't.

The two boys had discovered baseball together, just the year before. It was the Braves' first year in Milwaukee and David and Andy spent hours listening to games on the radio, and started collecting Topps bubble gum cards. They invented their own two-man game, chalking in a strike zone on the depot wall at the train station and working out elaborate rules—anything hit over the railroad tracks was a homer, anything off the gas storage tanks a triple, anything that hit the ground short of the pitcher an out. They kept detailed box scores, complete with cumulative ERAs and batting averages. David was usually the Braves, Andy the Dodgers, and the Braves nearly always won.

Twice a week they would round up the younger kids in the neighborhood, all the losers and oddballs, all the mama's boys who weren't signed up for Little League either, and play games with five or six boys on each side in the big lot across from the graveyard. There were no uniforms, no coaches, no freshly limed foul lines, no bleachers full of cheering parents, but on the other hand, there wasn't anyone around to tell them they weren't Mantle or Mays.

Andy rolled the new ball down his forearm and tried to give it a flip with his bicep. It was a trick that needed work; the ball bobbled off his fingertips and dropped to the wet grass.

"Jesus, Andy, nice move."

Andy shot David a wounded glance, but retrieved the ball and handed it over. Sullen, David wiped the ball on his jacket. Sometimes Andy's goofing around got on his nerves.

"You want to go check out the flood?" David said.

"Sure. Let me get my bike."

David tucked the baseball back into the Spalding box as Andy loped around the corner of the house. It was a tiny place and the Danaceks occupied only half of it, renting from a mean old Baptist lady who had a tiny Chihuahua that yapped in the window from morning to night.

David had been inside the Danaceks' house only four or five times; it wasn't a place he enjoyed being. They had just two rooms and David had no idea where they all slept. Bedding seemed to be heaped everywhere, and there was always a smell that he'd never been able to identify. He imagined that only Eskimos lived in conditions like this, hut-like and dark. Andy's mother was kind but very large, and she never went out; his father never came in.

Andy pushed his bike across the wet lawn. "You ready?"

"Ready," David said.

They set off, pedaling past the elementary school and the city park. David knew he shouldn't have barked at Andy, but he had a lot on his mind. He'd been awakened during the night by the sounds of his parents' arguing, and the argument was still in him somewhere, churning.

He hadn't been able to hear all of it. His parents' bedroom was downstairs, and though he'd been able to make out most of what his father said, his mother's voice was muffled and far away.

"So what are you suggesting, that we pack up the car and go?" David lay under his quilt, his father's words circling around him like angry wasps. His mother murmured again, trying to be placating, but his father cut her off. "That's not the way the world works. It's not up to somebody like me." More murmuring. "Tell someone? Do you have any idea what would happen if I did? My job is to put food on this table."

His mother began to cry. Both voices faded and then there was silence. David lay awake for more than an hour; his little brother was asleep in the bed across the room. His father had been having more and more of his moods and David could only guess at the reasons. He knew that production was being cut back at the plant, now that the Korean War was winding down. People were being laid off and some were being transferred.

But why would his mother suggest that they leave? It made no sense. Even though David hated his father's anger—hated it when he shouted at his mother—it seemed wrong for her to question him. If he said something wasn't his business, then it wasn't his business.

David secretly believed his father was a cut above other men. He'd gone to college, even if he hadn't graduated, and had worked his way up to unit supervisor at the plant. Once when the minister was sick, his father had gotten up and delivered a sermon, off-the-cuff, that everyone said was the best they'd heard in years.

David's and Andy's bicycle tires hissed on wet pavement as they coasted towards the bridge. The sixty-foot span sat on the very western edge of town. On the south bank was the woolen mill, with its rows of broken windows, and on the north, flooded hayfields and swampland. The two boys propped their bikes against the concrete abutment and made their way to the center of the bridge.

They leaned on the railing and stared into the brown water of the Sauk River racing just a couple of feet below them. In the main channel the giant limbs of an uprooted elm vibrated like a tuning fork. Andy let a gob of spit drop and they watched it spin away in the muddy current. Debris floated past: two-by-fours, clumps of leaves and torn branches, a bobbing milk can, part of a wooden fence.

They threw sticks in the water and when they got tired of that, they crossed to the far side of the river. For an hour they wandered through pastures and woodland, exploring the margins of the flood. They pitched rocks and rolled a log over a high bank and listened to it splash. They found a dead dog stuck in some larches and came upon a cow and shivering calf stranded on a boggy island. In the shallows they could see swirls of trapped fish.

Water seemed to be flowing in every direction, without rhyme or reason. Why would his mother think they needed to leave this place? What could she possibly have said that would have made his father so angry? Andy lagged behind, swatting at the trunks of trees with a willow switch and singing, "Comin' to get you in a rickshaw, honey . . ."

On their way back they stopped at a gravel pile just below the bridge and had a stone-skipping contest on a quiet pond that had crept out of the swamp. Skipping stones was the one thing that Andy was better at than David. Maybe it was just his technique—he was so loose-limbed and his release so low that his knuckles seemed to scrape the ground as he let fly—or maybe it was just that he spent forever picking out the right rock.

Five times they threw and five times Andy won. Irritated, David searched in the damp gravel until he found a jagged bit of slate that fit snugly between his thumb and forefinger, a little bigger than an Oreo but with a plcasing hcft.

Andy threw first. His rock skittered across the water like a frightened duck and disappeared in some reeds after the fifth touch. David waited, pressing his piece of slate to his chest with both hands, like Warren Spahn holding the runners close.

"You ready?"

"Go ahead," Andy said.

David took a short run and flung his stone across the glassy pond. It sailed further out than Andy's throw had, skipped four times, ricocheted off a charred stump, and then, miraculously, skipped twice more.

David spun and raised both hands in the air, like a referee signaling touchdown. "Six! I win!"

Andy gawked at him, incredulous. "Aww, come on! It hit the stump!"

"So what? It's still six."

"It doesn't count if it hits a stump."

"Show me the rule book."

"You know there's no rule book."

"Well then?"

"Well then what?"

"Well then what what? I can't believe this. The one time in a million I beat you, and you start making up new rules."

Andy's eyes behind his huge Buddy Holly glasses were starting to smart. "I gotta go," he said. He turned and began to climb the embankment.

David held his ground. Andy could be such a baby. Somewhere a plane droned in the sky. This was all so stupid, but there probably was no point in turning it into World War Three.

David lumbered up the incline and trotted to catch up to Andy on the bridge.

"OK, you win," he said.

"It doesn't matter."

"Maybe it doesn't, but you're still the champ. I was just kidding you anyway." Andy gave him a wary glance. "But I'll bet I can do one thing you can't do."

"What's that?"

David put a knee up on the railing and, after a couple of hops, pushed himself up. The metal beam was eighteen inches across, and every few feet there was a row of bolts, the heads rounded and slightly raised. He took a few seconds to steady his nerves, and then he rose, stooping at first like an old man and then straightening up, triumphant. He beamed down at Andy.

Andy shook his head. "No way. Forget about it."

"What do you mean, no way? It's a piece of cake." David began to walk across the bridge, placing one foot in front of the other. He focused on the woolen mill on the far bank, trying not to look down at the fast-moving water. When he was halfway across, he heard a scuffling behind him. He glanced back. Andy had somehow managed to scramble onto the railing and was perched like an ungainly bird, not quite sure how to get up or down.

"There you go," David said. "You can do it. Just take it slow."

Andy lifted a hand off the railing and quickly put it down again. He raised the hand a second time and began to come out of his crouch. Both arms were extended but unsteady, like the wings of a balsam glider.

"Just relax, you've got it," David said. Suddenly Andy was upright, swaying for a second, and then rock-solid. "Way to go."

David nodded and Andy nodded back. David turned, shifting his focus to the far side of the bridge. He could see their bikes now, leaning against the concrete abutment. The clouds to the north looked ominous. David prayed for the rains to hold off for just a few more hours, until they got their ball game in. He could hear Andy singing behind him. "Comin' to get you in a rickshaw, honey, I'll be by about a quarter past nine . . ."

There was a tiny splash, like a bluegill jumping in the river. David wouldn't have thought anything about it except that the singing had stopped. He stopped too, stock-still, for five seconds and then for ten, listening for the scuff of a tennis shoe, for a hum or a cough, for anything.

"Hey, Andy."

There was no answer. David glanced over his shoulder; the gray metal railing stretched out behind him, empty. He leapt off the railing and ran to the far side of the bridge. He saw Andy, going down the river backwards. His glasses were gone and he was gulping for air, both arms flailing. The current seemed to be pushing him toward the south bank and David ran off the bridge, past their bikes, and down the grassy incline.

For a moment it seemed as if everything was going to be all right. Andy had come to rest in the shallows, sitting chest-deep in the water. He looked, without his glasses, like a wet, shivering rat.

"Just hold on," David shouted. He scanned the bank, then ran to a huge downed tree, but the first branch he tried to snap off was so rotten it came apart in his hands, and the second he couldn't break at all.

"It's going to be OK." He scrambled back down the slope and splashed into the water. He stopped shin-deep; the river was icy cold and already he was in far enough to feel the tug of the current. Andy was no more than ten feet away, shoulders hunched, wet hair plastered across his forehead.

"Just take my hand." Andy stared dimly at him. "You can do it! You think I'm going to stand here all day? Come on!"

Hand extended, David edged another foot out in the water. Andy's lips were turning blue. He rocked forward three or four times and then tried to heave himself to his feet, but instead fell backwards into the river. He slid slowly on the seat of his pants into the main channel. David scrambled back onto the bank and ran along the weedy slope.

"Keep your head up! Don't fight it!"

David had no idea whether Andy could hear him or not, but Andy did manage to twist himself around in the water. He swam a few strokes as he was being swept downstream, but then a floating island of brush obscured David's view, and when it passed, Andy wasn't there any more.

David continued to trot along the bank, scanning the water. His heart leapt at every dark form, every submerged log, every clotted mass of debris. A hero would have thrown himself into the water, but the water was too muddy to see anything, and the truth was that David was too poor a swimmer to complete a single lap at the city pool.

When he came to a high barbed-wire fence, he finally stopped and crouched on his haunches, watching the flood roll past. He'd come a good quarter of a mile down from the bridge. Blue jays quarreled in the trees on the far side of the river. His socks and shoes were sopping. He began to shake from the cold.

Years later, when he first told Peggy the story, she asked him what he was thinking as he sat on the bank. He told her that he couldn't remember; it was as if everything went into a cloud.

All that he was able to remember was what he did. He went home. His mother was horrified at how wet he was and made him go upstairs and take a bath. Running hot water in the tub, he could hear *Sky King* playing in the next room. They'd only had the television for a few weeks, their first one, and his sister had been glued to it night and day.

They ate grilled-cheese sandwiches for lunch. His muddy jeans clunked and thumped in the washing machine while his mother stood at the sink, slicing tomatoes. She joked with David's sister, her mood light and playful, without a trace of whatever had made her weep the night before.

Drinking his milk, David scrutinized her. If anyone would understand, it would be his mother, but he hated the idea of making her cry again. Besides, he wasn't utterly sure anything had even happened. Everything was already getting so hazy. He felt that if he put his head down, he would be able to sleep for hours. As long as he didn't put the event into words, in some way it wouldn't really exist.

A squirrel clucked on a low-hanging branch outside the kitchen window, its tail pulsing like a snake about to strike. David knew he was going to have to say something. He made a silent pact with himself: as soon as his sister left the room, he would tell his mother everything.

It didn't work out the way he'd planned. His sister was off to her first babysitting job ever, and she was all aflutter. Even though it was just down the street, she asked her mother if she would go with her, just for a little while, and her mother said she would.

"You'll be OK?" David's mother said. She sucked some tomato juice off her thumb and wiped her hands on a towel.

"I'll be fine," he said.

"I'll be back in a little bit," she said. "There's some ice cream in the refrigerator if you're hungry." David didn't look up as she came over and gave him a kiss on his head.

After they'd gone, David set his dishes in the sink and looked up at the clock. It was nearly one; he had a game. He pedaled his bike to the field. Even though the grass was damp, the field was on high enough ground not to be muddy. The other kids began to arrive:

Jerry Wilkins, Tom Fass, Billy O'Neill and his two brothers. After a half hour they had fourteen boys, which meant they had enough, as long as they pitched and caught for themselves.

Billy O'Neill asked David where Andy was, and David said he didn't know.

"Should we wait for him then?" Billy asked. Tom Fass was setting out pieces of cardboard for bases, weighing them down with sticks.

"No, I think it will be OK," David said.

On the wet field the new ball quickly became as heavy as a rock. On his first time at bat, David fouled off the first two pitches and then, on the third, swung and missed by a foot. Everyone hooted; no one had ever seen him strike out, not in a game like this. He did better his second time up, lining a double into the pine trees down the right-field line, but he still felt strangely disconnected. He forgot to tag up on a long fly ball, and when Billy O'Neill got caught in a rundown between first and second, David just stood in center field, watching with the idle interest he might have shown toward a moth fluttering helplessly against a lamp.

As the teams changed sides to start the fourth inning, a police car pulled up. David couldn't recall the name of the policeman who got out, but he had seen him somewhere before, maybe on the canoe trip with the Boy Scouts. He was a large man with a George Gobel crew cut and hands the size of shovels. All the kids stopped to stare as he picked his way through the maze of bicycles.

"Is one of you David?" he asked.

"I am," David said. He was swinging two bats, letting them hang down between his shoulders. He was supposed to lead off the inning.

"Can I talk to you for a minute?"

"Sure. Should I bring my glove?"

"Whatever you want."

David flung the bats aside and scooped up his glove. They walked to the car and the policeman held the door for David to get in. David had never been in a squad car before; he sat forward on the black vinyl seat, staring at the radio with its looping cord. The policeman slid in behind the steering wheel and yanked his door shut.

"So were you with Andy Danacek this morning?"

"Yes," David said.

David didn't try to hide anything. He told the policeman about the rock-skipping contest and Andy's fall from the bridge and how David had tried to save him, how he'd run along the bank, trying to get him to swim.

The policeman frowned, running a hand over his close-cropped hair. "So why didn't you tell anyone?"

David stared mournfully out the window. Jerry Wilkins was circling the bases and Tom Fass was waving him home. The ball had rolled under one of the bikes and Billy O'Neill was trying to retrieve it.

"I don't know," he said.

They drove to the police station and called his parents. Andy's body had already been found, washed up in some willows about a mile down from the woolen mill. David had to repeat his story to two other policemen and a woman who wrote everything down. One of the policemen kept asking if David was sure he hadn't pushed Andy, if there hadn't been some sort of scuffle.

David kept saying no, there hadn't been. The policeman grew more and more frustrated and began pacing the room. "So what do you feel about this? You feel bad?" "Yeah." "Then how come you don't show it? How come you just sit there like a bump on a log?" David knew everything would be all right if he could just cry, but he couldn't do that. The policeman spun a chair across the floor and slammed out of the room.

The whole town turned out for the funeral. David and his father arrived a little late and had to stand in the back. David had never been in a Catholic church before, and the candles, the Latin incantations, and the genuflections of the congregation all smacked of the forbidden, the idolatrous. Every now and then he caught sight of someone looking his way, tugging a neighbor's sleeve to discreetly point him out.

Andy's brother and his parents were up at the front, and David was able to catch glimpses of them only at the very end when they came down the center aisle, following the casket. It was the first time David had ever seen Andy's mother out of her house. She was so large it looked as if it was painful for her to walk. Her breast was heaving, whether from grief or exertion it was impossible to tell. She clung to her son's arm, while her husband, bringing up the rear, had the frantic look of a lost dog trotting through an unfamiliar neighborhood.

As they passed the last pew, Andy's brother spied David stationed against the wall. He came to a dead stop, shaking off his mother's arm like a boxer shaking off his robe. His thick neck colored above his white collar. For a moment it seemed certain that he would launch himself, fists flying, but his father put a hand on his shoulder, whispering something in his ear, and even though Andy's brother brushed the hand away, it was enough to hold him. The three of them continued on their way out of the church.

Early that summer David and his family moved to California. The reason they gave all their friends was that the plant had cut back to a skeleton crew, and there were lots of good jobs in the aircraft industry on the West Coast. David knew better; he knew they were leaving because of him, because of the shame he had brought on the family.

All spring David had endured terrible things at school, none of which he ever told his parents. Andy's brother had been unrelenting. He would stare David down in the lunchroom and make a point of bumping into him, accidentally on purpose, whenever they passed in the hallway, knocking David's books to the floor. A couple of the older kids started calling him "killer" as if it were his new nickname. "Hey, killer, let me see your homework for a sec," and, "Hey, killer, lend me a nickel for the milk machine."

Not everyone was cruel. There were teachers who would keep him after class for a few minutes to ask him how he was doing. There was Joann Barker, whom he'd had a crush on for two years, pulling him aside before Sunday school class to tell him she knew he was too good a person to have done what everyone said he'd done. The minister came to the house a couple of times to see if he wanted to talk. But David had no way of talking about it. Andy had been his best friend in the world. He was going to miss Andy more than anyone else, more than all those kids who were ragging him day after day.

How could he make people believe that he hadn't been trying to get away with something? That the reason for his silence had not been cowardice or callousness or fear of facing the music? How could he make people understand that there were things that could happen to you that were just too big, that were like entering a vast cloud, that could overwhelm any reaction you could have? That in less time than it took to flip a light switch, the world could go unreal? He'd always heard the phrase "struck dumb," and he'd never understood what it meant. But he did now. He'd been struck dumb.

Worse than anything anyone could do to him was the shame he'd brought on his family. Long silences and forced conversations marked their dinners. His father brooded, retreated every evening behind his newspaper, and sometimes, late, David would look out the window to see him standing in the driveway, having a smoke, the ember of his cigarette glowing in the dark spring night.

His mother was the one who kept trying to find ways to get David to talk, ways to comfort him. One day after school, as he sat at the kitchen table having his afternoon snack (chocolate pinwheels and milk, the cold glass beaded with tiny drops of condensation), she took a chair opposite him.

"David, we want you to know . . . Your father and I, we know what happened was an accident. You're a good boy. You're the best son we could ever have. We believe in you and we're going to get through this. All of us . . ."

Her eyes began to tear up, and she wasn't able to continue. David stared at his plate, squashing a bit of flaking chocolate with the tip of his thumb. His mother left the room without a sound.

Maybe it was just that they were all so Swedish. It was a home where unpleasant things were almost never addressed, where a grandparent in North Dakota might die and no one would ever mention it. It was a home where his mother's optimism and lightness of touch served as a counterweight to his father's darker moods, where orange juice was drunk out of small glasses and no one left the lights on in a room he wasn't occupying.

One Saturday David walked into his room to find a book of poetry lying open on his bed. He knew it was his mother who'd put it there. She had written poems from the time she was a teenager growing up on a farm outside of Fargo, and had even had a couple published in small magazines. She loved Emily Dickinson and the writings of Anne Morrow Lindbergh. David had always gotten books at Christmas, and for the past several years they had become increasingly literary—the essays of Emerson, a volume of Tagore.

The poem lying open on the bed was *The Hound of Heaven* by Francis Thompson. The book, checked out from the local library, included a commentary by Francis P. Le Buffe, S.J., Professor of Psychology, Fordham University. The spine was cracked, the boards badly bowed, and the cover the color of a grocery bag.

David sat down at his desk to read.

I fled Him, down the nights, and down the days;
    I fled Him, down the arches of the years;
I fled him, down the labyrinthine ways
    Of my own mind . . . and under running laughter.
        Up vistaed hopes I sped;
        And shot, precipitated,
Adown Titanic glooms of chasmèd fears
    From those strong Feet that followed, followed after.
        But with unhurrying chase,
        And unperturbèd pace,
    Deliberate speed, majestic instancy,
        They beat—and a Voice beat
        More instant than the Feet—
    "All things betray thee, who betrayest Me."

The poem went on for seven pages and he read to the end. Through the open window he could hear Mrs. Ohlendorf's clattering lawnmower and smell the freshly cut grass. His cheeks were burning.

His mother thought he was lost. What else could the poem mean? His mother had always been the one person he could count on, the one person who'd always believed in him, and now even she had given up.

He ran a trembling hand over his face. Maybe he was taking it all wrong. Maybe she'd meant the poem to be consoling. Maybe the idea of God never relenting, never abandoning the chase for your soul, was supposed to make you feel better, but how could his mother be so sure what God was like? What if he wasn't patient and plodding and gentle? What if he was filled with vengeance? It was just as likely. More likely. Maybe David's mistake had been not running soon enough. Maybe he should never have come home. His mother thought he'd betrayed God; that's exactly what the poem had said. Maybe, as soon as Andy's head had disappeared under that dark water, he should have just gotten on his bike and ridden and ridden.

They left for California on a Wednesday evening. They always started their long trips at night; his father liked to do as much of the driving as he could late, after the children had fallen asleep in the car. An hour before they were to take off, David told his mother he was going out for a walk, he would be back in a minute. His father had gone downtown to get the oil changed.

It had just turned dark and the streetlights were flickering like fireflies. David walked for maybe a block and then began to run. He broke into a full sprint, suddenly wild with grief. He pounded down the pavement until it felt as if his heart was about to burst. It took him less than ten minutes to get to the river.

He went to the middle of the bridge, running his hand along the railing. He knew his father would be furious if David wasn't there when he got back. No one had ever disobeyed his father; it was impossible to imagine what would happen the first time someone did. The water below was the color of iron, the banks an inky black. Frogs chanted in the swamp. The stump where he had ricocheted his skipping stone stood in a hayfield, six or seven feet high, a dark sentinel.

He put his knee on the railing and pushed himself up. He paused, and then rose to his feet; it was a joke, how easy it was. A light breeze rattled the leaves on the far bank. Looking out across the tree line, he could see the last red sliver of sunset in the western sky.

He dug in the pocket of his jeans and pulled out a thick wad of papers. He took a half dozen of the pages, lifted them over his head, and let the breeze catch them. They fluttered in the darkness, descended like ghostly white birds, and settled on the water. On the bank the abandoned woolen mill looked like something out of ancient Egypt. He took a second handful of papers and did the same. What was the point in keeping them? They weren't real box scores anyway, despite all the ERAs and batting averages and won-lost records, neatly listed in pencil. They had just made it all up, imagining themselves to be Eddie Matthews and Joe Adcock, Duke Snider and Roy Campanella. What they hadn't been capable of imagining was being nothing—one second balancing on a rail, singing a stupid song about a rickshaw, and then the next second being gone.

David threw the last batch as far as he could, nearly losing his balance. Some of the papers had already sunk, but others were still drifting like a doomed armada down to the bend in the river where Andy had disappeared.

The sound of a car made him turn. Headlights flared on the long hill. David hopped down from the railing and walked quickly back across the bridge. The station wagon stopped twenty feet short of the bridge, and David heard the door open.

His father stepped out. David's heart pounded. Squinting, he cupped his hand to his eyes. In the dim ceiling light of the five-year-old Chevy, he could see his mother's frightened face, and in the back seat, his brother and sister engulfed by pillows. His father was in darkness, unreadable, standing behind the open car door like a matador behind a cape.

"So what is this about?"

"Nothing, Dad, nothing. I just didn't know you were going to be back so soon."

"Just get in the car," his father said. There was no anger in his voice, only the low, discouraged tones of shame. "We've got a long way to go."

four

In the morning, a dull pain in his hip woke him. He reached down in his pocket and pulled out his keys and wallet. The polished log beams of the dance hall glowed in the early light. He rolled onto his back, careful to keep the blankets up to his chin. It was Christmas morning and fiercely cold.

He laid his keys on the floor. When he opened his wallet, three or four cards fell on his chest. It was a hopeless wallet; he'd had it for years, and Maya was always on him to buy a new one. He gathered up the cards—ATM, gym membership, driver's license. In among them was one of Maya's old school photos.

He held it up to the light. It was her kindergarten picture, and it was badly dog-eared. She was so little, and she looked as if she were afraid of the photographer. She sat on a wire chair, wearing red stockings, and her hands were folded demurely in her lap, her dark bangs coming almost down to her eyebrows.

David shifted onto his side and dug the rest of his cards out of his woebegone wallet. There were twenty or thirty of them, and he went through the stack quickly, pulling out all of Maya's pictures. He'd never thrown any of them away. There was one of her in her pink jumper, wearing a pink ribbon in her hair, and one in the fifth grade, when she'd first gotten her glasses, and then there were the defiant high school pictures.

He laid them out next to him on the floor and tried to put them in order. He wasn't quite sure which was the fourth grade picture and which the sixth. They were all so real to him; it was as if no time had passed at all. The shy kindergartener was as vivid to him as the teenage rebel. He remembered a writer he'd represented once telling him, after meeting her, that she had such clear eyes. "You can just tell she's been well brought up," he'd said. "With eyes like that, you can tell she just trusts the world." There had been a time when that was true, but it was long gone.

It was more than he could stand. He scooped up the dog-eared pictures. He pressed them between his palms and held them to his lips, as if to warm them, as if he could somehow breathe them back to life.

Grief was a room he couldn't allow himself to fully enter yet. He pushed the pile of blankets aside and hobbled across the floor, his feet sore and swollen. There was a series of closets in the front hallway. He found nothing in the first three, but with the fourth he got lucky. A bulky pea green Forest Service coat sagged on a wire hanger, and crumpled on the floor were gloves and a green Forest Service cap.

There was a full-length mirror on the back of the door, and as he bent over to retrieve the gloves, he caught sight of his reflection. It was a shock. He had always prided himself on being rather put together. He was not an unhandsome man, with small, rather fine features and a powerful physical presence that belied the slightly wounded quality of his expression. He was as stocky as a blocking back, wore a neatly trimmed beard, and his clothes had always been carefully chosen. But now, with the bloodstained jacket, his thinning hair unwashed and sticking up in all directions, and great bags under his eyes, he looked deranged.

David unzipped his jacket and slipped out of it. He scanned the cavernous dance hall for several seconds and finally stuffed the jacket under the bar, sliding a couple of heavy cartons of plastic cups against it to hide it from view.

He pulled on the Forest Service coat. It was musty, icy cold, and maybe one size too big, but he could have done worse. He put on the fur-lined gloves and then the hat with the pine-tree-shaped badge, tugging down the earflaps.

He went back to the cooler, hoping to fortify himself with another carton of cheese curds, but the cooler was empty. What he did find, after a little nosing around, were three Snickers in one of the cabinets. He stuffed two of them in his coat pockets and ate the third. The candy was frozen and brittle, but a minute of hard chewing reduced it to a warm, reviving goo of syrup and peanuts.

He went to the front door of the dance hall and stared out at the blanketed parking lot and the boarded-up kiosk where in the summer they sold Cracker Jacks and suntan lotion. The morning had the cathedral-like hush that always followed a big snow. If Maya were alive, the two of them would be out skiing now, it would be perfect . . .

At the end of the hallway, beyond the bathrooms, was an office. It was locked, but barely; one solid shove was enough to knock it open. The room had the sour smell of old socks. A shellacked bigmouth bass gaped from a plaque on one wall, and on a bulletin board were tacked a sheaf of job listings, a poster on water safety, and an out-of-date Packers schedule.

A cell phone lay on the desk. David picked it up, expecting it to be dead, but miraculously it wasn't. He called his office in Manhattan, but just got voice mail. After a moment he remembered it was Christmas Day.

He hung up and punched in Mike and Annie's number in Rye. Besides being David's best friend, Mike was a high-powered lawyer and PR man in the city, with enough testosterone and righteous vindictiveness to bust just about anyone's ass if he took a mind to it.

The phone rang five or six times—David was on the verge of hitting OFF—when Ann picked up.

"Hello?"

"Annie?"

"David?"

"Yes."

"Oh David." He knew instantly from her tone that Danacek must have gotten the story to the press. His eyes clouded with tears. He knew the kitchen where Ann was standing now, the kitchen where the two couples had spent so many Saturday mornings, gossiping over coffee. He could just about see it—the long butcher-block counter, the cut flowers, even in winter, the pictures of everybody's kids up on the refrigerator—a whole civilization.

"Where are you?"

"Listen, is Mike there?"

"He's just getting out of the shower. Michael? Michael! Get on the phone!"

There was a long pause. The bigmouth bass on the wall shimmered with unholy life. "David?" It was Mike.

"Yeah."

"Jesus, man, are you all right?"

"No. I don't think so, no."

"We heard on the radio this morning. I just can't believe it."

"I know, I know."

"What they're saying . . ."

"You believe what they're saying, Mike?"

"No. Of course not."

"Then just listen. I want you to know who did this. In case anything happens to me. There's a sheriff out here by the name of Doug Danacek. His brother . . . his brother was the boy who drowned."

"Yes, I remember."

"This is just payback. That's all it is."

"David, you've got to turn yourself in."

"Listen to me! Danacek killed her, and now he's trying to turn the whole thing around . . ."

"Did you hear me? This is really stupid. The only reason for any white man to be running from a cop in this country is because he's guilty, and that's what everyone's going to think . . . You've got all the resources in the world at your fingertips, and you'd be a fool not to use them. Let me call the DA out there; we'll set up a time and a place for you to surrender."

"I don't think you understand, Mike. They're not going to let me surrender."

"That's total horseshit and you know it."

"Doug Danacek, Michael. Remember the name."

"You think you're being a hero? This is no way to be a hero. This is the coward's way out, I don't care what you say. You're starting to sound like some jibbering country half-wit . . ."

David punched the OFF button. He heard other voices now, murmuring, and it seemed as if they were right under him, under the floorboards.

He moved quietly to the window. Through the partially lowered blinds he could see two police officers, a man and a woman, resting on skis almost directly below him, no more than ten feet away. The man intently scanned the distant shoreline with a pair of binoculars while the woman blew into her hands.

David stood motionless, his fingers touching the blinds. Between the windows lay a litter of dead flies. The two officers were just an arm's length from the stacked-up canoes. All it would take was a glance over the shoulder for one of them to spot the broken pane and he would be undone.

He slipped the cell phone into his pocket. He knew he couldn't flee. If he bolted out the front door, after all that had happened, or, more precisely, after all they believed had happened (a man, gone berserk, killing his daughter and then stealing a policeman's car), the two officers might feel perfectly within their rights to shoot him in the back. So what was he going to do? Hide in a closet? It was hopeless. Surrender, then. Surrender in a way that didn't take them by surprise: come out with his hands up and hope for the best.

The officers turned suddenly, as if their heads were somehow on a single swivel, and stared back into the woods. The man quickly capped his binoculars, skied swiftly across the snow and disappeared around the edge of the dance hall. The woman followed him.

David, his heart racing now, moved swiftly out of the office and down the hall. The front door, partially blocked by a bulky vending machine, had two narrow panes of glass where he could safely see outside without being seen. He spotted the two officers instantly, leaning on their ski poles, just twenty feet away, but it took several more seconds to make out what had gotten their attention: a snowplow rattling down the long hill, blasting a wide swath through the glistening drifts. The two officers waited while the snowplow wove its way across the parking lot and finally came to a stop in front of the boarded-up kiosk.

There were three men crowded together in the cab, and two of them tumbled out. They were dressed exactly like David, in heavy green Forest Service coats and the hats with the earflaps. The woman officer glided over to speak to them.

The conversation went on for some time, along with a good amount of gesturing and pointing (toward the lake, back up the hill), and eventually the second officer joined in. David could guess what the problem was: the police wanted them out of there and the park employees wanted to get on with their work. To David's surprise, it was the police who relented.

One of the maintenance men unlocked the kiosk and dragged out a half dozen gleaming snow shovels. He took one and tossed one to his partner; the other four they left leaning against the door of the kiosk as they trudged off toward the stone bathhouse.

David peered at them, his hands tight on the corners of the cigarette machine, silently cursing himself. He'd slept too long, and now he'd blown it. The two officers went on talking to the snowplow driver for a couple minutes, and then the driver leaned forward to turn the key in the ignition. The ancient yellow machine, solid as a tank, coughed to life amid a cloud of black smoke. The snowplow wheeled around and clanked through the parking lot and then up the road, clearing the other half of the pavement.

After the snowplow finally disappeared, the woman officer turned and casually surveyed the dance hall. David was too far back from the glass to be seen, but the woman officer was taking so much time David began to doubt himself. Maybe it was some trick of the light, maybe she could see him, or maybe she heard something, but then her partner spoke and she pivoted away. The two of them skied out of sight to David's left.

David scrambled quickly back to the office. Making the narrowest crack in the blinds with his fingers, he was able to locate them almost immediately. They had stopped fifty yards down the lake-shore, and the woman was talking into a cell phone or a walkie-talkie.

David returned to the front door. I am like a rat in a cage, he thought, scuttling to and fro. He stared at the four remaining snow shovels leaning against the kiosk. His guess was that the snowplow would be back soon enough, with a fresh crew of reinforcements. He walked onto the dance floor, gazing out the broad windows at the end of the enormous room. He could see one of the workmen on top of the stone bathhouse, shoveling off the snow to keep the roof from collapsing. But where was his partner? David didn't see any sign of him. He looked again at the four shovels.

If he had any chance of getting out, he decided, it was now. The two officers were fifty yards to his left, the workman fifty yards to his right (maybe his buddy had just gone into the bathhouse to take a pee). There was a narrow bridge on the far side of the parking lot, and if David could somehow get there and drop down to the creek, he'd be out of sight again, he'd have a real shot. Maybe it was crazy, but there was no time to come up with anything better. At least he was wearing the right clothes; he looked like any other poor schlub shoveling snow for the state.

He pulled the brim of his cap down and jerked the drawstring taut under his chin, then stood for a full minute clutching the door-knob, trying to gather his nerve.

He took one big last breath and eased the door open. It had been cold inside the dance hall, but outside was worse; the morning met him with a fierce arctic slap. He pulled the door quietly behind him. He could hear the rasping of a shovel on the roof of the bathhouse. The key was not to look, to appear to be nothing more than a man going about his business, but as he came down the front steps, he couldn't resist. He took one quick glance; one of the officers was pointing up to the nearby bluffs, while the other rested her hand on her revolver.

David picked up one of the shovels and swung it onto his shoulder. His boots crunched on the snow as he headed for the parking lot. Somewhere in the distance he could hear a faint barking. Christ, he thought, dogs. The man on the roof of the bathhouse had his head down, concentrating on just keeping his balance. David's hands were sweating inside his fur-lined gloves. At least he wasn't leaving any tracks on the shoveled parking lot; he was halfway across it, following the curving path of the snowplow.

He heard the scraping of a shovel start up again, and then he heard the scraping of two, the sound oddly syncopated. He was only thirty feet from the bridge. It was the oldest trick in the book; what David was counting on was that no one ever looks in the place they've just been.

He made the mistake of taking a second peek over his left shoulder. The male officer was down on one knee now, adjusting his ski bindings, but his partner was staring right at David. David looked away, keeping his head down, trudging along at the same steady pace. He prayed that all she saw was just another working stiff, no one to take note of. His heart trip-hammered in his chest. He had only twenty feet to go. Ten. He waited for the shout, but it never came.

Once he reached the bridge, he glanced back one final time, but the officers had vanished. David slid down the steep incline on his rump. He stabbed the shovel, handle-first, deep into a powdery white drift, scooping great armfuls of snow around it, burying it completely.

The frozen creek came down the hill, cutting an erratic path from the deep woods to the lake; its sheltering banks were a good ten feet high. Heading upstream, David fought his way through a snarl of roots and briars, and then, once he was past it and onto a stretch of clear ice, he began to run.

five

He followed the creek upstream as far as it would take him and then headed into the woods. Like a bather battling through ocean surf, he slogged through the drifts, his lungs burning with the exertion. A squirrel chattered from a lightning-shattered oak, and David could hear a siren, far off. If he was lucky, they hadn't yet found his tracks leading down from the bluffs. If he was lucky, he might still have another half hour.

Coming to the border of the park, he stared through a stand of birches at the curling neon sign for the Piney Woods Motel. There were a dozen units, modest log cabins trimmed with green, arranged around a couple of ice-coated picnic tables. A miniature-golf course lay just down the road. A fifteen-foot-tall statue of Paul Bunyan stared blankly into the winter sky, snow decorating his shoulders like white epaulets, his axe raised high. A police car sat next to a red pickup, its bed stacked with firewood. Leaning against their vehicles, sipping coffee and chatting, were a wizened farmer and the Pit Bull.

David needed a plan. The whole notion of making his way to Danacek's now seemed, in the light of day, not just reckless, but seriously lunatic. All the same, he was not about to surrender. There was no one here he trusted and too much he had to understand. For the moment, the only thing that made any sense was putting some distance between himself and his pursuers.

Staying a healthy distance inside the margin of the woods, he followed the county trunk road for nearly a mile. Through a screen of trees, he saw a tractor rigged up with a plow, clearing a long driveway of snow, while cattle huddled in the barnyard like dispirited refugees awaiting passage to a new world. Everything seemed strangely distanced, as if he'd had a concussion.

His hamstrings were beginning to tighten and his hips ached. Feeling the energy draining out of him, he finally stopped, leaned against a charred stump and tore the wrapping from another Snickers bar. He bit off great hunks of the candy and chewed slowly, letting the sugar restore him.

He wrestled the cell phone from his pocket and started tapping at the tiny silver ovals. George Kammen's number was one he knew by heart. George had been the caretaker for the cabin for the past several winters. In his mid-seventies, George hadn't done the best job of it, but if there was anybody who might have a clue about what had happened out there, George was the one.

The phone picked up halfway through the first ring. "Hello, Kammen."

"George, it's David."

"Oh my God, oh my God."

"I know George, I know."

"Are you all right?"

"No, not really, but I need your help. I'm trying to get to the bottom of this. I thought maybe you might have spoken to Maya."

"I did, yes." His voice was low and dispirited.

"When?"

"Yesterday." George, a bachelor, lived with his sister, a retired music teacher. They had a small place on the edge of town with a single milk cow that could usually be seen in their front yard, its hooves long and curly from years of immobility. George was the gentlest of men, but he was afflicted with the maddening midwestern habit of never wanting to say anything bad about anybody.

"When yesterday?"

"David, where are you?"

"It doesn't matter. When yesterday?"

"About noon. She came by to pick up the key."

"Was she OK?"

There was another long silence. "I don't know if OK is the word. She seemed pretty out of sorts."

"What do you mean, out of sorts?" David crumpled the Snickers bar wrapper and stuffed it in his pocket.

"I don't know exactly. Just seemed PO'ed. The whole time she kept getting up and looking out the window. She needed to use my phone."

David was half tempted to ask George to come pick him up at some safe, out-of-the-way location, but he didn't quite trust George enough. George was a worrier, and even if he agreed to come get him, he'd probably say something to his sister, and the sister would call the cops in a flash.

"For what?"

"She was trying to get hold of Larry Gillette." Larry was a wildlife biologist at the Wolf Center, more than a little crazy, but the most steadfast of Maya's friends.

"And did she get through to him?"

"No. She called, but there was no answer. She said if I saw him to have him call her out at the cabin as soon as possible. She said it was urgent." Through a tangle of dead branches, David could see a milk truck rumbling down the road, its long silver tank gleaming in the morning sun.

"She wouldn't tell you anything more than that?"

"Not really. It just seemed like she really didn't want to leave. I told her she could stay if she wanted, at least until the snow let up, but she said no, she needed to go. I offered to lend her this extra set of chains I had, but she said she'd be fine."

"What else, George? What else do you remember?"

"Nothing, really." The phone had gone staticky, cutting in and out. "Just that she gave me . . . big hug. Tell you the truth, it sort of surprised me, but I figured maybe . . . the way the girls are up in New York . . ."

"And that was it?"

"Yeah. Well . . . one other thing. About fifteen minutes . . . some guy called, asking for her."

"Was it Danacek?"

"I'm sorry, I'm having trouble hearing you."

"Was it Danacek?"

For several seconds David thought he had lost the connection altogether, but then George's voice came back again, stuttery and far off. "She was different . . . I know you went through a lot with her."

"George? George?" The phone had gone dead. David punched the ON button three times, but couldn't even get a dial tone. Cursing, he tossed the phone into the brush.

Thoughts rattling like coins in a beggar's cup. If Danacek had called George's, it meant he must have been keeping track of every move Maya was making. Would he have followed her out from town? Something didn't compute. There had been no sign of any other vehicle at the cabin, and the snowmobile most likely had been hidden behind the snowy ridge before Maya arrived. Someone had been waiting for her. Could it be that he'd had help, that it hadn't been just Danacek?

And why had it been such an urgent matter, getting hold of Larry? He was her closest friend here; if she'd known she was in trouble, he was the one she would have turned to. But if she'd known she was in danger, wouldn't she simply have gone to his house? She certainly wouldn't have driven out to the cabin alone. She'd told George that it was urgent that Larry call her. There must have been something she needed to say to him, some piece of information she needed to convey. David was going to have to find out what that was.

Larry and Maya had dated for a time, right after she'd gone to work for the Wolf Project. For nearly a year he'd followed her around like a puppy dog. Though her interest in him had never really been romantic, she had been delighted by him. He knew an enormous amount about zoology and botany, and every time he came back from the woods, there was a story: how he'd spotted a black bear, even though none had been seen in that part of

Wisconsin for fifty years, or how he'd been attacked by a rutting eight-point buck, or found a rattlesnake den high in the bluffs. No one was ever sure how much of it was true, and yet no one would ever have thought of calling him a liar. Larry was just blessed by an active imagination, his own way of seeing things. He had raised an orphan fawn he'd found in a farmer's field—Maya had helped him bottle-feed it—and from time to time he kept wild ducklings in his bathtub at his trailer. Socially, he was a hopeless mess, impossible to tease.

When Maya started seeing the infinitely more sophisticated Seth Carswell, Larry had been crushed. It had taken some time to repair their relationship, but they had pulled it off, or at least had seemed to; at the moment, David trusted nothing, wounded male pride least of all.

David set off again, but after a couple hundred yards, ran into a problem. The woods came to an end at the river—his guess was that it was the upper branch of the Sauk—and beyond it was nothing but pastureland. Even though there wasn't a farmhouse in sight, he knew that once he was in the open, it would be only a matter of time before he was spotted. His only option was to stay along the river. Its banks were low, but intermittent thickets of willow would afford decent cover.

He slipped down under the bridge and disappeared into a tall stand of marsh grasses. He continued on for perhaps a quarter of a mile, pushing through head-high willows, thorns catching at his jacket. Footing was treacherous and made for slow going. The brush was riddled with paths that cows had churned up on their way down to drink. In the summer the paths had been mud, but now they were frozen into snarls of potentially ankle-busting ridges and shallow holes.

Coming to a sharp bend in the river, he ascended a broad, gentle knoll to take stock of how far he'd come. To his astonishment, a number of vehicles were gathered on the road—a couple of police cars, lights flashing, and a trio of three-wheelers. An officer talked to a small group of hunters in fluorescent orange jackets.

David crouched, hiding himself behind a tangle of blackberry bushes. A second officer appeared, laboring up from under the bridge. As he gave his report to the others, his partner got on his cell phone. The second officer pivoted and gestured across the pasture and the meandering river. One of the hunters trotted to a wooden gate set in the barbed-wire fence and began to unravel the heavy chain. The others ran for their three-wheelers.

David stumbled down the knoll, across the ice, and thrashed his way through the willow thickets on the far side. They had found his tracks.

Coming out of the dense brush, he spied a smaller, tree-lined pasture just ahead of him. Three horses—a roan mare, a yearling, and a gaunt white stallion—stood at the fence, staring at him. Twenty yards behind them was a battered wooden feeder surrounded by straw and trampled snow.

David slowed to a walk. It was a cockamamie idea, but it came to him nonetheless: if he could catch one of the horses, he might have some chance of riding to safety without leaving any tracks of his own and without leaving a scent.

He held out his hand. "Hey, girl, hey. How you doin'?" He moved slowly towards the horses, but after his third step the mare and the yearling spooked, wheeling and galloping off. The white stallion whinnied and trotted back to the feeder, then stopped and gazed soulfully at him.

David climbed the fence and dropped down on the other side. The horse was as still as a statue, his breath plumed and visible in the cold air. David edged across the stomped-down snow, pausing after every step, murmuring low reassurances.

There was no way of knowing how much time he had. If his pursuers mucked around in the willow thickets, trying to retrace his every step, it might take a while, but if one of the hunters on the three-wheelers was smart and ranged out ahead, looking to cut David off, it could be a matter of minutes.

He took the last Snickers bar out of his pocket and tore off the wrapper. "Hey, boy. Hey. Look what I've got for you."

The spavined old horse shook his head. David took a step closer and leaned forward. With his shaggy white coat set against the white snow, the stallion looked like a dying polar bear, the last of a species. There is just not time enough for this, David thought. Crows called in the woods, and then the horse surrendered to temptation, clopping towards him.

David extended the candy bar out as far as he could. The horse's breath warmed his hand. The stallion took half of the Snickers in one bite. His chewing was loud and sloppy. David sneaked his left hand onto the horse's rough coat. He could feel the nerves quiver, but the stallion didn't bolt; instead he came back for more. David flattened his palm to avoid being nipped by the huge yellow teeth. One more pass of the horse's head and all that was left in David's hand was a sticky slime. David could hear sirens, far off.

David's move to grab the mane was gentle enough, but the stallion wasn't having any part of it. He snorted and reared. David held tight to the mane. The horse flung him in a complete circle. Coming out of a stumble, David ran alongside the stallion and then, after three quick hops, leapt on its back.

It was a less than perfect landing. He nearly pitched off the other side, but somehow managed to get an arm around the horse's neck and right himself. The stallion bucked once, trotted off a few feet, and stopped.

David leaned forward and whispered into the horse's ear. "Come on, boy, come on." He kicked the stallion hard in the ribs, but there wasn't even a hint of a response. David kicked again, harder, and still the horse didn't move. He wiped a trembling hand across his face, as helpless as a twelve-year-old at a county fair pony ride. He made a third try, raking the animal's belly with the toe of his boot, and finally the horse began to move, meandering towards the fence line and the trees. In the distance, he could hear the whine of the three-wheelers. All that was keeping him out of sight of his pursuers was the broad knoll and a few trees.

David kept drumming at the bony rib cage with his heels, yanking at the mane, trying to turn him, to no avail. Far down at the north end of the pasture, the yearling and the roan mare stood watching.

David desperately needed someplace to hide. To his left was pasture and to his right, woods and swamp. A couple hundred yards further on, a deer stand perched in an oak, but that would be the first place anyone would look.

Emitting a series of prolonged farts, the old stallion clopped through the brambles and into a grove of trees on the near side of the fence line. He led David under the lowest-hanging branches, trying to scrape him off. David ducked under the first two and batted away a third.

Shouts rose from below the bend in the river. David's instinct was to leap off the horse and run for it, but then he spied, just ahead, a massive sycamore, one of the biggest he'd ever seen. The stallion was headed right for it, not about to pass up an opportunity to unseat his rider.

As the horse led him beneath one of the drooping limbs, David grabbed the branch with both hands and held on, letting the stallion walk out from under him. He hung for a moment, arms trembling. The pain in his collarbone was excruciating. The stallion snorted, free finally of his burden, and galloped off to join the mare and the yearling. The three of them raced over the ridge of the pasture and out of sight. "Just go," David whispered, "the further, the better."

Swinging his legs, he moved hand over hand, lurching like the class fat boy on the jungle gym. He finally worked his way close enough to the trunk to get a foothold on one of the lower branches and pull himself to safety.

He reached up for a higher branch to steady himself and surveyed his surroundings. It was as he had hoped. In the crook where the trunk divided was a dark, rotted-out hollow. It was the nature of sycamores, when they got old, to decay from the inside. It was what made them such ideal homes for possums and coons, skunks and hibernating bats. He remembered a grade school teacher telling them once—maybe it had been in his Wisconsin history class—that in the old days the sycamores had grown so large that the early settlers had used them as barns. David didn't need a barn; he needed a few narrow feet, and it looked as if he'd found them.

He rose carefully, one hand still clamped on the limb above him, and edged along the low-hanging branch. Though the decaying recess was still filled with snow and leaves, it looked as if it went down at least five feet, maybe a little more. Shouts were coming from the swamp off to his right, louder and more distinct. They couldn't be more than a football field away.

David lowered himself into the hole the way another man might have lowered himself into a hot tub. There was a sudden explosion, a great whirring just below him, and a black bird jetted out of one of the sycamore's many crannies and winged its way across the marsh.

David kicked at the snow and the leaves, making as much room for himself as he could. He worked his boots from side to side until he was neck deep. By scrunching he was able to work his way down another six inches, and tucking in his chin gave him a couple more. He pulled his hood over his head. From the ground, at least, he would be utterly out of sight.

For what seemed like the longest time, he was alone with the pounding of his heart and the musty ammoniac smell of decomposing wood. There was a spot of stinging cold where his left knee pressed against the inside of the tree trunk, but after a couple of minutes it melted away. The muffled shouts came closer, faded, and were replaced by the whine of three-wheelers.

He could only guess what was going on. He imagined them at the feeder, at the spot where his tracks vanished. He imagined them trying to puzzle it out. They would probably follow the hoofprints of the horses, at least at first, but sooner or later they would be back. The question then would be whether something would click for one of them as it had for David. Meanwhile, the more they tromped around playing fox-and-goose, making a mess, the better it would be.

It was surprisingly warm in the tree. Out of the wind and tucked in as snug as a cartridge in its chamber, David eventually felt a tiny trickle of sweat roll down the inside of his arm. He heard the baying of the dogs—once it even sounded as if they were snuffling at the base of the sycamore—and the thudding of a helicopter.

It was very hard to keep track of time. He knew he could be in for a long haul. If they were certain they had him, they would be perfectly willing to wait him out. They could be sitting out there in a ring of pickups for days.

He tried to empty his mind, to mentally pull back to a place where he could maintain some sort of equilibrium, but his mind wouldn't obey. It gave him a small, mean pleasure, imagining how he was frustrating his pursuers, imagining how furious Danacek must be.

Everything kept orbiting around Danacek; the questions were endless. Maya and David had been coming to the cabin for four years. If Danacek had murdered Maya in retaliation for his brother's death, why would he have waited until now? Just before she'd gotten off the phone, Maya had said something about there being a lot to say. Could she have known that Danacek was on his way? She had it in her to be such a provocateur—could she have said something to set him off?

David wiggled his toes and squeezed his fists, trying to keep his extremities from going to sleep. Voices floated in from the outside, drifted and disappeared, and every now and then came the high, excited yip of deer dogs and the growling, almost comic complaints of the hounds.

He fought back the periodic waves of panic and claustrophobia, imagining himself a ship in a bottle, an insect preserved in amber, a caveman buried in ice.

He tried not to think about Maya. He knew it would be the worst thing, but the thoughts came anyway, unbidden. Out of nowhere, he remembered the Christmas presents still in the trunk of the rental car: the sack of H & H bagels, frozen hard as rocks by now, the Peter Carey novel, the little bottles of lotions and perfumes he'd bought at the French store on Madison Avenue. She would never open them. They were the last presents he would ever buy for her.

Eventually his knees began to ache and the swelling around his collarbone began to throb, beating as if it contained its own small heart. He tried to move a little to relieve the pain, but when he did, something gave way under his right foot. He heard a bit of rotten wood trickle down inside the hollows of the sycamore. He didn't try again.

He stayed inside his hole for the entire day. He was incredibly hungry. He regretted giving his last Snickers bar to the horse. There were the sounds of trucks, shouts, and once he thought he heard Danacek's voice. Late in the afternoon he broke his vow of stillness and pulled back the corner of his hood. He twisted his head around just enough that he could make out, with a single eye, the tiny seed clusters clinging to the tips of the zigzag branches and the rotors of a helicopter tilting across the river.

Night came and the temperature dropped. Hunger began to work on him. He was roused out of a fugue state by a tickling on his neck. At first he thought it was just an itch, but then he realized that it was moving, creeping along his jawbone. He worked a hand free and gave a quick slap, squashing a fat spider just under his ear.

It had been some time since he'd heard any voices. At least an hour. Maybe two hours. It was hard to tell. His guess was that the searchers had withdrawn for the night and were concentrating their efforts on sealing off any possible escape routes.

He knew it was dangerous to double-think things, but maybe trying to outlast them wasn't the brightest idea in the world. Without food or drink, he was only going to grow weaker and less able to make a decisive move. They could wait forever; he couldn't.

He pulled his hood back and slowly raised his head, surveying the surrounding treetops, drinking in the crisp night air. The moon glowed behind ominous clouds; it looked as if they could be in for yet another storm. He pivoted, scrutinizing the woods. He saw no one. The wooden stock feeder sat in its circle of frozen mud, and hundreds of tracks crisscrossed the snow around it. Through the trees it looked as if thc riverbank were awash in light, bright as a baseball diamond, and in the other direction, he could see the halos of car lights beyond the ridgeline of the pasture. For the moment at least, it seemed as if his pursuers had abandoned the chase.

He wriggled his way silently out of his hole. He got one knee up and grabbed a scaly branch with his left hand. He blew a bit of rotten wood from the corner of his mouth, then leaned forward to shake his other leg free. As he did, he glanced down at the base of the sycamore and saw two tiny embers of light, maybe three feet apart, pulsing in the darkness. Two men sat under the tree, having a smoke.

David froze, poised ten feet above them. One of the men coughed, the sound rich with phlegm, and spat into the snow.

"So what time you getting off?"

"I don't know, man. I've been out here since five this morning, and I'm starting to get pissed. I didn't even get to open presents with my kids. This is getting bad." Both men had rifles cradled against their shoulders, and David was close enough to smell the drifting smoke from their cigarettes. "You got anything to eat?"

"Half an egg-salad. If you don't mind that I've been sitting on it all afternoon."

"Lemme see."

A cigarette was snubbed out against the trunk of the tree. The ember of the other jigged as one of the men wrestled the sandwich from his side pocket. There was a soft crinkling of cellophane.

"So I hear Danacek's calling in the marines tomorrow morning."

"That's what I hear, too."

David shifted his left hand to get a better grip. It was a mistake. A tiny flake of sycamore bark spiraled downward and landed softly on the snow.

"You ever met that girl? The one that got murdered?"

"Mmm." It sounded as if the man had a mouthful of egg salad. It was several more seconds before he could speak. "I saw her out at the Pizza Hut once in a while."

"And what did you think?"

"I don't know. Seemed like a real New Yorker to me. What about you?"

"No. I never met her. But I heard she was really spreading it around town."

The second man's laugh was incredulous, a guffaw. "Buddy, sometimes you're really full of horseshit, you know that?"

David crouched, curled like a silent tongue in the tree's mouth.

The first man pushed to his feet, using his rifle as a crutch. "I'm going home. I don't care what Danacek says. Seventeen hours, it's enough."

"You can't do that."

"I'm going to just tell him. So where is he?"

"I don't know. I thought he was back by the old bridge."

"You going with me or you staying?"

"Oh, I'm definitely going with you. I want to see this." He flicked his cigarette away, the ember tumbling through the darkness.

David didn't move, poised above them. What could the man have meant, that she'd been spreading it around town? If someone walking down the street had said something like that about his daughter, he would have slugged him. It was just stupidity, small-town mean-spiritedness. Or was it? What does any father know of a daughter's life?

He watched the men stroll away, and when they were a good distance off he took a firm grip on the lowest of the overhanging branches and eased himself down. He swayed for a moment and dropped silently to the snow. The two men never looked back.

Later, he would not be able to tell anyone exactly how he had managed to escape. There were too many parts to it, too much blind luck, too much stumbling half crazed in the dark, trying to steer clear of the voices in the woods around him, too much waiting, too much guesswork. He remembered maneuvering past two bored volunteers in a truck, searchlights glaring from the far side of the river, and a reckless dash across the broken pavement of the old roadbed.

He lumbered across a frozen bog, thrashing through stands of cattails and winter weeds—dock and goldenrod and thistle. He was sure something would happen, that they would run him down in two minutes or four, but nothing did happen. He climbed a sagging wire fence and crossed a long cornfield. Once or twice he thought he heard a siren, but the sound quickly faded. The searchlights on the river dimmed to a dull pewter sheen.

He walked for nearly an hour. Slogging through the deep drifts was both exhausting and slow going, so when he finally spied a road he headed toward it. It started to snow, and then to snow hard.

The words of the deputy had fouled everything. Spreading it around town—what the hell was that supposed to mean? That she'd been picking up men in bars? It was laughable.

He was forced to think about things no father wants to think about. He didn't know for sure, but he had assumed that Maya and Seth Carswell had been sleeping together, though they had broken up at the end of the summer. Could there have been someone else? She had dated Larry Gillette for about ten minutes, but David doubted that anything had happened with that. So could there have been a third man? Or even more unlikely, a fourth? No. There was no way he could have been so obtuse.

The snow blew up in great sheets; for a moment the whole world went white. The truth of the matter was that Maya had possessed a certain seductiveness. She had been anything but girly—she'd always loathed makeup, fashion, teen magazines—and David had always been trying to get her to comb her storm of black hair. But she had been witty, beautiful, and possessed of her mother's gift for instant intimacy. From her teenage years boys had followed her around like little ducklings, and she had had a way with the wealthy older men who were the Wolf Center's major donors—the surgeons from Chicago, the investment bankers from Boston. After her semester abroad, letters had kept arriving at the house from some Algerian auto mechanic she'd met in Paris. David had once gotten a call, when she was home in Westchester during one of her holidays, from a young Macalester professor, male, who just happened to be in the city and wanted to meet her for dinner. David could still remember the false hardiness of his voice, the unmistakable ring of a guilty conscience, when he realized he was speaking to Maya's father.

The driving snow brought tears to his eyes. He wiped the ice crystals from his face, utterly lost.

He saw car lights just once, but from far enough off that he was able to leap a ditch and hide himself behind a corncrib before the pickup whizzed past. The truck's windows were rolled down, and for a second he was able to hear the two drunken farm boys, hooting and hollering and pounding on the door panels, and then the dark and the silence swallowed them, snuffing the receding taillights like dying birthday candles.

Making his way back to the road, he found himself following one of the pickup's tire tracks, placing one foot in front of the other, as meticulous as a high-wire artist above a sawdust ring.

In the swirling snow, the distant farmhouses, the narrow bridge he crossed, the machine-shed yard illuminated with a powerful all-night light, all seemed as alien as Siberia. He was supposed to have spent his childhood here, but he didn't recognize anything. A dog came down a driveway to bark at him, but then stopped, reconsidered, turned, and trotted back, satisfied that David posed no threat.

There was a long stretch of road where there were no farms or houses, just thick woods on both sides, and David felt himself tiring, ground down to a trudge.

Eventually the landscape opened up again, with rolling pastures, a barn, and a dark brick farmhouse sitting up on a hill. He cut across the pasture and a frozen slough. He circled around so that he could approach the barn from the back. He moved warily, watching for a dog or any sign of movement from the house, but there was nothing. He passed a low concrete building and made his way to the barn. He opened the low wooden door and slipped inside.

A single bare lightbulb hung from a cord in the middle of the cavernous space. There were a dozen cattle locked in their stanchions. Most of them were down and asleep, but one of them swung her head around, rattling her metal collar, and stared balefully at him. There was the familiar smell of milk and excrement. A cat appeared out of nowhere, purring and rubbing against his pant leg. David moved quickly across the splattered concrete and up the ladder into the loft.

He climbed to the very top of the mountain of bales, ducking the wooden crossbeams, getting as far from the ladder as he could. Right under the tin roof, in a spot where he figured he would be least likely to be discovered, he rearranged the bales, creating a refuge for himself. He lowered himself into it and stretched, trying to get comfortable, locking his hands behind his head.

A soft rustling off to his left made him jump. He turned quickly, thinking it was a rat, but two seconds later the tawny cat flowed out from between a pair of bales. David picked up the cat and put her on his chest. He stroked her fur, listening to her purr. It wasn't so cold; all those animal bodies below were warming them all, keeping them safe through the night.

six

For years David had carried within him the feeling that there was something missing in him, something that everyone else possessed. It made him wary. He was a good man, a devoted father and husband, but he often kept things secret for no reason. When he spent several hours a week tutoring the Albanian janitor who worked in his office, it was six months before David's wife knew. He never talked about his parents or where he'd grown up, and he wrote poetry that would never see the light of day, stashing it in the back of his desk drawer.

The month after Maya began eleventh grade they discovered that Peggy had cancer. For a year they fought it, with operations and radiation and the best medical help money could buy, hoping for a miracle, but there were no miracles.

Peggy's mother took the train up from Bronxville nearly every day to help. David found himself battling the blackest of moods and what was, at times, an incapacitating rage. It was Peggy, who they'd always teased about needing her comforts, who was the indomitable one. She joked and tried to keep everyone's spirits up, continued to sit in the bleachers during her daughter's soccer and volleyball games. Sometimes at night he would stand in the kitchen doorway and watch her at her desk, going through bills, writing thank-you notes, organizing all their lives. For the last several months she wore a kerchief, her hair destroyed by the radiation treatments, and yet under the soft light of the lamp she could still look as radiant as when he'd met her at eighteen.

At the very end, there was the hospital. He spent hours sitting by her bed, watching her sleep. He kept trying to find things that she could eat and keep down. One by one they had to be crossed off the list: Cokes from the machine in the lobby, then chicken soup, then tapioca pudding. Finally all that would work were two or three ice chips placed gently on her tongue. Even her remarkable fortitude began to break down. "I don't want to die," she would cry, "I don't want to die." She would weep and he would hold her. Sometimes after a long day in the hospital he would wander in the parking garage, unable to find his car.

The kindness of friends overwhelmed him. Coming home at ten at night, he would find that the neighbors had left dinner in a cooler on the front porch. They mowed his lawn and took Maya into Manhattan with a group of girls. Sometimes they would ask him, keen-eyed, "I know this must be tearing you up inside," and he wouldn't know how to answer.

The night Peggy died, Maya was at an out-of-town volleyball tournament—David had insisted that she go. He came home from the hospital and went out back to water the yard. As he stood in the dark, he was struck, with a terrible fierceness, by the thought that he had no life without Peggy. Everything—the flowering vines she'd planted by the back door, the pictures on the wall, the garage she'd remodeled so that Maya could have a place to be alone with her friends—was entwined with her. And now she was gone.

In the morning he sat alone in the house, unable to make the call to his daughter. In his mind, he was somehow sparing her. He even toyed with the idea of waiting until she returned home with the rest on her team on Sunday. Two or three times there were knocks on the door, neighbors or friends who had heard the news, but he made no move to go see who it was. A little past three in the afternoon, he finally picked up the phone. He got hold of one of the assistant coaches and told him what had happened.

"I'm so sorry," the coach said, "so sorry." In the background David could hear girlish cheers and the shriek of a referee's whistle. When Maya's game was over, the coach said, he would pull her aside; he was sure he could arrange for one of the parents to drive her home.

An hour later, David was standing by the kitchen window as the gray Suburban pulled up. He went outside and crossed the lawn. Maya got out of the van, tugging her gym bag out from under the seat. She was bare-legged, with her shiny purple team jacket over her uniform. At the far end of the block, one of their neighbors carried leaf bags to the curb.

As Maya came towards him, he could feel his lips twitch, the beginning of tears. She had the stride of a warrior.

"Hey, honey . . ."

He reached for her, and she broke past him, racing into the house, letting the door slam behind her. The driver of the van, a huge, wispy-haired father whose name David couldn't quite place, stood on the far side of the Suburban. David nodded to him. "Thank you," he said, a little too loudly. "Thank you."

David found her in her room, pulling a weekend of dirty laundry out of her bag. He could see a long red floor burn, just above her knee. "Can I get you anything?"

She pivoted, face flushed, her black hair tangled behind a white headband. "You should have called me!"

"Maya . . ."

"She was my mother!"

"You were with your friends. I didn't want it to be awkward . . ." A balled up sock tumbled onto the floor and rolled under the bed.

"Awkward? Somebody's mother dies and you think it's awkward?" On the bookshelves behind her were the copies of *Pippi Longstocking*, *The World of Pooh*. "You couldn't even tell me yourself? You had to have a coach tell me? A coach?"

"Maya, please, honey." He put a hand on her shoulder, but she slapped it away.

"Just get away from me! Just get away!"

For the next several months, he tried to keep things just as they had been, for Maya's sake. He got up at six to make her a hot breakfast, and asked his assistant for recipes so he could have a good meal ready for Maya at night. He did endless loads of laundry, took her to the mall on Saturdays to shop for shoes, and spent a week with her touring universities.

For Maya's part, she was sneaking out of her bedroom window at night to go off with her friends, smoking on the sly, getting suspended for two days for sassing her history teacher. She came home one afternoon with a butterfly tattoo on her ankle and, for a time, dated a local gas-station attendant who took her for ninety-mile-an-hour rides out on the interstate on his Harley. Between David and Maya there were terrible scenes. The low point was when he got a phone call at three in the morning; she had passed out from too much alcohol at a frat party at the local college.

In the spring, he arranged for her to go to an outdoor school in Maine that taught everything from boat building to wilderness tracking. Maya sent him one postcard the entire semester, and when she came back in May, she was a changed person. The school had promised to teach her self-sufficiency and it had done that. She washed her own clothes and picked up after herself. In the evenings she would say an early good night, go to her room, and read for hours. Sometimes David would still see the light on under her door as late as one in the morning. She was still listening to the Doors and reading Baudelaire, but other than that, there was little sign of the old trouble. It was a huge relief. The only cost was that she had moved away from him, gone emotionally underground; she would never again turn to him when she was in trouble.

She had plans for the summer. Her favorite teacher at the outdoor school was working at a project in Wisconsin, helping restore wolves to the wilderness, and had offered Maya an internship. The project's headquarters were ten miles from Black Hawk, the small town where David had grown up.

David's first reaction was that it had to be some sort of cosmic joke. There was no way he was going to let this happen. Unwilling to reveal his true objection, he came up with others. Hadn't Maya agreed to be the assistant manager at the local yogurt shop for the summer? Was she just going to leave them in the lurch? What about their plans to go to the Adirondacks with Maya's cousins?

Maya was astonished at being opposed and then, when she realized how serious he was, furious. Did he really prefer that she spend the summer in a yogurt shop? They went to the Adirondacks every summer, and invariably David was the one who complained about how boring it was. Wasn't he always telling her about the moral superiority of the Midwest?

In the end, she wore him down. As long as he wasn't prepared to tell her the whole truth, his arguments had a slightly preposterous air to them, even to himself. The week before she left, he was hardly able to sleep. What was it he was so afraid of? He wasn't quite sure. She was just going to be there for six weeks, stuck out in the woods—what really could happen? Several times he vowed that he was going to tell her the story of what had happened there, so long ago, but each time he came close, he found himself pulling back. They'd been through enough trauma for one year.

She ended up having the best summer of her life. Every time they talked on the phone, there was a lilt to her voice. She loved the people she was working with, and even though most of her time was spent with school groups, twice a week she would go out in the field with the wildlife biologists. One afternoon they had found a den and crouched for an hour behind a stand of birches, watching a trio of wolf pups tumbling and playing, trying to catch grasshoppers in the rocks. Another time she went along to check traps and helped attach a radio collar to a huge sedated alpha male. She told David how her hands shook as she reached into the thick gray fur.

He drove out in August, his car jammed to the ceiling with all of her things for college. She would be going to Macalester in St. Paul. He arrived late on a Thursday afternoon and went directly to the Wolf Center. Maya was in the parking lot, seeing off a busload of children. Some of the kids had rolled their windows down and were waving and calling out to her. Maya walked alongside the bus as it began to pull away, reaching up to give the children's fingers a last-minute squeeze. Her dark hair was in braids and she was tanner than he had ever seen her; she looked half-Indian.

She gave David a brief tour of the center, leading him through the new exhibition hall. There were artfully done dioramas and a collection of photographs of wolf hunts, Russian and American, from the turn of the century, but what impressed David most were the drawings reproduced from old books of fairy tales and fables, the pen-and-ink renderings of wolves as demons, cunning killers, and abductors of children, the sharp-toothed repositories of all our worst fears.

That night they ate in a small country restaurant. A hunched farmer at the next table stared at her through the entire meal; whether it was the butterfly tattoo on her ankle or her bare midriff, there was no way of knowing. Afterward, on the way back to the car, Maya said, "You know what I'd like to do?"

"What's that?"

"I'd like to go see the house where you grew up."

Tires crunched on the gravel behind them. David pulled Maya out of the way of a slow-moving pickup.

"It's sort of late, isn't it?" David said. "We could go tomorrow."

"I'd like to do it now," she said. "Unless you're too tired."

Driving into Black Hawk for the first time in thirty years, he felt his head fill with so many things. There was a half-mile stretch of new fast food restaurants and farm equipment lots on the outskirts, but once they got downtown, everything began to get familiar. David leaned forward on the steering wheel, peering out, his stomach in knots. The old Rexall's was still there, and the Merchants Bank and the hardware store. Everything seemed so much smaller. The old theatre was gone, he saw that, and it looked as if the Brinkley Hotel had been converted to apartments.

He turned down Maple, bumped across the tracks, and passed the abandoned brewery sitting up on the hill. He knew all the houses now. There was where the Dickman twins lived and further on, Mrs. Ohlendorf. He remembered how furious she used to get when the squirrels ate all her corn. She must have been dead for at least twenty years. He slowed his car to twenty miles an hour, then to ten, and pulled to the curb.

Maya looked over at him. "This is it?"

"This is it."

They both stared up at the white two-story house. Someone had made the decision to trim it in an unfortunate lime green, and the front porch had been enclosed, but the old barn out back that his father had used as a garage was still standing. David could see the tin roof shining in the moonlight.

"So, which was your room?" Maya said.

"There. The furthest one on the left, upstairs."

Lights were on inside the house, and the shadows of children flitted behind gauzy curtains.

"So, how does it make you feel?" she asked.

"I'm not sure," he said. "It just seems like such a long time ago."

"You want to get out and take a look?"

"No, this is fine," he said. Her eyes were on him, intent and assessing. A boy sped by on his bike, a playing card whirring in his spokes.

"You know, Dad, I was talking to the people in the office today. They've offered me a job for next summer. I'd be in charge of all the interns."

"Would it pay?"

"It would pay pretty well."

Someone had come to the living room window and was staring out at them from around the corner of a shade.

"We should think about it," David said. "First thing we need to do is get you off to college."

Maya had agreed to put in a half day on Friday, leaving David with a morning to himself. He got up early and went for a drive. The leaves had begun to turn and there were brilliant flashes of red and yellow on the hillsides. He had forgotten how beautiful it was here. He drove for two hours, drinking it all in: the cattle grazing around a reedy pond, the tractor crawling along a distant ridge, the deep wooded valleys, the small brick farmhouses and faded barns.

Around eleven o'clock he went back into town to fill up the car with gas. Afterward, he turned down Main Street and then, without quite knowing why, pulled over to the curb. He sat for a moment before getting out. He began to walk down the block.

The day was warming up. In front of the hardware store a man sat in a folding chair, eyes closed, hands clasped across his ample belly, face lifted to the sun. A group of middle-aged women said hello as David passed, and David said hello back. Hurrying out of the bank, a ruddy-faced farmer in a tractor hat nearly bumped into him, muttered an apology, and moved on without a second glance.

David crossed the street. Pausing in front of Rexall's, he could see Olson Braidwood showing a girl in tight jeans how to operate the cash register. David continued on, past the café and the hotel. No one paid him any mind: not the retarded boy limping out of the post office and lurching onto his bike, not the policeman writing a ticket across the street, not the two teenagers swiping each other's hats in front of the video store. David might as well have been invisible. Nobody remembered.

He drove out to the edge of town. He parked on the shoulder and walked onto the bridge. The river was low, the exposed banks caked and hard; the waitress at the restaurant had said there'd been almost no rain all summer.

He ran his hands over the eighteen-inch-wide railing, the metal warm to the touch. Rust flecked the rivets; David scraped some of it away with his thumbnail. This was where they had stood, the two of them; this was where Andy had fallen.

A combine crept along the perimeter of a cornfield on the far side of the river, the clatter carrying in the still air. Birds rose and fell in its wake. It looked to David as if a lot of the swamp had been cleared over the years, but willows still clung to the riverbank. He stared down at the water. Green with algae, it was barely moving. Hard to imagine that it could have ever done harm to anyone. Here and there, turtle heads dimpled the surface.

A rumble of tires made him turn. A maroon and gray SUV bumped onto the bridge. The driver raised two fingers off the steering wheel in greeting and David raised two fingers in return. After the car had passed, David turned and began to walk back toward the near bank.

Someone had tucked an empty glass bottle into the recess of one of the girders. David bent down to retrieve it; the label read Nehi

Grape. He rolled the bottle in his hand, then pivoted and hurled it as far out onto the river as he could. It made a hollow plunking sound when it hit and bobbed quickly to the surface.

At first it just seemed to sit there, but then there was a whisper of movement, the most sluggish of currents pushing it downstream. David stood watching the sunlight flash off the slowly rotating glass. Insects sang in the yellow weeds, and from far off there was the drone of the combine. The bottle finally drifted around the bend of the river. David began to weep.

Three hours later, David and Maya were on their way to Macalester. He drove while she went through a packet of freshman-orientation materials. As they got closer to the Twin Cities, the traffic got bad, and they began to spot more and more college stickers on the bumpers of overstuffed Subarus.

"So about this job next summer," David said. She looked over at him quickly. She had a Minnesota map spread like an accordion across her lap. "I think you should do it."

"Really?"

"It's what you want to do, right?"

"Yeah."

"Then do it." David glanced in his mirror; they'd been stuck behind a toilet-paper truck for a mile, but nobody was letting him change lanes. "I had this other idea, too."

"What's that?"

"I wondered what you'd think if I looked for a place out here."

"What do you mean, out here?"

"Somewhere around Black Hawk. There are some nice old farmhouses; I'm sure you could pick them up for a song. Or maybe a cabin. Someplace we could use during the summer. That is, if you're sure you're coming back."

She lifted the unwieldy map warily and began to try to fold it. The skyline of Minneapolis rose ahead of them, sharp against a cloudless sky. "And you'd come too?"

"For part of the time. But I wouldn't do this if you thought I was crowding you."

She reached across and patted his shoulder. "Sounds great, to tell you the truth."

It took two trips back to Wisconsin that fall to find the cabin. He had Maya come down for the day to give her approval. The cabin hadn't been occupied for a couple of years and a lot of work would need to be done, but it was clearly a grand place. Maya was both delighted and shocked by the suddenness of it all. Over lunch she grilled him. Was he sure he wasn't going through some sort of midlife crisis? Wouldn't it be wise to take a few days to think things over? He cut her short. The only question as far as he was concerned was whether she would enjoy it. Her answer was yes. He put down the earnest money that afternoon.

For the next two summers the decision to buy the cabin seemed like the best thing he'd ever done. David's work at his literary agency made it impossible for him to spend the whole summer in Wisconsin, but he would fly out for long weekends and then come for all of August. Maya was at the Wolf Center from nine to five while David read manuscripts at the cabin and made his rounds of phone calls. But sometimes, late in the afternoon, the two of them would go for long runs around the lake. At least once a week they would play killer games of hearts with her friends out on the porch.

Not that living with a twenty-year-old was a piece of cake. She still had her moods, and sleep was sometimes in short supply. If he wasn't lying awake worrying about her being out on the country roads at night, he was being jolted out of slumber at three in the morning by the slamming of doors, Maya and her friends raiding the refrigerator, rummaging through closets, trying on clothes, God knew what. There was an incident when a roach clip was discovered on the floor of her car, and a run to the emergency room when one of her coworkers, seriously looped, had fallen out of a canoe and opened a six-inch gash in his scalp.

But there was never any question whether it was worth it or not. Often, after supper, they would walk down to the pier to watch the sunset, and she would take his arm. He would tell her stories about her mother, about how they'd met, about their courtship and early years in New York. Maya's intelligence was so quick, she saw so deeply into things, that it was almost surprising to discover, despite all the grief she could give him, how much she thirsted for his advice.

Sweetness had stolen back into his life. Sometimes he would get up in the morning, knowing that she'd gone to bed at four. He would creep into the kitchen, make his coffee, and then head out to the porch, putting his hand behind him to ease the screen door shut, being careful not to wake her.

When things took a turn, at first it seemed as if it had nothing to do with the two of them. From its beginnings, the Wolf Center had excited controversy. Over its five-year history, a number of people had lost dogs (one, a small cocker spaniel, had been snatched off its owner's back porch), but in David and Maya's third summer at the lake, things began to escalate. A farmer discovered one of his calves, mauled but still alive, its anus torn out, in a far pasture. A pair of sheep were killed. A month later, a wolf was discovered poisoned; two weeks after that, a second was found dead in a ditch, without a mark on him, eyes bulging and discolored.

seven

He awoke in the barn to the soft calling of a child, very close. "Smurkus? Smu-u-u-rkus . . ." Opening his eyes, he stared up at the rippled tin roof of the barn, momentarily disoriented. His heart pounded. The cat was no longer on his chest.

He lay very still, but didn't hear anything more. He moved his left arm slowly across his body, careful not to make a sound, and turned onto his side. He peered up again. Above the wall of hay bales was a child's face. He was maybe seven or eight, blond and ruddy cheeked, and he gaped down at David with eyes as wide as an owl's.

"Who are you?"

David decided it was best to lie. "Steve," he said. "Who are you?"

"My name's Bobby. What are you doing here?"

"Just getting a little rest. I won't be staying long."

"Did you ask my Granny if you could sleep here?"

"No, I'm sorry. I would have. I'm leaving soon, I promise. Just don't tell anybody, OK?"

Bobby knew better; in a flash he was gone. There was a rustling of hay, a thump, and then the patter of feet across the loose boards of the loft.

"Granny! Granny!"

David lurched to his knees just in time to see the boy disappear down the ladder. David half scrambled, half tumbled down the mountain of bales and then, hand over hand, climbed quickly down the ladder himself. The stalls were all empty now, and the child was nowhere to be seen. The wooden door David had entered by the night before hung open, but there was a second open door as well, at the far end of the stanchions, leading out into the barnyard. He hesitated, but there was no real choice.

He ran down the concrete aisle, sprinkled now with fresh lime, ducked through the door out into the middle of a herd of cows. Glancing over his shoulder, he could see the little boy and his grandmother, hand in hand, running toward him, running toward the fence. The grandmother, a woman in a baggy blue sweater, carried what looked like a twelve-gauge shotgun in her free hand.

David dodged and darted like a broken-field runner, trying to sprint through the milling cattle, but he slipped and fell into the fresh slop of the barnyard. The cows scattered, parting like the Red Sea.

"Don't you move! Do you hear me? Don't move!"

He did as she said. His right elbow throbbed; it felt as if he'd cracked it in his fall. Finally he sat up and wiped his hands, sticky with green muck, on a fresh patch of snow. He turned and looked back at the woman. She wore black rubber boots and faded blue jeans. The shotgun was at her shoulder, aimed right at him, but after a moment, it began to lower.

Thirty-five years, he thought. He didn't know which was more remarkable: how much she'd changed or how much she seemed the same. In her eyes he didn't see the slightest flicker of recognition.

A small black dog bounded down from the house, late for the party, but still barking wildly. The little boy held tight to his grandmother's sweater. The cattle had retreated to the far end of the barnyard, bunching along the fence line and staring at David like students on the very slow track.

David unbuckled his Forest Service cap and pulled it off.

Bareheaded, he stared up at her, saw the trouble come into her steady gaze. The barrel of the shotgun dropped another six inches.

"Granny . . ." the little boy said.

"Go back in the house," the woman said. In the driveway was an old Pontiac.

"But Granny . . ."

"Just do as I say! Get back in the house!"

Ruefully, the little boy turned and trudged up the hill. David got to his feet and wiped his hands a second time, this time on his trousers. He was an utter mess.

"So," she said.

"So."

"I read about you in the paper," she said.

"And what did it say?" She didn't answer. One of the cattle began to moo, the sound long and distressed. "It isn't true," he said. "What you read." There was a long silence.

He and Joann had been in a Christmas pageant together. She had been Mary and he had been Joseph. He'd nearly kissed her once, in the Sunday school basement. He'd worked up his nerve and he would have done it too, if Vern Zander, strange and endlessly lurking, hadn't come down the stairs at exactly the wrong moment.

A couple years after that, jealous of her affections, he'd beaten a boy up, or at least wrestled him to the ground, to keep him from coming to Sunday-night youth group and claiming too much of her attention. When Andy Danacek had died, she had been the only one brave enough to come to David's defense.

At thirteen she'd been beautiful and even now, middle aged, in work clothes, with a red kerchief tied around her hair, she was a striking woman, though there was an inevitable solidity to her features and a wariness around the eyes.

"He called you Granny," David said.

"Yes. He's my daughter's child." Her mouth still tight, she reached down to shush the barking dog. "So, what are we going to do?"

"I don't know," he said. "If you want me to leave, I'll just leave."

"And where would you go?"

"I don't know."

The dog's eyes were bright, and he was poised for a chase. "Why don't you come into the house?" She saw his hesitation. "My husband had to go into town. We can't just stand here. I have to drive Bobby into school in a minute anyway."

David followed her up to the house. There was a glassed-in back porch—a mudroom—and on one wall hung a row of coats and vests, tractor hats and misshapen wool knit caps. Several pairs of skis were carelessly stacked in the corner like stray tipi poles.

"You can leave your jacket here," she said.

"Thanks." He slipped out of the bulky Forest Service coat and draped it over the back of a yellow folding chair. She was still carrying the shotgun and she saw him glance at it.

"Unless I plan to use it, I suppose it's a little ridiculous, isn't it?" she said.

"I'll leave that up to you to decide."

She laid the shotgun on a rack above the mounds of winter garb and gestured with an open palm. "After you," she said.

Bobby sat at the kitchen table, sulking and eyeing them suspiciously.

"Bobby, I want you to pick up all those puzzle pieces in the TV room and get your backpack," Joann said. "We'll be going in just a little while."

"But Granny. . . ."

"Don't 'but Granny' me. Come on, let's go."

She took her grandson by the hand, helping him out of his chair, and gave him a pat on the rump. The little boy trotted off.

In the four summers that David had been back, he'd thought several times about looking Joann up, but each time had decided against it. He'd asked a few people about her, and what he knew was that she'd married young, to a farmer, one of the Meineke brothers, had children, and didn't see much of her old friends. He'd assumed that sooner or later he would run into her at the post office or in a supermarket parking lot, but that hadn't happened. He wasn't exactly sure why he'd resisted trying to find her. Part of it was simply that he'd been busy, focusing all his energy on Maya, but part of it too was that it made him feel vaguely disloyal to Peggy's memory, if not foolish. It was easy to misinterpret the motives of middle-aged men who started calling up the women they'd had crushes on when they were twelve.

"You want some coffee?" Joann said.

"Yeah. Sure."

"You can wash your hands in the sink," she said.

While she got a cup from the cupboard, he went to the faucet and turned on the water. He let it splash over his hands and wrists, giving it time to heat up, then squirted some liquid soap into his palms. He worked the soap into a lather, scrubbing off all the grime and cowshit and blood of the last two days. Joann stood at the stove with his mug of coffee. He could feel her scrutinizing him. There was something she was looking for and he couldn't imagine what it was. He bent low to the tap, scooping some of the water into his face, feeling the sting of it, and then reached for the towel on the towel rack.

"So how many kids do you have?" he asked.

"Three." He wiped his face and hands and then draped the wet towel over the wooden rods. "My youngest is going to Whitewater. My son is in the air force. My other daughter works for the phone company and lives just down the road. So I take Bobby to school for her." She placed the mug of coffee warily on the table, keeping her distance. "Please, sit." David sat, wrapping both hands around the blue cup, letting it warm his red, cracked fingers. "Are you hungry?"

"Yeah, I am. Pretty," he said.

She undid a square of tinfoil and got a long knife from the roundabout. He watched her cut the banana bread with slow, even strokes. The kitchen window rattled in the wind. She let the slice collapse into the palm of her hand, slid it onto a plate, and set it before him. The plate had tiny red flowers rimming the border and one small chip.

"Hold on, I'll get you a napkin," she said. She yanked open a drawer, found a paper napkin, and handed it to him. He unfolded it on his knee. "Your daughter. She was your only child?"

"Mmm," he said.

He stared down at the banana bread, at the bits of chopped walnuts embedded in the dark, moist cake. He broke off a corner, put it in his mouth, but didn't swallow. He sat perfectly still, and when he finally looked over at her, his eyes were blurred with tears. She looked away quickly, staring out the window. The ticking of the clock seemed strangely amplified in the silent room.

"I didn't do it," he said.

"I'm sure you didn't," she said, but she didn't sound that sure. "I saw the man who did," he said. "He ran out of the cabin maybe five minutes after I came in, he must have been hiding there. I went after him . . ." Hearing the words coming from his mouth, he finally just stopped. He was making himself sound like a fool.

Joann stared blankly at him, pinching her lower lip between her thumb and forefinger. A 1991 calendar from the local feed store hung above the counter; the December photo was of two skaters racing on a frozen pond, their hands clasped behind their backs.

"You need to go to the police," she said.

"You mean to Danacek?" he said. He saw her color. "You know I can't do that."

"Why not?"

"You don't know why not?" She was not happy, having the question thrown back at her. "Joann, I saw him. Coming out of the cabin."

She was incredulous. "You're sure?"

"I'm very sure."

"Did you see his face?"

"No. He was wearing a ski mask. But I know it was him. Who else could it be? Who else had a reason?"

"Granny, I can't find my backpack!" came the little boy's voice from the other room.

"Well, you just look for it!" Joann shouted. "You had it this morning. We'll go as soon as you find it."

"You believed in me once before," David said. "You were the only one. Please. I don't know anybody else I can turn to."

She turned away, refusing to meet his steady gaze. "My husband had to go over to Utica to look at a bulldozer. He won't be back until at least noon. You can rest here. I don't suppose there's any harm in that." Without warning, her voice was suddenly husky with emotion. "You must have been very proud of her."

"How so?"

"It sounds like she wasn't ever intimidated by people. Daughters are hard, I know, but it seems like she was quite something." She wrapped the tinfoil tightly around the loaf of banana bread. "There's a little boy here who's about to be late for school. I'll be back in an hour."

David stood at the window, watching Joann help her grandson into the station wagon. She slammed the door and then leaned over the hood to whisk away the snow on the windshield with a plastic scraper. David wiped his hand across his face. The radiator in the far corner of the kitchen sounded as if the world's most furious Ping-Pong match were going on inside.

He watched as Joann backed the pickup around and headed down the long drive. The small black dog ran alongside for a while, biting at the tires, but finally surrendered the chase to charge a row of sparrows huddled on a barbed-wire fence. The birds burst into flight, winging their way across the gleaming white pasture.

Was he crazy, or were people trying to tell him something? First George, now Joann. Daughters are hard? Where had that come from? Was there something they were tiptoeing around, trying to spare him, out of kindness? It wasn't kindness he needed now; it was the truth.

He glanced at the phone on the wall. He needed to find Larry Gillette. He picked up the phone and was halfway through dialing the Wolf Center number before he heard the squawks of protest.

"Hello? Excuse me!"

"We're on the line here! Ethel, there's somebody . . ."

He set the phone gently on its hook, his heart racing. It was just his luck; Joann was on the last party line in America. Even though there was no way the two country women could know who he was, he still felt panicky and trapped.

He scanned the room, the Christmas cards pinned to the refrigerator door by dime-sized magnets. The morning paper lay folded on a kitchen chair. He leaned over to retrieve it.

The first thing to catch his eye was the photo of himself and Maya, standing on the lakefront, pulling a rowboat out of the water. They were both grinning, both bundled in life preservers. The headline read:

MANHUNT FOR SUSPECTED MURDERER

Maya Neisen, 22, was bludgeoned to death sometime Tuesday afternoon at a cabin on Sauk Lake. Local law enforcement officials have organized an all-out search for her father, David Neisen, 50, who is the prime suspect in the case.

After being questioned by Sheriff Doug Danacek, Neisen stole a police car and escaped. According to other officers, Neisen was first spotted carrying a metal poker, which has since been identified as the murder weapon. State and county authorities are cooperating in the search and Neisen is still believed to be in the area.

Mr. Neisen and his daughter have spent the past several summers on the lake and she had been volunteering at the Wolf Restoration Project. According to one of her fellow workers, she had not spoken to her father for several months. Sheriff Danacek warned that if anyone should see Neisen, they should contact his office immediately.

"In my thirty years of law enforcement, this is the most vicious murder I've ever seen. I'm no psychiatrist, but what would it take to kill your own daughter? I can promise the people of this county that we will smoke him out of whatever hole he's hiding in. Until then, Mr. Neisen should be considered extremely dangerous."

David ran a trembling hand through his hair. He folded the paper carefully and set it on the chair. He lifted the phone from the receiver; the two women were still on the phone.

"There they are again! Excuse me, but this is so rude! Would you mind? Who is this?" David slammed the phone down on the hook. He felt sick and dazed.

He wandered through the dining room and the small front living room. Under the Christmas tree, green needles were sprinkled across a red drop cloth. The furniture was mostly clunky hand-me-downs, but hanging in the hallway was a beautiful silk screen, a montage of tractor tires, plowed fields, and animal skulls, all in rich tans and golds.

He stared out the living-room window at the snowy cornfields. How many people would be reading that article? Ten thousand? Twenty thousand? He could just see Danacek spouting off to the reporter, putting on his best Sunday school face, the poor man's Eliot Ness.

He turned to face the room. A narrow bookshelf was jammed with old albums and porcelain horses. He pried loose one of the albums and sat down on the couch.

He flipped absently through the brittle pages, trying to calm himself. The pictures were old. There was one of Reverend Pond beaming on the steps of the church with his wife and kids, another of Joann's father sitting behind the wheel of his milk truck in his white Dolly Madison Dairy uniform and hat.

He leaned forward to examine the yellowing wedding pictures of Joann and her husband. They'd been teenagers, so incredibly young, though there was no denying that this Meineke boy she'd married had a certain raw-boned appeal, grinning goofily as she stuffed a huge piece of cake in his mouth. Clarence—was that his name?

A dog barked. David sprang to his feet and went to the window, his heart pounding. The black dog ran in mad circles around the elm tree in the front yard, terrorizing a cat perched on a limb just above him. David ran a hand over his mouth and gave a long, shuddering sigh of relief.

He returned the first album to the shelf and took another. Too edgy to sit, he leaned against the doorframe, thumbing through the pages. The second collection was more recent. There were gawky teenage children now, and Clarence had put on weight, acquired a certain sadness in the eyes. It caught David's interest, the workings of time.

Joann had changed too, and it wasn't just that she was older. There weren't many photos of her—she was obviously the picture taker in the family—but the ones she was in weren't marked by a lot of buoyancy. There was a shot of her in her garden, picking summer squash; a blurry shot of her and one of the kids wheeling a mammoth white rabbit around in a wheelbarrow; a shot of her and the whole family gathered in front of the Christmas tree. In all of them, David could see the coiled wariness in her; in one or two she almost looked like a person in shock. Something had happened to these people; David was not making it up.

As he turned the pages, a handful of photographs slithered to the floor. David bent to retrieve them. On top was a color print of Joann and Danacek standing next to the bleachers of a Little League game. Danacek had one arm draped around her neck. With his free hand he thrust a bottle of Miller High Life in the direction of the photographer. He looked tipsy and typically belligerent.

Joann's eyes were downcast, a trace of a smile on her lips. There was no sign that she was enjoying the beefy arm around her neck, but she wasn't objecting to it either. What made the picture chilling wasn't just what was in the foreground. Five or six feet behind them, Clarence stood on the lowest step of the bleachers with a look of bruised grievance on his face.

David slammed the album shut. Maybe Danacek wasn't making the kind of claim he seemed to be making. Maybe she and Danacek were just good friends, but there could be no mistaking the easy familiarity of the gesture.

How stupid could David possibly have been? To accuse Danacek in front of her without thinking twice about it? He needed to get out of here, and he needed to do it now.

He moved quickly through the house. Almost as an afterthought, he picked up the phone. To his surprise, the line was finally clear.

He dialed the number. It rang and rang. He glanced at the clock on the wall. Just a little past eight. It was very possible that no one was even in yet. Just as he was about to give up, someone answered.

"Good morning, Wisconsin Wolf Center."

"Good morning," David said. "I'd like to speak to Larry Gillette."

"Mr. Gillette isn't here right now. Can I take a message?"

David hesitated. Leaving a message was the last thing he wanted to do. "No, that's all right. When do you expect him in?"

"I'm not sure."

David didn't recognize the voice. They usually had interns working the front desk, and they were never there long enough for David to get their names.

"How about Gloria?"

"She doesn't come in until nine."

"What about Kim?"

"She might be here, I'm not sure."

It was all David could do not to get testy; he had no time to waste. "Could you put me through to her then?"

"Who should I say is calling?"

"Just tell her it's an old acquaintance."

"One second, please."

David waited, one hand pressed against the wall. Kim Minor had been a friend of Maya's, though they couldn't have been more different. She was five years older than Maya, in charge of the center's newsletter as well as school programming. She'd grown up in Spooner and gone to school in Eau Claire. She liked sexy clothes, big hair, bawdy talk, and seemed to go through three boyfriends a month without it ever denting her confidence.

"Hello?"

"Kim?"

"Yeah."

"This is David Neisen."

"Hoo-boy."

"Kim, I need your help. I'm trying to find Larry Gillette."

"I don't think I should be talking to you."

"I didn't do it, Kim. I promise."

"Maybe you didn't. I don't know. I'm just so upset. Why would you call me? I can't help you. I mean, where are you?"

"I'm sorry, I can't tell you that. Please just listen to me. The morning before she died, Maya was desperate to get into touch with Larry. Do you have any idea why?"

"No." Through the kitchen window, David could see the cows in the barnyard, swaying slowly through the snow and muck.

"You didn't see her that day?"

"No."

"Do you know anyone who did?"

"I swear, if anybody finds out I've been talking to you, they're going to arrest me . . ."

"What about this fall?"

"She was here a couple of times for board meetings."

"And that was all?"

"Well, yeah . . ."

"What do you mean, well, yeah?"

"You know this guy I was going with? Harold? Who works over at the Y? He goes running early, pretty much every day. Anyway, one morning, he said he saw Maya in a canoe out on Teide's Pond. And she had a little girl with her."

"What do you mean?"

"I don't know what I mean. But Harold said she was singing the little girl show tunes. Weird, huh? Seven, seven-thirty in the morning, paddling around in the mist."

"Maybe it was somebody else."

"That's what I told him. But he said no. He was sure it was her. Mr. Neisen, I've got to get off."

"Kim, please. What time is Larry coming in? Do you have any idea?"

"I told you, I don't know. I think maybe he said he was feeding this morning."

"And where would he be feeding? Last summer they were up on the bluffs."

"No, they're not there any more."

"What about the Forest Preserve?"

"It could be. I'm sorry . . ." There was a series of clicks, silence, and then a busy signal. David slammed the phone down on the receiver.

At least now he had a place to start. David moved quickly onto the back porch, grabbed a heavy coat off one of the pegs, and strode outside. He didn't like the idea of stealing somebody's coat, but he didn't have a lot of options. As he headed up the slope to the machine shed, the black dog bounded at his side, his buddy now.

David surveyed the shadowy, cavernous space, the faded red tractors, the barrels of insecticide, the cannibalized remains of old combines. The only vehicles of possible use were a battered Subaru truck and a muddy three-wheeler, but this time he wasn't so lucky; after a furious ten-minute search he still wasn't able to come up with a key. Then he remembered the skis on the back porch.

He loped to the house, pushing the dog away with his leg to keep him from coming in with him. He flipped through the stack of skis, running his hands over the smooth wood, until he found a pair with a decent surface.

He went into the kitchen and scooped the tinfoil of banana bread off the counter. He opened the refrigerator and quickly gathered a square of cheese, a salami, and an apple. He stuffed the food in his jacket pockets and then, on the way out, added a blue knit cap and a pair of ski poles to his take. Somewhere down the road, he thought, he would have to make all this up to her.

Crossing the barnyard, he swung the skis onto his shoulder and then headed up the slope. The good news was that the hatch-work of tracks in the snow, animal and human, would make it difficult to pick up his trail. The dog followed him nearly halfway up the steep hill before finally stopping and trotting back toward the house.

David followed a narrow, oak-filled gully until he got to the crest of the bluff. He knelt to strap on his skis. Rising, he pulled the knit cap down over his ears. It had been nearly a year since he'd skied, and at first he felt awkward and out of shape, but after a few minutes he found a rhythm and began to pick up speed, the slick wood hissing over the fresh snow. It was a beautifully clear morning, the sky cobalt blue, the patchwork of farm and woodland unfolding beneath him. The ridge he was following ran parallel to the road and rose perhaps a couple hundred feet above it. There was no sign of traffic in either direction. On his right the ridge fell away into a heavily forested basin.

An impossible thought came to him. Maybe the little girl in the canoe had been Maya's. Maybe she'd had a child and hidden the fact from him for all these years. It was laughable. She would've had to have a child at what? Fifteen? Sixteen?

She'd always been great with children. At parties, she'd been the one people could turn the younger kids over to, the one who would organize treasure hunts and games of Monopoly.

David had always imagined that she would have children of her own one day, that he would be a grandfather. There was going to be none of that now.

It was all preposterous. They didn't know any children here. He would have dismissed the whole business, except for one thing. Maya did sing show tunes. All the time. Songs from "Kiss Me, Kate", "Annie Get Your Gun", and "Oklahoma!"—songs her mother had taught her.

He had gone for about a mile before he stopped to catch his breath. He felt the first twinges of misgiving, of second thoughts. Maybe he was being a fool. Maybe he'd have been better off staying right where he was. Maybe Joann would have protected him.

But then he saw, in the distance, two cars coming fast. As they got closer, David could see that the first was a police car, the second a black Dodge Ram. They must have been doing close to eighty. David watched, leaning on his ski poles, as the cars whizzed past and disappeared around a curve in the road. He hadn't been wrong after all. There was no one who was going to protect him. He'd better get used to it. As he turned, he got his skis tangled for a second and nearly fell, but he righted himself and pushed off, gliding down into the trees.

eight

The week after the second of the wolf poisonings, David attended one of the community meetings, organized by the mayor and the state Fish and Wildlife Department. It quickly deteriorated into a shouting match: the farmers and townspeople on one side, all of Maya's friends on the other. An old man missing several of his uppers stood on a chair and spouted Bible verses, accusing the Wolf Center of unleashing the devil in their midst.

Halfway through the meeting, Maya took the microphone. She was eloquent and articulate, but there was something in her tone that bothered David, something acid and self-righteous. On the ride home, he tried to speak to her about it.

"I thought you were very impressive tonight," he said.

"Thank you," she said.

"My only thought is, if you're going to make this work, you can't afford to make people feel like fools."

"Even if they are?"

"Particularly if they are."

She was silent for a long time. The cones of their headlights swept across the great stone pillars flanking the entrance of the park, and they were quickly swallowed up in a tunnel of maples. "I don't know why anyone should be shy about speaking the truth," she said.

"That's because you're young, honey," he said.

In July, two more pups were found poisoned and the relationship between the Wolf Center and the town burst into open warfare. Accusations flew. David watched Maya grow angrier and angrier, and sometimes it felt as if the anger was directed at him.

She broke up with Seth Carswell in August, the troubled but brilliant boy she'd been seeing for over a year. It wasn't clear which of them had ended it, and Maya had always been too proud to ever admit that anyone had hurt her. Several nights she didn't come home. She would call the cabin at one or two in the morning to say she'd decided to sleep over at a girlfriend's. David didn't know if she was lying or not. She was twenty-two; he had no right to pry.

The last weekend of the summer they went to a small fair in town. They left their car in the Lutheran church parking lot and walked the two blocks to Firemen's Park. It looked as if the whole town had turned out. A merry-go-round spun slowly in the open area next to the tennis courts, and people bellied up three-deep to the American Legion beer tent, their laughter raucous and good-natured. The smell of bratwurst permeated the night air.

David and Maya walked through the park, neither of them speaking. On the drive in, she'd been in a particularly black mood, and he wasn't altogether sure why. There had been yet another of her meetings, he knew, but she had chosen not to go into it. Lights strung in the trees dappled everything; it was as if everyone were strolling through a masked ball. David was aware of people being aware of his daughter: a deputy leaning against his squad car, a sad-eyed alcoholic adjusting the stirrups for the pony rides, a group of teenagers licking runny ice-cream cones.

Near the bandstand they were waylaid by Dainty Gunlock in her wheelchair. Well into her eighties and badly arthritic, she had run David's vacation Bible school, thirty years before.

"My, oh my," she said. "This does my heart good!" Her nails dug into his forearm like claws.

"Dad, I'm going to run on," Maya said. "I'll be right up here."

David gave her a look, trying to send the message that he wanted her to stay, but she gave him no mind. "It's nice to meet you."

"And it's nice to meet you, too," Dainty said.

The two of them watched Maya walk off, passing the corndog and lemonade stand.

"Such a beautiful girl," Dainty said.

"Thank you," David said. In the distance, calliope music wheezed and whistled.

"I've heard so many things about her."

"Good, I hope."

"Good," she said, but it was clear that good wasn't what she meant. "I would worry about her a little if I were you."

"How do you mean?" David said. He could see Maya at the shooting gallery, watching farm boys shoot at wobbly metal ducks and try to win stuffed bears for their girlfriends.

"She needs to be careful. You know what it's like here. People don't like it when things get too different."

On the drive back home, Maya worked on a candy apple she had bought for herself. When she was finished, she rolled down the window and tossed out the stick.

"You know, darling," David said, "you really need to speak to people."

"What do you mean by that?"

"People like Dainty Gunlock."

"I spoke to her!"

"Not really." They flashed by a machine shed where a father and son were working on a combine, the rutted ground etched by floodlights. "She told me that people have been talking about you, Maya."

She wiped a bit of caramel from the corner of her mouth. "People are talking about you too," she said.

"And what do they say?"

"They say that you let a boy drown. A long time ago." They rumbled over a small bridge. Cows' eyes glowed in the pastures, demonic. "Is that true?"

"It is true."

"Why didn't you ever tell me?"

"I suppose I wanted to protect you."

"Protect me? How were you protecting me?"

"Children don't need to know everything," he said.

She didn't answer right away. "But they need to know some things, don't they?"

"Like what?"

"Like when their mother dies."

David did not look over at her. The gauntlet was thrown, but he was not picking it up. A grasshopper splatted against the windshield. Here and there across the dark fields he could see the lights of distant farmhouses. His daughter, no more than a foot away, sat still as a statue.

The evening that he flew back to New York, David called and left a message on Maya's answering machine at school. When three days passed without a response, he sat down to write her a letter. It took him an entire afternoon, laboring through a dozen drafts.

The letter was over four pages long. In it he told her, in as much detail as he was capable of, about the death of Andy Danacek and the incident on the bridge. Only in the last paragraph did he take on his other purpose for writing.

> I confess that I was pretty stung by what you said in the car. The thought that for all these years you've felt that I had somehow kept your mother's death from you is profoundly upsetting. I did the best I could. I know I botched a lot of things back then, but, honestly, I was just as lost as you were for a while. I know I'm too private a person for anyone's good. It used to just exasperate your mother. I'm not even sure I can change—but I'm willing to try. You are my heart. You have to know that.

A week after he mailed his letter, he got the briefest of e-mails in reply.

> Dad, I'm sorry. Sometimes I just say things. You shouldn't take them so seriously. You know how irritable I can get. This is no excuse, but we were together all summer. There are times when a girl just needs her space. Please, Dad, don't get needy. Give my love to Mike and Annie.

For most of the fall they didn't speak. He was profoundly angry. If it was space she wanted, space was what he was going to give her. What she'd said to him in the car had cut to the bone, and now she was trying to wave it off as if it were nothing. When he got most down about it, he was convinced that she had lost some essential respect for him, that she'd decided that he was just too wounded and weird for her to deal with.

The first week in November, Maya sent him an e-mail saying that she was swamped with schoolwork and wouldn't be home for Thanksgiving. Trying to keep his temper in check, he e-mailed her back, saying that would be fine. He'd paid the bill from the college bookstore, he said, and he would be sending along a packet of mail that had come to the house.

Thanksgiving morning he called. Her roommate said that Maya wasn't up yet. Just tell her I'll be out all day, he said, I'll be home tonight.

He ate dinner with Mike and Annie and their two kids, back from Colby and Amherst. David got a chance to hold court a bit; he had a book on the best-seller list, a memoir by one of the original *Saturday Night Live* writers, and he regaled everyone with stories. After the pies and the chocolate icebox cake and the coffee, he and Mike watched some of the Cowboys-Lions game in the den. By the middle of the second quarter, the Cowboys were running away with it and Mike was snoring in his recliner.

David tiptoed out, went to thank Annie, and made his way home. It seemed as if half the neighborhood was outside. Some were striding off their meals, elbows pumping, while others gathered at the curb, saying their goodbyes to grandparents, nephews, and nieces. Mr. King was raking his leaves. A pair of boys with lacrosse sticks fired hard rubber balls into a net set up on their front lawn. David passed unnoticed, a man without a family, of no more importance than a locust husk.

He spent the evening catching up on his work, flipping through a dispiriting thriller set in a presidential library in the Southwest and a terminally hip collection of linked stories. The only thing he found of interest was a manuscript on rituals in pre-Christian Europe, written by a Columbia anthropology professor. David had only agreed to look at it as a favor to a friend. He didn't have a snowball's chance in hell of placing it with a commercial publisher, but it was the most absorbing reading he'd done in months.

There was a long chapter tracing the origins of the twelve days of Christmas, the period between Christmas Eve and Epiphany. For centuries, he learned, it had been a festal season, a time charged with the supernatural and the uncanny. For the Teutonic peoples, midwinter was a time of darkness, howling winds, and raging storms. It was natural that they would see mysterious shapes and hear the voices of the dead, which the living shun.

In the northern countries there was a belief in a wild horde, spirits that rushed howling through the air on stormy nights. In North Devon, the term for these spirits was Yeth, or the heathen hounds. In several of the Nordic countries, they were referred to as the hounds of winter. They were the ragged pack of despairing souls who died unbaptized or by violent hands or under a curse.

At ten o'clock David put the manuscript boxes aside, went into the kitchen, and had a glass of milk and a cookie. Staring out the window, he saw the wind swaying the tree branches in front of the gently rocking streetlight, the leaves scurrying across the pavement like frightened hares. Winter would not be long in coming, he thought, and, yes, he could almost see how people could believe in these things.

He was in bed by ten thirty. The phone rang a little before midnight, jarring him out of a deep sleep. Lunging across the bed in the dark, he knocked the receiver to the floor and had to scramble to retrieve it.

"Hello?"

"Dad?" It was Maya and it sounded as if she'd been crying.

"You OK?"

"I'm fine. I'm sorry I woke you, but I know you called earlier . . ."

"Yeah," he said. Rolling over, he snapped on the bedside lamp.

"So did you go over to Mike and Annie's?"

"I did," he said.

"And did Annie make her rolls?"

"Uh-huh." He squinted, eyes adjusting to the sudden light. Across the room on the bureau was a framed photograph of the three of them, taken the year before Peggy died. They stood huddled together in the parking lot at Logan Pass in Montana. It had been a ridiculous day to even be out, cold and wet, the mountains swallowed in fog. They were all wearing orange ponchos. They had gotten a German backpacker to snap the picture.

"So Ben and Caroline were there?"

"Yeah."

"And Caroline's liking Colby?"

"She seems fine about it. Everyone was asking about you." There was a long silence. The light pouring out of the top of lampshade cast a trembling circle on the ceiling. "Is everything OK?"

"Everything's fine." In her voice he could hear an undisguised yearning.

"You want to come home? I'll buy you a ticket right now."

"No, Dad. No. But I was thinking . . ."

"What's that?"

"I was thinking, maybe we could meet at the cabin for the holidays. We could go cross-country skiing."

"I think it would be great," David said. "If you'd like that, I think it would be great."

After she hung up, he wasn't able to go to sleep for a long time. He thought about ringing her back, but decided it would be a mistake. The greatest mystery was the one between parent and child; there was no way to plumb the depths of it. What was it that Annie always said? There are things you'd rather not know. What mattered was that he was going to see her; what mattered was that whatever dark cloud had been hanging over the two of them had somehow passed.

Monday at the office he was a new man. Clarissa seemed

almost alarmed at the change. Flying to Wisconsin on short notice was going to cost him an arm and a leg, but it didn't matter. He started putting in an hour every morning on the Nordic Track so he wouldn't make an utter fool of himself on the cross-country trails.

He gave Clarissa and the bookkeeper sizeable Christmas bonuses and, against his better judgment, agreed to represent a poet. The day before his trip he took the afternoon off to shop for presents for Maya. He bought Peter Carey's *Oscar and Lucinda* and the new Barbara Kingsolver novel; went to a French store on Madison Avenue, where a young woman with an insufferable accent helped him pick out a variety of shampoos and handmade soaps and lotions; and then took a crosstown bus to get a bagful of bagels from the H & H bakery, her favorite since childhood.

nine

David stood ten feet from the Fish and Wildlife van, hidden behind a tangle of briars. It was remarkable how close he'd gotten without being detected, but now he wasn't sure it was such a good idea; Larry Gillette wasn't a person you wanted to take by surprise. Larry sat behind the steering wheel, binoculars pasted to his eyes, staring into the meadow where three young wolves feasted on a dead deer.

David bent down and packed a loose snowball. He tossed it a little too softly, and it plopped silently just shy of the truck. Out in the meadow the young wolves flowed around the carcass like gray smoke. David knelt to pat together a second handful of snow. His aim was better this time; his arcing throw thumped squarely on the hood of the green van.

At first it seemed that Larry couldn't tell where the snowball had come from. He looked up into the trees, then to his left, and then back to his right, finally spying David behind the snarl of brush. David raised a gloved hand in greeting.

Larry stepped out of the truck. In the meadow the wolves were still as statues. David slid forward on his skis, pushing through the brambles.

"Hello, Larry."

"Hey." The grief in the eyes of the young wildlife biologist was so undisguised, David had to look away. The wolves drifted off toward the woods; one stood for a moment to stare at the two men. Larry rubbed at the nape of his neck with a puffy black glove. He was no more than five feet nine, but powerfully built, like a high school wrestler. David glided toward him, using just his poles.

"So, how you doin'?" David asked. Larry considered an answer and then turned, squinting off in the direction of the distant tree line, unable to speak.

"You know what I was thinking?" Larry said after a minute. "I was thinking how sometimes when we had a day off, Maya and me and a couple of the others, we'd pack a picnic lunch and hike all the way around Sauk Lake, the High Trail, up along the cliffs. And when everybody got tired and cranky she'd start trying to cheer us up. Telling jokes. Singing songs. She'd get us all laughing. She could be really funny. People didn't realize that about her, she could really crack you up . . ." Larry glanced over his shoulder, tears glistening in his eyes.

"The afternoon that she died," David said, "she was trying to get in touch with you. Did you know that?"

Larry seemed stunned. "Where'd you hear that from?"

"I want you to look at something," David said. He dug down in his pocket and retrieved the glass vial he'd taken from the snowmobile. Larry crunched across the snow and took it from him. He worked the cap loose, gave a sniff, and wrinkled his nose.

"Where'd you get this?"

"It was in the snowmobile of the guy who killed Maya."

David waited for a reaction, but there was nothing. If Larry was playing dumb, he was doing a hell of a good job of it. "You mean you saw him?"

"Yeah, I saw him. Running out of the back of the cabin."

"You saw his face?"

"No. He was too far away. He took off on this big Arctic Cat."

Larry pursed his lips, the muscles in his jaw visibly tightening. He snapped the cap back on the vial. "And what did it look like, this Arctic Cat?"

"It was black. And it had some kind of red detailing. Flames, maybe."

"Well, shit."

"Well, shit, what?"

Larry held up the vial of yellow liquid. "You know what this is?" His voice was shaking now.

"What?"

"Trapper's oil. Animal urine."

"So who traps around here?"

"Nobody. Not for years. But there's a guy named Kingsbury who owns a bar west of town. Three years ago the cops hauled him in after he shot a couple of wolves and hung them up on his fence post."

"I remember."

"The guy's been on our case forever. You've probably seen him. Every community meeting we have, he gets up and starts ranting about how it won't be long before there will be wolves walking down Main Street, stalking our children."

"So Maya knew him?"

"Oh, she knew him all right." Twenty yards off in the woods, a great clump of snow plummeted silently from the branches of a pine tree. "We've had six wolf poisonings just this year. Including the mother of the ones you saw out in the meadow. We haven't been able to figure out how they're doing it. It's not cyanide; it's not strychnine. Maya came over from St. Paul a couple of times this fall to help me collect blood and tissue samples."

"I didn't know that."

"Maya and Kingsbury got into it big-time, more than once. She pretty much straight-out accused him. She said she didn't know how he was doing it, but she was going to find out, he could count on it."

"And what did he say?"

"He said he was just waiting for the day. I told her, when I heard that, if he ever contacts you again, you call me." From somewhere far off, David thought he heard the baying of dogs. "Oh. And one more thing. He drives an Arctic Cat, one of the old ones. With a big red blaze."

"But what about Danacek?"

"What about him?"

"When he came into the cabin, just an hour after she was murdered, his trousers were wet."

"I don't understand."

"Just listen to me! When I came across the snowmobile, that vial I showed you wasn't the only thing I found. There was a packet of Red Man tobacco."

Larry was incredulous. "You think it was Danacek?"

"Until now, I was sure of it."

Larry rubbed at the side of his face, scowling. "Let's get this straight. What you're telling me is that Danacek went to the cabin, murdered Maya, took off on a snowmobile, cracked it up in some ravine, went back to his police car, changed his jacket and went back to the cabin. No offense, but that's horse-dukey. Danacek doesn't even own a snowmobile."

David leaned forward on his poles, his face burning. He had clung to the idea of Danacek being the murderer like a rock climber clinging to a fraying rope. If it hadn't been Danacek, David had made a grievous, unforgivable mistake. Seeing his daughter on the floor of the cabin, he had only been capable of seeing it as a sign, a sign that he was being punished, and now it seemed that it might have had nothing to do with him.

"So when she was trying to get in touch with you that morning . . ."

"My guess is she'd finally gotten the goods on these jerks. Kingsbury must have gotten wind of that."

"So what are we supposed to do?" David said.

"I think we go see him."

David looked over at him quickly. "Don't joke."

"I'm not joking."

"I don't know if you've heard, Larry, but I'm a wanted man."

"I know that."

David sucked on his teeth. "That's crazy."

"Is it? I'm not saying we do anything to him. We just talk to him."

"But what if you're wrong? What if it isn't him?"

"I promise you, it's him."

David looked away. The carcass at the far end of the meadow seemed like nothing more than a gray smudge in the snow.

"I need to think about this."

"Think about it all you want, but you can't stay here," Larry said.

"No. No, I guess that's right."

"There's no one at the old Nature Center. They close it over the holidays. I could take you there. Come back and get you later."

It sounded like madness, but David was so dizzy with fatigue, he really couldn't be sure. The thought of sleep was nearly irresistible. "You could go to prison for five years for hiding me."

"I know."

"How would we get there? What about roadblocks?" More and more David felt as if he weren't really the one doing these things, as if he were standing outside, watching some stranger.

"Those guys aren't going to bother me. I play pool with those fools. Let me show you something."

Larry walked to the rear of the van and yanked open the doors. With one push of his poles, David joined him. On the floor of the truck were a rolled-up tarp and a coil of heavy chain. A dead owl lay behind the driver's seat.

"You should be fine back here."

Everything suddenly seemed to be deteriorating into farce, David thought, some kind of Edward Abbey bad-boy fantasy. It was perfect Larry. The baying of the wolves had grown louder and more distinct.

"If you're not up for it, just say so," Larry said.

"With all due respect, this is nuts."

"And what do you suggest we do?"

"We've got to find a way to go to the cops. We've got to. There's no way you and I can settle this on our own."

"And what cops do you have in mind? Danacek? Or his cousin over at the state highway patrol?" For a moment, neither of them spoke. "I hate to rush you, but I think we need to get moving."

There was no way to go back and redo what had already been done. He bent down and undid his bindings. Larry held the skis while David clambered into the back of the van, unrolled the tarp, and pulled it up around him; it smelled of rotting meat. Larry slid the skis and poles in between the wall of the truck and the coil of heavy chain.

"You all right?" Larry said.

David shifted onto his side, trying to protect his tender ribs. "Fine and dandy."

Larry slammed the doors shut, walked around, and ducked in behind the steering wheel. "So here goes nothing."

They had gone perhaps a mile when David felt the truck begin to slow. His heart leapt. "What is it?"

"Nothing. This is only going to take a second."

Larry eased the van to the side of the road, stopped, and got out. David craned to see out the windshield. The empty road ahead shone with patches of ice. The rear doors of the van groaned as Larry swung them wide.

"What are you doing?" David said.

"Just sit tight. I'll take care of it."

Larry pulled out the skis and the poles and walked to the edge of the embankment. David, the stiff fabric of the tarp arranged around him like a rumpled sleeping bag, scanned the long country road behind them. If anyone comes along now, David thought, we're sunk. A sudden gust of cold wind ruffled the feathers of the dead owl in the corner of the van. Larry baby-stepped down into the ditch and rattled the skis into the far recesses of a concrete culvert. He tossed the poles in after them, slinging them underhanded, like spears.

He wiped his hands, looking over his shoulder at David. "That should take care of that," he said.

They drove on. They were about ten miles east of town, moving through open farmland. David leaned against the side of the van, arms around his knees. Silence grew between the two men like a geological fault. When Larry had said he wanted to go see Kingsbury, what had he meant by it? If it hadn't been such a ludicrous idea, it would have been frightening. What were they going to do, get in a shouting match? Shoot the guy in the head? It was chastening to be hooked up with someone more reckless than he was.

They passed a towering stand of pine trees, so thickly packed that there wasn't room for a man to walk down the rows; thirty-some years before, David and his Boy Scout troop had helped plant them. He could still remember the cloudy March afternoon they had done it, how cold and raw his hands had been, packing the soil in around the tiny, wet seedlings.

"OK," Larry said.

"OK, what?"

"There's a roadblock up ahead. Just get down. Let me handle this. Everything's going to go just fine." Larry might have been talking a good game, but he didn't sound that sure. David felt the tug of the brakes, the van beginning to slow down.

He yanked the tarp over his head and pulled up his knees. The smell became suffocating, but he couldn't make out what it was. The van slowed some more and came to a complete stop. Nearly a minute passed.

"Good morning!" David recognized the voice instantly; it was Young Burmeister.

"Morning, Tommy, how you doin'?" Larry said.

"Doing all right. How you doing?"

"OK. Just out cruising for roadkill."

"Oh, yeah. I talked to Kerry yesterday. He said somebody hit a deer out on old Twenty-seven, near the Samuels Brothers place. I don't know how much the crows will have left you."

"I'll go check it out."

His fist pressed to his mouth, David felt as if he were about to retch. He tried to imagine what it would be like to be yanked out by his heels, handcuffed, slammed into a police car.

"Better watch yourself though. As long as they've got this lunatic running around in the woods."

"You mean Neisen?" Larry said.

"Who else?" Larry had left the motor running and the fumes were slowly filling the rear of the van.

"You heard anything?" Larry said.

"Well, yeah. They nearly caught him this morning. Apparently he busted into the Meinekes' place."

"You kidding me?"

"No, I'm serious. Joann, she actually talked to the guy. She was lucky to get out of there alive. God, Larry, anybody ever tell you how bad this van smells? What you got back there?"

"A dead owl. You want to have a look? You're welcome to it."

"Thanks, but no thanks." There was a solid thump—the policeman hitting the side of the truck. "You going over to Goldie's for lunch?"

"Probably so."

"I'll see you there. Have a good one."

The van eased off, then shifted gears and began to pick up speed.

"Still breathing?"

David pushed the stinking tarp away, his face burning. "Yeah, I think so."

Reclining, he watched the tops of the trees slide by, the gray winter sky. Everything was at such an odd angle. All he could do was trust. It was like being a child again, lying in the back of his family's station wagon that night, thirty-five years ago, heading off for California. He could still summon it all up: the same queasiness, the same touch of motion sickness, the same dark fear of heading off into the unknown. He remembered pulling his blanket up around him, trying to sleep, listening to the hum of the tires on the highway, the murmuring of his parents in the front seat. He remembered how the lights of the passing cars had slid like liquid across the soft upholstered ceiling of the station wagon.

As they got closer to town, David spied the old county home, shut for many years, where Mrs. Eisenreich used to take their Sunday school class on Christmas to sing carols with senile old women and retarded children. A few billboards began to sprout up for Dairy Queen and McDonald's. They passed the Christian Day Care Center and a lot full of trailers, brightly colored plastic banners flapping over the entrance.

Black Hawk had changed a lot since David had lived here thirty-five years ago. Most of the young people had left for jobs in Madison or Minneapolis, and the once-thriving downtown was now riddled with fourth-rate antique emporiums. There was a Chinese restaurant run by a Vietnamese refugee who would ask if you wanted ketchup with your egg foo yung. As the dairy farms had gone under, one after the other, a small group of Amish had moved in, attracted by the cheap land prices, and it was no longer an oddity to see a black, horse-drawn buggy swaying down the back roads.

Larry turned at the golf course road and skirted the edge of town. Two kids in blue jackets labored over a snowman on the hill behind the elementary school. For David, the week after Christmas had always been the most dispiriting week of the year; old Christmas trees, their moment past, lay on the crusted banks along the curbs, and the sky became heavy and gray. A policeman stood at the gas pump at PDQ, scraping his windshield, never looking up as they sped past.

The nature center was a half mile back behind the football fields. In David's childhood this had all been swampland, but a generous gift from the town's first tycoon (he'd made millions investing in real estate in the Southwest) had turned it into a preserve, with well-groomed trails and a modest museum. It was a little too out of the way to ever get much use, except for school expeditions, and during the holidays even that stopped.

Larry pulled the van up in front of a corrugated-steel utility shed and came around to open the back. David tossed the tarp aside and climbed out. He inhaled deeply the crisp winter air; it smelled faintly of spruce. The center itself was a low barracks of a building, with icicles clinging to the eaves. Over the sturdy wooden sign announcing visiting hours, someone had tacked up a handwritten message—Closed until January 7.

David followed Larry up the newly shoveled walk. The lock on the front door was sticky, and it took Larry a minute to get his key to work. He shoved the door open and gestured for David to go first.

It had been a couple of years since David was last here. At one end of the building were lab tables and rows of tiny chairs for the grade school kids. Directly across from him were the display cases of local fauna—muskrats and duck, a beaver and a few tattered raccoons. Some joker had put a Santa Claus hat on a badly stuffed lynx. A turtle-filled aquarium bubbled softly under a row of cabinets.

"You going to be all right?" Larry said.

"I'll be fine."

"Just don't turn on any lights. There shouldn't be anybody coming by. Once in a while you get some joggers on the nature trail, but with all this snow, I don't think there'll be much of that."

"Larry, can I ask you something?"

"Sure."

"What did people think of her?"

"That all depends on what people you're talking about. The people I know loved her. There wasn't anybody smarter. Or funnier. And you should have seen her when she was working with kids."

"But she had an edge, right?"

"She knew how to push some people's buttons, that was for sure." Larry pulled a glove out of his jacket. "You know what she told me once? About why she loved wolves?"

"No. What was that?"

"It was that they didn't have any use for you. A funny thing to say, huh? But it always stuck with me."

After Larry left, David wandered through the building. He stopped at the big picture window to watch the sparrows and cardinals flitting at the empty bird feeders. Beyond the porch, a trail led down into the swamp. He stared out at the frozen marsh, imagined he heard the brittle branches clicking together like bones. As boys, he and Andy Danacek had built rafts and secret forts here, and once they had come upon a giant snapping turtle rotting on a log, an arrow through its shell. There had been a shack too, not far from here, with rattlesnake skins tacked to the wall. The story was that there was an old hermit who lived there, but no one had ever seen him—it may have just been one of those tales that twelve-year-old boys make up to scare themselves.

He found a knife in one of the drawers and cut slices of apple and salami, making a snack for himself. The apple was softer than he had hoped. He gouged out the brown with his thumbnail and flicked it into a wastebasket.

The only sound in the building was the soft bubbling of the turtle tank. On the wall next to the men's bathroom was a pay phone. David settled in with a stack of old *Natural History* magazines, flipping through the pictures of archeological digs and prairie dog colonies, Javanese masks and Mongolian herdsmen. He did a set of push-ups and sit-ups and, after a brief foray into the offices, found a radio.

He turned it on, hoping to pick up some local news, but there seemed to be nothing on but Christmas music. Keeping the volume low, he crouched in a chair, listening to Bing Crosby, Alvin and the Chipmunks, Nat King Cole singing about chestnuts roasting on an open fire.

Through the window he could see the wind picking up, swaying the trees out in the swamp, chasing twigs and pinecones across the snow. A low muttering came from a loose pane. The hounds of winter, wasn't that what they called it? The voices of the dead. He could have saved her. If he'd just gotten there fifteen minutes earlier.

He turned off the radio and went into the other room. The afternoon passed, and night came on. The one spot in the building that let in at least a little light was the big picture window, and David eventually settled there, his back propped against the cold glass. He finished the salami and cut himself a couple of slices of cheese.

He watched the moon rise slowly through the trees. Two hours passed, then three. He put together a makeshift bed out of a ratty quilt and a pair of cushions he found in one of the offices. Where was Larry? All David could hope was that there hadn't been more trouble.

The pay phone sat on the far wall, the silvery metal cord catching a glint of moonlight through the picture window, the receiver sitting on the hook like a gently curved question mark.

Larry's case for Kingsbury being the murderer had its points. David could imagine Maya standing up to some irate redneck all too easily. The problem was that Larry wanted so badly for it to be Kingsbury, just as David had wanted so badly for it to be Danacek.

How much could you ever really believe of what Larry said? As long as Larry was explaining raised-leg urination, he was rock-solid; once he got outside of that, things got a bit shaky.

David pushed up from his makeshift bed and hobbled to the phone. He stabbed at the tiny metal cubes: first the MCI access code, then the fourteen digits of his calling card, then the number he knew as well as his own. The phone rang three times before someone picked up.

"Hello?"

"Annie?"

"David? David, is that you?"

"Yeah."

"Thank God. Where are you?" The gallery of dead animals glared at him from the gloom of their display cases.

"Out here somewhere. Is Mike there?"

"No, I'm sorry, he's not." Her accent was soft, Alabaman, familiar.

"Where is he?"

"He left for Wisconsin this morning."

"Oh shit."

"What's wrong?"

"Nothing. What's he coming here for?"

"He spent all day yesterday on the phone. He thinks he's found something."

"What do you mean?" David turned, the metal cord tightening around his upper arm.

"Apparently there's this man, this farmer, who's been making these threats . . ."

"Yes, I know," David said.

"Kingsbury, I think his name is. It seems he was upset about wolves killing some of his cows . . ."

"Right." It was hard for David to control his impatience; he didn't need her telling him what he already knew. Turning again, he saw, through the picture window, a wash of light slide across the tops of the bare trees.

"Anyway, Mike talked to some boy's mother yesterday. Her son worked at the Wolf Center last year." In the distance, David could hear the low drone of an engine. "It seems he ran into this Kingsbury snowmobiling up in the bluffs."

"When?"

"Three days ago. He said that Kingsbury was acting very oddly, but the boy figured it was just that he was doing a little off-season poaching . . ."

"So where exactly did he see him?"

"I think Mike said it was maybe a half mile inside the main entrance to the park. At three or four in the afternoon." Moonlight shone off a display of dried insect galls.

"What else, Annie?"

"Maybe I shouldn't be telling you all of this."

"Please, Annie! What else?"

"The boy said the back of Kingsbury's trousers were spattered with blood."

David leaned against the wall, shutting his eyes. From the far side of the room, he could hear keys rattling in the door. "I'm going to have to get off," he said.

"David, please . . ."

He hung up the receiver. He pushed away from the wall. The misshapen lynx in the Santa hat grinned at him from his perch.

The door swung open and Larry backed into the room. When he turned, he seemed startled to see David standing there.

"Are you all right?" Larry said.

"I'm fine."

"Are you sure? You don't look fine."

"No, I'm OK."

For a moment neither of them spoke, the only sound the soft bubbling of the turtle tank. "So are we doing this or not?" Larry said.

"Let's go," David said.

ten

They took the van five or six miles up the river road, putting more and more distance between themselves and the roadblocks. It was the dead of winter, and all the brooks were frozen, all the pastures deserted. A small herd of deer, no more substantial than ghosts, drifted through a grove of evergreens. Neither man spoke, each lost in his own thoughts. David leaned forward, his arms wrapped around his chest, trying to stay warm. Eventually the road took them up onto a high ridge and then into Utica. A century before, Utica had been a thriving community, but now it was down to four or five hundred people, a post office, a feed store, and a couple of small cafés. Kingsbury's bar was a half mile on the far side of town, next to the graveyard. A couple of drooping strands of Christmas tree lights blinked over the front door, and the roofs of a dozen cars shone in the snowy parking lot.

Larry pulled to the side of the road, into the shadows of the trees bordering the graveyard.

"So this is it," David said.

"Yeah."

"I need to ask you something. You said you saw Maya a couple of times this fall."

"Yeah."

"Did she ever say anything to you about taking some little girl canoeing? Maybe one of the other workers' kids?"

"No. Why?"

"No reason."

"So what are we going to do?" Larry asked.

"I want you to just leave me."

"No way! I'm part of this deal."

"No, you're not. I'm her father. End of discussion. I want you to go home."

"Jesus Christ!"

"So which is Kingsbury's truck?"

"I think it's the red one, over by the back door." Larry was pouting now.

"And how will I know it's him, when he comes out?"

"Oh, you'll know. He's got a big beer gut and he doesn't have what you'd call a pretty face." David leaned on the handle and opened the door. "What are you doing?"

"To be honest, I don't really know." David stepped out of the truck. He could hear the wheezing of a faulty accordion coming from inside the bar, the familiar strains of polka music. Larry hunched over the steering wheel, looking rueful.

"Hold on for a second. I've got something for you." Larry flung himself across the seat and punched open the glove compartment. He fumbled around for a moment and finally pulled out a small handgun. He offered it to David, butt-end first. "Go ahead. Take it. You never know."

David hesitated, but finally complied. The weight of the revolver surprised him.

"The safety's there on the left. And the trigger's a little tight, so be careful. Oh, and one other thing. I thought I'd tell you." David turned, waited. "I would have married her." The accordion was still playing, worse than ever. "I know she wasn't interested in me. I was too goofy for her. But I would have. If she would have had me."

"Just go home, Larry, please. Just go home."

Larry pulled the door shut. David waited by the side of the road as Larry maneuvered the truck around. He made a sloppy job of it—ramming into a snowbank and bumping into a ditch—but finally lurched his way onto the blacktop. He raised a hand in farewell, and David waved in return as the van sped off.

David watched the red taillights recede in the darkness. He was on his own now. He turned the gun over warily in his hands, like an archeologist examining a find that fit into no logical scheme. It had a fancy carved-ivory handle, like something Tom Mix might have carried in some Pasadena parade.

It took David a few seconds to figure out how to open the chamber; it was fully loaded. He looked back at the bar; there was no sign of anyone yet. The music seemed to have taken a deeply Bavarian turn.

What the hell had Larry been thinking, giving him a hand gun? Maybe it was because he was so crazy, or maybe it was something else, something not so apparent, something David didn't fully understand yet. He considered throwing the gun in the ditch, but decided against it. When he slipped it in the pocket of his jacket, he could feel the sag.

Snow squeaked underfoot as he trudged along the line of trees. A rusted iron cherub stared blankly from the center of the graveyard gate. Bells jangled. The front door of the bar opened and David moved more quickly, taking cover behind a massive oak stump.

A man and a woman wove their way down the front steps. He had his arm around her and was jostling her, making it impossible for her to zip up her coat. She finally pushed him away, her laughter light as the notes of a cleanly struck xylophone. David, his cheek pressed to rough bark, watched as they got into their car. For a moment it seemed as if the engine wasn't going to turn over, but then it did, firing up with a great racket, and the mud-spattered Chevy crept out of the parking lot and down the road.

David climbed over the fence into the cemetery and moved along the row of trees to a spot where he could peer in through one of the windows of the bar. What he could see was part of the dance floor and one corner of the tiny stage. At first all he could make out was bits—the swirl of a colorful skirt, a sweaty, shiny face, a pair of linked arms. It seemed as if everyone was having a good time—a fleshy farm couple that looked as if they'd just stepped out of a Brueghel painting, a gaunt young man with long hair and a silver stud in his ear, and a young woman with more bounce than Tammy Wynette.

David shivered among the gravestones, staring in at a world he would never make his way back to. He hugged his arms to his chest, moving from one foot to the other, trying to stay warm.

He didn't see anyone who fit Larry's description of Kingsbury. The only person working, other than the musicians, appeared to be a rather grim-looking sixty-year-old barmaid who passed in front of the window a couple of times, clearing pitchers from the tables. What if Kingsbury wasn't here? What if Larry'd been wrong? Maybe the red pickup wasn't Kingsbury's, maybe he'd already gone home for the night. David would be in a fix then, stranded, without wheels or an ally, and the temperature plummeting. Just as he was about to abandon hope, a door behind the stage swung open, and David saw him—big belly, thinning hair, and a face like a boil—making his way through the dancers with a broom in one hand and a large plastic trash bag in the other.

David had to give Larry credit for one thing; he'd timed the bar's closing time about right. The band did one more number—a rousing version of "The Beer Barrel Polka"—and then everything began to break up. After a few minutes of milling about—back slaps and bear hugs, the hurried downings of the last steins of Old Milwaukee, the struggles with winter coats—people began to straggle out of the bar.

Two men swaggered to the edge of the parking lot to have a peeing contest; their female companions huddled by a Four Runner, complaining loudly for them to hurry up before they all froze to death. David still crouched behind the oak stump, his hands pressed between his thighs.

One by one the cars began to leave. The band members were the last to go, packing away their instruments, the barmaid rushing out to catch a ride with the accordion player. As the musicians' cars pulled onto the road, there was an exchange of honks, and then someone rolled down his window to shout something cheery and incomprehensible into the frosty air.

Suddenly everything was silent. Stars, millions of miles away, pulsed through the liquid darkness. David remembered how Peggy had always tried to get him to come out and look at the stars at night; he had never been much interested.

Only Kingsbury was left. Through the glowing pane, David watched him wiping the tables. Kingsbury's hands were the size of porterhouse steaks. Watching him wring out a wet washcloth, David tried to imagine those hands around an iron poker, the damage they could do.

He pushed to his feet. This was his chance; he had to act now. He climbed over the wrought-iron fence and walked quickly across the parking lot to Kingsbury's pickup. He got in on the passenger side and eased the door shut, careful not to make a sound. He opened the glove compartment.

He pawed his way through the usual random clutter—some oil-stained state maps, an out-of-date registration, a packet of dental floss, a few yellowing repair bills. He looked back at the bar. One of the lights had gone out. A moment later they all went out. David scrambled between the seats and crouched low behind the padded driver's headrest.

He watched Kingsbury come out and swing a couple of trash bags into the Dumpster. The bar owner turned, stopping for a moment to pull his cap down over his ears. He had a zippered bank bag in one of the pockets of his jacket. David's left knee ached, resting on what felt like a metal jack; he reached down in his pocket and removed the handgun, holding the revolver against his inner thigh.

Kingsbury shambled toward the pickup. David ducked down even lower, listening to the crunch of boots across the snow and then the creak of the door as it opened. Kingsbury tossed the bank bag onto the passenger seat and heaved himself in behind the steering wheel. David didn't breathe or move, the muscles in his back as tight as guitar strings.

Kingsbury didn't move either. "What the shit?" he muttered. He leaned across, one hand on the gearshift. In an instant David understood: either the glove compartment was still open, or something had fallen to the floor. Either way, Kingsbury knew. As the bar owner twisted to retrieve whatever it was that had dropped, David rose up and put the revolver firmly at the back of Kingsbury's head.

"Don't move. Don't even think about it," David said. Kingsbury gave a small shudder.

"The money's on the seat. Just take it."

"I don't give a damn about your money. You killed my daughter."

"Killed your daughter? Who the fuck are you?"

"Who the fuck do you think I am?"

Kingsbury raised his head a couple of inches, but one gentle push of the gun barrel against his rough, scaly cheek put him down again. David caught just a glimpse of his fear-filled eyes, rolling back like the eyes of a cow trapped in a catch pen. David could smell the beer on Kingsbury's breath. With his free hand, he grabbed the bar owner by the neck and shoved his head forward. "You were up in the park. The day she died. And you had blood all over your trousers."

"Buddy, I've got no idea what you're talking about."

"Somebody saw you. Monday afternoon."

"Monday afternoon?"

"Yeah, that's right. Monday afternoon."

"So, I got me a deer out of season, OK? You going to shoot me for that?" Kingsbury's voice sounded half strangled. "If you don't believe me, we can go to my house, the carcass is hanging in the backyard!" He put a hand on the dash to keep from rolling onto the floor. "I never knew your daughter! I saw her once in a fucking restaurant, and we got in an argument. Is that a crime? I never even knew she was back in town until I saw her the other night. . . ."

"What do you mean, the other night?"

"The other night. Over at the Carswells'." David's first reaction was to laugh—Kingsbury had to be lying, trying to save his skin, but it was a clever enough lie to serve its purpose.

"What do you mean, you saw her?"

"I saw her! I was delivering the liquor for a party they were having."

"I should shoot you right now."

"I'm telling you the truth, I swear!" All that was keeping Kingsbury from tumbling onto the floor of the pickup was the gearshift poking him in the gut.

"Did you talk to her?"

"No. I had to carry these cases of beer up to the kitchen and get everything set up. When I was finished, I went back to my truck. I heard these people arguing in one of the stone cottages they had down from the main house . . ."

"I know. I've been there," David said.

"I couldn't make out the man's voice, but I recognized hers right away, and I could see her in the lighted window." Kingsbury shifted his weight, getting a fresh hold on the dashboard; it was not the most comfortable position from which to be telling a story. "She looked a little crazy, to tell you the truth. Her face was all flushed. She'd be in the window and then she'd disappear, and then she'd be back again. She kept putting her hands over her mouth and nose. It was like she was trying to hold everything in . . ."

"And what were they arguing about?"

"I couldn't tell. The only thing, when she was leaving . . . She was in the doorway, and she just shouted out at him, 'How many times do we have to go through this? It was over then, it's over now.'"

"And that's all you heard?"

"Yeah."

The thought came to him out of the blue: if he was on the run now, Maya had been on the run, in her own way and for her own mysterious reasons, for months. "What happened then?"

"She went to her car and peeled out of there going a hundred miles an hour. Can I get up now? My leg is killing me here."

"So, how about the guy in the stone cottage? Did you ever see who it was?"

"Are you kidding me? I got the hell out of there as fast as I could."

David hovered above the fleshy bartender, one hand still pressing Kingsbury's neck, the other holding the gun. He wasn't sure whether the safety was off or on. Lying on his side, with his big belly rising and falling, Kingsbury looked like a beached and panicked whale.

"What about Carswell's son?"

"What about him?"

"Do you know if he was home?"

"I didn't see him. But when Carswell's wife and I were talking, she was telling me how happy Carswell was to be getting his boy home for the holidays."

"So how many days ago was this?"

"Lemme see. One . . . two . . . three. It was three."

"The night before she died."

"Whatever you say."

"One more thing."

"What's that?"

"You got a snowmobile?"

"Yeah."

"With a big red flame on the side?"

"Yeah. Me and about twenty other guys in town."

"So did you get a big kick out of poisoning those wolves?"

"I never did anything to those wolves!"

David righted himself, lifting the gun from Kingsbury's ear. "Just drive," he said.

"Where?" Kingsbury hadn't moved yet, afraid to risk it.

"I don't care where. Just get us out of here."

When Maya first announced that she and Seth Carswell were dating, David had misgivings. Seth's father was Black Hawk High's most famous graduate, a one-time governor of the state and a big-time operator; his mother, a socialite from Dallas. After his parents' divorce, Seth had gone to Texas, where, according to the rumors, he'd been kicked out of St. Mark's for having an affair with his junior English teacher.

Seth had had more than his share of troubles: bashed cars, a half dozen colleges, and a couple of run-ins with the police. The low point came when his father had to fly to Mexico to negotiate Seth's way out of jail after he and his buddies had trashed an Acapulco bar. Seth had no interest in politics. He wanted to be a novelist, and had recently been accepted into the graduate writing program at Columbia.

Maya and Seth saw each other several times a week during the summers when he was in Wisconsin, staying with his father and stepmother; during the year they managed a few visits in either New York or St. Paul. David had warmed to him a lot. He couldn't have been more different from the morally earnest types Maya was hanging around with at the Wolf Center. Maya, whether she admitted it or not, appreciated irony, and irony was something Seth had in spades. Though he fancied Jimmy Buffett–style Hawaiian shirts and had the air of a boy with his own margarita machine, Seth loved to talk books, the more arcane the better. He had brought David a couple of samples of his own fiction, stories that David found imaginative, heartless, and too clever by half.

Seth had his father's good looks and impeccable manners, even though he was the sort of kid who could call you sir and make it sound like an insult. Behind his presumptuous façade lurked a profound insecurity. About his father's up-and-down career, Seth could be as scathing as a stand-up comedian.

It was probably too strong a statement to say that Seth hated his father, but he hadn't forgiven him much. He had confided to Maya that when he was young, his father had taken a belt to him more than a few times. He had the feel of a wounded boy, and David always suspected that one of the reasons he was attracted to Maya was her strength. He was a kid on the lookout for a little mothering.

Maya had never spoken to David about the reasons for the split. All David knew was that one afternoon in early August, Seth had showed up at the cabin looking for her. When David asked him what was wrong, Seth burst out crying. There had been a rash of late-night phone calls, hang-ups at one and two in the morning. One morning David had found a sodden note on the front lawn.

He opened it. Some of the block letters had been erased by the morning dew.

FORG VE ME
FO T
VING YOU

The next evening Maya came in to say that Seth had flown to New York. Not a word had been uttered about him since.

They drove out into the countryside, the scattered lights of Utica fading in the rearview mirror. Kingsbury hunched over the wheel, David kneeling behind him, the barrel of the revolver resting lightly on the headrest. They passed a series of small farms and the Amish cheese factory.

He didn't trust Kingsbury any farther than he could throw him. Could the bar owner have invented the story about Maya on the spot, just to save his skin? Of course he could. Everyone knew that Maya and Seth had dated. Most people knew about their breakup. But what made Kingsbury's story convincing was the way it connected the dots, dots Kingsbury couldn't have known about: the teary phone call at Thanksgiving, the fact that she'd suggested coming here for Christmas rather than coming home, George the caretaker's report of her showing up at his house the morning before she was murdered, fearful and on edge.

How oblivious could a father be? He should have been smarter than to take Maya at her word when she said that it was over between her and Seth. David had been around long enough to know that every relationship needs to end at least twice—once politely and once not politely at all. Seth would not have been easy to say no to. Intense and easily wounded, he had a proven capacity for getting crazy.

So, could Seth possibly still be here? If he had killed her, most likely his father would have spirited him quickly out of town; David sure as hell intended to find out.

His immediate problem was Kingsbury. He still wasn't convinced that Kingsbury had clean hands in this, but if David kept him in the truck, he would be a ball and chain. Letting him out here wasn't the brightest idea either; Kingsbury would be at some farmer's door in no time flat, calling the police.

It took David a couple of minutes to come up with a solution. He leaned forward and pointed to the crossroads looming in the darkness. "I want you to take a left up here."

Kingsbury gave him a quick glance. "Where are we going?"

"Don't worry about it. Just drive."

They headed into wild, hilly country, passing a few jutting limestone cliffs and an occasional shack. Some of it was familiar to David, some of it wasn't. It was a strangely intimate act, holding a gun to a man's ear. When David's arm began to ache, he switched hands.

"Listen, I know your daughter and I had our differences, but I never wanted anything like this to happen, I promise. Not in a million years."

"Just shut up," David said. "There's a right up here. Take it."

They dropped into a long, mist-filled valley that was as remote as David remembered it; for five miles they didn't see a single light. Sensing what was coming, Kingsbury had become more and more nervous, reaching up from time to time to wipe the foggy inside of the windshield with his meaty hand.

"You can just pull over here," David said. Kingsbury glanced quickly at him "That's right, here." Kingsbury eased to the side of the road. The headlights shone on an ice-bowed tangle of brush. "Now get out. Just leave the motor running." Kingsbury hesitated, but when David nudged him with the revolver, the effect was galvanizing. The bar owner swung the door wide and scrambled down. David gestured with the gun. "Back. Go."

Kingsbury retreated, nearly tripping over his own feet. He was petrified, looking as though he thought David was about to shoot him and leave him to bleed to death. David climbed between the seats and slipped behind the steering wheel. Kingsbury backed off another step.

"Hey. Don't forget about this." David leaned over, retrieved the bank bag from the floor, and gave it a toss. The bartender caught it with both hands. "I don't want people saying I'm a thief."

"Now what am I supposed to do?" Kingsbury said.

David stared down at the burly, red-faced man. God, he hoped he wasn't making a mistake. "If I remember right, we passed a farm three, four miles ago."

"But I'll freeze to death!"

"You just keep moving, you'll be all right."

David banged the door shut and shifted into drive. As he sped away, he glanced in the rearview mirror; Kingsbury stood in the middle of the road, waving in disgust. The slog to the farmhouse would take Kingsbury a couple of hours; if things went well, that was more time than David would need.

David continued another mile or so down the valley, passing a pair of collapsed and long-abandoned barns. He was upset now in more ways than he could name. Part of it was being wrong, and part of it was that things were getting so much more tangled and cloudy than he had imagined them. But part of it was simply the upset over having held a gun to a man's head. What if Kingsbury had confessed to murdering Maya? Would he have shot him? There was still a knot in David's stomach, knowing how close he'd been. He felt so far from his own life, from everything he'd ever been proud of. It was as if he were standing outside a window, watching someone act in his stead.

At a narrow bridge, David pulled over to the shoulder, got out, and pitched the gun as far out into the reeds as he was able. Whatever kind of monster he was turning himself into, there was still a step he wasn't willing to take.

He wound through a series of back roads until he found his way to the interstate. As he headed onto the highway, the huge green sign reading EAST-MILWAUKEE-CHICAGO flashed overhead.

It was a nervy move, heading back into the eye of the storm, but his hope was that the interstate cut far enough to the north to be free of roadblocks. For fifteen miles or so a pair of semis kept him company, playing a lumbering game of tag with each other, but once he passed the Black Hawk exits, even they vanished. Rumbling over an overpass, he saw a police car parked outside a tiny cracker box of a house. All the windows were dark. It felt as if the whole world was asleep.

He had to work to keep his eyes open. He remembered Maya telling him that wolves could run up to eighty miles in a single night; it looked as if he was going to beat that all hollow. The billboards for The Narrows began to appear, advertising supper clubs, water ski shows, Indian casinos. He'd been to Carswell's place only once before. He was just going to have to feel his way.

As fatigue set in, he began to sense Maya's presence there in the pickup with him. It was as if she were somehow orchestrating all of this. One thing he knew for sure; she would not have wanted him to surrender.

eleven

The Narrows was a fifteen-mile stretch of the Otter River where surging waters had carved fantastic shapes out of the sandstone. For more than a century it had been one of the state's major tourist attractions. At the start it was little more than two-dollar boat rides to see the freakish rock formations with the fanciful names—The Devil's Chalice, Tubby's Torment, Sleeping Hiawatha, and Lover's Leap—and a few Chippewa Indians from the local reservation squatting by the sides of the roads, selling handcrafted baskets and beadwork. A hundred years later it had exploded into a midwestern Disneyland, with go-carts, water parks, Ripley's Believe It or Not! fudge, and soft-ice-cream shops.

But along the river, a little to the south, there were still some nice homes, and this was where Carswell lived. Leaving the interstate, David entered a rat's nest of twisting two-lane blacktops. At first none of it was familiar; it all seemed to be junk: tiny tourist cabins, trailers, and abandoned fishing shacks. He slowed to a crawl, leaning forward on the steering wheel to peer into the darkness. Twice he had to turn around; the one time he'd been to Carswell's had been in the summer and then he'd had directions. He passed two campgrounds and a small store. A deer looked up at him, startled, from the lawn of one of the big summer hotels. He was close; he remembered the hotel. He imagined his daughter on this road. What had Kingsbury said she'd been going? A hundred miles an hour? A bit farther on he came to the familiar trio of mailboxes and the driveway curving up to the right. He hadn't been as far off as he thought. He drove a hundred yards or so past the house, parked the truck in a turnaround under some willows, and walked back.

Tall pines lining both sides of the driveway masked David's approach, but he could still feel his stomach tighten, feel the electric flare of nerves. For someone who was as much a public figure as Carswell, it would make perfect sense for him to have some sort of alarm system—motion sensors, cameras, dogs even. The house was a famous one. It had been built in the thirties by Jeffrey Joseph Archbold, one of the giants of twentieth-century architecture, a man of flowing ties and utopian ideals. This house, one of his masterpieces, protruded from the hillside like some fabulous crag of limestone and glass. The long slope, which in summer featured beautifully tended gardens and terraces, now looked like nothing more than a wonderful toboggan run. Archbold's signature touch, the stream that gushed from the very heart of the house, was now frozen and still.

The house itself was dark, but a pale nimbus of light radiated from the far side of the hill. David crossed the narrow footbridge and moved into the trees, skirting the steepest part of the incline. He passed the wooden stakes of an old vegetable plot and the massive stone cisterns shaped like musical notes. Further back were the crumbling studios where Archbold's apprentices had done their renderings five decades before, where Kingsbury had seen Maya the night before she'd died. He saw that the light was coming from the gym that Carswell had had built for himself and his basketball buddies. The door stood half open, and as David moved closer, he could hear the bouncing of a ball.

He stopped a couple yards short of the door; he could see all he needed to from where he was. Carswell was shooting baskets at the far end of the court. He swished a ten-foot hook shot, retrieved the ball, and then threw up another hook, a long one from the corner that bounced high off the back rim and rattled the guy wires. He wasn't seventeen anymore, but as he ran down his miss, there were still traces of his old silkiness.

David stepped inside the door of the gym, but Carswell didn't see him at first. Carswell dribbled—right hand, left hand—spun, and then just as he was about to shoot, realized that he was not alone. He stared across the court, lowered the ball, and finally cradled it against his hip.

The two men eyed each other across the freshly waxed floor. For a moment David wasn't sure what it was he saw on Carswell's face. Shock? Fear? It would have made sense for him to be afraid, whether David was the killer or not, but there was something else on that face—more than fear, more than shock—and David couldn't make it out.

Carswell dribbled slowly up the court and David moved out across the free-throw line to meet him. The sound of the bouncing basketball echoed in the cavernous space. The building was cool—it couldn't have been more than sixty degrees—but Carswell had worked up a good sweat, his maroon turtleneck soaked through. He finally passed the ball, two-handed and crisp, the way they'd all been taught, so many years before, and David caught it chest-high.

"I see you've still got the hook," David said.

"David, my God, I'm so sorry . . ."

"Nobody shoots it any more, do they? It's such a shame. It's a hell of a weapon." Maybe it was just the hour, maybe it was just the strenuous workout, but Carswell seemed to have aged visibly in the two years since David had seen him. "I understand that Maya was here. The night before she died."

"Who told you that?"

"Does it matter? So, was she here or not?" He could hear his voice riding upward, growing shrill.

"Yes, she was here," Carswell said. "We've been trying to raise some more money for the Wolf Center. We had a Christmas party, and there were some people I thought she should meet."

"Like who?"

"The Wrights. The Johnsons. There's a new doctor in town by the name of Levinson."

"So did she enjoy them?"

Carswell gave a faint smile, wiping a bead of sweat from the side of his nose. "You never know about those things, do you? I'm not sure."

"You had a chance to talk to her?"

"A bit."

"So how did she seem to you?"

"Seem to me?"

"Yeah. Seem to you." David bent over and rolled the basketball into the corner. The melted snow from David's boots made small puddles on the gleaming hardwood floor.

"She was fine."

"Uh-huh. And how about Seth? How was Seth?"

"Seth wasn't here."

"No?"

"No."

"Then who the hell was she arguing with out in that cottage?" Carswell's face went ashen. He raised a hand for a second, but was unable to speak. "You stand there and lie to me through your teeth. Maya never met any of those people! Because she left before any of the guests arrived! Because she and your son were having it out . . ."

Carswell closed his eyes and gave a short, exasperated laugh. "Seth was not here, I promise you."

"So where is he?"

"I have no idea."

David stared down at the floor. His lack of sleep was making him even more irritable that he would have been. "But it's Christmas."

"The holidays have nothing to do with it. We have our differences, Seth and I. As you are doubtless aware." Carswell turned and surveyed the empty gym, the blank scoreboard, gathering himself. "David, what you're going through right now, I can't imagine it. There are not words. Everyone loved your daughter."

"Apparently not."

"How do you mean?"

"I understand a lot of people had pretty mixed feelings about her."

"She was incorruptible. Some people had a problem with that." Carswell plucked sourly at the stomach of his wet turtleneck. "David, forgive me, but I have to say, I think it's crazy, what you're doing. Let me help. I beg you. Let me call the DA and get this straightened out. We will find the person who did this."

David was silent for a second. Carswell had been covering for his son for how many years? The car wrecks, the dope busts, the early-morning phone calls from the police. Carswell was a real master at it.

"I've already seen him," David said.

Something changed in Carswell; it was as if the wind had just pivoted from south to north. "What do you mean, you saw him?"

"I saw him leave the cabin."

"I don't understand."

"When I came in, Maya was lying on the rug, all bloody. You could actually see, through the hair, where the skull was broken . . ." Carswell looked stricken, but he never took his eyes off David once, intent on every word. "I went into the kitchen to call the police. While I was talking to them, I looked out the window. There was a man running through the snow."

"What did he look like?"

"It was hard to tell. He was too far away." The basketball, on its own, rolled slowly back across the floor.

"Was he a young man or an old man?"

"Young enough to outrun me. I chased him across the meadow behind the house. He had a snowmobile stashed behind a ridge and he just about flattened me with it."

"And where did he go?" Carswell had the nauseated look of someone who'd just stepped off a bad flight.

"That's the question, isn't it?" David flexed his fingers, still stiff from the cold. "So you're telling me Seth didn't come home for Christmas. Does that mean he's still up at Columbia? You must have the phone number."

"Just leave Seth out of it."

"Leave him out of it? How can we leave him out of it? Seth was in love with her, Seth had a temper, Seth was unhappy about the way it ended, and now you tell me you don't even know where he is . . ."

"Jesus Christ, David! How dare you come in here and talk to me like this! My son has caused me a lot of grief in my life, but he is not a murderer! This is preposterous!"

"Right. It's so preposterous you just decided to get up at three in the morning and come out here to work on your hook shot."

"You want Danacek off the case? I can get him off the case. We'll get the best investigators in the country to go to work on this, if that's what it takes . . ."

It sounded like a wonderful idea; the only problem was that it was being proposed by the wrong person. David picked up the basketball and spun it in his hands. It felt slick and new. "I don't think it's going to take all that."

"Then what's it going to take?"

"All it's going to take is for you and me to go to the house and wake him up."

"David, how many times do I have to tell you? He is not here. My wife is asleep up there. I'm not going to . . ."

David passed the ball, hard, and Carswell caught it around his face. "I'll see you later."

"Where are you going?"

"I'll be damned if I know," David said.

David drove toward The Narrows. At three in the morning there was absolutely no one out, but he still found himself cross and edgy. Everything had toppled into confusion. Carswell had been so evasive, so clearly hiding something, but when he'd said that his son hadn't been at the Christmas party, he'd sounded as if he was telling the truth. Things were not matching up. Could Kingsbury have been lying to David, after all? It had been a mistake, letting him waltz off into the winter night.

David rolled down his window, listening for the faintest sound of sirens, but there was nothing. His guess was that Carswell wasn't going to be calling the police.

Coming up out of the woods into a stretch of small stores, he spotted a pay phone sitting between a 7-Eleven and a Laundromat. Both buildings were dark. He pulled over, opened the glove compartment, and scrambled around until he found a pen and a yellow repair bill. He swung down from the truck. Through the front window of the Laundromat, he could see the scattered wire baskets, the ghostly rows of dryers. Going to the phone, he punched in all twenty-five digits of his long-distance code, then entered the number for New York City Information. The operator did not have a listing for Seth Carswell.

David hung up and just stood for a moment, staring out at the ice-slicked road. What now? He was utterly out of ideas. He probably had Seth's number on his Rolodex in Westchester, but a lot of good that was going to do him. Then it came to him, a story Seth had once told him about meeting his roommate. It was one of those tales of social embarrassment: when they'd been introduced, Seth had been convinced that the name the kid gave him was a big put-on, a joke, but it wasn't. It was one of *those* names, a real mouthful. Oberholtzer. Oberbeck. Oberdorfer. That was it. Ray Oberdorfer.

Turning his back to the cold, he redialed the number for New York Information.

"What borough, please?"

"Manhattan. Oberdorfer. I'll spell that for you. O-b-e-r . . ." He went slowly, hoping the operator wouldn't think it was some late-night prank. "D-o-r-f-e-r . . . First name is Ray. On the Upper West Side."

There was a long pause and then she said, "Please hold."

David scrunched up his shoulder, cradling the receiver to his ear as he quickly scribbled across the yellow repair bill. He hit the metal tongue of the phone, got a dial tone, and tapped in the stream of numbers.

It took eight or nine rings before anyone picked up, and then there were several more seconds of fumbling around—it sounded as if the receiver was being bounced along the floor—but finally a sleepy voice answered.

"Hello?"

"Is Seth there?" David asked. A huge raccoon had come around from behind the Laundromat and was up on his back legs, inspecting the contents of a large trash basket.

"No, this is his roommate."

"When do you expect him in?" The raccoon froze for a second, realizing that David was there, and then dropped to all fours, eyeing him warily.

"I think he's out of town."

"Where out of town?" The raccoon scurried quickly out of sight.

"I don't know. He took his sleeping bag and some camping stuff. God knows where he was going in the middle of the winter."

twelve

David sat in Kingsbury's truck for a long time. No matter how many ways he tried to think about it, he kept coming to the same conclusion: Seth was here and his father had lied to protect him. It was now almost too easy to imagine what had happened—the rejected boyfriend waiting for her as she entered the cabin, his trying to plead his case, her getting angry, things getting out of hand.

David jiggled the key into the ignition. The motor bucked a couple of times before it caught. He turned the pickup around and headed back toward the river. He retraced his route, once again passing the tourist cabins and the old fishing shacks. The only other car out on the road was an ancient Dodge Dart, creeping along at about twenty-five miles an hour. As David edged by, he caught just a glimpse of the driver, drunk as a skunk, hunched over the steering wheel.

David turned in at the old hotel. The snow in the parking lot was pristine; the place had been closed for several months. He drove around behind and left the truck under a small wooden bridge, far from the sight of passing motorists.

He trudged the quarter of a mile to the old Tudor mansion

adjoining Carswell's estate; a domed observatory rose above the steeply pitched roofs. In back was a long slope that had been used for sledding, and David labored up it, his tracks lost in the welter of a million children's footprints. As he climbed over a barbed-wire fence at the farthest corner of the property, one of the strands broke and he bumped down, tearing his trousers on a metal spur. He cursed and felt his calf, making sure he hadn't drawn blood.

He was in a grove of pines, and through the dark trunks he could see two of the crumbling stone cottages that had been used by Archbold's apprentices back in the thirties. He slipped through the trees, wet needles brushing against his face. Both of the cottages were bolted shut, but the wooden door frame of the one nearest the gym was in such bad shape that he was able to pop the lock with the slightest nudge of his shoulder.

Inside it took a minute for his eyes to adjust to the dark. There seemed to be a closet on his right, and on the left, a telephone table that he nearly knocked over, banging his knee. A desk, set up with computer, printer, and fax, sat under the lone window. Through the rippled glass David could see Carswell's house looming at the top of a hill like a giant ocean liner. It was not much more than sixty yards away.

The cottage was very cold. He found a heavy wool serape hanging on a nail on the back of a door. He ducked into it and sat down in a big oak swivel chair in front of the window, propping his feet up on an old computer box.

The vigil began. He knew he had several hours before anyone in the house would be stirring. He slumped in the chair, his arms folded over his chest, moving in and out of an uneasy sleep. Two or three times he jerked awake in horror, thinking that he was still in the cabin, standing over Maya's body, viewing the terrible wound at the back of her skull. Now and then he would get up and squint through the window, believing that he'd heard someone moving out on the lawn, but there were only the still shadows of the pines against the snow, the moon hanging low above the house.

Dawn arrived, cold and gray. A solitary raven croaked in a nearby tree, sounding like an old man clearing his throat. David had a bad crick in his neck; when he tried to move it, it felt like gravel grinding in the gears of a car. He got up and wiped his hand across the misted windowpane. The house on the hill was still dark, but there was enough daylight for him to make out the Christmas wreath still hanging on the front door.

He bent down, reaching for his toes, and then swung his elbows from side to side, trying to get his blood moving. For the first time it was possible to inspect his surroundings. The closet was filled with top-of-the-line ski equipment—boots, poles, a shelf of expensive waxes, a rack of down jackets, parkas, and scarves. The stone walls were lined with photographs, fifty or sixty of them.

Some of the pictures were quite old—a black-and-white print of the flood of '32; pictures from Black Hawk's horse-and-buggy days, the streets raw and muddy; yellowing images of Chippewa Indians selling baskets along the roadside. Most of them were from Carswell's youth—his high-school team photos, the picture from the *Capital Times* of Carswell holding aloft the MVP trophy at the state tournament, a snapshot of Carswell and his father unloading pea trucks at the canning factory, another of him in his Eagle Scout uniform, the framed poster from his campaign for college president.

To say that David had known Carswell while they were growing up would have been an exaggeration, but he had certainly known of him. Chet had been the reigning deity of the high school when David was a lowly freshman—a high-scoring forward who had led the basketball team to the state championship with his deadly hook shot, a movie-star-handsome class lothario renowned for his way with the girls. His father owned the local canning factory, sponsored the Little League, and saw to it that the Danaceks were taken care of after Mrs. Danacek was hospitalized. If a small Wisconsin town like Black Hawk could be said to have had an aristocracy, the Carswells were it. Not that it mattered; if anything was clear in those days, it was that young Chet had far grander worlds to conquer than their little burg.

David and his family moved at the end of his freshman year, and it was twelve years before he heard of Chet Carswell again. David could still remember precisely how and when. It was the fourth of November, and David was taking the 7:12 train from Scarsdale into his office in Manhattan, trying to discreetly scan the *New York Times* election results without jabbing his fellow commuters in the ribs with his elbows. On the front of the second section, there it was: a photograph of a beaming Chet Carswell standing with Senator Gaylord Nelson before a roomful of campaign workers. The two men stood side by side like victorious boxers, hands clasped, arms raised. Chet had just been elected governor of Wisconsin. The article beneath the picture sketched in the dozen years of missing history. Chet had graduated from Northwestern, earned a Purple Heart in Vietnam, and then returned to work for McGovern's presidential campaign and speak out against the war.

He had the whole package. He was both patriot and rebel, a politician with the common touch who could quote Marshall McLuhan and Teilhard de Chardin without stumbling. Daniel Patrick Moynihan dubbed him one of the rising stars of the Democratic Party.

His rise was spectacular and brief. Three years into Carswell's first term, a wealthy developer was accused of bribing state officials, and Carswell was caught in the cross fire. Though it was never proved that he had taken any money, several of his aides went to prison, and the ensuing scandal was enough to destroy any political future he might have had.

But if he dropped out of politics, he scarcely dropped out of the public eye. After a couple of years as a lobbyist in Washington, he emerged again as the partner of the heir of one of Chicago's largest department-store fortunes. For a time it seemed as if they had a finger in every conceivable pie, but they got caught in the S&L crisis of the mid-eighties. It was a debacle of stunning proportions.

To fail once in such a public way would have been enough to do in most men, but to survive two such humiliations seemed almost unimaginable. Yet somehow Chet Carswell did it, shaking off defeat the way a setter shakes off water. The summer that David came to Wisconsin to close on the cabin, Carswell had returned as well, this time to put together a consortium that was trying to sell the old army ammunition plant to a Korean chip manufacturer. The price under discussion was several hundred million dollars.

Every indication was that he was about to pull it off. It was all he was focused on: one grand triumph, a final blaze of glory, one last chance to laugh in the face of his enemies. To have it all unravel because of yet another scandal, because of a renegade, lovesick son, was more than even the strongest man could stomach.

David reached out and wiped a finger diagonally across the glass of the campaign poster; his fingertip came up black. As he wiped it on his pant leg, he heard a door slam. He turned quickly and peered out the window. Carswell's wife hurried down the front steps in a blue nylon running suit. She stopped in front of the cars and did her stretches with the matter-of-fact thoroughness of the trained athlete.

Irina Carswell was an impressive-looking woman, tall, broad shouldered, and blond, ten years younger than her husband. She had once won an Olympic bronze as a member of the Lithuanian ski team, and some local quipster had cracked that not only had Carswell found himself a trophy wife, he'd found one with her own trophy. Many of the Black Hawk residents considered her haughty and standoffish, but David, the one time he'd met her, had found her, behind the insolent exterior, to possess a quick and nicely jaundiced wit.

She shook her arms and legs out after the last of her hamstring stretches, rolling her head from side to side, and then struck out down the driveway with long, powerful strides.

It was another half hour before the garage door rattled open and Carswell emerged, hauling a pair of huge plastic garbage cans behind him. He maneuvered them down the long driveway, looking, in the early morning light, like just another rumpled middle-aged man who hadn't gotten the best night's sleep. He vanished behind a curve of trees and reappeared in another minute or so, hands jammed in his jacket pockets, hurrying back to the warmth of the house.

David was prepared to wait, all day and all night if he had to, and it began to seem more and more as if he were going to have to. The morning dragged on without incident. Irina returned from her run and Carswell, all slicked up in suit and tie, zoomed off in his dark blue Mercedes. A UPS truck arrived with a stack of packages; Irina came out to fill up the birdfeeder. Just before noon, a housekeeper showed up, a large woman with painfully bowed legs. Moments later David heard the drone of a vacuum deep within the bowels of the house.

As the hours passed, tedium began to take its toll. David's stomach was growling from lack of food, and his back throbbed from his standing so long at the window. There was no sign of anyone in the house other than Carswell's wife and the housekeeper. David stared at the cardinals and sparrows squabbling over birdseed, the snow beneath the feeder littered with dark hulls.

He flipped through the correspondence on the desk; there were a lot of letters from surveyors and state agencies, a pair of thick packets from the Defense Department, but nothing personal, nothing of use to him.

Late in the afternoon Carswell returned and disappeared into the house. David had begun to lose heart. Maybe Seth wasn't there after all. If he had murdered Maya and confessed the act to his father, wouldn't the smartest thing have been to get the boy on a plane and fly him as far away as a ticket would take him? Or even if he was here, he could be staying somewhere besides the house; there were a million possibilities.

He was reluctant to leave—what did he have to go on, other than the phone call to Seth's roommate and Carswell's awkward attempt to shield his son? But he knew that his position was becoming increasingly untenable. Sooner or later someone was going to spot Kingsbury's pickup behind the old hotel, and once they did, it would take the police five minutes to track him here.

But how to extricate himself? It was not even supper time. The roads would be crawling with people coming home from work. It was too early to make a move.

He sat down on the floor with his back against the wall and pulled the serape snug around him. His mind drifted. He wondered about Clarissa, his assistant in New York, and if she knew yet. She must, he thought; everyone must know. He was going to lose some clients over this one. They all must think he'd gone insane.

And maybe he had. He thought about the book auctions he was supposed to be setting up, the e-mail messages piling up, the stack of unread manuscripts in his office. He thought about his favorite Japanese restaurant on Columbus Avenue and how good it would feel to hold a warm bowl of miso soup in his hands, how pleasant to run into his friends on the street. Even the thought of sitting at his desk and listening to his authors explain their impenetrable plots filled him with an odd longing.

He'd started to shiver. He got to his feet and did a couple dozen jumping jacks to get his blood moving. He felt an almost irresistible urge to sing, to hoot, to do something. He paced back and forth in the narrow office, blowing into his curled fingers.

The housekeeper left about six; an hour or so later the front door opened and Carswell and his wife came out. They did not seem particularly happy with each other, and took off in separate cars—she in a gray van, he in his blue Mercedes.

David rubbed his forehead, a cold draft whispering through the cracks in the ceiling. The house on the slope above him was dark. It was all his, if he dared.

He slipped out of the cottage. Elbows tight to his sides, he trotted across the frozen lawn and climbed the stone terraces. The garage door was still ajar.

As he stepped inside, he nearly tripped over a riding mower. The musty, airless space was cluttered with snow shovels and mountain bikes, huge plastic trash baskets and stacks of window screens. He picked his way through it all and silently ascended the wooden stairs that led to the main part of the house.

He eased open the door to the kitchen. The clock on the stove blinked the time: nearly seven-thirty. Gleaming kitchen utensils hung above a long and spotless butcher-block table. Blowing air hushed like rustling silk; otherwise the house was perfectly still.

He moved into the living room. A moody Russell Chatham painting of a Montana canyon at dusk hung above an antique Italian sofa. The picture window seemed to embrace the dark woods. On a side table were two photos, one of Carswell standing with Walter Mondale, the other of Irina soaring on her skis through the winter sky, on her way to Olympic glory.

The bedrooms were at the far end of the house. David edged down the carpeted hallway, passing a nook with several shelves of colorful Mexican dolls. He gave the first door on his right a silent push with his foot.

Except for Carswell's running clothes tossed over the back of an Eames chair, the room was immaculate, one of those places you might see profiled in the *New York Times Magazine*. There was a Mark Rothko on the wall, walk-in closets, and a king-size bed dwarfed by a carved wooden headboard that looked as if it had been commissioned by a Bavarian lord.

The house creaked, tightening in the winter cold. David turned, trying the doorknob across the hall. The second bedroom was a different story altogether. It was a boy's room and it was in use: a B. B. King poster taped to the closet, paperbacks and CDs strewn across the bed, an open suitcase on the floor.

David stepped inside and snapped on the desk lamp. On the bookshelf, next to a row of yellowing baseballs, was a framed photo of Maya and Seth. They rested on their bikes, posing in front of a dark railroad tunnel. Seth had his helmet on—it made him look a little silly, as if he was wearing a Frisbee—and he held a plastic bottle over her head, squirting her with it. It was horseplay, both of them laughing even as she held her hand out, begging for him to stop, wincing from the shock of cold water.

David pivoted, scanning the room. On the floor next to the closet was a green backpack. David picked it up, unzipped it, and poured the contents onto the bed. It was a rat's nest of odd scraps of paper, computer disks, balled-up socks, two or three stapled manuscripts.

He could feel B. B. King scowling down at him. He sat on the edge of the bed and began to go through it all. He rifled through the soiled credit card receipts, deposit slips, and crumpled syllabi, looking for a boarding pass or a ticket, but all he came up with was an empty American Airlines envelope. He leaned over and flipped the lid of the suitcase; the baggage tag had already been ripped off.

David felt as if he were deep underwater, fathoms from light and air. So where was Seth if he wasn't here? He hadn't gotten into the car with Carswell and his wife. Maybe he was still in the house.

Maybe he was sitting in the living room right now, or standing in the hallway, listening to David go through his things. It was impossible. David had been watching the place for an entire day and there had been no sign of him.

He picked up a couple of the computer disks. The scrawled labels read—NOVEL NOTES—1/12/90 and IDEA FILE—COMPLETE—5/25/89.

He pitched them aside and sat for a moment, trying to regather himself. He stared absently at one of the manuscripts on the bed, and then turned it so he could read the title. It was another one of Seth's jokes: *The Seeing Eye Dog with an Eye for Women.*

It was a one-act play, and it had Seth's name on it. As far as David knew, Seth had never written plays. He picked it up and turned to page one.

It was a black comedy about a blind man, his guide dog, and a woman they encounter in the park. The conceit of the play is that the guide dog can talk, not just to his owner, but to the audience as well.

The blind man uses his dog to strike up a conversation with the woman; it's clear that this is a well-oiled routine. The blind man is a seducer, by turns provocative, prying, or pitiable, working the woman's sense of guilt.

The dog airs his complaints in asides to the audience. He doesn't approve of what the blind man does to these women, any of them. He doesn't like being a party to it. But what can he do? He's a domesticated animal. Like a cow or a chicken. He has his fantasies, sure—running with the pack, the other guys calling him Fang. He would bound in for the kill, tearing a gaping hole in the throat, blood gushing from the wound, steaming red on the white snow.

The blind man invites the woman up for tea. Back in his apartment, he tells her a lurid, horrendous story of how he lost his sight as a child. By the time he finishes, she is in tears. He begs her forgiveness for upsetting her. Is there any reason for you to be afraid, he asks. No, she says. He takes her hand and leads her into the bedroom, leaving the dog alone with the audience.

Once they are offstage, the blind man tells her another, even darker story, about a woman who betrayed him.

BLIND MAN

I called her up the day after I found out who it was she'd been seeing. I said I was doing fine, but I'd run across a few things she'd left in the apartment, wouldn't she like to come pick them up? And it would give her a chance to say goodbye to the dog. She came by that night. I made her a cup of Folgers. We talked a long time. I finally told her I wanted to make love to her one last time. It would have been nearly impossible for her to refuse . . . given my condition. We came into this room. And after we made love on this bed, I whispered his name into her ear. I reached up to touch her face. There were tears. Like your tears now.

WOMAN

I'm not crying.

BLIND MAN

I can feel the tears with my hand. I can feel the wetness.

DOG

(Whimpering.) A dog is friendly, loyal, trustworthy, helpful, and kind . . . knows how to tie a square knot. I hate my master. I love my master . . . He takes me to the vet . . . ain't no fleas on Poochie . . .

BLIND MAN

What choice did I have? She pitied me. She would only love me if she pitied me, and if she pitied me I hated her and had to kill her . . .

DOG

How can I go? Who will feed me?

(The DOG turns and faces the bedroom door.)

BLIND MAN

Who can help but pity a blind man? Stumbler, sleep-walker . . . We each sink into our own blindness, over and over, one way or the other. We carry our tin cups with us into the future, pressing dirty coins into the sockets of our eyes. I'm sorry that you were blind too. What kept you from seeing?

(Pause.)

Can you hear me?

(Whispers.) Can you hear me?

(Pause. The BLIND MAN appears at the bedroom door. The MAN and the DOG stare at each other. Neither gives.)

BLIND MAN

Poochie? Come here, Pooch.

(The DOG turns and leaves the room.)

Here, dog. Pooch!

(HE moves across the floor, groping.)

Dog! Heel! I'll beat you! Pooch!

(HE becomes more hysterical, stumbling across the room, knocking over furniture, calling out for the dog. The lights dim into darkness.)

THE END

David tossed the play onto the bed. He stood up and ran a shaking hand over his mouth. David knew all about the games writers play, the masks they hide behind, the way they mix the real with the imagined, but there was no way of disguising the lethal malice of what he'd just read.

He grabbed the play off the bed. The date on the title page was November 18, just a month ago.

He heard a car coming up the drive. He moved to the window and brushed back the curtain. At first all he could make out was the glow of headlights, but then as the car eased to a stop in front of the garage, David could see it was the gray van. The garage door stuttered open and the van disappeared inside.

David stared at the upended backpack on the bed, the scattered disks and notebooks. Should he run or not? What would running get him? This was the moment he'd been waiting for; he was unlikely to get another.

A door opened at the far end of the house. He stepped over the suitcase and snapped off the desk lamp. After a moment, a pale strip of light appeared magically on the rug in the hallway.

"If you're hungry, you can get something from the fridge. I forgot something in the car. I'll be right back." It was a woman's voice, traced with a European accent.

David felt something catch in his throat, a fishbone impossible to dislodge. He thought for a moment he heard running feet, but then there was nothing. There was a second sound now, a rhythmic squeaking coming from the living room.

He stepped into the hallway. A girl in white angel wings bounced up and down on the antique Italian couch. She was a chubby little girl in blue tights, a red blouse, and a twisted-tinsel headband.

She didn't see David at first. He'd known that Carswell and Irina had a young daughter—Seth had certainly mentioned his stepsister more than once—but David had somehow put it out of his mind. She had never been part of the equation.

Cardboard wings flapping, she bounded higher and higher, her face rosy with glee, free at last from being too good for too long. There was a sound of someone ascending the stairs from the garage; they both heard it. The girl hopped to the floor just as David was making his move for the kitchen. It was then that she saw him.

Her mouth made a perfect O of astonishment. She thought she was the one who'd been caught. She scrunched up her face, pushed her glasses up on her nose, crossed her blue-stockinged feet.

David glanced over his shoulder, looking for a way out. Beyond the butcher-block table was a door opening onto some sort of deck.

"Excuse me," David said.

He strode through the kitchen, bumping against the stove. The door was secured by both a dead-bolt lock and a chain. It took him several seconds of fumbling to get it open.

"Mommy! Mommy! There's a man in here!"

David leapt over the railing of the deck. There was an eight-foot drop to the slope beneath and he turned his ankle slightly when he hit. He pushed himself up, hobbled around the side of the house, and began to run through the stone terraces. He looked back just once and saw mother and daughter standing at the picture window, staring down at him. He was the one who needed wings now, not that little girl.

He ran along the lane of snow-laden pines and onto the road, past the trio of mailboxes and the Tudor mansion with its domed observatory. Out of breath, he had to slow finally to a walk. He broke into a trot, turning in at the old hotel. Kingsbury's truck was still there under the wooden bridge, its windshield webbed with frost.

He got in, turned on the engine, and slapped on the defrost. Making a wide U-turn, he rattled his way out to the main road.

Once he was on dry pavement, he floored it. He figured he had ten minutes, fifteen at most, before there would be police. The narrow road rose and fell like a roller coaster. Every so often he passed the lights of a house set back in the trees. He zipped past the 7-Eleven and the Laundromat where he'd made his phone call. Off to his left, a narrow glen that in summer would have been thick with ferns and moss and dripping rock faces was buried in undulating curves of snow.

When he got to the main highway, he pulled into the parking

lot behind one of the old Indian trading posts and snapped off his lights. It was a good thing he did. He hadn't been there for more than thirty seconds before two police cars, sirens wailing, came flying down the highway, turned onto the two-lane blacktop, and bounced into the dark woods.

David turned his lights back on and crossed the highway. Finally, he was in open farmland, on a road as true as an arrow. He pushed Kingsbury's truck up to seventy, the old pickup shimmying as if it were about to explode. He blew past cornfields, a small Christmas-tree operation, a set of collapsed stables. It was only then, leaning forward over the steering wheel, peering down the two trembling cones of light, that it came to him: the girl in the angel wings had to be the same girl that Kim's boyfriend had seen that morning, sitting in a canoe, listening to Maya sing.

thirteen

There was a roadblock a mile or so north of Black Hawk, but David picked up the flickering police lights far enough in the distance to be able to take the cutoff past the old quarry and the cheese factory. He kept checking his rearview mirror, but no one seemed to have come after him.

If some of his questions had been answered, the answers had only led to more questions. The pain in the play had certainly felt fresh; every line had reeked of sexual rejection and rage. But just how to read it? Some of the jibes had clearly been aimed at Maya—the cracks about nature girls and piney scents and moral rigor, the guide dog's fantasies of running with the pack, chasing down deer in the snow. But if David was going to try to interpret everything literally, then who was it that had poisoned the well? Whose name was it that the blind man had whispered into the doomed woman's ear? There were worlds within worlds here. What was making this so hard, he realized, was that Maya, like her father, had been a master at hiding her tracks.

It took him twenty minutes to thread his way through the forest preserve, finally coming out on the highway where Larry Gillette had finessed their way past the Young Burmeister. He slowed to thirty miles an hour and rolled down his window to peer out into the darkness.

Everything looked so different at night. He drove one mile, then two. Just when he was convinced that he'd gone too far, he spied the culvert. He pulled the pickup to the side of the road and got out. There was a smell of silage in the air. He shuffled quickly down the incline and dropped to his knees. Reaching into the black hole as far as he could, he fished around until he finally felt the hard laminate finish of the skis.

He pulled out the skis and the tangled poles, tossed them into the back of the truck, and drove on. The high, wooded bluffs were on his left. He increased his speed, pressing on into the night, retracing his path. He bumped over the railroad tracks and crossed the tilting highlands, where bales of hay in their plastic wrap glowed in the fields like rows of giant marshmallows. For the moment at least, he had outmaneuvered his adversaries. He dropped down again and followed the meandering creek through the long valley. The world felt utterly abandoned.

A wind came out of nowhere, buffeting the truck from side to side. He made a right, taking the state highway south, skirting the edge of the park. His immediate problem was how to get rid of his vehicle.

The only possibility he could think of was Cider Hill, the apple orchard smack up against the boundary of the park. It was owned by Ole Swenson, a hard-bitten Swede in his early seventies; he spent six weeks every winter in Florida and was too cheap to pay anybody to look after his place. Ole was an old-style Goldwater Republican—the two or three times he and Maya had actually had a chance to talk, they'd gotten into ferocious political debates—but David got a kick out of him, even considered him a friend.

He took a right off the state highway and headed up an icy gravel road. Behind the tall wire fences David could see the rows of gnarled apple trees, pruned way back for the winter. The faded red barn where Ole's wife sold cider and fresh-baked pies to the tourists every summer was boarded up, and the parking lot was empty. David drove past the barn to the machine sheds.

All the sheds were locked, but after a brief search he found a long-handled bolt cutter in a toolbox under Ole's front porch and snapped one of the chains. He unraveled the chain, put his shoulder to the sliding door, and heaved it open. Inside were an ancient John Deere tractor, Ole's ten-year-old beige and brown station wagon, a pair of rusted sprayers, and a stack of plastic insecticide buckets.

As he was moving the buckets, David froze suddenly, thinking that he heard voices. It was someone singing. It took him several seconds to locate the source: a small portable radio sitting above the workbench, its tiny yellow light shining in the darkness. It was perfect Ole, the old man's idea of taking security measures.

David maneuvered the pickup in behind Ole's station wagon. He prowled through the shed, desperate for food, and under a threadbare yellow couch found a red Igloo cooler with a couple cans of Miller High Life and a half-eaten tube of braunschweiger. Sitting on the couch, he tore away the plastic with trembling fingers. God knew how long the lunch meat had been sitting there. He gave it a sniff, then scraped away about an inch of rock-hard crust with his thumbnail. He'd always hated braunschweiger—for years his mother had put sandwiches made with the soft, liver-smelling spread in his school lunch box—but now it tasted like caviar. He wolfed it down, licking clean the folds of plastic wrapping, and followed that with the two beers.

When he was done, he sat with his elbows on his knees, feeling dopey and a little bilious. He belched softly. After so many hours without food or rest, the alcohol was hitting him hard.

He pushed to his feet. At the back of the shed was a small room with a toilet. David took a pee, fatigue spots whirling before his eyes. An ancient copy of *Marathon Man*, two-thirds of the text ripped out, sat on a rough wooden ledge; Ole had apparently been using it to wipe himself.

David zipped up and retrieved the book. The cover was from the movie version, showing Dustin Hoffman running through Central Park, pursued by Nazis. Man on the run. David had sold a hundred novels like it, and now he found himself trapped inside one.

He flipped through the brittle pages. Sixth printing. Not bad. U.S. price, $3.95. How many years ago was that? David remembered reading the book in a single night. It was a funny thing how Americans always liked to think of themselves as such stand-up guys, when in truth there was probably nothing more American than to bolt. Cary Grant running from the crop duster, Cool Hand Luke slipping away from the chain gang, Huck and Jim poling down the river. His father, too, piling them all into the station wagon that spring night and driving them off to California. And now David had joined them, all those other marathoners.

Maybe it didn't matter who you were fleeing—Nazis, Southern prison guards, bounty hunters—maybe that was all just a pretext, an excuse. Maybe the point was just to keep running: as long as you were running, there was no time to look back and see what doors were being quietly closed to you forever.

David tossed the book away, went back, and curled up on the couch. He told himself that he was just going to take a short nap, then fell into a dead sleep.

When he awoke, he could hear barn sparrows twittering and thumping under the eaves. He lay still for a minute, pinching the corners of his eyes, letting his mind drift.

What was he going to do? He'd hit a dead end. He wasn't capable of rooting Seth out on his own, and even if the boy was the murderer, David could scarcely come striding into a police station with a one-act play as proof.

He needed an ally. The obvious choice was Mike, who, according to Annie, was here. David needed to call her and get a number.

Where to call from was the question. He supposed he could bust out a back window in Ole's house and see if the phone was working, but something in him balked at the thought of breaking into the house of a friend. Besides, it was morning now. There would be people coming by on the road, and if Ole were on the same party line that Joann was on, all it would take for David to be discovered was one person picking up at the wrong time.

His cabin was no more than a mile or a mile and a half away, through the woods. On the face of it, it was a foolish idea, but if the police weren't there, he could at least have some confidence that the line was secure. It was strange. The cabin should have been the last place in the world he wanted to go back to, but there was some comfort in the thought of being in a place to which he had some right. He would need to get there before dawn, before people were stirring. He pushed up from the couch.

He got the skis and poles from Kingsbury's truck and carried them outside. He shoved the sliding doors shut behind him and looped the chain through the handles. The moon still hung on the horizon.

He walked to the fence, tossed the skis over the sagging barbed wire, and then climbed over himself. There was a cross-country trail that circled the edge of the park, and the good news was that even though it was only three days after the big snowfall, there were plenty of tracks; David's would be indistinguishable from anyone else's.

He set down the skis and nudged his toes into the bindings until he heard them click into place. For nearly a mile he followed the trail and then cut into the woods. Atop a jagged granite outcropping he could make out two or three ghostly forms watching him, then melting away into a pine grove as he drew closer: wolves.

It took him twenty minutes to work his way to the top of the rise; after that it was easier. He glided down through the silent trees, his skis droning like wasps. He used his poles only to brake himself, trying to avoid the giant boulders. He began to see tracks again, floating past on either side of him, strangely dream-like—the tread of snowmobiles, the slender grooves of skis, the plunging holes left by men on foot. Some of the rocks were familiar to him now, even some of the trees; he was on home ground.

He slowed as he came to the edge of the bluff, stabbing his poles into the snow to stop himself. The roof of the cabin loomed below him. He saw something fluttering on the kitchen door. It took him a minute to figure out what it was: a strip of yellow police tape. Maya's car was still there; so was his.

The windows of the cabin were all dark, but he waited another five minutes just to be sure no one was there, then coasted down the long slope and across the meadow. He took off his skis and left them inside the shed.

He tore away the yellow tape, opened the door, and stepped inside the icy-cold house. The kitchen seemed just as he'd left it, except for a paper coffee cup and the remains of a sugared doughnut wrapped in a napkin, sitting on the table. A policeman's snack, no doubt.

He lifted the phone from the wall and cradled it in the palm of his hand; it was hard, harder than he'd imagined. On the floor of the pantry, he could see several small kernels of popcorn. He lifted his eyes to the window and stared out at the meadow where he'd seen his daughter's murderer lurching through three-foot drifts. There was nothing out there now, just the predawn half-light and a solitary squirrel digging frantically in the snow. David's throat thickened; for the moment, he was in no shape to talk to anyone.

He set the receiver back on its base and walked to the living room. The police had marked the floor with tape where Maya had fallen and the smell of ashes was still in the air. David could feel the cold air pouring in through the broken window, brushing his cheek like a chilled hand.

He was not a person who believed in ghosts, but there was still something of her presence in the room, he was sure of it; it was as if she were trying to make herself known to him.

He moved into the hallway and gazed up the stairs. It came back to him now: when he first discovered her, he had seen her duffel bags on the landing and something else, something odd. A *Field and Stream* magazine. Did they even publish *Field and Stream* any more? And who would have been reading it? Not him. Not Maya.

He stood for a moment, trying to puzzle it out. If the duffel bags had been on the landing, it meant she must have gone upstairs before she was attacked. Could there have been someone else up there? Gripping the banister, he felt his way up the warped wooden steps.

It was very dark, but he was afraid to turn on any lights. He edged along the second-floor landing and stopped in the doorway of Maya's bedroom. There was just enough gray from the window for him to spot one of her blue duffel bags sitting on the bed.

He found a kerosene lamp and an old box of matches in the hall closet. It took him a couple of tries to get the ancient wick lit. He set the glass chimney carefully in place, the low blue flame flickering through the curved surface.

He set the lamp on Maya's dressing table and surveyed the room—the oak chest in the corner; the amps for her sound system propped up on her desk; the bookcases with their dog-eared college anthologies, collections of nature writing, slender volumes of poetry by Lawrence Ferlinghetti and Gary Snyder, Mary Oliver and Adrienne Rich. Turning, giving everything a second look, he spied something he hadn't noticed before: on the floor, under the windowsill, was a dark, irregularly shaped stain. He went to inspect it, going down on one knee. It was slick to the touch, almost greasy, and when he put his fingers to his nose, the smell was rank.

Sitting on his heels, he squinted to his left and then to his right. He spied something along the base of the wall. He had to stretch out to retrieve it: a ragged, discolored toenail.

He examined it and then flicked it away. He pushed to his feet. Someone had been there. But who? He yanked open the closet doors and then, finding everything in order, slammed them shut again.

Unwilling to give up, he went to the duffel bag on the bed and unzipped it. It was filled with winter things: gloves, thick woolen socks, a nubbly vest from REI, clunky hiking boots. He took the items out, one by one, and set them on the bed. There was an Irish scarf he'd given her for her birthday, a collection of essays by Rick Bass.

He picked up the duffel bag and gave it a final shake. He heard something else slide inside. Mystified, he patted the interior of the bag, found nothing, and then realized how basic his error had been. He unzipped the side pocket of the duffel bag and lifted out a large manila envelope.

He crossed the room and held the envelope to the light of the kerosene lamp. The postmark said Madison, Wisconsin, but there was no return address.

Fumbling, he managed to tear the package open. Inside was a thick sheaf of papers, seventy-five to a hundred pages, and it was all chemistry. He examined the sheets, one by one, but couldn't make hide nor hair of any of them. He sat down on the bed, trying to decide what to do next. The muscles in his back were cramping from the cold.

He finally recrossed the room and knelt by the butane heater. He pressed down the metal lever, turned it to the open position, and heard the rush of gas. He tried to strike a match, but the tiny sulfurous tip crumbled like moldy bread. He tried a second match, with no more success.

He cursed softly; the box must have been old or damp. As he leaned over to turn off the heater, he glanced up. In the mirror of the far wall, he saw Danacek's reflection—the bulky policeman standing in the doorway with his gun drawn.

"So if it isn't Harry Houdini," Danacek said. "Get up." David rose slowly. "Put it down."

"It's just matches," David said.

"Put it down."

David tossed the box of matches onto the bed. He could still hear the hiss of gas. It seemed as if Danacek stood without speaking for an eternity.

"So I guess I'm not as dumb as you thought, huh?" the policeman said.

"I never said you were dumb," David said.

"No? The way you were showing me up, people were starting to think I was Barney Fife."

Danacek sat on the bed, pushing some of the clothes to one side. The manila envelope was on the floor at David's feet. David made a move to turn off the heater.

"I said don't move," Danacek said. David straightened again. The policeman still had his hat on, but even if he couldn't hear the gas, how could he not smell it?

"So what were you looking for?"

"Nothing," David said.

Danacek laughed. "You know what I really want to know?" The flame in the kerosene lamp glowed more brightly. "I want to know how you could not say anything. How you could just go home and eat lunch and go play ball with your pals when my brother was still out in that river. I've spent too many goddamned years thinking about that. Did you push him? Or maybe he just fell and you were too much of a chickenshit to go after him. Tell you what. I'll make you a deal. You tell me what happened to my brother, and I'll tell you what I think happened to your daughter."

David glanced at the manila envelope on the floor. "What's that?" Danacek said.

"What's what?"

"On the floor."

David bent down and picked up the envelope. "Nothing. It's just mail. . . ."

"I want to see it. Hand it over."

David stared dumbly. He was too tired to obey. He'd come so far. Danacek took a step toward him, holding out his hand. David jerked the envelope away, putting it behind him like a kid trying to keep his milk money out of reach of the schoolyard bully.

"Are you crazy?" Danacek said. "You want me to fucking shoot you right here? I said hand it over!"

David retreated another step. It was more than Danacek could stand. He lunged clumsily for the envelope, banging his hip against the dressing table. The kerosene lamp tipped and fell, smashing to the floor.

"Shit!"

Danacek turned to look back at the mess he had made. For a couple of seconds it seemed as if there were no harm done—the tiny blue flame guttering, nearly winking out, the viscous fluid creeping across the floorboards—but then everything went.

The boom was of concussive force and a wave of flames engulfed the room. There was no time for David to even get his hands up; the blast caught him directly in the chest and face, throwing him backwards. The space that had been so dark was now bright as day, curtains and bedspreads and bookshelves burning like Mexican altars. David rolled on the floor, flailing his arms over his head. His coat and hair were on fire and his face was seared, deeply, beyond anything he'd ever felt before. He heard Danacek moaning somewhere nearby, but he didn't see him. The room began to fill with smoke.

As he rose to his knees, he spied the manila envelope at the foot of the bed. He retrieved it, bending low, and scrambled for the door. He vaulted down the stairs and out of the house. He was ten yards beyond the front porch when he heard the second explosion.

He stopped and looked back. The windows on the second floor had been blown out, and flames now licked under the eaves. A length of burning curtain floated through the air as lazily as an eel and settled finally on the snow. For a moment, David was caught—if Danacek was seriously hurt, David could scarcely leave him—but an instant later all was resolved. He heard the policeman's bellowing, full-throttled and as mad as hell.

A squad car was parked behind Maya's Bronco and David's rental, blocking them in. David glanced through the squad-car window; this time Danacek had been smart enough to take his keys with him. David had a problem: if Danacek had both wheels and a radio to call in reinforcements, and all David had was skis, it wasn't going to be much of a contest.

He turned and stared at the curtain still burning on the snow. He set the manila envelope on the hood of the police car, pried open the circular fuel-tank door, and quickly unscrewed the gas cap.

He lifted the burning length of curtain, tied the unignited end into a knot, and then shoved the knot deep into the gullet of the gas tank. The burning fabric hung as limp as a donkey's tail, the flames still a good eight inches below the open hole.

He retrieved the manila envelope and stuffed it into a jacket pocket. He moved to the shed and snapped the tips of his boots, one at a time, into the ski bindings. His face felt like raw meat. He fumbled with his poles for a moment, wrapping his hands into the plastic straps. He could feel the heat from the burning cabin through his jacket and there was the sound of great beams cracking, giving way. Just go, he told himself, don't think.

He pushed off, gliding into the meadow. He was nearly across when a shout made him turn. Danacek stood on the porch. The blaze above him was spectacular—the old, dry logs had gone up like kindling—but it wasn't the fire that concerned the policeman. Danacek saw what David had done. The makeshift fuse was still burning, just an inch or two from the gas tank.

The bulky policeman lumbered down the stairs; it looked as if he had injured his right leg. He ran for his car, but tripped and fell in the snow. The explosion lit up the hillside, the sound volleying across the meadow like the sound of an ancient cannon. Both men watched as flames engulfed the car—David leaning on his ski poles at the far end of the meadow, Danacek still on all fours, looking as forlorn as a castaway on a desert island eyeing a ship sail over the horizon. David finally turned and coasted into the dark woods.

fourteen

Fleeing half blind from the burning house, David knew there was almost no real chance of escape, yet he kept on. He labored up the hills as best he was able, even though his left hand was severely burned and closing his fingers around a ski pole felt like wrapping his fingers around a red-hot poker. He skied through the mist-shrouded woods, pushing himself until his lungs were nearly bursting with the effort.

He figured it might be minutes, a half hour if he was lucky, but it wasn't going to be long before Danacek had every cop in the state roaring in with sirens wailing. What he hadn't counted on was a miracle. Coming out of the park, David stared; fifty yards ahead of him, slumped on the buckboard of a horse-drawn hay wagon, was an Amish farmer. The wagon swayed away from David at a snail's pace. The farmer's back was turned.

David hesitated a moment. He wasn't going to have another chance, not like this. He punched the tips of his ski poles into his bindings and jammed the skis and poles under a pile of brush.

He began to run down the road, trying not to make a sound.

Whether he succeeded or whether the farmer was just as deaf as a post, there was no way of knowing, but the man in the heavy black coat never turned, not even when David eased himself onto the rear of the rickety wagon and burrowed into the loose hay.

David's heart thudded like a muffled drum. For a long time the only sound was the clopping of the horse's hooves on the freshly plowed blacktop and an occasional "gee-haw" from the driver.

The wagon went down a long hill and then ascended again. Curled up in a ball under the hay, David kept waiting for the distant wail of sirens, but it never came. He didn't understand. Maybe something had happened to Danacek, something worse. David found a way to protect his seared face in the crook of his arm, but even the slightest jarring, the faintest brush of straw across his blistered neck, was enough to make him want to scream.

Nearly delirious with pain, he had no clear idea of how far they went. A mile? Two? More? It began to seem as if they were rumbling on forever. They finally pulled to a stop, and he heard the driver clamber down from the wagon. David's heart leapt to his throat. He was sure that he'd been found out, but when he raised his head, he saw the Amish farmer limping stiff-legged toward a green metal gate. In the morning mist, the black-hatted figure seemed spectral and unearthly. Maybe I am already dead, David thought; it would be better if I were. The farmer unlocked the gate and the metal moaned as he pushed it open. David dived back under the hay.

After a minute he heard the farmer climb back into the wagon, then they were moving again. They drove on for another five minutes, lurching over much rougher terrain. There was a loud thunk—for a second David thought they must have broken an axle—and suddenly they were descending a steep incline. He knew he couldn't wait any longer. Pushing the hay aside, he slipped noiselessly off the wagon like a swimmer sliding into a pool.

He stood for a moment watching the wagon rattle down a snowy lane and finally disappear behind a sickly stand of birch. He was maybe fifty yards below the crest of a high ridge; farmland stretched out in the valley below him. He wasn't quite sure where he was, but something about it—the abrupt turn of a distant creek, a lightning-blasted oak still standing in the middle of a pasture—was strangely familiar.

He made his way back to the top of the bluff. Ravens croaked in the surrounding brush, as guttural and malevolent as trolls. There was a fresh snowmobile track, hard-packed, and he began to run. He ran for as long as he was able, and when he couldn't run anymore, he stopped, resting his elbows on his knees. When he stood up again, he realized where he was. The barn where he had spent a night lay below, no more than seventy yards away and still engulfed in shadow. He walked softly down to it.

The door of the shed was open six inches and David stood, staring in at Joann. Down on one knee, she fed a hungry calf out of an enormous plastic bottle. The wobbly baby bull was so eager that he kept threatening to pull off the rubber nipple, and Joann had to hold on with both hands. A half dozen other calves watched from nearby pens, bumping against the railings, their eyes lustrous with envy.

David leaned an elbow against the corner of the building, bracing himself against the next wave of pain. The morning sun was just beginning to break over the high ridge. The searing on his face, neck, and hand felt like the worst sunburn he'd ever had, multiplied by twenty. His eyes were nearly swollen shut: everything was blurred and he had almost no peripheral vision.

The young bull calf finally managed to wrestle the nipple off the plastic bottle, and pale formula spilled onto the concrete floor. Joann did a quick sidestep to avoid the splash; she didn't utterly succeed. She cursed softly and then stood, brushing her hands across her wet jeans. She looked up.

"Oh my God," she said.

"I'm sorry," David said. "I had nowhere else to go."

For a second she did nothing. It wouldn't have surprised him if she had just run. But she didn't. She came to the door and slid it open, ancient rusted rollers growling in their metal track. "Come in," she said. "Come in."

He did as she told him, and she quickly closed the door behind them. Maybe it was just the movement from light to dark, but suddenly everything was spinning; he thought he was going to faint.

"What happened to you?" she asked.

"There was a fire. At the cabin. Danacek was there . . ." He stood in the middle of the low-beamed room, six or seven feet away from her, keeping his distance. He tried to read her expression, but she was giving nothing away.

"You need a doctor," she said.

"No," he said. "I can't. I can't." The calves all gaped at him. Pain was hitting him like a ton of bricks.

"Then what are you going to do?"

He could feel something wet on his face, but it wasn't tears; something was seeping. "I don't know."

At her feet, the barn cat lapped at the spilt formula. Joann picked up the fallen rubber nipple and brushed off the straw. She wore a faded denim jacket and black boots, and a knotted red kerchief held her hair.

"I think you'd better come up to the house. We need to get those burns tended to."

David waited while she herded the calf back into the pen. He followed her out, ducking low to avoid hitting his head. The driveway had been freshly plowed, and in the front yard a snowman stood watch, carrot-nosed, a broomstick angled across his glistening white belly.

They entered the house. As she led him into the upstairs bathroom, he caught a glimpse of his reflection in the mirror. He looked as if he had been slammed by a baseball bat. His eyes were nearly swollen shut, and the area of the burn was a deep dark red. Blisters ran down one whole side of his face and neck, and some of them were open and weeping.

When she reached for the zipper of his jacket, he instinctively jerked away. "What are you doing?"

"We have to clean everything."

"With what?"

"Soap and water first. If you want to take a pill before we start, you can."

"You have one?"

"I think so. Let me help you with your coat."

They maneuvered him out of his jacket, careful to slip the sleeve over his burned hand without letting it touch. She set the coat on the back of a wooden chair and opened the medicine cabinet. She rummaged for a minute and came up with a tiny, amber-colored bottle. She shook out a pill and handed it to him.

"What is it?"

"Demerol," she said. "It should do the trick."

She turned on the faucet in the sink, ran some water into a custard-colored cup, and offered it to him. He put the Demerol on his tongue and took a sip of water. Two hard swallows and he had it down.

"We should give it a few minutes," she said.

He sat on the edge of the tub and she leaned against the counter. He could hear a clock ticking in the adjoining bedroom; the moment felt strangely illicit.

"I hear you put a gun to Kingsbury's head," she said.

"I did, yes." A green plastic alligator grinned up at him from the bottom of the tub. "But that's not all."

"What do you mean, not all?"

"I went to see Chet Carswell." The Demerol was starting to take hold; he felt as if he was falling through pillows.

"Why did you do that?"

"Because Maya was at his house. The night before she died."

Joann pushed away from the sink, picking up the bottle of Demerol. "I don't understand."

"Maya used to go out with his son. She tried to break it off last summer. I thought it was over. Apparently it wasn't." Joann stared at him. David didn't know if he was explaining it badly or if she was just slow. "Carswell's son was there the other night, at the party. Carswell swore to me that he wasn't, but he was."

"How do you know that?"

"Kingsbury heard them fighting. In one of the stone cottages next to the house."

She seemed unimpressed. "So you think it was him, then? Carswell's son?"

"I know it's him. I'm not sure I've got enough yet to make it stand up in court, but I know it's him." A radiator ticked at the far end of the house.

"But you were sure before."

"Yes, I was sure before. But I was wrong then."

"Uh-huh."

He could tell that she had her own opinions and that she intended to keep them to herself. She put the pills back in the medicine cabinet. "Let me help you with your shirt," she said.

He stood and held both hands in the air as she undid his buttons. It made him feel as if he were ten years old. With her assistance, he wriggled free of the shirt.

He leaned against the counter while she filled the basin with warm water. She wet a cloth, rubbed it with soap, and very gently began to wash his neck and face. Every touch made him wince, but it wasn't nearly as excruciating as he'd expected; the Demerol was doing its job.

It was an odd moment to be concerned with his vanity, but it occurred to him that it had been more than thirty years since she'd seen him with his shirt off—not since their youth group had gone swimming at Sauk Lake with the exhausted Mrs. Eisenreich. It was scarcely the same. He was a fit man, but he suffered from the inevitable middle-aged sag—the slight feminine suggestion of breasts—and a tracery of white through his chest hairs.

She rinsed out the washcloth and draped it on the towel rack. David relaxed, thinking she was done, but she wasn't. She took a sterile gauze pad and began to scrub at the blisters on his neck. He straightened up instantly.

"Ahh!" he cried out.

"I'm sorry," she said. "I've got to get rid of all the loose skin. We've got to make sure you don't get an infection."

His hands were trembling. "OK," he said. "OK."

He held on as best he could, gritting his teeth, focusing on the gleaming glass droplets of the old-fashioned chandelier that hung from the ceiling. She tried to be a little gentler, but at the same time she worked intently, professionally, seemingly oblivious to anything other than the task at hand. Her face was no more than six inches from his. He could smell her hair. It was the first time since Peggy had died that he'd been touched by a woman.

She picked up a towel and very lightly began to dry him. "I need to put some ointment on this," she said. "Just come with me."

She led him into the adjoining bedroom, had him lie down on the bed, and propped him up with pillows. He stared upward, trying to get his eyes to focus; the ceiling looked as if it were sliding away, launching itself like some massive ocean liner. Joann sat on a chair next to the bed. She squeezed some silvery ointment out of a tube and spread it along his neck and onto his face.

"None of what you're doing will bring her back," Joann said.

"Maybe not," he said. He laid his cheek on the pillow, felt her fingers along his neck, the salve cooling the blistering flesh. "But she was a stranger to me when she died. And she'll stay that way until I know why this happened."

Out of the corner of his eye, he saw something flicker across her face. She squeezed a fresh curl of ointment onto her fingertip.

The phone rang, the sound magnified in the empty house. David pushed himself quickly up on one elbow.

"Excuse me," she said. She rose from her chair and slipped out of the room.

David listened to her trip quickly down the stairs. After three rings there was silence. He sat up and leaned forward. Straining, he was finally able to make out the distant murmur of her voice.

He turned cautiously, surveying the room. A blue and white Shaker quilt hung on the wall; an exercise bike was tucked away in the corner. A pair of dirty overalls was draped over the back of a chair. A copy of *The American Dairyman* lay open on the nightstand. Framed family photographs were everywhere, like prairie dogs standing on alert at their holes—pictures of children and grandchildren, grinning uncles and dour maiden aunts, weddings and baptisms.

He saw now how wrong it had been for him to come here. He had no right to ask her for help, to make a shambles of her life. For what she'd done already, she could go to jail for a decade.

He eased up from the bed and hobbled across to the bathroom. He retrieved his shirt and edged down the stairs, taking them one step at a time. He made it as far as the front door.

"What are you doing?"

Her voice made him jump. He turned. Joann stood in the dining room. The knotted kerchief in her hair had come partially undone.

"I'm going," he said. "I can't make you part of this. It's not fair."

"That was my husband. Someone called over at his brother's. Apparently your cabin . . . it's burned to the ground. The fire trucks came, but way too late. They've taken Danacek to the hospital. They're trying to round everyone they can find to join the search . . ."

"So call them then. Turn me in."

"I can't."

"Why not? You called them before."

"It isn't the same as before," she said. "Wait here. I'll be back."

She disappeared into the kitchen and a moment later David heard a door close. He sat down on the stairs, his shirt balled up in his fists. He shut his eyes; everything had started to swim again. God knew what her scheme was. Maybe she was getting the car, maybe she would drive him somewhere. He thought he heard another door bang, but he wasn't sure. His eyeballs, behind closed lids, felt like heavy, aching stones.

He drifted off into a light sleep, then woke with a start when a cardinal fluttered at the dining room window. He had no idea how much time had passed. Ten minutes? Fifteen?

"Joann?" he called. The house was silent, the only sound the rattle of a loose windowpane in the wind.

He pushed to his feet, moved swiftly through the kitchen and onto the back porch. He stared out at the rippling plastic at the tractor shed; all the cars were still there. It wasn't until he turned that he saw her, coming around the corner of one of the small outbuildings next to the barn. He opened the door with his good hand and squinted at her. She gestured silently, as if she wanted him to follow her. He hesitated, not thinking she could be serious. She gestured again.

He moved down the steps and across the freshly plowed driveway. It occurred to him that he must look like some barbarian, naked from the waist up, covered with blisters and salve. She led him around the side of the small shed and opened a three-foot-high latticed door to a crawl space beneath.

"Go ahead," she said.

Shivering in the frigid air, he bent down to take a look. The shed was on a bit of a slope, so there was, at the front at least, nearly enough room to stand. There was a dirt floor and a haphazard walkway of sodden cardboard. A massive heating unit took up most of the space, and in the corners were a few battered packing boxes, a bag of bone meal, an old lawnmower, and some piles of discarded lumber.

"See what you think," she said. "Just be careful not to hit your head."

He ducked down and stepped through the low door. It wasn't until he was five or six feet in that he saw what she had done. Behind the heating unit, at the narrowest end of the crawl space, she had set up a pallet for him, with clean white sheets and a pillow. She'd even created the equivalent of a bedside table, an old wooden crate draped with a starched white dishtowel, next to the pallet. He looked back at her with wonder. She'd put all this together in record time.

"Go on," she said.

"You really think this has a chance of working?" he asked.

"We'll see. Lie down. I'll be right back."

He crouched low, stepping carefully from one piece of cardboard to the next. He kept his good hand above him, making sure not to bump his head. He tossed his jacket onto the ground, reached out for the pallet and lowered himself onto the clean white sheets. He twisted around to look back at her, but his view was blocked by the massive heating unit.

"Joann?" he called.

There was no answer. He heard the latticed door shut; whatever gradations of light there had been were instantly extinguished. It felt as if a coffin lid had just closed over him.

He laid his head back on the pillow. He was trapped. He was scarcely able to think clearly, but how could she possibly imagine they could pull this off? Three days ago she'd tried to turn him in; now suddenly she was willing to risk everything to protect him.

It made no sense. Warmth percolated through the pipes over his head.

No more than a couple of minutes passed before the low door opened again. David turned on his side as Joann made her way to him. She was carrying what looked like an old gym bag over her shoulder.

She knelt beside him and unzipped the bag. She removed a plastic water bottle with a flexible straw.

"Here," she said. "You're going to need all the fluids you can get." She held the bottle for him while he drank. He finally waved it away, wiping the excess from his lips.

"Thank you," he whispered.

"I'm going to set it here, all right?" She set the bottle in the wooden drawer and then searched the gym bag for a moment, finally fishing out a container of pills. "And here is more Demerol. Ordinarily I'd say one every four hours, but if it gets bad, don't wait. It's important not to let the pain get out of control."

"Why are you doing this?"

"Just lay back," she said.

He did as he was told. She took a strip of damp gauze from the bag and laid it carefully across his eyes. "Just be still," she said. Strip by strip she covered his face, his neck, and his burned hand with gauze. "This will keep the swelling down. We just have to keep everything moist and clean."

"You didn't answer my question," he said.

He felt her lay a blanket carefully over his bare chest. She patted his arm and he heard her slip away. The latticed door closed. He felt a stab of panic, but he knew that if he moved he would make a mess of things. He reached out, groping for his jacket. He retrieved the manila envelope from the pocket, slipped it under the mattress, and lay back again. After a moment the panic began to subside, replaced by a rolling fog that obliterated everything.

fifteen

He woke to the sounds of voices and of a tractor starting up, yet everything was dark. It bewildered him, but then he remembered the gauze masking his face. Very carefully he pulled the strips of soft fabric from his eyes. Everything was still utter blackness. Far off a door slammed, and then a dog barked.

His face still felt as if it were on fire. He stretched across for the wooden crate—the slightest motion unleashed fresh volleys of pain—and fumbled around until he found the pillbox. He held the bottle inches from his nose, hoping to read the label, but he couldn't make out anything. He put the bottle on the sheet next to him. He took a moment to calm himself and then reached up with his good hand. The lightest touch of a fingertip felt like a glowing poker, but it was enough to tell him what he needed to know; his eyes were swollen shut.

He lay still for a long while, fighting back panic. He had screwed up big-time. He should have let Joann take him to the doctor when he'd had the chance. The sound of the tractor receded and then disappeared altogether. He retrieved the bottle of Demerol, fished out a tablet, and washed it down with a swallow of water.

Everything got very silent. Some of the gauze strips flapped from his forehead. He was blind and he was trapped, as defenseless as a baby chick. He tried to fight back the feelings of claustrophobia, the impulse to get up and run. His heart raced. He tried to remember the tricks he'd learned in yoga class years before, focusing on his breathing, waiting for the painkiller to kick in.

It was maybe fifteen minutes later that he heard the latticed door open and the sounds of someone shuffling across the crawl space.

"Joann?"

"How are you doing?" she said. Her voice was wary.

"I don't know," he said. "I can't see."

There was a rustling as she sat down next to him and then she touched his arm. "When did you take the gauze off?"

"Just a few minutes ago. I . . ."

"Let me look," she said. The first time she brushed his eyelid he jerked away. "It's all right. I'll be very careful," she said. She touched him lightly in three or four places on each eye. Each touch felt like a tiny electrical prod. "We should have taken you in."

"Maybe so," he said.

"It looks as if the lids are just swollen shut, but I'm not a doctor."

"So how long will they be like this?"

"A day or two. Maybe longer. I don't know. But if a doctor doesn't have a chance to look at this, you're taking a really big gamble. You know that."

"I need you to help me, Joann."

She was silent for several seconds. "I thought I was doing that."

"That's not what I meant. I want you to find out if Seth Carswell's in town, if anyone's seen him."

"I'm doing all I can do," she said, her voice on the verge of breaking. "Please, don't ask me for more than that. I've brought you some Gatorade. If you sit up, I'll give you some."

He heard a soft snap as she undid the plastic ring around the neck of the bottle. He propped himself up on both elbows and she held the container to his lips. He drank what he could and then lay back again.

"Did you take another pill?" she asked.

"I just did," he said. "So where is your husband?"

"He went down the road to work on a combine with one of the neighbors."

"You didn't tell him?"

"Tell him?" her voice was tinged with contempt. He heard her screw the top back on the Gatorade. "How could I possibly tell him? I'll be back," she said.

Day blurred into night and back into day again. Two days could have passed, or four. She would come to change his bandages and put more salve on his burns. She brought a warm quilt and a plastic bottle for him to pee in. Pain and painkillers ebbed and flowed in an uneasy truce. He could not see, and he had to lie as still as an entombed Egyptian king so that he wouldn't disturb the strips of gauze on his face and neck.

His only handle on the outside world was aural: the lowing of cattle, birds chirping in the morning, the rumble of a milk truck arriving and departing. There was a howling wind that blew all one night, moaning like a wounded beast, rattling the latticed gate. The sounds of the wind worked their way into his sedated dreams, becoming the voice of his daughter, calling to him, becoming the voices of people he did not know.

Joann had made herself his accomplice and he didn't know why. She had put herself in terrible jeopardy, and not just with the police. The smallest thing could trip them up; all it would take would be for her husband, Clarence, to notice a few too many footprints in the snow leading down to the shed or an extra plate in the sink or a missing hot water bottle. Where, for example, did Joann go every day with the leavings of his slop bucket? He was too humiliated to ask, but he imagined it poured into the muck of the barnyard, with the excrement and urine of the cattle. For all her saintliness, Joann was also clever. She was good at deception—so good, in fact, it made him wonder. He remembered the picture in the album of her and Danacek together.

All the same, they were utterly at the mercy of Clarence's comings and goings. When he spent the day working in the machine shed, it made it impossible for Joann to get to David. For hours there were the sounds of pneumatic drills, whining saws, men's voices, and pickups arriving and departing. Without food or anyone to tend him, David found himself plummeting to new lows of despair, feeling his chances of tracking down Seth growing more remote with every passing day. David's rage was the rage of a child. He was blind, he was helpless, a mad dog chained under a porch.

Late one afternoon she brought with her part of a chicken potpie in a tin and it was piping hot. He sat up on his pallet and she held the tin in both hands so he could dig in with a fork. Ravenously hungry and in too big a rush, he spilled some of it on his shirt.

"Damn," he said.

"It's fine," she said, "just hold still."

He heard her set the tin down on the wooden tray, and a minute later she was scrubbing at his shirt with a wet rag.

"I'm sorry," he said.

"It's not a problem," she said. "What's this?"

"What's what?"

There was a rasping sound, from under the corner of the pallet. "Some sort of envelope."

"I found it at the cabin. It was in Maya's bag," he said.

Papers rustled. "It's all chemistry," she said.

"Yes."

"I don't get it."

He felt himself growing impatient; all he wanted was something to eat. "You know what she was doing, right?"

"She was working with those wolf people."

"Yes. And a lot of the wolves have been dying. No one knows why. They think they're being poisoned, but it's not arsenic and it's not strychnine."

"And you think this is about that?"

"I don't know."

"So how were you in chemistry?" she said.

"Not great."

The dog barked outside. There was a slithering of paper, a stillness, and then a soft nudge under his left elbow; she had put the envelope back.

"Me either," she said.

At some point he realized that he was not alone, that he was sharing his low-ceilinged quarters with some sort of animal. He had noticed a smell that would come and go, and once, at night, he heard a great clatter from the direction of the house, as if a garbage can had been tipped over. Some of it might have been his imagination, but it seemed as if there were, from time to time, scratchings and soft rustlings, no more than a few feet away. Whether it was a raccoon, a skunk, or just a large rat, he envisioned the animal looking him over, curious and perhaps even angry at this great motionless body that had invaded his den.

As gentle as Joann was, there were times when having his wounds cleaned would take his breath away, when it was all he could do not to scream. Afterward, when he was exhausted, lying on his back on his pallet waiting for the painkillers to kick in, she would wait with him and they would talk—or rather he would talk, rambling on like some barroom drunk, summoning up random fragments of the past.

He told her about how he and Andy Danacek used to hide in the ditch next to the graveyard during harvest season, waiting for the tractors hauling their wagonloads of peas to the canning factory. He and Andy would crouch low, their hearts pounding, and then, just as the tractors chugged by, they would dart out, snatch a handful of vines, and race all the way back to the Danaceks' house, where they would hide under the porch and gorge themselves on raw peas until they were sick.

He told her about the rafts they built that would always sink, and the cardboard traps they would set out on the ice in their futile attempts to catch muskrats, and the time his father shook hands with Senator Joe McCarthy.

Because he couldn't see, he had no way to gauge her reactions to his stories. She said almost nothing, sitting just a few feet away. He imagined her with her head resting on her knees, her arms wrapped around her shins. His eyelids still felt as swollen and hard as mussel shells.

One afternoon, at the end of one of his slurred rambles, he tried to turn on his side, fumbling for her hand. She took his fingers for just a second and then set them gently on his quilt.

"Can I ask you something?"

"Of course."

"Do you remember when I was here before? You said that Maya wasn't intimidated by people. What did you mean?"

"I'm not quite sure."

"But you wouldn't have said it if you hadn't heard something. Please, Joann, I need to know . . ."

"Honestly, I don't know that I meant anything by it. It's just that in a small town like this . . . people talk about people. Someone like your daughter's going to stand out."

"In what ways?"

"She had lots of boyfriends . . . or admirers, anyway. People didn't approve of her bumper stickers. Someone told me once . . . I guess they had seen her at some bar, dancing with her girlfriends . . . It's not that girls don't dance with their girlfriends here . . . I guess it was just the way she did it . . ."

"Jesus Christ."

"I know. People can be narrow here. Do you remember Reverend Pond? And Vern Zander?"

"Of course. How could I not?"

"I've always thought if you could leave this place, it would be better never to come back." He heard her moving around, preparing to go. The afternoon was getting late and it was cold; Clarence had driven over to his brother's to drop off a generator. "When I heard you'd bought a cabin here, I thought you were crazy."

David remembered being a little afraid of Vern Zander. He was three years older than David and lived out at the county home. Reverend Pond, who spent a couple afternoons a week working with the people out there, was the one who'd invited him to church.

Vern was a strange boy, unsmiling and slow on the uptake. At fifteen he was as strong and tall as an adult. The other kids at church gave him a wide berth. "Sometimes if you ask him a question," Jimmy Gunlock said, "you can look him in the eyes and see all the way to Lake Superior." David's mother thought they needed to be more sympathetic. "Vern is an orphan," she said, "and his life has been harder than any of us can imagine."

It wasn't long before Vern was coming to church every Sunday, taking up the collection and singing, rather badly, in the choir. People were generous, giving him clothes, having him over for meals.

After six months, Albert Bensen took Vern out to his farm and put him to work as a hired man, letting him help with the milking and the hauling of manure.

Everyone in the church seemed pleased and said how much happier he seemed. He didn't seem happier to David; if anything, he seemed to be getting angrier and stranger, but David knew enough to keep his thoughts to himself. Just because grown-ups told you to feel sorry for somebody didn't mean you could. Just because someone was slow didn't mean he couldn't be nasty.

Every few weeks David and his family would go out to Albert's after church for dinner. Vern wasn't around that much—he was usually back in his room or out in the woods, squirrel hunting—but David did remember once when Vern took him and Jack, Albert's oldest son, down to the barn. He gave them cigarettes and told them dirty jokes. When David laughed at what was apparently the wrong time, Vern just guffawed at him.

"You don't know what it's all about, do you?"

"No," David admitted. It was winter and the barn smelled of rotting silage.

"You ever seen bulls and cows do it?"

David hesitated; he was a town kid and he didn't want to admit the depth of his ignorance. "Sure," he said. "Sure."

"Well, it's just the same."

Six months later, David was pedaling back from the baseball field, his new Stan Musial Louisville Slugger balanced across his handlebars, when he saw Reverend Pond's car coming down the alley behind the parsonage. He pulled his bike over to the curb. The green Nash Rambler slowed and stopped. Reverend Pond rolled down the window. His wife sat opposite him, and their two kids were in the back; they all looked stricken.

"I just wanted to say good-bye," Reverend Pond said.

"You're going on vacation?" David asked. Cicadas sang in the city park at the end of the block.

"No," the minister said. "We're going for good."

When David got home, his mother told him yes, it was true. But why, David wanted to know. His mother wouldn't say exactly.

"Did they fire him?" David asked. They stood in the kitchen. His mother was stripping corn from the garden, tossing the fresh shucks and silk into a Kroger bag at her feet. Arthur Godfrey was selling something on the radio in the most roundabout way; David had never understood why his mother liked Arthur Godfrey.

"No, they didn't fire him."

"Does he have another job then?"

"I don't know, honey," she said. She turned away, rinsing her hands in the sink. Ripening tomatoes glistened on the windowsill. "You should go take a bath. We'll be eating in just a little bit."

For much of the fall, intense adult conversations were cut short when children entered the room; the prayers at Sunday school became weirdly somber and gnomic. A student minister, a sandy-haired stutterer, came to conduct services while a search went on for a permanent pastor.

It was several weeks before David noticed that Vern Zander hadn't been in church. When he asked Albert about it, Albert just patted him on the shoulder.

"Oh, he's got himself a job down in Chicago," Albert said.

"He's doing OK?"

"Oh, he's doing fine. A guy like Vern, he doesn't ask for much."

Even though David's parents were too discreet to ever say what had happened, there were others who weren't. On a bus ride to the Indian reservation with the youth group, David ended up sitting near the back with Joann's cousin, Nancy.

"You know what Reverend Pond's problem was?" Nancy said.

"What was that?"

"He didn't like girls."

"I don't know what you mean," David said.

"You don't know what I mean?" she said. David had always found Nancy curiously nasty, but prim. She had once informed him that the name Jiminy Cricket was blasphemous because it had the same initials as Jesus Christ. "You don't know what happened?"

"No."

"Well . . . I don't know if I should tell you or not." She propped her saddle shoes up against the seat in front of her and patted her dress. David said nothing. He knew that if she was struggling over whether to keep something in confidence, it wasn't going to be a prolonged conflict. "You promise not to tell?"

"I promise."

Nancy slid a little further down in her seat. "Mrs. Truitt walked right in on them in the Sunday school bathroom after choir practice."

"Walked in on who?"

"Reverend Pond and Vern Zander."

"So what?"

Nancy's voice dropped to an exasperated whisper. "Reverend Pond was on top of him!"

"What do you mean on top of him?"

"They both had their pants down! Betty's aunt says that Reverend Pond had been doing the same thing with all these other boys out at the county home . . . for a long time. Only nobody believed them."

David didn't believe it either, whatever it was. Reverend Pond had been the one to baptize him, to lower him gently into the water with a white handkerchief pressed over his face. He had been the one to lift him up again, dripping wet and choking, and proclaim him one of God's own, in front of his parents and Albert and the whole church. Reverend Pond had been a kind man and the best preacher they'd ever had, that's what everyone said.

As the years passed, it was not a story David ever told much. One of the few times he did, at a Westchester dinner party, when everyone had started telling their religion stories, it was a mistake. It made him feel as if he had betrayed his own past, made fools and narrow-minded hypocrites out of people he cared about. What did he really know about what had happened anyway? All he had was a bit of gossip whispered by a spiteful girl so very long ago.

He stared at the rusted lawnmower in the far corner of the crawl space. He must have been thrashing in his sleep because a couple of the gauze strips had come loose, hanging from his cheekbones like the long ears of a basset hound. He sat up and pried the rest of the bandages from his eyes. With a touch as tentative as a safecracker's he explored his swollen lids. The slightest contact still burned and everything felt a bit gummy, but he could see.

Enough daylight glowed through the wire mesh of the latticed door for him to survey his surroundings. He inspected the tray and its medicines and tubes of salve, the rolls of gauze, the Gatorade bottle, and a plastic container of cold soup he had no memory of ever tasting. He stared at the piles of old lumber, the dirt-dauber nests, the coils of orange extension cord; everything seemed equally miraculous.

It was another hour before the latticed door opened. He rolled onto his side as Joann appeared around the corner of the heating unit. She stooped low, carrying a small bucket of water that sloshed at every step.

"Hey," he said.

"Hey," she said. The brightness of his tone was enough to cause her to look up.

"I can see," he said.

The shadows were too dark for him to make out her reaction, but she hesitated, switching the bucket from her left hand to her right. "Well, good," she said.

She made her way up the dirt incline, ducking lower in the tapering space. She set the bucket down and knelt next to the pallet. She wore jeans and a dirty blue down vest. "Let me look," she said.

He lay back on the pillow, scrutinizing her face—the stray bit of blonde hair loose across her forehead, the slight indentation in her chin, the guarded blue eyes. She ignored his gaze, touching the edge of his cheekbone and the puffiness under his eyebrows, poking gently.

"Ouch," he said.

"This is better," she said. "A lot better. We just need to clean everything."

She peeled the gauze away from his neck and the side of his face. He jerked two or three times when he felt something tear or catch; the good news was that scabs were starting to form.

She washed everything with a sponge and then dried him with a fresh towel. He lay still, trying to be a good patient, watching her face as she worked. He could hear the steady dripping of melting snow from the roof.

"Turn on your side," she said.

He did as she asked. She applied the salve to the area of the burn, spreading the cool ointment with her fingertips.

"I don't know if it was last night or the night before," he said, "but I thought I heard someone walking around, right over my head."

"It was probably me."

"I don't understand." She tore strips of gauze and began to lay them gently across his eyes.

"It's my studio."

"You mean an art studio?"

"The last two or three years," she said, "I've been doing some silk-screening. I don't know that I would call it art."

Layer by layer, the world returned to darkness. Her touch was as soft as moth wings. The pallet swayed a bit as she pushed herself back on her heels. There was a plop. A washrag, he guessed, dropping into the bucket of warm water. The gauze across his eyes felt like drying papier-mâché.

"Can I tell you something?" he asked.

"Of course."

"I could have saved her," he said.

"There's no way you could know that."

"No, I do know it." He heard a metallic rattle as she picked up the bucket and began to move down the dirt incline.

"Please don't go," he said. She didn't answer, but the movement had stopped. "At the end of the summer, we had this . . . I guess you'd call it a confrontation. She brought up all this stuff about her mother's death, about the way I handled it. They really have your number, these kids, you know? I made a stab at being big about it, but not really. What I did was back off. I don't think I spoke a word to her for three months. If I hadn't been so goddamned thin-skinned . . ." The silence stretched out for so long he thought she must have slipped out without his having been aware of it. "Joann?"

"I have to go now," she said. There was the creak of the latticed door opening and shutting again, the soft click of the metal hook, and then, further off, the barking of the dog.

He felt a hand stroking his hair, waking him from a deep, drugged sleep. He made a lazy attempt at swatting it away; the hand disappeared. He lay still. Under the layers of gauze, the scabs on his face itched like tiny, crawling ants. It was several more seconds before he was conscious enough to realize that there was someone lying on the pallet behind him, a body pressed against his own. He gave a quick, involuntary shudder and reached back, touching a coarse denim sleeve.

"What are you doing?" he said.

"Nothing," Joann said. "Nothing."

Neither of them spoke. He could hear melting snow from the roof splattering on the ice below. He had no idea how long he'd been asleep or what time it was. Noon? One? Her forehead rested against his spine. He reached up and carefully peeled the gauze from his eyes. He stared into the gloom at the stacks of discarded lumber, the bag of bone meal, the dark rafters. Joann put her hand on his hip.

He spun around and grabbed both of her wrists. Pain darted along the left side of his face, as quick as minnows. "What is this?"

She wouldn't lift her head. He touched her cheek. He could feel tears. He put his arms around her. Through his stocking feet he could feel the hard leather of her boots, the sharp metal eyelets. After a moment, she yanked the tangled sheet that separated them and tossed it away, then nudged a knee between his legs. He did nothing to resist; they lay that way for a long time. He could feel himself becoming aroused. He had not slept with anyone since his wife died. He would not be betraying any vow, but she would. What would it mean, allowing himself to be a party to that? She accidentally brushed his face with her fingertips and he jerked back like a skittish colt.

"I'm sorry," she said.

"It's OK," he said.

She rolled away from him and sat up. For a moment he thought it was over and was relieved, but then he saw that she was unlacing her boots.

"Joann, are you sure you know what you're doing?"

She gave the faintest of nods; her face was turned away from him. He watched her slip out of her down vest and unbutton her blue denim shirt. He felt a terrible sadness. Sparrows quarreled outside the shed. This was no place to make love, no matter how desperate, down here in the dirt and the pus-stained sheets. He unbuckled his belt and tugged off his trousers and underwear. It felt as if the two of them were buried a mile beneath the earth.

She got on top of him. There was a moment of awkwardness, but they weren't children. At first it was painful and dry, but then it became easier. His hands were on her waist, and he squinted up at her through eyes as crusty as an old alligator's. Above her head, nails protruded from cob-webbed beams. Her face was flushed and mask-like, her lips slightly parted. It came to him that she was not trying to console him, but to be consoled.

He reached up and cupped one of her breasts tenderly. "Hey." He said. "Hey."

The sound of his voice stopped her. He put a hand on her face, trying to get her to look him in the eye, but she wouldn't. Instead she laid her head on his chest and began to sob. He put both arms around her, his chin high, trying to keep the scars on his face untouched. He stroked her hair, listening to her cry. After a moment or two, she raised her head and glanced quickly toward the latticed door.

"What?" he said.

She put a finger to his lips. At first all he could hear was the syncopated drip of melting snow, the endless twittering of sparrows, but then he heard what she heard: the distant cough and whine of a tractor.

The sound surged, faded, and then surged again. The tractor was coming up the driveway. Joann tried to move away from him, but he grabbed her arms, unsure what she intended. The low, gutting sound grew closer, swept past the shed and into the yard next to the house. It cut off. David released Joann's arms; cold air raised goose bumps on his bare legs.

A door slammed. Joann slid off David and reached for her clothes. Clarence must have gone into the house. Maybe he was looking for his noon meal, maybe he was just looking for her. Joann snapped the buttons on her denim shirt; they made a series of sharp pops.

The door banged a second time. "Joann? Joann!" Clarence's voice echoed in the stillness. A whiff of gas fumes drifted across the narrow crawl space. Still barefoot, knees up, Joann covered her eyes with her hands. After a moment, the tractor sputtered back to life and made its way back down the long drive. The drone faded to nothing and all they were left with was the bright sound of sparrows.

David retrieved the sheet and covered himself. Joann pulled on her boots and put a hand down to push herself to her feet. Stooped, she made her way down the slope, moving from one sodden piece of cardboard to the next.

"Where are you going?" David said.

"I've got to go to town," she said. "I'll be back."

David sat up on his elbows. "Now hold it a minute. What just happened here? You need to talk to me about this."

"If there was any way in the world I could, I would," she said. She opened the latticed door. As she ducked through it, David caught a glimpse of a dazzling winter day, but then the door swung shut and he was once again plunged into darkness.

She was gone all afternoon. He finished off the two cold egg tacos she'd left him and tore new strips of gauze, applying more salve as best he was able. For the first time he could touch some of the scarred areas without it hurting. Every so often he could make out the shadow of the dog trotting past the latticed door.

He was unnerved. Utterly faithful in his marriage, he had never been understanding of people who weren't. Even though Peggy had been dead for more than five years, he felt as if, by a single act, he had profaned her memory. He felt dirty and cheap and angry at himself for going along with it. But if that was what he felt, what about Joann?

Even if Clarence didn't know, even if he never found out, how could she do that to him? It had been, almost literally, right under his nose. How estranged would she have to be to do something like that? How despairing? How angry? He didn't know. All he knew was that she had taken him in, nursed him, protected him when no one else would, and treated him with infinite tenderness, and now they had been launched into uncharted darkness.

Hours passed. He lay on his pallet, staring at the padded heating ducts and the dirt-dauber nests in the overhead beams. Late in the afternoon he was roused out of his stupor by the sound of something whisking across the snow. He scrambled down the dirt incline and peered out through the latticed door.

At first he saw nothing, even though the sound had grown more distinct. Finally he spied Clarence pulling a Christmas tree toward the machine shed, the dog dancing at his heels. Clarence stopped next to an ancient mower, lifted the tree, and heaved it into a trash barrel.

A single match was all it took to set it on fire. The whoosh of flames made Clarence take a step backwards. The cows, lined up at the barnyard fence, stared like out-of-town tourists at a Fifth Avenue parade.

After perhaps a minute, the dog turned, ears perked, staring in the direction of the road, and then began to bark. Clarence turned and David did too, craning to see through the angles of the latticed door.

A familiar gray van rolled up the driveway. It stopped next to the machine shed and Irina Carswell got out.

David stared, thunderstruck. It wasn't until she opened the back door and Joann's grandson tumbled out that David understood at all. The interior light was on just long enough for David to make out three other children still squirming in their seatbelts.

Bobby ran up the slope to his grandfather as Irina Carswell slammed the van door shut. She watched Clarence give Bobby a hug, the dog scampering around them, and then began to move up the incline herself.

David crouched before the latticed door, peering out. Clarence took off a glove to shake hands; in her elegant, long black coat, Irina looked as if she was three or four inches taller than he was.

They talked for several minutes, gathered around the barrel for warmth. Bobby grew restless and finally ran for the house.

The scene reminded David of something out of a Nathaniel Hawthorne story: the darkening day, the dumb, watching animals, the dying fire. What could have been more innocent than a woman driving a carpool, delivering children after some extracurricular event? But it was impossible for David to believe that anything was innocent anymore. She was asking Clarence questions and the questions were making him uncomfortable. He folded his arms across his chest, shrugged, and began to poke at the fire with a short board, but she pressed on. He turned finally to point out the bluff above them, turned again to point out the road.

As the fire began to settle, one of the top branches, still aflame, broke and fell to the snow. Irina stooped and picked it up by the unlit end. The dog, thinking it was a game of fetch, dashed off a few feet, stopped, and looked back, tail wagging.

Irina stared down at the burning pine bough. Sparks danced and disappeared in the late-afternoon gloom. In the fitful light, David could finally see her face, see something both brutal and dissatisfied playing across the perfect Nordic features.

One of the children was calling from the van, but Irina paid the cries no mind. The dog began to bark, dancing at her feet. Irina turned and with one easy motion, pitched the flaming torch into the sky. It landed in the snow of the barnyard and guttered out before the frantically scampering dog could get within ten feet of it.

After Irina left, David went to lie down on his pallet. Seeing her had upset him, set gears in motion, all over again.

How unlikely was it that Joann's grandson and Chet Carswell's daughter would be in the same church or school group? Probably not very; this was small-town America. All the same, Irina Carswell had been grilling Clarence, and there was only one thing she could have been grilling him about. Her family had been threatened and she wanted David caught. She was no fool. If anybody would be able to figure out where David might be hiding, she would likely be the one.

David knew that Joann would never have given him away intentionally, but the reality was that when you've got a secret, it changes you in ways you're not even aware of. Sooner or later, people were going to notice.

So where was Joann? It was late now. She'd been gone for hours and the temperature was plummeting.

As he turned on his pillow, he felt something wet and sticky. He touched his neck; he was bleeding. She had warned him that this could happen; by moving around too much, he had cracked open some of the newly formed scabs. He covered his wounds with fresh strips of gauze, took another painkiller, and was asleep within minutes.

He woke to the sound of munching, only inches from his left ear. His first thought was that it had to be his imagination, then he realized it wasn't. As soon as he pushed up on his elbow, the animal was off and running, knocking over the plastic food container on David's tray. David pulled the gauze from his eyes, grabbed the bottle of Gatorade, and threw. His aim wasn't good. The bottle bounced off an overhanging beam as the animal rattled under the latticed door.

David sat for a moment, his heart pounding. It disgusted him, the idea of sharing food with some scavenger. He carefully pulled the rest of the gauze from his neck. Everything was itching; he supposed that was good, but the urge to scratch was nearly irresistible.

He groped his way down the dirt incline to retrieve the bottle of Gatorade. He rolled the plastic container back and forth in his hands, set it down, and crept to the door on all fours. There was just enough room between the frame and the door to poke his finger through and flick loose the hook.

He stared out at the barn and the pastures beyond. The moon was nearly full, and layers of fog were drifting down from the hills. It was remarkable how much had melted: even though the snowbanks were still high, the trampled barnyard was a sea of black mud. David sat on his hands, looking for his tormentor, and finally spotted him: a fat raccoon perched on top of an old hay rake, maybe twenty yards away.

David reached down and pried a flat stone from the cold ground. It was roughly the circumference of an egg. He moved slowly, not wanting to scare the animal, bending low and then stepping out of the low door. His throw was better this time; the rock dinged off the rusted farm machinery, just a foot below the raccoon. The fat, ghostly animal leapt down and scooted off into a nearby grove of trees.

David was shirtless and the air was cool against his skin; it relieved the endless itching, at least momentarily. He stood for a moment, drinking in the moonlight gleaming off the tin roof of the barn, the wisps of fog settling on the distant road. He was afraid of waking the household, but he wasn't ready to go back in; he'd been cooped up for what felt like an eternity.

He shuffled carefully along the ragged border of ice, keeping one hand on the side of the shed for balance. After days without moving, his joints were creaky and stiff. Coming to the corner of the shed, he could see the farmhouse, just sixty yards away. A single light burned in an upstairs window.

He waited a few minutes. The last thing he needed now was for the dog to come barking down the hill, but no dog appeared. There was no sign of any movement, anywhere.

What did it mean, he wondered, for her not to have told her husband about him? It was a question that, with each passing day, loomed larger. Car lights crept along the road, a mile off, and finally vanished into the fog.

He reached for the wooden handrail and stepped onto the shed's narrow porch. The shed looked as if it must have been, at one time, a children's playhouse. A leather belt of sleigh bells was tacked to the door, and on the walls someone had scrawled BULLETT EXPLORERS—KEEP OUT in what was now badly faded paint.

When David eased the door open, the sleigh bells jingled softly. He stepped inside. The room smelled of strange inks. It took a second for his eyes to adjust, but there were big windows facing south, and with a full moon he could see a lot. Scissors, rolls of tape, and metal rulers cluttered a long worktable in the middle of the studio.

He spied a Swiss army knife in an open drawer. He picked it up, tried to work loose the rusted blades, and then just stuck it in his pocket. Silk screens were stacked against the wall, and on the shelves were paint jars and various odds and ends: bits of antler, a cow skull, crumpling oak leaves, corroded pieces of old farm implements.

He flipped through the silk screens, looking for some clue to her life, some way of understanding this woman who had become his protector. A number of the pieces were variations of the ones he'd seen mounted in the house—montages of country life, oak leaves and ferns superimposed on old photographs of threshing crews and enigmatic scraps of headlines. They were all lovely, but what did they tell him? Nothing, until he went into the adjoining room and found, jammed behind a paint-stained bathtub, just what he was looking for.

He carried it to the broad windows so that he could see it more clearly in the moonlight. It too was a silk screen, but the images were simple and sharp-edged, almost as if they'd been cut out of paper. It was a picture of a child's room, mobile hanging above a crib and little fluorescent stars dotting the ceiling. A mother's hand gripped the door frame. There was no child. What there was, was a raven sitting on the top rung of the crib, a single drop of blood on its beak.

In the morning when she came to him, David was already sitting on his pallet, waiting for her, his swollen eyes freshly salved but free of gauze. It gave her a bit of a start, but she said nothing. Tucked under her arm were a clean flannel shirt and a bulky blue coat. She tossed them both onto his mattress.

"What are these for?" he asked.

"I want to take you for a ride."

"I don't understand."

"You will soon enough," she said. "Please, David, we don't have that much time. I've got to go put some gas in the car."

After she left, he sat for a moment, pondering what to do. He didn't like her manner and he wasn't altogether sure he trusted her. She hadn't said a word about what had passed between them the day before. It was all getting too crazy. Whether he chose to go with her or not, his time under the shed was over.

He reached across the pallet for his boots, and then ran a hand under the edge of the mattress—the envelope was gone. Lying on his belly, he dug farther under the lumpy bedding, checking up and down, growing more and more frantic. He got off the pallet finally, lifted one corner of it, and stared down at the hard-packed earth. Nothing. He let the mattress drop. Questions piled on questions: who had done this, and why? It had to have been Joann.

He sat down again, brushed off his socks, and then yanked on his boots. He took a few deep breaths to calm himself. What he needed now, more than anything else, was to keep his wits about him.

He changed his shirt and pulled on the oversized blue coat. Making his way down the dirt incline, he ducked through the latticed door into dazzling sunlight. Joann stood at the ancient pump next to the tractor shed, filling up the Pontiac. The green and gold letters of the GO PACKERS bumper sticker shimmered. It was the first time he'd been out in the sun for days and everything seemed etched in light: the bare branches of the elm trees, the white curtains in the kitchen window, the rotting fence posts in the barnyard.

He moved across the snow, his pace measured and deliberate. The dog that had been nosing around in the margins of the tractor shed looked up, spotted him, and froze, unsure whether he was friend or foe.

"When did you take it?" he said.

"Take what?"

"The envelope." She pivoted away, not answering, hooking the metal nozzle back on the rusting gas pump. The dog started to wag his tail as David moved closer. "You showed it to somebody."

Her mouth was tight. She retrieved the gas cap from the roof of the car. He grabbed her by the arm and spun her around; the gas cap fell to the snow. Her face was averted as if she expected to be hit. "God damn it, Joann, I trusted you."

She looked up at him, her eyes dark with anger. "And you don't think I trusted you? I risked everything for you." The dog was barking now, but kept his distance. "Please, David, just get in the car."

"Where are you taking me?"

"Not far," she said. "Just to the top of the hill."

He was silent for a moment, but there seemed to be no point in arguing further. Getting into the car, he glanced in the rearview mirror. He was scarcely recognizable to himself. A solid sheet of scabs with the pebbly texture of a leather basketball angled across the left side of his face and neck. His left eye was still terribly swollen and discolored. He wasn't quite sure what he looked like—some cross between the Snake Man in the circus and Zorro, maybe.

They drove out to the main road and after a couple hundred yards turned into a gate. Both of them were too angry to speak. The old Pontiac groaned and moaned up a steep tractor path through a cornfield to the top of the bluff. Ice-glazed pastures glistened in the sunlight. They got out of the car, and she led him to a small grave next to a pond, set back in a grove of birch trees. A bedraggled wreath leaned against the granite headstone.

He glanced over at her, but she refused to meet his gaze, staring down instead at her jumble of keys. He approached the grave and knelt so that he could read the inscription: In Memory of Our Daughter, Mary Ellen Meineke, Rest In Peace—March 7, 1964—January 24, 1967. He put a hand out to balance himself and looked back at her again. Along the tree line, several of the fence posts had rotted away, like decaying teeth still clinging to the barbed wire.

"This is your daughter?"

"Yes," she said.

"She was very young."

"Yes."

"What happened to her?" A squirrel bounded across the gleaming snow.

"She was born with terrible problems." Joann put the keys in her pocket, drawing herself up.

"What kind of problems?"

"Her face wasn't like other children's."

"I don't understand."

"It was cleft. It was as if the two sides didn't match. She was underweight, she had seizures—you name it, she had it . . . When the doctor came to my room in the hospital, he didn't even want to show her to me, but I insisted. She was my baby . . ."

"Did you bring her home?"

"Not at first, it was impossible. But later, yes."

She had chosen to bring him here, yet now it was nearly impossible for her to speak. David saw that it was going to be up to him to press, to pull it all out of her. "Did people help you?" he asked.

"My mother did."

"But what about other people? People from church?"

"I stopped going to church."

"And why was that?"

High up in the cobalt blue sky, a fighter plane was leaving a stuttery trail of white. "You remember Susie Johnson?"

"Yes."

"She kept calling me. For months. Asking me to come back to church. But I was afraid. I didn't know if I could face it. I knew this town well enough to know that people had to be talking. 'You don't understand,' she said. 'Everybody's been praying for you. If there's ever going to be a time in your life when you need a church, it's now,' she said."

"So you went back."

"Yes."

David still crouched by the gravestone, the knuckles of his right hand in the crusted snow. Tucked back in the grove of birches, they were safely hidden from view, but he wasn't so sure about the tan Pontiac, parked a few yards farther out along the ridge. What if someone spotted the car from the road? Or worse yet, what if Clarence did?

"I remember walking up to the church that morning. Susie was on the front steps, waiting for me. And all these other people too, you know them, Bobby Statz and Janet Brannon. . . . It was wonderful. Everybody hugged me and there were tears . . ." She stopped for a moment, rubbing her hand across her mouth. The dry winter husks of sumac rattled at the edge of the woods.

"We all went in for the service. At first I thought, it's just like always. . . . Mrs. Truitt singing a little too loud in the choir, Charlie Turpin secretly adding up his hours at the lumberyard on the back of one of the visitor envelopes. But I was wrong. It wasn't like always."

"And why not?"

"It wasn't any one thing. Little looks. Little nods. People looking away a bit too quickly. I remember during one of the prayers, glancing over at these two boys, they were probably eleven or twelve. One was trying to keep from laughing and the other had his tongue hanging out of the side of his mouth, with one hand scrunched up by his shoulder, and he was twitching his head. What was it we called it back then? Being a spaz?"

"But maybe that had nothing to do with you."

"You don't think so? As soon as they saw that I saw them, they went all guilty and white. I had to get out of there. I'd left Mary Ellen with my mother; it was nearly the longest time she'd been out of my sight in a year. I got all panicky. I was sure something had happened. I slipped out just before the prayer ended.

"I was standing at my car, trying to find my keys, and I looked around and there was Mrs. Dederick in her white gloves and hat. I don't know how she got there . . . it was as if she'd just appeared. She stood on the sidewalk, staring at me. 'Mrs. Dederick, I said, 'How are you?' 'It was God's will,' she said and just walked away."

"What did she mean, 'God's will'?"

"Because of my sin." David stared at her. "Because I was pregnant when I got married." She looked at him swiftly, angrily, sensing his astonishment. "You don't believe me? You've forgotten what it can be like."

"Did you ever go back to church?" David said.

"Not for a long time. We made a life out here."

"It must have been hard."

"It was."

What was required of him, he wondered. Should he go to her? Hold her? She didn't look as if she wanted to be held, by anyone.

"And did your husband help you?"

For a second he thought he heard the drone of a plane over one of the hills, but the sound faded.

"We were so young. Just eighteen years old, both of us. He was so ashamed and so angry. If it had been up to him, I think he would have just let her die in the hospital. We used to argue. There were places equipped to handle children like this, he said, but I had been to those places, I couldn't bear the idea of it. He just became more and more walled off from me."

"So you did everything yourself."

"Essentially. But it wasn't what you think. We had some wonderful, wonderful days. On summer afternoons I would bring her up here. I would swing her feet in the water and she would squeal and cling to me. I would lie with her on a blanket. We would listen to the birds in the woods, and I'd see her eyes going this way and that. Sometimes, lying there, I'd think about what Mrs. Dederick had said, about it being God's will, and I'd think maybe it was God's will for me to have the joy of raising this child, a joy that no one in the world could fathom. . . ."

At the far end of the pond, among the cattails, was a patch of discolored ice where a spring emptied out. “And so what happened?”

“She got sick. It was just a cough at first, but with her, everything had the potential to escalate, and it did. I took her in the next day, as soon as she developed a fever, but it wasn’t soon enough. She died a week later of pneumonia.”

“You can hardly blame yourself.”

“But I did. Until yesterday.”

“I don’t understand.”

“I went to see Mr. Sinclair.”

“To who?”

“Mr. Sinclair.”

“Our old chemistry teacher? Why would you go to him?”

“The chemicals that your daughter wanted identified. They were nerve gas.”

“What are you talking about?” He rose to his feet. “What does Mr. Sinclair know? He must be a hundred and ninety years old. This is crazy.”

“Is it?” She turned away from him.

The knees of his trousers were damp and cold from kneeling in the snow. “No one ever made nerve gas here. It was a powder plant. My father worked there, your father worked there . . .”

She pivoted to face him again. “My baby wasn’t the only one. A year after Mary Ellen died, Dori Bakke had a little boy born with no brain at all. And Joyce Paschke’s sister . . .”

“Come on, Joann.”

“There were others, David, lots of others. You want to know just how crazy I am? I kept a record in the house. When my husband found out, he was furious with me. He said it was ghoulish. He said there were runts born in every litter—it was just the way the world was. But now wolves are dying and we know better.”

He stared at her, disbelieving. Her husband’s old barn coat, a couple sizes too big for him, drooped from his shoulders as if he were some sort of skid row bum. “And what are we supposed to do with this?”

“I’ve already done something.”

"What is that?"

"Do you remember Albert Backstrom?"

"Yeah. From church."

"He used to be a welder at the plant," Joann said.

"I know."

"The day before your daughter was killed, she didn't just go see Chet Carswell. She saw Albert too."

"How do you know that?"

"Mr. Sinclair told me."

"Jesus, Joann, what did you say to him?"

"He has no clue about you. I promise." She pulled her keys out of her pocket. "I want to go see Albert Backstrom and I want you to go with me."

"How can I do that?"

"How can you not?"

"Damn it, Joann, look at me!"

"I am looking at you." The silence between them grew long and painful. He cocked his head, the icy glare making him squint.

"What could Albert possibly tell us?"

"He could tell us whatever he told your daughter. And maybe he could even tell us why she died."

sixteen

Albert Backstrom worked part-time as a handyman at one of the water parks over in The Narrows and, according to what his wife had told Joann, would be there until noon. Alone.

"And how are we going to get there?" David said.

"I'm going to drive you." The cattails moved in a soft breeze.

"What about the roadblocks?"

"We're not going that way."

"Yeah, but . . ."

"I drive in every day. They haven't changed their checkpoints in a week. It's going to be OK." His look was dubious. He wasn't at all sure that he trusted her confidence. "Unless you'd rather get in the trunk."

"No, that's all right," David said.

She drove him down back roads David hadn't known existed, down narrow, rutted lanes, past abandoned brick farmhouses, past cows lined up against faded barns to catch the reflection of the winter sun. It was the first David had seen of the world in weeks and it made him feel a little drunk.

The Pontiac splashed through mud holes and rumbled over

loosely planked wooden bridges. They passed a slow-moving tractor and then a mailman, leaning out of his car to jam a bundle of newspapers in a metal box, but otherwise they saw no one. Joann had picked her route well.

He looked across at her. Her face seemed almost serene. He found it a little unnerving. "You all right?" he asked.

"I'm fine."

"Can I ask you a question?"

"Sure."

"Why did it happen?"

"Why did what happen?"

"Between us. Yesterday."

"I'm not sure," she said.

He looked away, staring at the gleaming white bluffs. The world was so bright, it was almost painful to take it all in. Was it possible to know anybody? he wondered.

"We were in a Christmas pageant together once," he said. "Remember?"

"Yes," she said. "I remember."

"I was Joseph and you were Mary. I remember standing out on the stage in this silly bathrobe and you were kneeling down over the crib. I remember totally forgetting what Mrs. Dederick had told me to do, so I just knelt down next to you and three or four people out in the church started laughing. You remember that?"

"Sort of."

He glanced over at the speedometer; it felt as if everything was flying by.

The countryside began to open up, and they crossed the interstate into cornfields and wide pastures. The road ahead was empty except for a yellow school bus.

"So what's your life been like?" he asked. "Since your daughter died?"

She didn't answer at first. "It's hard to say. For a time, I suppose I just ran. Maybe not that different from the way you're running now. I did some things I'm not proud of. I kept searching for an answer, something that would make the pain go away. I talked to ministers, to doctors. I went to this women's retreat up at Green

Lake, where everyone told their sad stories and we all hugged and cried together. Nothing really helped. But then we had other children. And that changes everything. When there's someone else you have to think about."

"And you and Clarence?"

"I may not have been the best person for him," she said.

They both fell silent for a moment. "So why did you take me in?" he asked.

"What do you mean?"

"The first time I showed up, you called the cops on me. But the second time you didn't."

Sunlight flashed across the windshield. "When I saw you . . . burned like that . . . There was no way I could send you away."

"Why not?"

"Because it was as if I was looking at my daughter's face."

As they approached The Narrows, the signs began to sprout up for the casinos, the boat rides, the Indian trading posts. For the first time, clouds appeared in the sky, drifting in from the east. He thought about touching her, decided against it, and then changed his mind. When he put his hand on her shoulder, he did it softly, like the gentlest of benedictions. She did not pull away, and after a minute she reached across and covered his hand with hers. Neither of them spoke. Their fingers twined together, tentatively at first, and then with a fierce desperation. When she had to switch lanes to pass a blue bread truck, she took her hand away and he did the same.

A half mile or so before they got to the bridge, David spied the mock-Bavarian castle rising high on the bluff above the river. Hauptmann Gardens was the oldest of all the waterslides in The Narrows, a throwback, a landmark of midwestern kitsch.

Joann exited onto the access road, and they passed a boarded-up pizza parlor, a go-cart track, and the dark windows of Ripley's Believe It or Not! As they turned into the parking lot, David leaned forward, pressing his forefingers to his lips, scanning the low row of buildings and the curving blue plastic chutes that towered above them. Joann eased to a stop thirty yards from the ticket office.

"Maybe he's not here," David said. "Maybe he's gone already."

"Maybe so. You want me to go in to look?"

"Not quite yet," he said. "Let's just wait."

She turned off the engine. David folded his arms across his chest. If Albert wasn't here, what were they going to do? This had been a fool's errand; he saw that now. He should never have agreed to come.

After a couple of minutes had passed, David thought he heard the distant whine of a saw, but when he rolled down his window to be sure, the sound stopped. A couple minutes after that, a man with a fur hat and a bad limp came out, hauling a huge plastic trash basket behind him. He rolled it up against the wall of the office and then turned, cupping his hand to his eyes, squinting in the bright winter sun. He was an old man, too old to be Albert. Tufts of white hair sprouted from beneath the shapeless hat, and he had the air of a befuddled bear.

"Is that him?" David asked.

"Yes, that's him," Joann said.

She cranked down her window, waved, and then turned on the ignition. Albert wiped a grimy work glove across the bib of his overalls as the station wagon rolled toward him.

"Hey, Albert," Joann said.

"Hey. My wife said you might be coming by. She didn't tell me you might be bringing anybody."

"I guess I didn't tell her," Joann said. "You know who this is?"

Albert leaned forward, hands on his knees, and stared through the open window.

"Oof-dah," he said.

"How you doin', Albert?" David said.

"OK, I guess." A hearing aid coiled snugly inside his left ear.

David leaned across the seat. "Can we talk to you?"

"I don't want to get into any trouble now."

"You're not going to," David said. Albert didn't look convinced.

"You want to go for a ride with us, or do you want to go inside?" Joann asked.

Albert squinted, wiped the squint away with a callused hand,

and squinted again. "How about inside," he said. "But one of you should stay here. Just in case."

Joann looked back at David. "You go," she said.

"Are you certain?"

"I'm certain."

David unsnapped his seat belt and stepped out of the station wagon. An eagle tilted high above the dam. "It's been a while, Albert," David said.

The older man just stared at him, then turned on his heel and limped towards the row of low buildings. David followed him across the parking lot. The phone was ringing as they entered the office.

"Excuse me a minute," Albert said. He pulled off his heavy work gloves to answer the phone. "Hello, Backstrom. Yeah. Uh-huh." David stared at him, looking for some sign of who it was. The lobby smelled vaguely of coconut suntan lotion, and fluorescent boogie boards were mounted on the walls like trophy skins.

"I could do that, sure, if you could get me a load of two-by-fours up here. Uh-huh."

There was a morning newspaper on the counter. David spun it around so he could make out the headline: GOVERNOR TO ATTEND GALA. Beneath the headline was a photo of Chet and Irina Carswell standing between a white-haired army general and a somewhat ill at ease Asian businessman.

"Yeah," Albert said, "I'll be here till five."

David picked up the paper and read.

> Governor Stan Woodson announced this morning that he will be on hand for the signing of a $200 million agreement between Chilsung, the Korean chip manufacturer, and the state of Wisconsin. Former Governor Chet Carswell, who has been in charge of the negotiations, said he expects a crowd of more than 400 at the Sentinel Bluff Ski Resort. "This is a great night," he said. "A great night for Wisconsin and an even a greater night for this town." Chilsung expects to be in full operation on the site of the former Sauk munitions plant within 18 months.

"That'll be fine, you betcha," Albert said. "Tell Harriet we'll see you on Sunday. Good-bye." He hung up the phone and picked a Styrofoam cup from a stack on the counter. "You want coffee?" Albert asked. "Anything?"

"No," David said. He pointed to the paper. "You see this?"

"Yeah, I saw it," Albert said. David could feel Albert's wariness. He doubted that Albert believed he was a murderer, but there was no way he could approve of all of David's well-publicized shenanigans. Albert was one of those people who, if the speed limit said fifty-five, you'd never see them going sixty. "You look pretty bad."

"I guess I do."

"So, does it hurt?" Albert gestured to his neck.

"Yeah. Sort of." Albert set the Styrofoam cup back down on the counter. "So, what they got you doing here?"

"Little of this, little of that. Let me go get my toolbox and I'll show you."

Albert led him through a set of sliding glass doors onto a spacious planked landing. A maze of stairs and twining plastic chutes spilled down the hillside to the river. A series of drained swimming pools lined the bank.

David trailed the older man silently up a series of walkways toward the Hansel and Gretel tower. Albert moved cautiously on the icy steps, using the railing. His bad leg was giving him a lot of trouble.

It was disturbing to see Albert diminished like this. Growing up, David had viewed Albert with something close to awe. Strong as a plank, Albert would arm-wrestle David and his friends three and four at a time and never lose. He'd been a farmer and a welder, worked at the plant, sold Christmas trees, and done a stint as a meat-packer. Things did not always work out, but Albert's spirit had been indomitable. David remembered a Fourth of July picnic, just a month after Albert had lost his farm, when he'd tried to convince David's father that they could make a hundred thousand dollars a year raising frogs. He had been the pillar of the church, a deacon, the only one in the choir who could carry a tune, and a one-man welcoming committee. He brimmed with generosity: he was the one who'd brought Vern Zander in from the county home and given him a job as a hired man, the one who would ferry all the old ladies in the congregation to Wednesday night Bible study, and if you ever went to his house for dinner, he'd always give you heaping bowls of ice cream for dessert.

He had set up an improvised workstation two landings up from the office. A giant sheet of plywood lay across two sawhorses, and a couple of freshly cut planks leaned against the railing. Tools were scattered everywhere.

Albert bent down to retrieve his tape measure. He had to fiddle with it for a minute before the long metal tongue came slithering back.

"I understand my daughter came to see you," David said.

"Yes."

"And what did she say?"

"I'm sorry, but I can't afford to get myself in the middle of this."

"I'm afraid you already are in the middle of it, Albert. What did she say?"

"She wanted to know what it was like. Working in the plant. Back in the old days."

"And what did you tell her?" Albert dropped the tape measure into the toolbox. They were high enough above the buildings that David could see the parking lot, see Joann leaning against the hood of her station wagon. "Did you tell her about the nerve gas?"

Albert slapped the lid of the toolbox shut. "I didn't know it was nerve gas! Nobody knew!"

"How could you not know what it was?"

"I was just a welder! All I know was that there was a rail line and that toward the end of the Korean War there were shipments coming in . . ."

"What kind of shipments?"

"I don't know. I heard one of the other guys say that they were storing it in some of the old bunkers . . ."

"And you're telling me nobody knew what it was?"

Albert blinked, beginning to falter. Memory was a barrel of eels. "All I heard was, there were some little rockets . . ."

"What do you mean, little rockets?"

"You know. Two, three feet long."

David leaned against the railing, his back to the parking lot. "Oh Albert," he said.

"You don't understand. It was just so different back then. We did what they told us. If they said to burn something, we burned it. When we bulldozed stuff into the ground, nobody questioned it. We were trying to win a war. Once a week they'd send a truck down to the slough to take out all the dead carp. They gave gas masks to the farmers who lived next to the plant so they could do their chores . . ."

David felt something trip, deep inside him. "Did my father know about this? About these little rockets?"

"I don't know. It's all so long ago. Who can say?"

"One week we were here, two weeks later we're packing up and moving to California."

Suddenly Albert was hot. "There were jobs in California! Things were closing down here! Your father wanted a better life for you! We should all have done what he did!"

David pushed away from the railing. It was all coming back to him now, his parents' murmured fights at night. He wanted to laugh, but the joke was too monstrous.

"Maybe you're forgetting what it was like that spring."

"No, I think I remember pretty well," David said.

Albert was not willing to let it go. "Your parents were worried sick about you. We were all praying for you . . . for you and that boy who died, both . . . We were trying to understand the best we could. I remember your mother coming over to our house one afternoon to have coffee . . . She was sitting at our kitchen table and she just burst out crying. She felt as if she had no way to reach you."

"But that wasn't why we left, was it, Albert? That wasn't why we left."

Albert started to answer, but then stopped; something in the parking lot had gotten his attention. David turned. The station wagon was flanked by a pair of police cars; Joann and Danacek stood by the front bumper. The sheriff was leaning on a cane, but otherwise there was no visible sign that he'd come through a fire. He was pressing her with questions and she kept shaking her head no. When she tried to walk away, Danacek grabbed her arm, spinning her around.

"I think you better go," Albert said. "I think you better go right now."

He willed himself to walk, not run. He kept his head down, determined not to do anything that would arouse suspicion. He slipped through a clutter of go-cart tracks and parking lots, around a concrete ramp where, in summer, life-jacketed tourists would be launched on their sightseeing tours in spiffed-up World War Two amphibious vehicles.

Escape seemed impossible. He was on foot, in a town he didn't know. There would be no sycamore trees to hide in here, and probably no more cars sitting around with the keys in the ignition. He turned up a long alleyway, looking for a refuge. A teenager knocking icicles off the eaves of a video arcade with a shovel paid him no mind.

David took a right at the end of the alley and slowed to a stop. Thirty yards ahead, a train blocked the street. David stared at the blinking lights, the swinging metal pendulum, the zebra-striped wooden arms barring the way across the trestle.

There was just one vehicle waiting, a muddy, red Ford pickup. David kept his distance, but through the rear window of the truck he could see what looked like a farmer in a tractor hat, working intently on his molars with a toothpick. The train slid forward a bit, made a long screeching stop, and then began to back up. There were the sounds of couplings and uncouplings.

David looked over his shoulder, not quite sure what to do. There was the smell of cinders and diesel fuel; an emaciated dog foraged among mammoth storage tanks. He knew that uncertainty could be fatal. He couldn't imagine either Joann or Albert deliberately giving him away, but Danacek was no fool. If he figured it out, it wasn't going to be long before there would be cop cars screaming all over town.

The farmer in the red truck had finally had enough, backing around and driving off. As the pickup passed, David rubbed his cheek, trying to hide his scars.

The train slid forward again and shuddered to a stop. The boxcar sat right in front of him. It seemed empty except for a few busted hay bales.

When he was growing up, there had been so many trains. They were almost all gone now, the old roadbeds converted into bike paths for weekend exercise nuts from Chicago. When David had been twelve, there'd been an older boy, Dwayne, gap-toothed and muscled and rough, who claimed it was as easy as pie, riding the rails. "I do it all the time," he'd said. "Hop a freight car, you can be in La Crosse in forty-five minutes, and back again before supper." David never had gone with him. Not that he hadn't been tempted, but he knew it was against the law, and he'd never broken the law.

The train shuddered again and began to inch forward. David broke into a run. The train was still moving at a crawl, and he was able to catch up quickly to the open boxcar, but he wasn't quite sure what to do next—what to hold onto, how to pull himself up. He finally put his palms flat on the rough-planked floor and lunged forward. The landing was sprawling and ugly, but he made it. He wriggled forward on his elbows and pulled his legs in.

He rolled over on his back, gasping, listening to the soft clacking of the rails. He had no idea where the train was headed, but at this point it scarcely mattered. He'd been flushed out of his hole, and he was on the run again.

As the train picked up speed, the wind whipping through the open door grew colder and more cutting. He sat up, brushing some of the loose straw from his trousers, and got to his feet. The train lurched to one side and David staggered for a moment.

He stared out at cornfields and blue silos. If what Albert had said was true, he thought, it changed everything. If Maya had found out there was nerve gas on the site of the old plant and had been about to go public with the information, it would have created havoc. Not only would it have destroyed the two-hundred-million-dollar deal with Chilsung, but Maya would have been putting a bull's-eye on her back.

The problem was that he still wasn't ready to believe it. Who died for a cause these days in America? A few kooks who chained themselves to redwoods, maybe, but not normal people. People had died for causes once. He and Peggy had met, in fact, at a civil rights march in Washington, but that had been decades ago. David still gave his ten dollars to the Clean Air Action canvassers when they came around, but the truth was that he no longer believed in politics. It would have been nice to dismiss some of the harder, more disturbing thoughts he'd been having about his daughter and himself, nice to imagine that she had died a heroine, allied with the forces of light rather than the forces of darkness, but he wasn't there yet.

The train moved through a small fishing village. A couple of the bars already had their Pabst Beer signs on, pulsing in the gray afternoon, three or four mud-spattered trucks parked outside. At the far edge of the village a pair of shaggy horses drank at a rusted trough. The tracks gradually curved away from the river and began to climb into the bluffs.

David knew he couldn't ride the train forever. There was a good chance there would be police waiting at the next station; it wasn't something he could risk. For the first time he noticed snowflakes in the air. As the incline grew steeper, the train began to labor. The hillsides were studded with limestone outcroppings, and the dense piney woods looked sodden and forbidding. When they finally reached the crest, David leaned out of the train to see.

On the plain several hundred yards below him lay the plant. David stared at the rows of green-roofed still houses that stretched on for miles, the wilderness of roads and pipelines, the massive fuel tanks. In some of the more distant buildings he could make out a few twinkling lights. There it was, he thought, the past, laid out before him like a big birthday cake, waiting for someone to come along and blow out the very last candles.

Under the strain of a hundred cars, the train was reduced to a crawl. If he was ever going to make a move, it had to be now. He leaped from the boxcar. As soon as he hit the ground, he covered his face with his arms, rolling down the icy embankment.

He lay motionless in a stand of mullein and steeplebush as the rest of the train chugged past and then disappeared around a bend. He felt the scar on his neck and then checked his fingers; there was just the tiniest trace of blood. He got to his feet, gimping a bit on a tender left ankle. He crossed the tracks and picked his way down the steep slope.

David's father had been one of thousands to come to work here in the early forties. There had been farmers, truck drivers, housewives, out-of-work salesmen, Indians from the reservation at The Narrows, anyone with flat feet or bad eyesight who hadn't been able to enlist. They had come to make powder. The pay was scarcely extravagant, but for everyone who'd lived through the lean years of the Depression, it felt like boom times. David remembered an old picture of his father with some of his fellow workers, posing in front of the huge sign that hung above the front gate. The sign read simply KEEP 'EM SHOOTING. In the picture they all seemed happy and loose, their arms draped around one another's necks as if they'd just won the World Series.

The plant closed shortly after V-E Day, geared back up for Korea, closed again, and then reopened for Vietnam. Though his father had moved the family to California in the late fifties, never to return, David had never sensed that the move had been prompted by any moral qualms about what his father had been doing. He'd been part of a war effort that had defeated Hitler; he'd supported his family and been good at his job, working his way up to unit supervisor. In the sixties, when University of Wisconsin radicals tried to drop homemade Molotov cocktails into the plant from a two-engine Cessna, David's father, reading about it from the safety of his sunny patio in the San Fernando Valley, had been outraged. "We are not the enemy," David remembered him saying. "I don't know what they're teaching them up there. We are not the enemy."

David had never heard anything about nerve gas, at least not in relation to the plant. He'd read grisly articles in the *New York Times* about chemical and biological weapons, and he remembered a manuscript coming across his desk (one he chose, in the end, not to represent), claiming that the United States had experimented with germ warfare during Korea. Though turgidly written, it had been filled with vivid details: cholera-infected clams, anthrax-infected feathers, yellow-fever-infected lice. It also explained how bombs were used to disseminate the bacteria. It had seemed perfectly credible. But nerve gas stored here in Wisconsin? Without anyone ever knowing about it, or, if they knew, never telling? It was preposterous.

It had been nearly thirty years since the plant had last been in operation, and during that time its eight thousand acres had been scoured over by every regulatory agency in the government, every feasibility-study guru, clean-up crew, and environmental watchdog group. How could they have missed nerve gas? Wouldn't there be records?

He edged down the slope, his boots crunching through the icy snow. They pinched a bit, but if the cops were as hot on his trail as he suspected they were, a different set of tracks couldn't hurt.

He scanned the bluffs behind him. Sauk Lake was maybe ten, fifteen miles away, on the far side of the range of hills. Where, he wondered, had Larry and Maya found the dying wolves?

He remembered, as a boy, driving by the plant with his family on summer afternoons, hearing the booming, seeing the smoke rise in these bluffs. He knew that they tested rockets by firing them into sandy embankments all along here; there were caves and long, rocky dells.

The snow was coming harder now. When he reached the bottom of the slope, he began to walk along the fence line, staring back up into the dark woods. What was he going to do, search for evidence of nerve gas in every nook and cranny? It would take a hundred men, not one, and it would take time. He had no time.

Who was the enemy? It kept changing: the fascists, the communists, the Germans, the Japanese. But there were no enemies anymore, wasn't that the whole point? America had won. The plant was a relic, as much of a museum piece as a rusted Revolutionary War musket or a pitted Civil War cannon.

He bent for a moment to pull a burr from the cuff of his trousers, and as he did, he glanced back over his shoulder. He spied lights moving slowly through the plant, a good half mile off but moving in his direction. He straightened up and cupped a hand to his eyes. The lights disappeared behind a row of mustard-colored buildings and then reappeared, drifting closer. He could make out the headlights of three vehicles.

It hardly seemed possible that it could be the police. David had heard that the plant kept a skeleton fire crew on the premises for emergencies, but this definitely didn't look like fire trucks.

He lumbered through a field of yarrow and milkweed and clambered back up the steep, rocky slope. A pair of chickadees darted ahead of him, filled with alarming life, dancing from tree to tree. He hid himself under the wide, full boughs of a towering spruce and then peered back through the falling snow.

The cars, he could see now, were all black stretch limos, and they bumped slowly past the warehouse and the salvage yard. They came to a stop about thirty yards shy of the fence, next to a frozen nitro pond. Three chauffeurs got out, as neatly synchronized as three carved gnomes popping out of three Swiss clocks, and moved around to open the doors.

A number of men got out—seven, eight, nine, David counted. The tour leader, an imposingly large man with a shock of white hair, pointed off in the direction of the river and then swept his arm across to the bluffs in the slightly grandiose manner of a high-school band director. No one seemed to be paying him much mind; they all appeared a bit uncomfortable, being out in the snow, and concerned about getting their shoes wet. They were in standard business garb—knee-length eight-hundred-dollar overcoats, either navy blue or gray—and they all had expensive haircuts. The most remarkable thing about the group to David was that three of the men—the three to whom every comment seemed to be directed—were Asian.

seventeen

David stared down through the falling snow at the figures huddled a hundred yards below. When the portliest of the three chauffeurs pointed back toward the still houses, one of the Asian men fished a pair of binoculars from his jacket pocket, raised it to his eyes, and surveyed the receding line of yellow buildings.

After several seconds he swung the glasses around, scanning the bluffs. Suddenly the binoculars stopped their slow crawl. Instinctively David retreated a step. It looked as if the glasses were trained right on him, but surely he was out of range, the canopy of cedar branches more than thick enough to hide him.

The man lowered the binoculars and raised an arm, gesturing. One by one the other men turned to look. Maybe they hadn't seen him. Maybe it was just some limestone outcropping that had gotten their attention, or the rail line further up the hillside. There was no way of knowing for sure, but David wasn't taking any chances.

He backed slowly out from under the drooping cedar branches and half slid, half stutter-stepped down a shallow ravine. He began to run up the rocky throat toward the ridgeline, bending low, stopping every thirty yards or so to catch his breath. When he reached the railroad tracks, he looked over his shoulder and saw that the stretch limousines had disappeared. He didn't know if that was a good sign or a bad one. If the men had seen him and called the police, he knew he had no chance, not on foot.

He trudged along the rail line, his hands thrust deep in the pockets of his jacket. He had never felt so alone. He had gotten what he deserved. He had run from the police, run from anyone who would have helped him.

Far off in the woods he could make out the broken walls of what he guessed must have been an old quarrying operation. This was part of the bluffs he had never seen before. The snow continued to fall steadily and everything was very still.

He had walked a mile or so along the tracks when the sound of running water made him lift his head. On the slope below him was a partially frozen stream, bordered by dense blackberry thickets. He left the tracks, wading through the bushes with his arms held high. Hanging upside down from a bramble at the edge of the stream was a tiny, frozen sparrow, its claws, even in death, still clenched tight to its perch.

David knelt on the snowy bank and drank several handfuls of icy water. When he'd slaked his thirst, he sat back on his heels, resting, staring at the rippled surface of the water. His gaze gradually drifted upstream, where the swiftly moving current foamed around a partially submerged log. Except it wasn't just a log; impaled on the splintered branches was the half-eaten carcass of a deer.

The animal must have been dead for several days; the exposed hindquarters were frozen and dusted with snow, but the head was totally submerged in the stream. The eyes had been gnawed away, as well as the soft meat around the nose, giving the carcass the demeanor of a snarling, rabid dog.

David put a fist to his lips. He rose to his feet and stepped back from the stream, trying not to puke. He spat again and again, as if that might somehow cleanse his mouth. He turned and stared at the tiny frozen sparrow, still swaying from the brambles like a small brown coin purse.

What was this place? He snapped a dead branch from a mammoth oak and surveyed the uneven ground around him. He poked at one small mound—it was nothing but grass—and then poked at a second—all leaves and rotting bark. But when he jabbed at a third mound, he heard a solid thunk, like an eight iron hitting a golf ball.

He got down and brushed the snow away, uncovering the scattered bones of a small mammal, a squirrel or a rabbit, he wasn't sure. He searched for several minutes more, swinging the oak branch through one ice-glazed protuberance after the other, and discovered four more caches of bones: the shattered skull of a young fox, the wing of a large bird with some of the velvety black feathers still attached, the perfectly intact pelvis of another deer.

He turned and scrutinized the hillside covered with blackberry bushes. He stared steadily for a full minute, then two, until a shape began to emerge from beneath the dense tangle of thorns. Halfway up the slope there appeared to be something like an Indian mound, only larger than any Indian mound he'd ever seen, and boxier.

He thrashed his way through the thicket to the top of the mound. He cleared away some of the brambles, stomping them flat with his boots. He knelt and whisked away the snow with his hand, exposing sodden brown leaves and frozen earth. He patted his pockets, reached down, and took out the Swiss army knife he'd stolen from Joann's studio. He opened the biggest blade he could find and began stabbing at the icy ground.

It was slow work, but he kept at it. When the blade folded on him, nearly slicing his thumb, he put the knife away, switching to his dead oak branch. He used it the way a farmer might use a post-hole digger, raising it with both hands and plunging it downward into the shallow depression he'd carved out, stopping from time to time to scoop out the slowly yielding soil.

It took him a good ten minutes before he hit metal. He tossed the branch aside and went back to work with the knife, scraping and digging, gradually exposing an oval of corrugated steel.

He closed the knife blade and wiped at his mouth with his wrist. In spite of the cold, he had begun to sweat. He stood up and scanned the mound dropping away from him on either side like the great curving back of a whale. It was clear to him that he was standing on some kind of bunker.

He retrieved the four-foot length of branch and hammered at the rippled metal. The booming echoed in the silent woods, but all his effort got him nowhere. On the fifth or sixth swing, the makeshift club broke neatly in two.

Farther off in the trees a woodchuck slipped across the snow. David stumbled down the slope to what seemed to be the base of the mound, thorns grabbing at his jacket and trousers. If there were an entrance to the bunker, he guessed that it was most likely here, but it looked as if he would have to tear apart the entire hillside to get at it.

As he turned, he nearly tripped across a badly rusted rod in the snow. He bent and picked it up. It looked like something that must have rolled down from the railroad. He tapped it in his open palm. It was a lot sturdier than a broken tree branch, but what he really needed was a bulldozer—either that or a witching stick.

He paced back and forth across the mound, using the metal rod as a scythe, knocking down brambles. It occurred to him that anyone who had seen him striding to and fro, thrashing at the bushes, would have thought him quite mad. He must have passed it three times before he saw it, concealed by snow and sumac: a gentle depression, a small "V" filled with rocks and rubble, where years of erosion seemed to have created a natural sinkhole.

Using the metal rod as a crowbar, he began to pry some of the rocks free. One by one he picked them up and tossed them down the hillside, sent them crashing through the blackberry bushes. Once he got started, he saw that the fissure was much larger than it had seemed at first glance.

He worked mindlessly, like some madly burrowing animal. Every so often he would stop to rake the sides of the crevice with the metal rod, widening the hole. Though the earth was frozen at the surface, a couple of feet down it was wet and slick where water had carved its own narrow, erratic passage. It didn't surprise him. The geology of the bluffs was notoriously unstable; on their summer hikes, it had not been at all uncommon for David and Maya to find two or three new springs where there had been none the year before.

After twenty minutes he stood thigh-deep in what had become

a trench, his trousers and camouflage jacket streaked with mud. The passageway seemed to be corkscrewing into the hillside, but it was impossible to tell if he was headed toward the bunker walls or not. He had no intention of giving up. They had broken into his house, whoever the bastards were; now he was going to break into theirs.

As he wrestled a large quartzite boulder out of the fissure, his right foot slipped and caught between two rocks. He nearly fell, but still managed to hoist the boulder onto the slope, where it rumbled slowly through the blackberry bushes and came to rest next to the stream.

David leaned against the side of the muddy trench, staring blankly at his trapped foot. He tugged, gently at first, and then harder, without success. He cursed softly. The metal rod lay in the snow, seven or eight feet away, just out of reach. For weeks he'd managed to elude police, dogs, and helicopters; what a hell of a way this would be for it to end.

It took him a minute to gather his wits, to realize that the solution was a simple one. He knelt as best he was able, undid the laces, and wagged the cracked leather tongue back and forth to loosen everything as much as he could.

He stood and tugged again. The results were no better than before. His ankle throbbed; he hoped he hadn't done anything worse than twist it. His breath hung in great white clouds in the freezing air. He rested for a moment, then leaned back, gritted his teeth, and gave one last yank. His trapped foot popped out like a cork from a bottle.

Hopping on his good foot, he retrieved the metal rod and went to work, jimmying loose the rocks around the trapped boot. What he succeeded in doing was accidentally poking the scuffed footwear and sending it tumbling down into a still-deeper crevice.

"Well, God damn!" he muttered. He was turning goofy with fatigue. He got down on his knees and peered stupidly into the narrow cranny. Eight or nine inches down, the boot had come to rest, not against rock, but against a section of an olive green metal doorjamb.

He retrieved the boot, pulled it on and laced it up with trembling fingers. The snow was coming harder. He went to work with a fierce new energy. It took him another fifteen minutes to clear away enough rock and dirt to expose a sizeable triangle of the bunker door.

He lowered himself into the muddy pit and began to kick at the olive green metal. On the third blow, he heard the ancient metal groan; on the fifth, it began to give, the upper left hand corner of the door curving back from the frame like the lid on a tin of sardines.

Once several of the rivets had torn free, David was able to bend the metal with relative ease, creating more than enough space to crawl through. He stepped back, puffing his cheeks. He had no idea how far down the floor of the bunker was. If he did drop down into the darkness, what guarantee was there that he could climb back out? And what would he be dropping into? Whatever had created this animal boneyard was no doubt down there, in even more concentrated doses.

But what other choice did he have? To clear away the entire door of the bunker would have taken another couple of days of digging, and he was tired of digging. His knuckles were raw and the muscles in his back and arms drum-tight.

He remembered the matches in his pocket. He took them out, lit one, and held it as far into the inky black opening as he could reach. He strained to see beyond the tiny halo of light, but could make out nothing but more yawning darkness.

He tossed the smoldering match into the snow behind him. He owed it to his daughter to find out what was down there. He wanted to know beyond a shadow of a doubt. If it was dangerous, could it be any more dangerous than what was already out here, in the water that had killed these animals, in the water he'd swallowed himself?

He went in feetfirst, like a timid swimmer afraid of the water, lowering himself inch by inch, feeling with his boots, hoping to find a toehold on the inside of the bunker door. He found none.

He closed his eyes, muttered a brief, jumbled prayer, and let himself drop. To his surprise, the floor of the bunker was just another couple of feet down. He stumbled to his knees when he hit.

He reached a hand out tentatively, first to his left and then to his right. Though he knew there was still a dim triangle of light somewhere over his shoulder, the darkness seemed about to swallow him. He could hear a slow, echoing drip of water.

He fumbled in his pocket for the book of matches. He tore one free and quickly struck it. It turned out to be pretty much of a dud, fizzling for a couple of seconds before going out, but those two seconds were enough for him to make out the pale oblong shapes hanging from the curved roof of the bunker. David's first thought was that they were somehow alive, that he had walked into a den of great hibernating bats. Before he could have another thought, the match was out.

He quickly lit another. In the steadier light, he stared at row upon row of rockets suspended from what looked like sturdy metal wine racks. The rockets were all two and a half to three feet long, and a number of them had "USCC" stenciled on them in block letters. It took a minute to figure that one out: United States Chemical Corps.

He moved under them, staring up at the tapered nose cones. He could see tiny rivulets of water racing like frightened mice along the rusted metal seams in the ceiling and, further back, a place where a tree root had actually broken through, white tendrils grasping at the air.

David felt something sting his thumb. He gave his hand a quick instinctive shake, tossing the burnt-out paper stub aside. He lit the third of his matches. He spied, in the corner, a crumpled pack of Chesterfields and a grey, paint-stained work glove, the kind his father used to wear. How long had it all been here? Forty-five years, if Albert was right, but it could have been even longer.

The air had a strange pungency to it, like an old grain silo. He tossed the glove aside and lifted the flickering match up as high as he could; the tips of the rockets were still a good two feet above his head and as softly rounded as the noses of baby seals. This time he tossed the tiny sulfurous flame away before it burned his fingers.

He felt for his matchbook and flicked open the frayed cover. He had just one light left. He tore it free and scraped it across the rough graphite strip without success. He tried a second time with the same result. A drop of something cold splashed on his forehead.

Rattled, he wiped his forehead with the sleeve of his jacket. He tried the match again and this time it caught. He held it aloft, but had trouble keeping it steady. Maybe it was just his imagination, but the spot on his forehead seemed prickly, even a little numb.

He took a step backwards and nearly fell. Instinctively he put a hand out to catch himself and dropped the match. It fizzed and winked out in a damp spot on the floor. He could feel his heart speeding up; it was as if he'd suddenly drunk twenty cups of coffee.

He turned. The triangle of sunlight at the upper corner of the bunker door was blurred, and everything swayed as if he were standing on the deck of a ship. He began to run toward the triangle of light, but without warning his knees buckled and he pitched forward, landing on his open palms in a thin puddle of water.

He staggered to his feet. He tried to wipe his hands on his trousers, but his trousers were sopping wet now. It was all poison; everything was poison. He begged God not to let him die in this hole.

Standing on tiptoe, he could just reach the bent corner of the door, first with one hand and then with the other. He pulled himself up, his boots scrabbling on metal and finally finding a toehold on a wooden crossbar. His ears rang and his muscles were like jelly. He rested for a moment and then heaved himself toward the dim winter light. His jacket caught on a jagged edge of metal. He could hear it rip, but he was in too precarious a position to do anything about it. He gave one final lunge, and suddenly he was out, gasping on the muddy rocks.

He scooped up snow, rubbing it on his hands, face, and neck. His head felt as if it were about to explode, and his vision was blurred. Mucus poured from his eyes and nose. Why he wasn't dead already, he didn't know. He got to his feet and careened like a drunk, pushing his way through the blackberry bushes to the stream.

He quickly tore off his jacket, shirt, and undershirt and flung them away. He bent over the creek, plunged his arms in up to the shoulders, and then ducked his whole head in. The shock of icy water was more than he could stand; he pulled back and roared into the silent woods. He fumbled for his undershirt and rubbed his wet hair with it, then shook out his jacket and wrapped it around him.

He sat at the edge of the stream, clutching the lapels of the thin coat, his teeth chattering. He tried to slow down his breathing, even though he knew that will had nothing to do with it; what it had to do with now was what was being fired across a billion tiny nerve endings. Ten yards upstream the dead deer seemed to be staring at him curiously with his gouged-out eyes.

He could feel himself getting sick. He finally crawled to the base of a tree and propped himself up against it. He closed his eyes and listened to the gurgling water. What a strange place to die this will be, he thought, among all these bones. He tried to remember the faces of his wife and daughter, but all he could see were pinwheels racing like Roman chariots across a dark field.

He must have passed out, because when he opened his eyes again, he was lying on his side, his cheek pressed to a rotted slab of bark. A crow called from somewhere deep in the trees. David pushed himself upright. There was a tiny spot of blood in the snow. He wiped the mucus from his nose and eyes and briefly inspected the flecks of red on his fingertips.

He was still weak, but his breathing was almost normal and his vision was clearer than it had been. He shivered uncontrollably. He got to his feet. His left leg was numb, but after he hobbled a few yards, it got better. He retrieved his shirt, put it on, and then slipped into his jacket. If he was going to survive, he knew he needed to keep moving.

eighteen

He shambled up the slope, just trying to put one foot in front of the other, trying to draw one breath and then the next. He had no idea how much time he had before another spasm might send him sprawling face forward in the snow. He kept waiting, but for whatever reason it didn't come.

He followed the rail line for more than an hour. From time to time the tingling would return to his left leg, and he would start to sweat, but then it would pass. His nose and eyes continued to run. A light wind came up from time to time, swirling the snow around him, almost as if Maya's spirit was hovering, brushing his face, whispering things to him he couldn't quite make out. Once he thought he heard the flapping of a helicopter, far off, but the sound quickly faded. Maybe nobody's after me anymore, he thought. Maybe they've all given up. Maybe there's a Packer game on. He tried to remember what day it was, but couldn't.

The next step was to tell the world what he'd found—policemen, lawyers, judges, journalists, anyone who would listen. The trick was to not get himself shot first.

When the tracks ascended to the top of the bluffs, David could finally see the surrounding farmland—the distant silos, the vast white cornfields, a light twinkling in a far off machine shed—but he still had no clue about his location. The snow had not let up, and a late-afternoon gloom seemed to have settled over the entire earth.

In his dazed state, it seemed as if it were all slipping away from him like a ship cut loose from its moorings: his whole life, this world that he had known and grown up in, this midwestern world of farmers, and the sons and daughters of farmers, with their Christian forbearance and Scandinavian silences and delicate kindnesses, this Cold War world, this white-bread world. It receded like the Ice Age had receded, leaving behind its own rubble, its broken citadels and buried secrets, leaving him stranded on this terminal moraine, high up in the mist and the rocks. In the dirty suburban slush of Westchester how he had yearned for the clean, white expanses of this place! But in a few more decades, all the weather experts said, there would be no more winter at all.

After a few hundred yards, the tracks dropped off the ridgeline into a grove of sugar maples. Fifteen or twenty minutes later, David caught a bit of movement out of the corner of his eye, but when he turned to stare at the frozen marsh off to his right, everything was still. He waited for a moment or two, scanning the cattails and the purple loosestrife, and then he saw it again.

On the far side of the marsh, a small weasel, its front paw caught in a snare, thrashed this way and that, trying to free itself.

What was it that Larry Gillette had said? "No one has trapped here for years." David guessed that showed how much he knew. He remembered the vial of yellow liquid he'd found in the overturned snowmobile.

The animal was exhausted. It would fight the wire furiously, writhing in the snow, and then stop and rest, lying on its side, panting. As far as David could tell, the copper wire seemed to be wound around a nearby sapling. It was all so cruel and pointless. What could a weasel pelt be worth? To anybody?

David felt for the Swiss army knife in his pocket. He was three steps down the embankment before the worn-out animal finally raised its ears, staring at him with tiny black eyes. David could see a spattering of blood on the snow; the weasel had been trying to bite off its own paw, to gnaw its way to freedom.

The sound in the beginning was so small and so distant that David scarcely noticed it—it was like the low intermittent whine of a gnat—but it didn't go away. Instead it grew louder and more insistent, finally becoming recognizable: it was the drone of a snowmobile, somewhere in the woods below him. The weasel had heard it too, lifting its mangled paw and sniffing the air.

David turned, looking for a place to hide. On the far side of the tracks was a low quartzite cliff topped by a dense stand of birches. He moved quickly up the slope, scrambled over the rocks and found a place where he could lie down among the spindly white trees and still have a view of the marsh below him.

It was another three or four minutes before a blue and white snowmobile finally flitted out of the dark woods. It slowly circled the trapped weasel and came to a stop on the marsh bank. The driver stepped out. He had on a bulky olive green parka, and a red scarf was wrapped over his nose and mouth. He approached the animal warily, something small and dark hanging from his left hand.

The wounded animal edged away from him, its back arched like a cat's. When the man reached down for the copper wire, the weasel leapt at him suddenly, sinking its teeth into the sleeve of the heavily padded coat. The man spun around, pulling the animal off with his free hand, and then stumbled backwards into the snow and fell on his rear.

It had been an amateurish mistake, but now the man's adrenaline was flowing. He got to his feet and moved in cautiously, feinting with the short black club. He whiffed on his first couple swings, when the weasel hopped to one side and then the other, but connected on his third.

The weasel twitched on the snow. It tried to crawl away, but couldn't use its back legs. The man hit the tiny animal again and again, bashing it down into the freshly fallen powder. David lay on his belly, clutching the papery bark of a birch tree. The thought came to him, unbidden: was this how my daughter died?

The animal had ceased to move. The man bent down and loosened the snare. He lifted the weasel by the tail, walked to the snowmobile, and tossed the dead animal into a gunnysack under the front seat.

The man's scarf had come loose. As he turned to tuck it in, David saw his face for the first time. There was no doubt in the world who it was. It had been nearly thirty-five years, but even though the face was jowlier and unshaven, there was still the odd vacancy in the eyes. It was Vern Zander.

David trudged through the snow, following the packed-down tread of the snowmobile. For a while he could hear the whine of the engine in the distance, but eventually it faded and disappeared altogether.

The trail meandered and looped through the woods, stopping along streams and drainage ditches and narrow rabbit runs through the thickets. Two or three times he spied bits of blood and fur in the snow, broken brush where a dying animal had fought desperately to free itself, but most of the snares were undisturbed. When he found a huge double-spring metal trap lightly covered with leaves at the bottom of a gully, he snapped the jagged teeth with a stick and tossed it into the branches of a nearby tree.

In the bunker, in the flaring match light, David had thought he'd finally understood everything, but now he realized he knew nothing. Everything seemed to fit, yet nothing fit. It had to have been Vern Zander whom he'd chased across the meadow the afternoon of Maya's death. But why would Vern Zander want to kill his daughter? What had Joann said? That Vern had been smart enough to leave and not come back? Some things she got right and some she didn't.

Fatigue was threatening to pull him under. He kept stumbling in the snow and red rings spun before his eyes. He hadn't heard the motor for a long time, and he assumed that Vern was miles out ahead of him, so it took him by surprise when, coming through a dense stand of basswood and red oak, he saw a small shack sitting in the middle of a clearing.

Sparks drifted above the tin chimney, blinking like fireflies in the winter gloom. The blue and white snowmobile was parked next to a giant woodpile, and a pair of chained-up deer dogs lounged in a pen. Just beyond a small garden plot sat a battered pickup.

The shack had a single frosted window; David could see a light on, but he couldn't make out anyone moving around inside. He squatted on his heels among the red oaks, not certain what to do next.

After a moment, the light snapped off and Vern came out, fumbling with the zipper on his jacket. The two dogs roused themselves and trotted to the chicken wire, whining for attention. Vern paid them no mind, crossing the garden plot, pulling himself in behind the wheel of the pickup, and driving off.

David waited three or four minutes, just to be sure, then rose and trudged across the clearing. The dogs gaped at him, uncomprehending, and then began to bark wildly. They charged at him, only to be snapped back by their chains. David knocked at the door. When there was no answer, he let himself in.

He patted along the wall until he found the light switch, then snapped it on. The place reeked of fish guts and stale tobacco. A great pot-bellied stove sat in the middle of the room, and through the cracks in the cast-iron door, David could see the flames billowing upwards.

There was a scarred chest of drawers, a small Formica table, and, on a high shelf, a stuffed beaver, its stitching pulling apart. Old newspapers had been packed into the walls for insulation. A girlie calendar was tacked above an unmade bed, and there were a refrigerator and a sink set in an alcove.

David walked across the narrow room, stepping over old boots and a couple of empty Jim Beam bottles. In the back sink he found the dead weasel and a couple of bloody rabbits iced down in a caramel-colored plastic bucket.

He opened the refrigerator door and knelt down to look. There wasn't a whole lot there: a couple of bars of cheese, milk, eggs, pickles, a discolored head of lettuce. He moved the jars and cartons around, inspecting them one by one, and then, at the very back, he found what he'd been looking for: a cardboard container with six vials of yellow liquid. He removed one of the vials, uncorked it, and took a quick sniff. Urine. Or what had Larry called it? Trapper's oil.

He put everything back just the way it had been, closed the refrigerator door, and stood up. He scanned the room; it was very warm.

He spied some mail on the scarred chest of drawers. He retrieved it and quickly flipped through the stack. There was a two-year-old disability check, an empty envelope from a hospital in Maryland, and a thick packet from Publisher's Clearinghouse.

He went through the drawers, rifling through socks and sweaters, some old Badgers T-shirts. In the third drawer down he found a packet of Red Man tobacco. Behind it, wrapped in a faded turtleneck, was an old Ferragamo shoebox. He sat down on the bed and took off the lid.

He stared for a moment and then began to take out the contents, putting them on the rumpled quilt next to him: the tiny Balinese locket that Maya's first boyfriend had given her, a creased black-and-white photo of Peggy and himself standing in front of the Tetons, a smooth stone from the coast of Maine that used to sit on their windowsill.

Everything in the shoebox came from the cabin. Some of the things David hadn't seen for two or three years. A few he remembered missing; most of it he'd never even noticed being gone.

A dog barked and then barked again. David went to the window. Night had fallen and he could see, high in the trees, a pale flickering light. Someone was coming.

He started to put everything back in the shoebox, but then realized how stupid that was. What was he going to do? Run? He picked up a stick of firewood from the stack next to the pot-bellied stove, snapped off the light, and stared out through the frosted glass.

A minute later the pickup bumped into the clearing. Vern got out of the truck with a couple of six-packs under his arm. He walked over to the pen and rattled the wire, saying something to the eager, tail-wagging dogs. He turned finally and trudged, head down, toward the shack. David flexed his fingers on the splintery stick of firewood. Ten paces from the front door, Vern stopped and surveyed the snow. He put the two six-packs down and glanced at the window. He had seen David's tracks.

With an almost laughable pretense of casualness, Vern moved off to his left, disappearing around the corner of the shack. David glanced wildly around the room, looking for a place to hide, looking for a real weapon. There had to be guns here somewhere, but where? He gaped at the back door; if Vern was coming in after him, that had to be the place he would most likely enter.

David moved quickly, wedging himself into the corner between the back door and the sink. Several seconds later he heard a soft thump, very close, as if someone had just moved up onto the back porch. There were scrapings and creaks, as if something was being taken out of a closet, and then, just inches from his ear, the unmistakable clicking of a gun chamber opening and closing.

What came next was utter stillness, a quiet so complete that David could hear the gentle shifting of the logs burning in the stove. Nearly a minute passed. David didn't know what to make of it: either Vern had vanished in a puff of smoke, or he, too, was waiting and listening, his ear pressed to the rough two-by-four that separated them. David worked his fingers on the raised stick of firewood to keep them from going numb. A bead of sweat rolled down the inside of his arm. It felt as if it was a hundred degrees in the tiny shack.

The silence was so excruciating that when he finally heard a single soft tick, at first he thought it was just his imagination. But when he looked down, he saw the doorknob moving, a little to the right and a little to the left.

The door flew open and Vern hurtled into the room, a shotgun raised and cocked at his shoulder. His focus was all ahead of him, and he was two strides past David before he realized he'd overshot his mark. He tried to swing the gun around, but he wasn't quick enough.

David clubbed him alongside his face with the stick of firewood. The glancing blow was enough to send Vern sprawling. The shotgun went off, the sound deafening in the enclosed space.

David jumped on Vern's back, trying to pin him, as cheap insulation floated down from the ceiling like tickertape in a Wall Street parade. The shotgun had spun across the floor, out of reach.

It was not a fair fight. David was too banged up to play superhero and Vern was alarmingly strong. David held on for dear life, but Vern kept bucking, trying to scrape David off against the potbellied stove, the side of the bed, the wall. David could feel his grip giving way. Outside, the dogs were baying. With one giant heave, Vern slammed David down on the woodpile.

For a second David was sure his spine was broken. He rolled onto his side, gasping for air. He tried to crawl away, but Vern tackled him, flipping him over the way he might have flipped a dead mink.

Pressing his knee in David's chest, Vern retrieved the shotgun and poked David's temple with the end of the barrel. David winced, closing one eye.

"What the hell was that for?" Vern cried. "What did I ever do to you?" Blood trickled from the corner of his mouth.

"You killed my daughter."

"It wasn't me." Insulation still drifted down around them like confetti.

"What do you mean, it wasn't you? If it wasn't you, who was it?"

Vern stood up, breathing hard, and backed off a couple of steps, the shotgun still trained on David. Vern wiped the blood from his chin. He looked troubled for a moment, running his tongue around inside his cheek, then reached inside his mouth and gingerly removed a long yellow molar.

He held the bloody tooth up for inspection. "Look at this! Look at what you did!" He sounded as if he were about to break into tears.

David propped himself up on an elbow. "I saw you run out of my cabin," he said. "You tried to run me over with a snowmobile."

"I know, but it wasn't me that killed her." He put the finger back in his mouth, making a quick dental examination. "Jesus Christ, now what am I going to do?"

"If it wasn't you, who was it?"

Vern retreated another two steps, turned, and spit a mouthful of blood into the sink. "Somebody. A man." The beaver grinned from its shelf, button eyes gleaming.

"What do you mean, a man?"

"I saw him."

"How could you see him?"

"I was upstairs."

"In the cabin?" David asked.

"Yes." Vern wiped his tooth on his trousers, rueful.

"Doing what?"

"Hiding."

None of it made sense. Vern sat down on the bed and rested the shotgun across his knee. A welcome stream of cool air poured in through the hole in the ceiling left by the shotgun blast.

"You saw this man hit her?" David asked.

"No. But I heard. I heard them fighting. I heard her cry out . . ."

David sat up, clasping his hands around his knees. He's lying, David thought, he's lying to save himself. At the same time he thought, Vern never was smart enough to lie.

"And what did you do?" David asked.

"I was afraid. I didn't do anything. Not until he left the house." Vern dug down in his pocket, retrieved a jumble of keys on a key chain, and tossed them on the Formica table.

"And then?"

"I went to the window." With his tongue, Vern mournfully probed the hole where his tooth should have been. The last thirty years had not been kind to Vern. With his swollen jaw, a couple days' stubble, and stringy hair going every which way, he looked like one of those whipped dogs you see trotting along the turnpike.

"He was right below me," Vern said. "He had a ski mask on, a pale blue ski mask . . ."

David felt something tighten in his chest. "So you didn't see his face?"

"No."

"Was it a young man or an old man?" He wiped at his eyes with a knuckle; they had started to run again.

"I couldn't tell."

"Was it Danacek? Come on, Vern, you remember Danacek. You remember how he used to move. He's a big guy . . ."

"I don't know."

"Was it Chet Carswell?" Something whirred in David's left arm.

"I don't know who Chet Carswell is! I told you, I don't know. It was a man in a blue ski mask! That's all I saw!"

David leaned forward, one hand on the floor to steady himself. The dogs had finally stopped barking. "This man. After he left the cabin. What did he do?"

"He went behind the garage and when he came back, he had a pair of skis. He put them on and then he just pushed off down the hill. He moved like the wind . . ."

"And what did you do?" The dark cabin had begun to flicker with strange light.

"I went downstairs. I saw her lying there. . . . I'm sorry. I'm so sorry."

"No, go on."

"I didn't know what to do. I was scared. I went to the bathroom and got a towel, and I put it under her head."

"And why did you do that?" David leaned forward, pressing his hands between his knees, trying to control the ticking in his bladder.

"I thought maybe it would stop the bleeding."

"You mean she was still alive?"

David could see the panic in Vern's eyes. All his life, people had been tricking him into saying the wrong thing. "I don't know."

"Was she breathing?"

"No." Under his knitted brows, Vern's eyes looked like badly smeared jelly.

"I'm afraid I don't understand."

"I told you. I don't know why I did anything. I was just so scared. I went into the kitchen. I thought I should call somebody, but I was afraid nobody would believe me . . ."

"And then what?"

"And then I heard a car . . ." Vern was still talking, but somehow it had all turned to gibberish. Was he explaining where he'd hidden? There was something about his sleeping bag. What did his sleeping bag have to do with it? There was something about glass breaking. David's nose was running; he wiped at it with the side of his thumb. The Jim Beam bottles glimmered like precious diamonds. He felt his brain corroding. He had finally found someone who could tell him about how his daughter died, and he couldn't understand any of it.

He pushed to his feet. Vern swung the shotgun around, but when he saw the puddle on the floor, his face crinkled in disgust. "Jesus!"

David lurched to one side as if he'd been kicked by a horse. He reached for the bed, trying to regain his balance, but missed and crumpled to the floor. The poison had him in its jaws and was shaking him like a dog shaking a rat.

Vern stood over him, watching him flop; finally he'd found someone weirder than he was. David's head sang. The last thing he remembered before he lost consciousness was Vern wrestling to open David's mouth, trying to keep him from swallowing his tongue.

When he came to, Vern was gone. David had no idea if ten minutes had passed or ten hours. He stared up at the newspapers insulating the walls, thinking he was too weak to even lift his head, but after a moment, the room steadied around him.

He rolled onto all fours, put a hand on the Formica table, and rose to his feet. The fire in the pot-bellied stove had died to embers. He knew he would not be able to survive a third attack. His eyeballs felt as if they'd been scraped by a Brillo pad.

He hobbled to the sink, wiped his wet trousers with a dirty dishrag, and washed the dried mucus from his face and neck. He retrieved a mug from on top of the refrigerator and stood at the tap, drinking and drinking, until it felt as if he'd downed a gallon. Through the window he could see that the snowmobile was gone, but the truck was still there, outlined against the dark woods. Turning, he spied the mass of keys still on the table. There was no way of knowing if Vern had gone for help or just fled, but either way, he had not left David stranded.

The dogs bounded to the chicken wire, whining for food, as David left the shack. The truck was a mess, upholstery in ribbons, but the good news was that it started on the first try.

David followed the tire tracks, his headlights flitting down an endless gauntlet of trees. The cab reeked of unnameable animal fats. He had no idea where the road would lead, but sooner or later he figured it would have to lead him out.

Like snowflakes, bits and pieces of what Vern had told him began to settle. Vern had been hiding in the house; perhaps he'd even been living there. What mattered was that he'd seen the murderer skiing away from the cabin, a man in a pale blue ski mask, moving like the wind. It couldn't have been Seth. Seth wouldn't have given a damn about the reports of nerve gas; he might have even been glad. The person it could have been was his father.

A white owl flapped through the trees as if drawing him on into a dream world. Cold air poured through the holes in the floor of the rattling truck. His mind was still not right. David popped the clutch as the truck began to ascend one of the bluffs; the gearshift was so loose it was like waving a wand through water. Beyond the crest of the ridge, he could see a pale nimbus of light. The wipers clacked, out of sync.

When he came to the top of the bluff, the valley opened beneath him. He tapped the brakes, easing the truck to a stop. Leaning forward, he wiped at the fogged windshield with an open palm. To his left were cornfields and the impenetrable winter darkness, but to the right was Sentinel Bluff, the resort lit up like Coney Island on the Fourth of July.

Torches dotted the ski slopes, and the cars coming off the interstate were lined up for nearly half a mile. There were people in evening dress getting out of stretch limos in front of the hotel, and police with orange batons, spaced out every thirty yards or so, were waving the traffic through. There was some sort of commotion as well. David was too far away to be sure of what it was, but it looked like protesters, a handful of people with signs, yelling at the cars as they turned into the parking lot.

The spectacle of it all baffled David for a minute, but then he remembered the newspaper on Albert's desk at the water park. Tonight was the night. The night all the interested parties would celebrate the closing of their long-awaited deal.

David sat for two or three minutes, just staring. If it was just a doctor he was after, he was sure there was a doctor there, in a crowd that size. But if it was Carswell he wanted, Carswell would be there too. The hotel glowed like a beacon.

He turned out his lights, rolled the truck another couple hundred yards down the slope, and parked alongside the remains of a collapsed hay barn. He got out and crossed a barbed-wire fence into a pine grove. Scattered among the trees were a series of small chalets with scalloped Hansel and Gretel shutters. As he got closer, he could make out, at the base of the ski slope, several massive snow sculptures. He could hear the booming of a drum.

He passed through the trees and stopped at the far edge of the woods, staring at the front of the hotel. Ruddy-faced men in their Sunday suits and women in ball gowns scurried up the steps. Cordoned off a safe distance away were the demonstrators. Some were Indians; others, long-haired young whites with caps pulled down over their ears. A portly man in a feathered headdress stood on a snowbank, pounding on a painted drum. David was only able to make out a couple of the sodden, hand-lettered signs—BRING BACK THE BUFFALO and YOU CAN'T SELL WHAT YOU DON'T OWN—WE WANT OUR LAND BACK.

It was going to be no mean feat, getting inside. There was a kitchen entrance around the back, but unless he found a bucket to put over his head, there wasn't a person in there who wouldn't recognize him. The other choice was to wait it out, try to catch people as they left, though there was no telling when that might be.

A county sheriff's van rolled past the demonstrators and made its way around the side of the hotel. Its headlights flashed across the trees. David turned, retreating, afraid of being spotted, and began a stroll of calculated ease into the safety of the woods.

On the porch of one of the chalets was a row of snow-encrusted boots and, sitting on a picnic table, a set of gloves and a ski mask. It took a second for the idea to register. If a ski mask had been disguise enough for Maya's murderer, why shouldn't it be good enough for him?

The chalet's outside light was on, but inside everything was dark. He scanned the other units. From one of the larger cabins, farther back and obscured by the pines, there was the jangle of Garth Brooks's music, but all the others were silent.

David strode quickly onto the porch and scooped the ski mask off the picnic table. He vaulted over the railing into the snow and hurried down a shoveled path. He stopped finally at an ice-coated swing set, his head pounding. He pulled on the ski mask, the cold, rough wool scraping over his still-healing flesh.

nineteen

Through a stand of young birches he could see the rear of the hotel and the door to the kitchen. Soggy cardboard boxes with "Moët & Chandon" stamped on the sides were piled high in an overflowing dumpster. The sheriff's department van was nowhere in sight. David trudged across the snow to the kitchen door and stared in. A trio of gawky teenage girls wobbled down the corridor, lugging massive steel vats; a corpulent man in a stained apron herded them along with wagging hands. The three girls disappeared through a set of swinging doors. The man in the stained apron held one of the doors open, shouting further instructions, and then, realizing that teenagers should never be trusted, disappeared inside himself, leaving the hallway empty.

David opened the glass door and moved quickly down the hallway. As he passed the kitchen, he could hear the clanging of pots and pans, the hiss and sizzle of the grills. The service elevator was just ahead, right where he remembered it, waiting for him.

He stepped inside and scanned the buttons: LOBBY, BALLROOM, MEZZANINE. It was hard to know. He punched MEZZANINE, and the doors slid shut. As the elevator ascended, he glanced at his reflection in the small curved mirror in the upper corner of the car. In his grungy camouflage jacket and ski mask, he looked more like Travis Bickle than some upscale skier from Highland Park.

After a soft ping, the doors floated open. Two white-jacketed busboys were loafing by their metal carts, joking around, but when they saw David, they both fell silent.

"Excuse me," David said, pushing past them, trying to act as if he knew where he was going.

He was on a balcony, looking down at a magnificent ballroom. It looked like something in one of those old hotels built by the railroads in the national parks, complete with great shellacked beams and a roaring fire in a massive stone fireplace.

A couple hundred people had gathered on the dance floor, some in black tie and tails, but most in jacket and ties, their Sunday best, their wives in the middle-aged equivalent of prom dresses. After all the time he had spent alone, the sight of all these people in one spot was nearly overwhelming.

Kingsbury was refilling his glass at the punch bowl. The high school principal and his hefty wife chatted with the owner of the Cadillac dealership. Near the door, Young Burmeister munched on what looked like a chocolate-covered strawberry. The Pit Bull stood next to him, arms folded across his chest, as if he were guarding Buckingham Palace. The manager of the creamery was having an animated conversation with one of the elders of the church, discussing the price of milk, no doubt. Danacek, whom David had not seen at first, he finally spotted sitting on a chair next to the fireplace, leaning on his cane, one leg extended out in front of him; he looked like a man struggling with pain. There was no sign of Carswell.

David strolled to the far end of the balcony. Part of him felt as if he were somehow floating above the room. The more he stared at the people below, the smaller they got.

A sudden clatter made him turn. A boy and his father had just emerged from the elevator and were headed toward him. They had just gotten off the slopes; their bright down vests still glistened with moisture, and the boy, in a green ski mask, struggled manfully with his skis and poles. His father moved on ahead, key in hand, to open their room, which was on a short corridor just off the balcony.

The boy finally gathered his unwieldy bundle under his arm and then, as he turned, spotted David. They stared at each other in their ski masks like two raccoons.

"Jimmy, let's go!" His father had the room open. The boy galumphed across the rug, stacked the skis and poles outside the door, and disappeared quickly inside.

A smattering of applause rose from the floor of the ballroom. David pivoted and stared down. Carswell moved through the gathering tuxedoed, greeting people, reaching across someone's shoulder to squeeze someone else's fingertips. He looked a lot older than he had just a week or so before, and radiance was not coming without effort. His wife was at his side; with her silver tiara and her blonde hair coiled up on her head, she could have passed for a princess in some nineteenth-century novel. She waited, perfectly composed, as her husband worked the crowd. Behind the two of them were a tall, jowly man who looked a lot like the politician, perfectly coifed, and the Asian businessmen David had seen that afternoon at the plant.

As Carswell made his way through the throng, people seemed to rearrange themselves like iron filings shifting on a magnetized field; there was no doubt about whose night it was. Carswell stopped and spoke to a group of local businessmen until someone took him by the elbow and ushered him up to the stage at the far end of the room.

There was a smattering of applause as Carswell stepped to the podium, and then the applause grew. Someone shouted out, "Go, bro, go!" Carswell smiled, tapping lightly on the mike to be sure it was live.

"Thank you. Thank you. I'm glad to see how many of you have braved the storm, because this is a great night . . . a great night for the state of Wisconsin . . . a great night for this town . . . I want you all to enjoy your party, so I'm not going to interrupt you for long, but I just wanted to welcome a couple of people without whom none of this would have happened. First, my good friend and one of the finest governors this state has ever seen, Mr. Stan Woodson . . ." The man with the wonderfully coifed hair raised both hands in the air, acknowledging the fresh round of applause.

"And I would also like you to welcome Mr. Lawrence Kim, the president of Koto Industries, and his associates . . . Mr. Kim, where are you? There you go. . . ." Carswell pointed into the crowd, and Mr. Kim, not as comfortable with working the crowd as the governor had been, gave an embarrassed nod.

"Perhaps I'm belaboring the obvious," Carswell went on, "but when I was growing up here some forty years ago, there was a war going on between Korea and America. Many of the munitions that were produced at this plant were exploded just miles from Mr. Kim's hometown. As children, we always used to read in the Bible about hammering swords into plowshares . . . and although it's taken an awfully long time, maybe we've finally figured how to do that.

"We've gone through a bit of a tough patch, out here in Middle America. Jobs have been lost. Our children have been moving away after high school. Some people claimed that it was over for us economically, that there was no hope. But if there's one lesson I've learned in my life, it's that you don't ever let anybody tell you that it's over. As long as there's the will and heart and the ingenuity, it's never over . . ."

It was an applause line and it achieved the desired effect. Everyone clapped madly; even Danacek, seated near the fireplace, struggled to his feet to join in. Kingsbury, slurping down another glass of punch, slapped at his lapel with his free hand. David gave him a long look, glanced back at Carswell, then back at Kingsbury again.

What was the line again? The one thing Kingsbury had claimed to hear Maya say as she left the stone cottage, the night before she was murdered? "How many times do we have to go through this? It was over then; it's over now."

Carswell stepped down from the podium. David glanced over his shoulder; a security guard stood by the elevator with his arms crossed. David looked quickly back at the ballroom floor. Carswell shook hands with the governor, the two of them heading toward one of the exits. David took a second peek over his shoulder. The security guard hadn't moved. Maybe the two busboys had alerted someone, or maybe the kid in the ski mask had told his dad there was a weirdo in the hallway; either way, this wasn't good.

David crossed the balcony as casually as he could and gathered the pair of skis and ski poles leaning against the wall. He tucked them under his arm and clomped off towards the stairwell.

He moved quickly down the steps, the skis banging at his side. A clutch of locals laughed and talked at the bottom of the stairs: two of the nuns from the Catholic School, the manager at Mr. Gatti's, and old Mrs. Rood on her walker. A woman David didn't know froze at the sight of him in his ski mask, a cheese cube on a feathered toothpick just inches from her bared teeth. David ignored them, scanning the ballroom. Waiters maneuvered through the crowd, balancing trays of champagne on splayed fingers.

Carswell had vanished. David began to panic, but when he turned back, he caught a glimpse of perfectly coifed hair disappearing into an elevator at the end of a long corridor.

David hurried down the hallway. The floor indicator above the elevator read "Four." He leaned the skis and ski poles against the wall and banged open the door into the stairwell. He took the steps three at a time, grabbing at the handrail.

When he got to the fourth floor, he eased open the metal door. He could see Carswell and the governor shaking hands in front of one of the rooms. A legislative aide with the cheeks of a cherub stood watch, beaming, hands clasped behind his back. The governor gave Carswell a friendly cuff on the cheek and then the young aide led the older man away. Carswell watched them for a moment, oddly pensive, and then went into the room. He didn't bother to close the door.

David waited, still catching his breath. The governor and his aide chatted at the elevator. Thirty seconds passed, then a minute. Finally there was a soft ping and the two men disappeared inside the shuddering doors. David pulled off his ski mask and moved swiftly down the hallway.

He slowed as he approached the room. He peered in. Carswell stood in front of a mirror, patting his hair, fiddling briefly with the pin of his corsage. It looked as if there had been a private party here before the big party downstairs. There was an ice bucket, empty champagne glasses perched on every available surface, a tray of abused hors d'oeuvres on the dresser, a black dress coat draped across the bed. David stepped into the room and pushed the door quietly shut behind him.

Carswell spun around, startled and then angry. "What the hell . . ." David tossed the ski mask on the bed. "My God, look at you."

"You didn't think you were rid of me, did you? You must have known I was going to figure it out, sooner or later."

"Figure it out? Figure what out?" Somewhere a band had started to play.

"Somebody saw you, Chet."

Vexed, Carswell ran his palm across his forehead. "I have no idea what you're talking about."

"They were there. Upstairs. He heard you hitting her. He heard her cry out. And when you left, he went to the window and saw you skiing down the hill. You had on a light blue ski mask." Carswell laughed, the sound harsh and incredulous. "You think *that's* funny? I know about the nerve gas."

The smirk on Carswell's face vanished. There were several large baskets of flowers set in front of what looked like a working fireplace, tiny white envelopes tucked in the cellophane.

"She came to your house, the night of your party. You had an argument, out in the stone cottage. She told you what the reports had said. Maybe she gave you some sort of ultimatum, I don't know. She was just twenty-two, compromise wasn't exactly her thing. . . ."

"Reports? I see reports all the time. You think I would kill somebody over a report? I can't tell you the cockamamie theories I've had to listen to about the place up there . . ."

"It's no theory, Chet. I found it."

"What did you find?"

"Up on the bluff." Depleted, David sat down on the bed. "In one of the old bunkers. Rows and rows of these three-foot-long rockets."

"You're making this up."

"Am I?"

Carswell stroked the edges of his mouth with a thumb and forefinger. There was a sadistic pleasure in watching that perfect façade begin to crumble, but David was beginning to grow faint again, the colors of the flowers beginning to pulse.

"You're just like her, you know that?" Carswell said.

"And how is that?"

"You both like to imagine yourselves slaying some dragon, but there is no dragon. We're all on the same side here. Maybe I wasn't as honest with you as I should have been, but there are some things . . . All of us . . . Do you hear what I'm saying?"

"I'm not sure."

"None of us are perfect. I'm not perfect. But we all have to live in the world. We can't all go careening around like Attila the Hun destroying people's lives . . ."

There was the sound of feet running in the hallway, and then fierce pounding on the door.

"Mr. Carswell? Mr. Carswell? Are you all right?" It was Young Burmeister, and his voice was frantic. David and Carswell turned together, looking at each other.

"Go ahead," David said. "Answer it. I don't think I'm the one in trouble here."

Carswell picked up the ski mask and moved slowly to the fireplace. He turned the ski mask inside out, musing. For a moment David thought he was going to come up with something, snatch the poker and make it look as if there'd been a struggle, try something crazy, but when he turned back to stare at David, his eyes were filled with the dull hatred of a small, trapped animal. There was something more he wanted to say, but he never got it out.

"Mr. Carswell!" The hammering grew more insistent. "Are you in there?"

Carswell tossed the ski mask on the bed. He went to the door, opened it, and gestured to David on the bed with an open-handed wave. "There he is. He's all yours."

Crowded in the doorway, the two officers gawked like kids at the zoo, the Pit Bull peering over Young Burmeister's shoulder.

"Jesus Christ," Young Burmeister finally murmured. They were both still winded from what must have been a sprint up four flights of stairs.

David rose to his feet as the two young officers rushed into the room. The Pit Bull fumbled with his holster, trying to draw his gun, but Young Burmeister restrained him.

"I want you to turn around!" Young Burmeister barked at him. "Hands on the wall!" David did as he was told and let Young Burmeister pat him down. "OK, now, hands behind your back!" Again David obeyed. He winced as his arms were yanked together and the handcuffs bit into his wrists, but in some strange way, it almost made him feel safe.

"So what the hell has been going on here?" the Pit Bull said. "Did he threaten you?"

"The man is deranged," Carswell said. "Just get him out of here."

"Oh, we'll be happy to do that," the Pit Bull said.

"And take him down the back way," Carswell said. "It's a mob scene downstairs." The balance of power was off in the room and they could all feel it. David was too unresisting and Carswell too on edge.

"Come on," the Pit Bull said, grabbing David's elbow. "I can't believe you made it so easy for us."

"He killed my daughter."

"What did you say?" the Pit Bull said.

David turned so he could face Carswell again, straight on. "He killed my daughter and I can prove it."

"This is all hogwash," Carswell said. "Honest to God, I've had about all I can take . . ." He was not doing a good job of acting and even the Pit Bull, who wasn't the swiftest guy in the world, could sense it.

"I have a witness," David said. "Carswell killed her because she had the goods on him. Those bluffs up there are poisoned. You're not going to be selling them to the Koreans. You're not going to be selling them to anybody . . ."

David could see uncertainty play across Young Burmeister's face, but the Pit Bull knew what needed to be done.

"Buddy, we'd love to stand around all night talking about things, but I'm afraid we can't do it," the Pit Bull said. "Let's move it!"

As the two young officers hustled him out of the room, David caught a glimpse of Danacek getting off the elevator. Leaning on his cane, the sheriff stared stone-faced at the three of them. In the glow from one of the exit lights, David could see the scars just above Danacek's collar, the marks of the fire.

The two young officers hurried David down two flights of echoing stairs to the basement. They were moving too fast for him to protest, too fast to argue, too fast to do anything but keep from tripping. All the cooks and waiters were lined up in the corridor, staring wide-eyed and solemn as they passed.

A squad car waited by the Dumpster. The Pit Bull clamped a hand on David's forehead and shoved him into the back seat. Young Burmeister slid in next to him and glanced up at the Pit Bull.

"Why don't you call the station and tell them we've got our man and we're on our way in. All right?"

"All right," the Pit Bull said. A policeman with a handlebar mustache hunched behind the wheel; David could see his grave, assessing eyes in the rearview mirror. Young Burmeister slammed the door shut.

"Let's go."

The overhead lights flashed red and blue across the snow as the squad car slowly ascended the slope, following the driveway around to the front of the hotel. A couple of black-hatted chauffeurs leaned against their long black limousines, having a smoke. Several huge snow sculptures were scattered about the front lawn; the intent had been to represent Vikings and bears and Rhine maidens, but the sculptures had melted some, and their loss of definition had only rendered them more mysterious and impressive. Torches still burned high on the slopes.

David twisted in his seat, staring at the hotel. Carswell stood on the front steps. As perfect in his way, David thought, as a plastic bridegroom atop a wedding cake. Carswell raised a hand, signaling to them.

"Slow down for a second," Young Burmeister said.

The policeman with the handlebar mustache tapped the brakes and Young Burmeister cranked down the window. Carswell moved down the steps and across the snowy drive.

Carswell put a hand on Young Burmeister's window. "I just

wanted to say," Carswell said, "it's going to be important to not turn this into some kind of media circus. They're bringing my car around. I'll be right behind you."

"Of course," Young Burmeister said.

David leaned forward, the handcuffs cutting into his wrists. The police car rolled slowly forward and Carswell kept pace. As they dipped down the driveway toward the main road, a derisive cheer went up from the remaining demonstrators. A single policeman leapt up from a snowbank to wave the protestors back. Carswell gave the squad car a final pat and turned away. Lights from the hotel glittered off the great icy gods, the half-melted totems.

"OK, let's step on it," Young Burmeister said.

Thirty yards farther down the driveway, a commotion had broken out among the demonstrators; one of them burst suddenly out of the pack and ran toward Carswell, bent low and hiding something behind him like a quarterback hiding the ball on a bootleg. A green knit cap pulled down nearly to his eyebrows made him hard to recognize at first, but as he sprinted into the glaring lights at the front of the hotel, David could make out the unmistakable chiseled chin, the spoiled, movie-star features: it was Seth.

Carswell wasn't looking. He didn't see his son coming, not until the very last second, not until Seth was nearly on him. It all happened so quickly, but David experienced it almost as if it were a series of slides, luminous and discrete: Carswell's glance over the shoulder; the delight that came into his eyes, as if this were all some sort of grand holiday surprise; someone on the steps of the hotel leaping up, shouting a warning; and then the single swift motion of Seth's arm as he plunged the foot-long knife into his father's back.

Carswell staggered forward a couple of steps, grimacing, both hands reaching for the wound. In his black tuxedo he looked, for just a moment, as if he were performing some incredibly intricate dance step, and then he stumbled and fell on his face.

"Holy Jesus," Young Burmeister said.

Seth started to run down the road, but the policeman who'd been overseeing the demonstrators was blocking his path. Seth turned and began to run toward the ski slope.

Young Burmeister fumbled with his seat belt and finally tumbled out of the police car. Chet Carswell lay curled up in the driveway, utterly still, the stricken valet standing over him.

"Stop!" Young Burmeister shouted. "Stop!" Seth never looked once, lumbering between the eroded snow sculptures.

Young Burmeister unsnapped his holster and took out his service revolver. The other policeman was already in pursuit, his gun drawn. David banged his shoulder against the near door of the police car, trying to open it. The handcuffs seemed to click one notch tighter. The policeman with the handlebar mustache whirled around in the driver's seat.

"Just stay where you are!" he shouted.

Seth had reached the bottom of the slope, and as he started up the incline, he began to slip and slide. Young Burmeister was gaining ground, but the other officer, older, heavier, had slowed to a walk.

Young Burmeister shouted something, but David couldn't make out what it was. The snow kept coming as heavy as ever. The second officer went down on one knee. He wasn't about to be made to look like a fool. He raised his pistol with both hands.

Again David slammed his shoulder into the door. The policeman with the handlebar mustache spun around a second time, furious.

"I told you once!"

"You've got to stop them!"

The first shot missed, but it made Seth stop and look back. He turned and began to run again, trying to zigzag, but as the pitch grew steeper, he kept falling. The second shot hit him as did the third. Seth began to slide down the slope and finally came to rest along one of the snow fences. David leaned his forehead against the cold glass of the window, shutting his eyes.

When he looked up again, he could see three or four young skiers high up on the slope. They seemed to have emerged out of nowhere, and they were clearly novices: a couple of them fluttered their arms, trying to keep their balance. They must not have seen what had happened, because they were headed right for Seth's motionless form, and in the brilliant arc lighting David could almost imagine that they were a band of slightly uncertain angels, coming to bear the prodigal home.

twenty

David opened his eyes a slit. The faces ringing the hospital bed seemed grave, but he quickly sank again into a dream. He was sitting on his haunches, watching the muddy floodwaters scroll by. It felt as if he had been here forever, as if he had never left this place, yet the river raged on, unabated. A scaly pine branch surged past, bucking like a horse, followed by a bobbing milk carton. He hugged his arms to his chest, his trousers sopping.

He rose and began to limp up the slope. Bothered by a stone in his shoe, he stopped and sat down on the wet grass. He undid his laces and shook out his sneaker. The stone was no bigger than a Grape-Nut; he flicked it away with his thumb. When he looked up, he saw a commotion in the water by the far bank, under some overhanging willows. At first he thought it was just a large carp caught in the shallows, but then he saw a stooped figure stagger out of the water, grabbing for the springy branches. It was Andy.

David stood, hopping on one foot. He shouted three or four times, but Andy never heard him. A small knot of people waited for Andy on the shore. David's initial impression was that they were strangers, but they weren't at all. David's father was there, and his mother and Peggy, standing arm in arm with Maya; it was all of his dead. David hobbled to the river's edge, carrying his sneaker in his left hand. He hollered again and again, but it did no good.

His father helped Andy pull his wet T-shirt over his head, and his mother wrapped a white towel around his shaking shoulders. The whole group turned and moved slowly through the thickets, making their way toward the station wagon parked on the road. David could see that the car was packed to the ceiling with suitcases, pillows, and blankets; he remembered that his father liked to start late in the day and drive through the night.

One by one they got into the station wagon. David was ankle-deep in the water, then knee-deep, waving and crying out. The doors of the car slammed in syncopation, and the station wagon began to slide down the road. David put a hand out to steady himself, staggered by the pull of the current. The river murmured around him, as if filled with voices, and then the voices grew clearer.

David opened his eyes again. There was a pair of doctors—the younger wore an elephant-hair bracelet around his wrist, and the older man's head was not much bigger than a rat's. Flanking them were a nurse and a familiar-looking man, bearded and fleshy.

It took David a moment to figure out who it was. Mike. What was he doing here? Why wasn't he in New York? Then it came back to him, his phone call with Annie. Had Mike been here all this time? The four people around the bed talked among themselves, oblivious of the fact that David was awake. He shut his eyes again.

"What these gases do is inhibit the enzymes needed to control the muscles." It was one of the doctors speaking. "The muscles start vibrating and then they seize up altogether. The pupils and the bladder constrict, the tear and salivary glands secrete . . ." David's mind was drifting again, slow and rudderless. "Basically what happens is that the body strangles on its own vital organs."

"So, is he out of the woods?" That was Mike; David could have picked out the Brooklyn accent anywhere.

"Let's put it this way: he's at least to the edge of the woods. His breathing is normal again, and we've got him on antiseizure medication. But I'd like to keep him for a day or two just to be on the safe side."

"Would you mind if I stayed?" Mike again. "Overnight? Here?"

"That would be fine. But you should understand that when he comes out of this, he's not going to be quite himself. There's going to be some irritability, some forgetfulness, some confusion . . ."

"I understand."

"Good. One of us will be back in the morning, but there will be a nurse here all night."

There was a rustling and a shuffling, the sounds of people on the way out, followed by a metallic creak, close by. David opened his eyes again. Mike sat in a green leather recliner by the window, looking like a large, sad bear.

"Hey," David said.

Mike gave a small start. "Hey."

"You all right?"

"Oh, I'm fine. You're the one."

A metal pole stood next to the bed, holding a glistening sack of liquid. "What day is it, anyway?"

"Sunday night."

Everything was hazy to him; his brain felt as riddled as Swiss cheese. All he could remember was gasping for air, going into convulsions on the floor of the squad car, a lot of shouting, the sounds of tires squealing on asphalt.

"So do they know?" David asked.

"Does who know what?"

"The police. Do they know what Carswell did? Do they understand that he was the one?"

"They're coming around." Mike leaned forward, his fingers, as thick as carrots, laced in front of his mouth. "I was over there, talking to them for two hours this afternoon. There's this woman who hid you . . ."

"Joann Meineke."

"Yeah. I spoke to her lawyer. She's in pretty deep shit, but she knows a hell of a lot, and it's helping. Plus, they found some crazy old woodchopper who claims he was there when Carswell did it. The guy may not be playing with a full deck, but he says he actually saw Carswell leaving the cabin."

"He did see him," David said.

"You know that?"

"I do."

Mike seemed skeptical. He rose from the recliner and retrieved his coat from the windowsill. He rummaged through the pockets and came up with a pack of Nicorettes. Mike had been trying to stop smoking for years.

"It's not going to matter anyway," Mike said. "They've got blood samples from the cabin. Apparently Maya put up a pretty good struggle. A window was broken, and they found blood from not just one person, but two. They've sent everything over to the lab and they should have the results sometime tomorrow. They get a match with Carswell, that's it."

Both men were silent. It all felt anticlimactic and unsatisfying.

"So, have you been in Wisconsin all this time?" David said.

"Yeah."

"Why?"

"I suppose at first I thought I could somehow find you, talk some sense into you. Once I got here, I realized pretty quickly that that wasn't going to happen."

Mike seemed strangely muted. Maybe it was just that he was one of those men who are ill at ease in hospital rooms. Mike's true element was the dinner party at which he could hold forth, open two-hundred-dollar bottles of wine, tell gleeful tales of political chicanery. One of the *New York Times* writers had dubbed him "Doctor Dirt," and it was a nickname Mike was proud of.

"But you stayed."

"Yeah. I remembered what you'd told me about Danacek, so I did a little nosing around. Not a very attractive package, that guy, but somehow it didn't make sense to me that he would have done something like this. So I started talking to people. Waitresses, the desk clerk at the motel, these old geezers who have coffee every morning at the drug store."

"And?"

"Everything kept coming back to Seth."

"How do you mean?"

"Don't you always start with the old boyfriend? It's a no-brainer. But no one knew where he was. He wasn't here, and he wasn't in New York. I went to see Carswell and his wife. They were both so cagey; it was clear that they were lying through their teeth."

A sound from the hallway made Mike turn. A young girl pushed an old man past the door in a wheelchair; he was slumped in his seat like a sack of potatoes, clinging to the metal armrests with a claw-like grip.

"So what did you do?"

"Our firm uses people who are really good at this stuff, so I called one of them. It took him maybe two days to find out everything I needed to know. It turned out that Seth Carswell took a flight from New York that arrived in Madison three hours after Maya had been killed. Two days after that, a car was rented in his name in La Crosse, and a week later an accident report was filed with Hertz for the same car up in Duluth."

Mike chewed warily on his Nicorette, as if he were afraid of breaking a tooth. On the wall above his head was an old black-and-white photo of the nuns who had founded the hospital, all looking kindly and Germanic.

"So I drove up and there he was, sitting in jail, serving four days for drunk and disorderly. I made the arrangements to get him out, but the boy was in bad, bad shape. He was happy enough to get out of the hoosegow, but he didn't want to have anything to do with me. It took everything I had to convince him to let me buy him a cup of coffee. But once I did, once we were sitting down in a booth, it all came pouring out . . ."

"So tell me."

Mike scowled, pursing his lips. There was something in the quality of his reluctance that David found a little scary. Mike turned away, tucking his shirttail in his trousers.

"So the day Maya was killed, Seth flew into Madison early in the evening. His father met him at the airport. On the drive home, there was a report on the radio. Seth was beside himself. You can imagine. He wanted to know if his father knew anything. He wanted to know if he had seen her. Carswell was not in a position to deny it—the boy was going to find out anyway, one way or the other—so he said yes, she'd been at the house, just the night before."

Mike hiked up his belt. "So did she say anything, Seth wanted to know. Did she seem frightened? Did she mention if she was going to see anybody else that night? Who did she leave with?"

At the far end of the corridor, a janitor shuffled from room to room, emptying wastebaskets with a maximum of clatter.

"And what did Carswell say?"

"Apparently he finessed his way through it just fine. But Seth was no dummy. The next morning after Carswell and his wife went out for breakfast, Seth turned the place upside down, looking for he didn't know what, something that would tell him something, and he found it, at the bottom of one of his father's filing cabinets."

"And what was that?"

"A letter. From Maya to Carswell."

"And what did it say?" Mike tongued his gum inside his lower lip. "Tell me what it said, God damn it!"

"Here," Mike said. "It's probably better if you read it yourself."

Mike pulled a folded piece of paper from his back pocket and offered it to David. David thumbed it open. The handwriting was unmistakably Maya's, as full and clear as when she was nine. The date at the top of the page was December 3.

Dear Chet,

What more can I say than what I said on the phone? It's over. What went on between us should never have happened. It is without doubt, the stupidest thing I've ever done.

For two months I've been walking around with a knot in my stomach. You told me once that there are certain relationships where the rules don't apply. Wouldn't it be nice if that were true? Maybe you can lead a double life. I can't. Having to lie to people makes me crazy. I feel like such a weasel and so cut-off—from my friends, from my father.

There are still times when I want it all back, what we had together, but then I think about what would happen if Seth or Irina found out. It gives me nightmares. It's not all your fault. I wanted it as much as you, for whatever the reasons. I know it hurts, but, honestly, we should consider ourselves lucky. At least we're escaping with our lives. There will always be a place in my heart for you. Maya

David folded the letter and set it on his lap. An incomprehensible voice blared over the PA system. His eyes blurred with tears.

"I'm sorry," Mike said.

David put a trembling fist to his lips. He was reeling. Of everything he had learned, of everything he'd unearthed, this was the worst. If it hadn't been in her hand, he wouldn't have bought it for a minute. This was not her. Having an affair with an older married man? The father of her ex-boyfriend? There were a lot of things he might have believed about her, but not this.

How could she have been so dumb? Hadn't he taught her anything? But coming up fast behind all the rage he felt was something else, the conviction that he was to blame. He had sent her out into a wilderness, unprotected. It was the story of Little Red Riding Hood, only the father had arrived too late to slay the wolf.

"Have the police seen this?" he asked.

"No," Mike said. "I didn't see any reason why they would need to. I wasn't even sure I was going to show it to you."

David picked up the letter and stared at it again, but the words were like minnows, darting here and there. He was so ashamed. If Maya had been in the room, he would have shouted at her. Maybe he hadn't known her at all.

"So when Seth found this letter . . ."

"It sounds like it was a total debacle. He waited until Carswell and his wife got home. There was a huge shouting match. Seth actually hit his father, knocked him to the floor. Seth told me he might have killed him right there, but his little stepsister came in, weeping and crying. Carswell's wife was there, trying to pull them apart. It was more than anyone could handle. Seth ran out of the house. He took one of his father's cars, drove it to La Crosse, and when it broke down, he rented another one. Went on a ten-day drunk." Rueful, Mike pawed at the back of his neck.

"So he came back with you then?"

"Yes."

"How did you manage that?"

"It wasn't easy. Basically, I browbeat the kid. I told him he'd been acting like a jerk. Shouting at his father wasn't going to solve anything, or punching him in the mouth, or running around and getting ripped. I told him it was time to stand up and act like a man. He needed to go to the police and tell them what he knew. He seemed to understand that. He was a tormented mess, but there was something I liked about the kid." Mike wadded up his gum and tossed it in the wastebasket.

"Coming back was the most dismal car ride I've been on in my life. It was like we were driving through Siberia. Nothing but pine trees and cranberry bogs. Fox farms and freezing rain. I kept checking on the guy. 'You OK?' I'd say to him. 'You still on board with this?' He'd nod and tell me he was fine, though he didn't look too fine.

"We got back into town about five. We stopped at the motel, and I left him in the car while I went to see if I could get him a room next to mine. When I came back out, there was some guy standing next to the window of the car, jawing away. He assumed that Seth was there for the big shindig at the hotel, and he was going on about what a god he thought Carswell was, about everything he'd done for the community, and how proud Seth must have been of him. Seth was just sitting there, looking pale as a ghost.

"After I got rid of this idiot, I took Seth to his room. He could barely speak. I could see how raw it was for him. I told him maybe it would be good for him to take a shower and relax, and I'd go out and get us some food. 'You're not coming apart on me, are you?' I said. No, he said, he was fine, I should go. I'll admit, it passed through my mind that it might not be such a good idea, leaving him like that, but I left anyway. When I got back, he was gone. How he got out to the hotel or where he found the knife, I have no idea."

A cart filled with dinner trays rolled down the hallway, pushed by an orderly in blue scrubs. Mike took one of the plastic cups from the table and poured himself a glass of water.

"How could she have?" David said.

"She was a kid. Kids make mistakes."

"Not mistakes like this. She knew better."

Mike didn't say anything for a long time, swirling the ice around in his glass. "Of course she knew better. But you've got to remember, Carswell was a powerful guy. He was not someone a lot of women said no to . . ."

"Jesus Christ, Mike . . ."

"OK, I'm sorry. But the point isn't whether she made a mistake or not."

"Then, what is it?"

"You see when that letter is dated?"

"December third."

"OK. Figure it out. Two, three weeks after she wrote this, she found out about the nerve gas. Not that it was manufactured here, but it was stored here. That kind of thing was going on with all these big defense operations. She could have backed down. Or she could have waited. She could have gone to some EPA lawyers and let them handle it. But she didn't. She went back and really put it to him. The girl never lacked for guts."

David put his fingers to his eyes, closing them. "Don't spin me, Michael. Please."

"I'm not spinning you! Maybe she wasn't your innocent little six-year-old anymore, but she was brave, God damn it, she was brave! You've got to give her that!"

The rattling curtain made them both look up. A nurse stood in the entrance to the room, a stethoscope around her neck and a blood-pressure cuff under her arm.

"Look who's awake," she said. She was middle-aged, with tight blonde curls and a Scandinavian forehead of major proportions. "I hate to break this up," she said, "But we should probably take your vitals."

Mike stepped out of the way as she came to the far side of the bed. She sat down on a wooden chair, and David offered her his left arm. She wrapped the vinyl cuff around his bicep and pumped it up, fixing the stethoscope to her ears. She leaned forward, as intent as a safecracker, listening to the thudding in his arm.

"This lawyer you talked to? Joann Meineke's lawyer?" David said.

"Yeah?" Mike said.

"How did he seem to you?"

"Competent."

"We're going to have to help her, Mike."

"All right."

"No, I mean it. We're really going to have to help her."

twenty-one

Stocking-footed, Mike snored softly in his recliner. His wallet and car keys lay on the table next to him. David had been trying to go to sleep for an hour. He still couldn't get his mind around what Mike had told him. It was almost too painful to think about, Maya and Carswell being together, the struggles she must have been going through. If she'd only said something to David, if she'd only given him some clue, he might have saved her. But he could see the logic to it. If there was one thing she would have learned from him, it was how to keep a secret.

As he lay there in the dark, it was as if Maya were more powerfully present to him than she had ever been before. She could be, he knew, quick to judgment, merciless, overly theatrical, but so quick, so fresh, so winning, when she chose to be. He could almost conjure her up, with her snarl of black hair and her startling blue eyes, the play of irony across her lips. She was a good girl. The best girl.

Maybe Mike was right. Maybe the point was that, in the end, she had seen through Carswell and stood her ground. It wasn't any ethical lapse that had gotten her killed, it was her fearlessness, but what consolation was that? It wasn't Joan of Arc he yearned for now.

He retrieved the remote control from the side of the bed and punched the power button, remembering to hit "Mute" just in time. The screen crackled and then filled with a giant weather map. A goateed weatherman glided like a ballroom dancer, pointing out the Arctic front moving down through Canada, the snow flurries over Lake Superior.

David was about to snap off the TV when there was a cut to the anchor desk and then a five-second clip of Carswell's wife in her living room, sitting under the Russell Chatham painting. There would be an exclusive interview as soon as they came back from commercial.

David pushed himself up on both elbows, his mouth suddenly dry. He tapped the volume control, edging the sound up enough so that he could hear yet not wake Mike. After a trio of local car-dealer ads, the anchors were back. David gave the volume another quick nudge.

"Tonight our state still reels from the tragic events of the weekend." The hair of the announcer gleamed with too much gel. "Former Governor Chet Carswell stabbed to death by his son, the son shot down as he attempted to flee. There are many rumors, many versions of what happened last evening, much to still be sorted out, but earlier today, KXEW's own Kathy Corlett was able to speak with Governor Carswell's wife, Irina."

It took a couple of seconds for the tape to click in, leaving the anchors hanging, panicky and blank, but then, there it was: the huge picture window overlooking the stone terraces, the roaring fireplace, the antique Italian couch. Two women sat facing each other—the interviewer, teacup balanced on her knee, and Irina Carswell, regal in a black dress and pearls. Everything was as artfully arranged as a stage set. There were two photographs at Irina's elbow, one of her in all her Olympic glory, leaning forward over her skis, soaring into the winter sky, the other of Carswell pushing his daughter on a swing.

"A terrible day," the reporter said.

"Yes, a terrible day."

"How is your little girl taking this?"

"I don't think it's real to her yet. I suppose it's not real to me yet either."

"There are all these stories going around. Some of them are pretty painful, I'm sure . . ."

"Seth was emotionally disturbed. He had been seeing a psychiatrist for a number of years. We tried to help him. We tried everything . . ."

"Some people have claimed that the young woman who was murdered several weeks ago, Maya Neisen . . . was very close to your husband."

Irina pulled herself up with Greta Garbo–like hauteur. "People will say anything. Chet worked with this young woman on an advisory board. What needs to be remembered is how hard he worked for this state and this nation . . ."

"But what is it that you'll remember about him? Can you tell us?"

It took a moment before she could answer. Mike sprawled on the recliner, like a prisoner on a rack, one arm draped over his eyes, the other hanging loose to the floor. His snoring had subsided to a series of gentle flutters. Light from the television licked the green walls of the hospital room.

"What I will remember most is the ten wonderful years we had together."

The reporter smiled, getting cozy. "Tell us where you met."

"In Aspen. Eleven years ago. Almost to the day."

"So did you meet on the ski slopes?"

"On the ski slopes?" The question amused her. "No. Chet's never been on skis in his life."

"Never?"

"Never." Irina brushed a strand of blond hair out of her eyes, as poised as a runway model. "Chet was one of those men who hate to do anything unless they're sure they can be the best at it." In her voice was the unmistakable ring of contempt.

The tape ended and one of the anchors announced that they would be back with sports right after the break. David snapped off the television.

He lay in his tangled sheets, stunned. How could Carswell never have been on skis in his life? It was impossible. What reason would she have had to lie about something like that? Suddenly it came back to him, the moment in the hotel room when he'd told Carswell that someone had seen him gliding away from the cabin. He remembered the incredulous look on Carswell's face, the low snicker. Everything had been there, right in front of David, and he'd missed it: the closet in the stone cottage filled with skis, poles, vests, boots. He had just assumed all of it had been Chet's, but he'd been wrong. There was only one skier in the family, only one person who could have fled down that hill that day.

David watched the night nurse stroll down the hall to the vending machine. The hospital was so still he could hear the quarters tumble through the machine's inner workings, hear the candy bar thump into the metal trough. The nurse stood for a moment, tearing off the wrapper, and then disappeared down one of the side corridors.

He turned to Mike, who was still sputtering in his sleep. For a moment, David considered waking him, then decided not to. David eased into a sitting position and then slid noiselessly out of bed. He slipped into his clothes and boots and then scooped Mike's car keys off the table.

He crept into the hallway, pausing for a moment when he came to the side corridor. Peering around the corner, he saw the night nurse absorbed in her candy bar. He pushed open the door under the glowing EXIT sign and stepped into the stairwell.

He was dizzy and out of breath by the time he reached the bottom of the stairs, and had to take a second before he shouldered through the fire door and into the chill night air. Everything in his body ached. He'd been through more than Rasputin: he'd been run over by a snowmobile, burned, gassed, and shot at, but he wasn't done yet. The plastic tag on the rental keys said TAN—CAMRY, and there was only one Camry in the lot. He crunched across the ice-slicked asphalt. The car's windshield was solid white with frost, and he tried to rub some of it off with his forearm, but there was not exactly time for a thorough scraping job.

He opened the door and slid in behind the wheel. The engine

caught on the first try. Shaking with the cold, he fiddled blindly with the levers, trying to get the heat and the defrost working. He leaned forward, peering around the edges of the icy windshield as he rolled into the street.

He was halfway down the block before he turned on his headlights. The heater was blowing full blast, and the sheet of frost quickly broke up and floated down the glass. He drove past the hill where they had all sledded when they were children, past the Lutheran church and the abandoned brick brewery that they had all thought was haunted. When he got to Main Street, the lights were all blinking yellow. He turned left, moving past the theatre and the old woolen mill and over the bridge where Andy had been swept away such a long time ago.

Just past the river, he glanced in the rearview mirror and saw car lights, half a block back. The car maintained the distance, neither speeding up nor slowing down. David felt a sudden gust of panic, sure it was the police, but then, at the edge of town, the car pulled into the Chevron station.

Suddenly he was in the country, fence posts flying by on either side of him, wooded hillsides looming in the dark. How could he have been so blind? If his hunch was right, at least two people had died for no reason, and he shared in the blame.

It took him twenty minutes to get back to The Narrows. Navigating the route felt like second nature to him now. He threaded the maze of two-lane blacktops, passing the tourist cabins, the fishing shacks, the Laundromat where he'd called Seth's roommate, the two campgrounds.

He parked the rental car behind the hotel, under the wooden bridge—the same place where he'd once left Kingsbury's truck. Before getting out, he checked the glove compartment and was pleased to find a yellow and black flashlight. He snapped it on and off to be sure it was still working, then stuck it in his pocket.

Pulling his jacket tightly around him, he walked back the quarter of a mile to the Tudor mansion that adjoined Carswell's property. There was a station wagon in the driveway and a single lamp burning in an upstairs window, but otherwise there was no sign of life. He skirted the far border of the lawn and crossed the barbed-wire fence into the grove of pines. He moved slowly through the trees, ducking branches. At the edge of the woods he stopped and stared up at the house cantilevered over the frozen waterfall. Everything was dark.

He crept across the snowy garden to the stone cottage. It had a sturdy new padlock, but by going around the back, David was able to jimmy a window open and climb through.

He cupped his hand over the head of the flashlight and snapped it on. In the muted glow, a dozen young Carswells stared down from their picture frames, like portraits of young saints in a Roman crypt.

He tried the closet door. He had it halfway open when there was a great clatter, and he had to reach quickly inside to keep everything from falling. He moved with the caution of a safecracker, setting the skis and poles back in their racks. All he could do was pray that no one had heard.

He fanned the beam of light across the row of coats and down vests. On the shelf above were all the hats and gloves, sweaters and goggles.

He took the hats down one by one, discarding them on the floor behind him. There were red ones and black ones, green ones and gold ones. There were even a few ski masks, but not the one he was looking for. He cursed softly. He began to slide the coats and vests down the metal rod, checking the pockets.

He went through them all, or at least he thought he had. He stood for a moment, all bollixed up, and then, almost as an afterthought, shone the flashlight into the farthest corner of the closet. A tan hunting coat lay crumpled on the floor.

Bracing himself, he leaned in on one foot to retrieve it. He shook the coat out and set it across the back of the chair. The right pocket was empty, but the left one wasn't; he pulled out a ski mask of the palest blue.

It was slick to the touch and tightly knit. He stretched it out between his hands, pulling the eyeholes into narrow slits. Holding it to his nose, he could still detect the faint smell of smoke. He turned the ski mask inside out and shone the flashlight on it; several long blond hairs glistened in the blue fabric.

There was a click, very close, and then an explosion of light. Momentarily blinded, he put an elbow to his face, shielding his eyes. When he was able to take his arm away, he saw Irina standing in the doorway, one hand on the light switch and the other holding a handgun with a monstrously long barrel.

"What are you doing in here?" David set the ski mask and the flashlight on the desk behind him. "How dare you come back here! After all you've done to this family. I have a child asleep up there . . ."

He'd forgotten how tall she was, how physically imposing. She was dressed as if she were about to take off on a midnight jog, in her blue and white running outfit and two-hundred-dollar Nikes, but there was something off about her, something sedated and slurry in her speech.

"You killed my daughter," he said.

She touched her nose, as if the accusation amused her. "Now why would I do that?"

"Because she and your husband . . ."

"Because of their little fling? If I'd had to kill every woman my husband made a pass at, I'd be quite a monster."

She kicked a green wool hat in the direction of the closet; the mess on the floor did not make her happy.

"Someone saw you leave the cabin," David said. "They were upstairs though the whole thing. They saw you get your skis from behind the shed. They said you took off down the hill like a champion."

She cocked her head to one side, almost as if she were flirting with him. "And you're sure it was me they saw?" David hesitated; she was not dumb. "Why didn't you go to the police then? Why would you need to come here?"

"Because I've been wrong so many times before. I needed to be sure."

"I think you'd better sit down," she said. David didn't move. "I said sit down!"

He eased into the swivel chair. There was a folding chair next to the door. She spun it around and straddled it, the move as graceful as a dancer's. She sat, chin resting on her forearm, the gun hanging loose at her side, her gaze dreamy. She nodded at the ski mask on the desk behind him. "Give me that," she said.

He retrieved the ski mask and pitched it underhand. She snatched it cleanly out of the air. She set the revolver on the small table next to her. Staring down at the woven mask, she stroked the fabric as if considering a difficult purchase, and then turned it inside out. Whatever had been playful in her was gone now.

"Smell it," David said. "You can still smell the smoke. It's amazing how hard that stuff is to get rid of. The flue wasn't working very well, remember? By the time I got there, the whole living room reeked of it."

"God damn you!" She threw the ski mask aside and grabbed the revolver. She sprang to her feet, knocking the folding chair to the floor. "God damn you!"

With a single stride, she was at him, pressing the gun barrel to his cheekbone. "I could have shot you the second I saw you. Nobody would have said a thing, you know that?" David leaned back in the swivel chair, both hands raised, his face turned to the side.

There was a flicker of light at the window. She glanced over her shoulder and backed off a step. David could hear the muffled sound of chains, a car passing on the road. Irina went to the window and stared out until she was sure the car was gone.

The mood broken, she leaned against the wall and closed her eyes. David could feel the cold air from the open door whispering around his bare ankles. She slid down along the wall and sat, knees up, gazing ruefully at him. She ran her free hand through her hair. A sound came out of her, something between a laugh and a wild cry. David pressed a fist to his mouth, eyeing her intently. After a moment, she pulled her hair back and rested her head against the cold stone.

They sat that way for a long time. In profile, her face looked like something he might see on an old coin. It was clear to him now that she was going to have to kill him. He didn't know what it was that constrained her. Maybe it was having a sleeping child so close. Maybe it was the sedatives she appeared to be on.

He could see her sinking. She set the gun on the floor between her legs. Carswell beamed down from the walls in all his guises:

the proud Boy Scout, the flushed and triumphant MVP of the state tournament, the crew-cut student body president.

She kept closing her eyes and opening them again. Wouldn't it be something, he thought, if she just dozed off and I could waltz out of here? There was a crash in the woods, a snow-laden branch breaking loose. She opened her eyes and stared at him and then up at the pictures.

"You Americans," she said. Her voice was more slurred than before; whatever she was taking was kicking in big-time. "So sentimental."

"Sentimental about what?"

"About everything. About your childhoods. He would talk about it all the time. What it was like, growing up here. Running around in the woods like some wild Indian." She was silent again for several seconds. "I never liked living here. You want to go out to eat, what is there? Friday-night fish fry. The only thing people know how to talk about is the Green Bay Packers. But he insisted that we had to come back here. Because he was somebody here. People remembered him."

Again they both lapsed into a long silence. "So when did it start?" David said. "Between Maya and your husband?"

She reached for her neck, grimacing as if she had a crick. "Start? Who knows? In the summer, Seth would bring her to the house from time to time. Chet and I were both charmed by her. Too good for that boy, anybody could see that. When they broke up, we were sad, but it was no surprise."

She picked up the gun and tossed it softly from hand to hand, like a pitcher tossing a rosin bag between throws. "In the fall she would come down from college for their Wolf Center board meetings. Chet suggested that she stay with us, and I was all for it. Some people might have thought it was odd, having your son's ex-girlfriend as a regular houseguest, but she was so much more interesting to me than all the mealymouthed sorts around here. She and I would cook together, go on long walks. Our daughter adored her. Maya would read to her at bedtime, teach her songs. She and Chet would go off for their all-day meetings. At night they'd sit up late around the kitchen table, conspiring . . ."

"You weren't even suspicious?"

"I certainly knew about him and all his women. But with her, it didn't feel like that. She was a part of the family. I know everyone thought she was fierce, but with us she was like a little orphan sometimes."

Outside there was a quick rustling, the strangled cry of a bird, a whirring of wings. "And when did you find out? For sure?"

She pulled her knee a little closer and rested her elbow on it. "Not until the night of our Christmas party. I could tell that there was something terribly wrong, and after everyone left, he came into the kitchen. He was as white as a ghost. He told me everything."

"It must have been difficult," David said.

She gave a short, mirthless laugh. "Difficult? Yes, it was difficult. We had been like sisters. We would tell stories about our old boyfriends. She would braid my daughter's hair. I don't think I've ever been played for such a fool. But, you know, men do these things. Chet certainly wasn't the first. Sometimes in life there are bitter pills you have to swallow. I think we might have been able to get through it if she hadn't intended to ruin him."

"And how was she going to do that?"

"She was going to the newspapers. About what was buried in those bluffs. After everything we had done for her, she was going to destroy us. She wasn't going to listen. You know how she could be . . ." She grabbed the knob of the open door and pulled herself up. "If you could have seen him that night. He looked like a little dog that has just messed on the rug."

"And you told him you would take care of it. That mess on the rug."

"No." She sipped her Dacron jacket tight under her chin. "I said nothing to him. But if it had been up to him, he would have let her do it. He would have lost everything."

There was a sharp, splintering sound, somewhere outside the stone cottage. She whirled, raising the gun. David rose from his chair. Over her shoulder, he could see a dark shadow amid the tilted stakes of the garden.

It was Danacek. He had a gun too, extended in front of him, and he was leaning on his cane. His hat was strapped tightly under the ample folds of his chin, earflaps down.

"Ma'am, I think you better put that down," Danacek said. Irina hesitated and then, after a long moment, lowered her revolver. As Danacek lurched forward, he got a boot stuck in buried chicken wire and had to kick free. "All the way. Just let it drop."

Irina stood motionless, the gun at her side, as Danacek crunched toward the cottage. The sheriff limped into the light. David could see the burgundy-colored splotches on his neck, souvenirs from the fire.

David retreated a step, intending to get out of the way, but he stumbled against the swivel chair and the sound made Irina swing around.

The first shot hit him in the right elbow. He grabbed for his arm, staggering backwards, and then, realizing that she was going to fire again, dove for the far corner of the room. There was a second shot, a shower of glass, a cry, the clatter of wood on stone, the thudding sounds of a scuffle.

It felt as if his elbow had been smashed by an anvil. He gasped for air, trying not to pass out. When he was finally able to roll over and prop himself up, he saw that Danacek had her pinned against the wall, a forearm to the nape of her neck. His cane lay crossways in the door.

With his good hand, David grabbed the corner of the desk and tried to pull himself up, but he wasn't strong enough. The flashlight tumbled to the floor. Danacek, furious, looked back over his shoulder.

"Don't touch anything, God damn it! Just leave everything the way it is!"

Danacek took her outside. David leaned his head against the wall, elbow cradled to his chest. He heard the voices rising, heard her protest, but the whole world was spinning, words flying into outer space. Eventually there was silence and then the slam of a car door, a good way off.

He stared at the pale blue ski mask, the hats, and the gloves scattered across the floor. One of the framed photographs had fallen, lying just beyond the leg of the swivel chair. It was the picture of

Carswell and his father shoveling peas out of the back of a truck. In the upper-right-hand corner there was now a bullet hole, poised above the canning factory like a black sun.

David began to wonder if Danacek had just left him to bleed to death. The good news was, there didn't seem to be much blood. The bad news was, when he tried to move his arm, the pain was excruciating. All the same, he knew he couldn't stay here. It was important not to let Irina be the only one doing the talking. Using his good arm to brace himself against the wall, he willed himself to his feet.

He shuffled to the front door and bent over to retrieve Danacek's cane. The house at the top of the hill was still dark. He stepped outside. The only sign of either of them was the footprints leading across the snow. It wasn't until he got to the driveway and stared down the alley of pines that he spotted Danacek's Jeep Cherokee on the main road.

David teetered along the driveway. Danacek leaned against the hood of the car, resting his bad leg and staring in the direction of the hotel. Irina was in the back seat and as David moved closer, he could see from the way she bent forward, arms pulled back, that she was handcuffed. Danacek didn't turn until David was almost on him.

"What are you doing out here?" Danacek said.

"I wanted to see what you were up to." David handed him his cane back.

"How's your arm?" Danacek asked.

"Pretty busted up. But I'll live."

"There's an ambulance coming. They should be here any minute."

One-handed, David pulled his coat more tightly around him. Across the road and through a line of trees, he could see the frozen Otter River and a couple of small, pine-covered islands. In the summer there would be tour boats and water-skiers, but now, in the dead of winter, he could imagine that nothing had changed in a hundred years.

"She's the one," David said.

"It doesn't surprise me."

"Doesn't surprise you?"

"It's a small town. You hear things."

David looked over at him. "So how did you know I was out here?"

"One of the deputies spotted the car leaving town."

"There's a little girl up in the house."

"I know. I just called one of the neighbors to come stay with her." He surveyed the empty road. "I just don't know what the hell's keeping them."

David pushed away from the hood and glanced at the car. Irina rested her head against the glass, but after a moment, sensing that she was being looked at, she roused herself and stared at David, her gaze baleful, unrepentant.

David turned to Danacek. Neither of them spoke for a long time. "You asked me a question," David said. "Back in the cabin. You asked me how I could not have said anything about your brother. How I could have just ridden my bike home, gone off to play baseball . . ." Danacek pulled his heavy gloves on, one by one, frowning. "The reason was that he would not have been up on the railing of that bridge if I hadn't taunted him. I couldn't stand the idea of his beating me at anything. I was just a stupid kid."

"We were all stupid."

"I guess so."

"That's what it means to be a kid, right? To be stupid. I'm going to try these guys on the radio."

"Sure," David said.

Danacek got into the car. There was a gust of wind off the river, a thin swirl of snow. David walked to the front of the driveway and stared up the long slope.

The house was still dark. It was a miracle that Carswell's daughter had slept through all this—the gunshots, the angry voices—but then that was the thing about children: they could sleep through anything. He remembered Maya at that age, how sometimes, coming home late from a school play or a soccer game, she would fall asleep in the car and he would have to carry her in. He remembered the heavy, warm weight against his shoulder. He remembered how he would lay her on her bed, take off her shoes, and pull the quilt over her. He remembered how he would sometimes stand for two or three minutes in the doorway, just watching her breathe.

Stars pulsed in the night sky. The world was silent, crystalline. In a few hours the child in this house would wake. His own would not. All he could do now was pray that there was someone, somewhere, watching over them both.